SABEL SECURITY #13

A **JACOB STEARNE** THRILLER

LIES

SEELEY JAMES

Published by
Machined Media
12402 N 68th St
Scottsdale, AZ 85254

LIES: A Jacob Stearne Thriller
First Edition, released December 20th, 2022
Print ISBN: 978-1-7373223-7-5
ePub ISBN: 978-1-7373223-6-8
Distribution Print ISBN: 978-1-7373223-8-2
Sabel Security #13 version 3.66

Formatting: BB eBooks
Cover Design: Jeroen ten Berge

SEE THE SEELEY JAMES COLLECTION

International intrigue, neo-Nazis, corruption, and justice
for the underdogs. Join the millions of fans who think
of Pia Sabel and Jacob Stearne as old friends and give
the series a full five stars.

VISIT SEELEYJAMES.COM/BOOKS
FOR BUNDLES, SALES, MUGS, T-SHIRTS!

LIES

For the best oldest sister imaginable

Susan

CHAPTER 1

JACOB STEARNE

EVERY COP IN LATVIA IS searching for me. I peer through the gap between a stack of splintery lumber and a cold brick wall in time to see a Riga police cruiser rolling down the street like a shark stalking a tasty dolphin. An officer in the passenger seat shines a sun-bright beam down my alley. I snap back behind the stacked wood and control my just-sprinted-two-miles breathing. Their voices float across the pre-dawn silence, pumping each other up in Latvian to hunt down the bastard who overpowered their comrade. Not that I speak the language, but the tone of voice, dripping with revenge, is a dead giveaway.

In my defense, they left me no other option. Things didn't go well after four young and eager officers spilled into the townhouse where I knelt above a college boy, my hands steeped in his spilt blood. They didn't speak English. I don't speak Latvian. I said, "I found him like this and tried to stop the bleeding." But they heard, "I'm a homicidal maniac here to slash the throat of every stinking Latvian I can find!"

With shoves, shouts, and sneers they booked me into a small suburban police station, took all my stuff—my clothes, my pistols, sound suppressors, spare magazines, tactical knife, belt with backup blade hidden in the buckle, a length of garrote wire, half a dozen Sabel Darts, three passports issued by different nations with different names under identical portraits of me, a questionable-looking satellite phone, and a significant number of five-hundred-euro notes crisp and fresh from the bank—and tossed me into a dank holding cell.

It seems, I failed to present myself as Jacob Stearne, the decorated veteran from Donnellson, Iowa, currently a special agent for Sabel Security.

Sometime after three in the morning, they made their first mistake: they assigned a lone patrolman to transfer me downtown, where they expected their grizzled elders to mete out justice in the old Soviet tradition.

Then they made their second mistake: the nice, baby-faced young man had me sit in the back seat of a car without a barrier between us. That's all the mistakes I allow. We got as far as Old Town Riga. At a stoplight, I pressed my fingers hard on either side of his neck, cutting off the blood flow in his carotid and jugular while pinching his nerve.

In seconds, the hapless patrolman passed out. I took his keys and gun and had him gagged and restrained before he regained consciousness. When he came around, I tried to explain how sorry I was for resorting to violence but, since I didn't have time to deal with courts and lawyers, it was all I could think of. I went on about how I was on an important mission on behalf of the President of the United States—and Pia Sabel, my billionaire boss—so I had to run. For a moment, I considered rephrasing all that in Arabic or Pashto, the only other languages I know, having learned them in the wars, but it didn't seem likely to help.

He definitely didn't speak English. He turned pale and clammy as I spoke. I emptied his magazine, hurled the bullets in a broad arc, slapped the mag back in his weapon and slid it back in his holster. I chucked the car keys a short distance away. I intended to show him I meant no harm, wasn't armed and dangerous, and just needed a head start.

The poor cop, desperate to escape my imminent and deranged onslaught, scrambled off his heels and pushed backwards across the console.

I held up my palms, resigned to being lost in translation, shook my head, and ran into the chilly summer night. I had more important things to worry about than a scared lawman. I had to get back to the coastal suburb of Jurmala—at night, wearing a jailhouse jumpsuit in Atomic Tangerine, without maps or a phone.

Before I'd been sidetracked by a murder investigation that barreled toward a hasty conclusion, I'd been inches from the first goal in my quest: to locate the missing movie star—and quantum electrodynamics physicist—Betty Bardon.

Um. Full disclosure: I did have a brief and passionate fling with the blonde genius deep in the Canadian Rockies a couple weeks ago—but I will not let that interfere with my assignment.

Why am I even on this mission? I've been asking myself that for the last week, ever since meeting with President Williams and Pia Sabel, where they asked me to be their pawn. They dressed it up with fancy words I had to look up later, but they meant pawn. A pawn in a battle over the future of civilization.

I don't mind being a pawn. I'm damn good at it. For years, I served in the 75th Rangers as a pawn. It's an ancient art and honorable tradition.

Knowing you're a pawn is the first step to spiritual enlightenment. It requires a metaphysical breakthrough: we may control our actions, but others control our lives. First, we must acknowledge the lies we tell ourselves to make our endeavors worthwhile. Lies like: Management will recognize my contribution soon; I'm going to get the next promotion, for sure; I work for the best, most honest human beings in the world. The fact is, we lie to ourselves so we can be pawns in the daily struggle we call life.

This mission is different. It's not nation against nation. It's not Conquistadors versus Natives. It's not Greeks versus Trojans. I'm a pawn in a battle between billionaires.

I'm not so sure being a pawn is honorable anymore. We can't achieve illumination when lies are presented with such boldness they look like the truth. I'm questioning my orders. I'm doubting the lies I need to convince myself that my billionaire would be any better a steward of the future than any other billionaire.

But. All that existential angst will have to wait. I have more immediate problems.

The entire Riga division of the Latvian Police is combing the city looking for me.

Beyond the stacked wood giving me cover, the cruiser stops. Car doors slam. The voices of two men echo in the empty streets thirty yards away. Their volume rises and falls as they twist in different directions, deciding where to begin their search.

They decide to start with my lane. Their boots clop on the cobblestones, their lights flash around the timber, illuminating the alley's dead-end. A ten-foot, vine-covered fence shields a construction site just beyond. They turn their beams away from my hiding place to examine the boarded-up warehouse forming one side of the narrow space.

While they're occupied, I toss a small stone overhead as far behind me as possible. It tinks off the roof of their car. As they bolt toward the sound, I run for the chain link in the opposite direction. Their pounding feet drown out my noise. I scale it and take a glance at a chasm of darkness below.

I can't make out what's down there. Behind me, the cops return their attention to the alley. I face an unpredictable future with zero visibility in front of me and an all-too-predictable future behind me. I opt for the unknown. I fling myself over and jump to the ground on the other side.

Only it isn't ground. I fall into a giant dumpster filled with detritus from the construction site that smells of sawdust and plaster. I pull myself up the side in time to see a truck bearing down on me, iron arms outstretched to embrace my sanctuary. Not wanting to be seen by the driver, I drop back into the broken glass, nails, and splintered wood.

Scraping clanks and groans surround me and I feel the steel box lift off the ground. What I know about waste management could fill a thimble, but I think this whole crate is going over the cab in an arc that will tip it upside down, spilling everything into the yawning maw of a backend filled with more broken glass, nails, and splintered wood.

Unfortunately, I'm right. We travel in a simple curve, twelve feet high at the apex. I grab the metal edge of the dumpster as the floor I'm standing on goes vertical and the debris beneath my feet slips into the dark. Everything crashes with a sound like breaking bones. My legs lose their purchase and swing over the dark abyss. I'm the only thing left, and my fingers are slipping free.

For a split-second, everything freezes. I hang suspended in midair. I'm good.

Then the machine gives a shake, banging the dumpster against steel stops to make extra-special-sure nothing gets stuck. My grip dissolves and I fall.

Only, I don't land on the same junk I stood on earlier. I'm standing on a large steel plate. That's when the compactor's hydraulics engage.

Making the greatest leap of my life, I grab the lip of the truck's overhead opening with two fingers. I barely manage to drag my feet above the compactor long enough to bring my other hand up. With both hands engaged, I get my chest up and flop over. I cling to the steel top of the growling machine by digging my fingernails under rivets.

Looking around for a way off this diesel beast, I spy a ladder on the side.

Police lights sweep across that side of the truck. Voices shout in Latvian over the car's public address system. The driver leans out of his window. Cops hop out and approach the driver's door. Pleasantries are exchanged, the garbageman answers questions, the patrolmen are satisfied. They drop back in their car. We back up, beeping loudly. We turn and rumble across ancient streets, heading out of Old Town, southeast toward the landfill. Not northwest toward my preferred destination: Jurmala.

I'm about to climb down and make a leap the next time the truck slows when the cruiser comes around the corner and follows us. Its headlamps light us up.

CHAPTER 2

BETTY BARDON

BETTY BARDON COMPARES THE PHOTO on her phone to the man sipping tea at one of the Future Café's sidewalk tables. Luxurious dark curls surround high-fashion sunglasses on a tanned face with high cheekbones and a strong chin. That's him, Joe Rouleau. He should be the movie star, not her.

Checking her outfit as she passes the café window, she sees her honey-colored mane bouncing with a hint of seduction that's muted by her banker's suit. Her pride swells. It's a beautiful June day in Riga, she looks professionally alluring, and her game plan is committed to memory. Makeup is light and summery. Sandalwood perfume sets the right tone. Betty thanks the gods she was able to coax two drops from the empty bottle. She's going to win over this investor and land the funding. She has to.

Striding straight toward him, her confidence builds with every step.

As she nears, he rises with a broad smile. He wears a white linen shirt untucked over drawstring pants. The jeweled watch on his wrist speaks to generations of conservative wealth. Sockless sneakers say the opposite. Something grips her center mass and pulls her toward him. Gravity?

With arms outstretched and a light French accent, he says, "Ah, Betty Bardon! You are more beautiful in person than on the big screen. Your hair is as spun gold and your fashion—impeccable."

Leaning in to prevent a whole-body hug, she lets him kiss both her cheeks. She savors his musky cologne. "Thank you. It's a pleasure to meet you, Mr. Rouleau. If we—"

"Please, it is Joe." He waves an admonishing finger with a laugh burbling in his voice. "No matter what we decide today, it will never be more than Joe for you. Let the others call me monsieur or even Your Highness, but never you."

With his perfect, sparkling teeth illuminating his face, he gestures to the empty chair. She takes her seat. He scrapes his closer to her and drops into it.

He doffs his sunglasses, tosses them on the table, crosses one leg over the other, slaps his thighs, inhales deeply while looking her over, then laughs. "I cannot believe I am sitting with such a famous movie star. Pardon me if I bask in my good fortune and act like a mad fan." He purposely waits for the awkward moment to stretch. As she's about to reply, he leans forward and covers her hand with his. "Tell me, what do you prefer, Betty Bardon: Should we get to know each other first, a little small talk about where we grew up and how we survived our lousy childhoods? Or shall we dive into business straight away?"

Off balance, unsettled by his brashness, she checks out his meaty shoulders before gazing into his vibrant brown eyes. There are flakes of gold in there.

With an inhale, she reins herself in. She's starving both financially and literally; she must stay on task.

"Let's start with business." She lets a flirtatious smile spread across her face. "If that works, we might explore more later."

"Ah," he leans back, satisfied, "I love how you think. It is possible we could ascend the highest peaks and achieve great things together."

After another breathless pause he says, "Your email explained much but allow me to summarize: You believe you are close to creating the Holy Grail of green energy: an advanced battery technology. And this solves the biggest problem of the future, how to store and transport solar, wind, or fusion energy. This is interesting—"

"Sorry to interrupt," she says, holding up her hand, "but it's not 'advanced.' We're talking about a quantum leap forward from where we are today. We use the term battery for simplicity. Technically, it's a metacapacitor a thousand times more efficient than a battery. Imagine a laptop that runs for years on a single charge. An electric car that can drive 300,000 miles. Remember the Texas power outage of 2021? Five million people went without electricity for nearly two weeks. Think about a few trailer-sized metacapacitors shipped from California to solve the problem overnight."

She hops off her soapbox as a flush of embarrassment warms her cheeks. She should never correct a potential investor.

His brows arch.

"Your passion is impressive," he says. "This is most admirable. Then it serves a larger market than green energy alone. This is a dynamic invention indeed. Remarkable."

She folds her hands in her lap and nods.

"And you worked on this in Russia?" he asks.

"No, here in Riga, at the University of Latvia. The Russians financed the *Chaac Project*, but the research was performed here."

He settles back with a curious expression. "You pronounce 'Chaac' as 'shock?' Pardon me, but I've only seen it in print. This is the same word in English as our French *choc électrique*? That is, the electric shock?"

"Nerd humor." She smiles nervously. "A little play on words by the man who did the original research. Chaac is the Mayan god of lightning."

"Ah, oui." Ripping his gaze from her, he laughs. "Clever."

For a moment, she's off her game plan. She's not sure where to take the conversation next.

His eyes wander the table as he rubs his hands. "Oh, but where are my manners? First, you must want something. Coffee and a croissant, perhaps? Allow me to—"

Hoping he hasn't heard her stomach growling, she says, "Nothing, thank you."

"You are certain?"

He waits for her to nod before continuing. "Your work at the university gives you an advantage over any competitors. And all your research is in your possession?"

This is the sticky part she hoped to avoid. If he invests his grandmother's money, telling him everything won't be a problem. If she tells him everything, but he doesn't invest, he'll know too much. That could make him as dangerous as the Chinese, Russians, or OPEC—all of them are ready to kill her for her research.

She explains, "There are three pieces to the puzzle: the *Chaac Project*, the outline for everything involved—is now in the hands of Pia Sabel. But I don't need that because I memorized it during my studies." She taps the side of her head with a finger. "Rafael Tum, a Guatemalan professor has the *Chaac Equation*—a thousand pages of physics theory which is the heart of the system. And then there is the *Edison Data*, ten terabytes of data from my experiments. My research represents 80 percent of the work needed to bring a viable product to market. I keep the *Edison Data* in a secure location until I can work out a deal with Professor Tum for the all-important *Equation*. Then I will have everything I need to finish the project."

He nods knowingly. "I see. So your value proposition is that you are closer to solving the problem than anyone else. All you need is capital to buy out this Rafael character?"

Truth be told, she needs capital for rent and groceries, not old man Rafael. The former guerrilla leader, who only recently came in from the jungles to take a professor's role, will never sell. The only way to pry the *Equation* out of his hands is to bash him over the head and steal it.

She answers, "Exactly, buy him out."

Joe purses his lips and frowns. "You mentioned Pia Sabel is involved in this as well. I did not know this before. Are we talking about Pia Sabel, the athlete-billionaire who killed her father for the inheritance?"

The ridiculous theories swirling around Pia Sabel came from the same cesspool of clickbait conspiracy sites as many an ugly rumor about Betty Bardon. She hates to give them credence, but answers, "Yes, *that* Pia Sabel."

"Why does she care?"

"Her birth father invented it. Assassins killed him and stole his work when she was four. She's been after it ever since. Now that she's inherited her adopted father's money, she can fund her adventure with unlimited resources."

"Have you contacted her about collaborating?"

"Uh … well," Betty hesitates. How did she let the conversation turn to Sabel? Big mistake. "We had a few discussions. They didn't go well."

"Oh?" He turns his teacup absentmindedly as he waits for her answer.

"See," Betty says and leans forward, "Sabel feels entitled to the whole thing. Gets a bit psycho about it, actually. Claims it's her birthright, Russians murdered her parents, it was stolen, and … all that." Betty finds her fist clenched. She relaxes and looks away. "So. Um, yeah. We couldn't come to terms."

He studies her, his stare making her nervous.

"Sabel's not the only one," she blurts out, her excitement rising with her volume. "This thing is huge. Whoever makes it work will blow right past Elon Musk and Jeff Bezos to become the first trillionaire. People would do anything for that much money. Do you want to live in a world where one person—Pia Sabel or Mikhail Yeschenko or Deng Zhipeng, or whoever—becomes so rich and powerful they achieve omnipotence? That's why we must complete the project quickly and make it public. Once everything is open-source, there will be nothing to fight over. We'll give the world a future that is not monopolized. Let the people have green energy without ultra-rich overlords charging us for the privilege."

Taking a deep breath, she calms herself again and reminds herself outbursts won't win the day. She must focus on the goal: make Joe Rouleau beg for a chance to invest.

"Are you sure you won't have a bite to eat?" he asks, sensing her embarrassment and attempting to change the subject. "I feel a poor host finishing a delicious tea while you have nothing."

"I'm fine, really." She hasn't eaten since breakfast yesterday. She's hangry and that's driving her eruptions. Sipping something might steady her nerves, calm her down. Too late now.

"So be it." He nods. "Let me come back to something you said earlier. You memorized the basis for this project. How does a movie star become so passionate about science?"

"Well." Betty flips her hair over her shoulder while she thinks for a moment. How much should she tell him? "It's kind of you to say that, but I had the lead in three box office bombs, and bit parts in a few other movies. I'm hardly a 'movie star.' Acting was merely a means to fund my education. My true calling is particle physics. I have a masters in quantum electrodynamics. QED for short. I came to Riga to read for my PhD when—"

"Quantum what? Masters? PhD?" His brows rise so high and fast he nearly rises from his chair. "This is not in your IMDB bio."

"Well, if a woman wants to work in Hollywood, she leads with boobs, not brains. Look what happened to Hedy Lamar. She pioneered spread-spectrum radio encryption, the foundation for secure communications to this day—and she only landed roles in B-movies after that. Well. Not to imply I ever rose above B-movies."

Betty's stomach clenches. She's blowing it. She's far too assertive for a woman seeking an investor. She should seduce him into the opportunity, not lecture him about the challenges of women in physics.

Joe Rouleau claps his hands and roars with laughter. "You are a woman of many talents, Betty Bardon. I like you! Graduate degrees in something I cannot even pronounce, much less understand. And you keep it a secret so men will not be intimidated. That is extraordinary. Quite extraordinary."

A wave of relief flows through her that quickly turns to excitement. She wonders why this man affects her so much. She imagined him as nothing more than another privileged Euroboy with a tenuous claim to Russian royalty. She needs him for his money, not his charm and looks. But is getting everything in one place so bad?

She chastises herself. She shouldn't let his electrifying presence distract her from her goal. Stick to the cash; anything else would just complicate matters. He can make her dream come true, it's time to close the deal. What was next in her script? Her research showed he seeks fame over fortune.

"Whoever brings this project to the public domain," she says, sitting up straight and staring into his gold-flecked eyes, "will be heralded like Jonas Salk. Joe Rouleau could be associated with the great philanthropists like Gates, Buffett, and Carnegie. We could call it the Rouleau Capacitor."

His eyes narrow. She's brownnosing shamelessly and he knows. She spreads a beguiling smile across her face. Acting comes in handy at times.

"My name would be synonymous with the man who made the polio vaccine free?" he asks. "A grand statement, indeed. But why would I associate with your rag-tag 'army' of ... what is the name?"

"Electric Liberation Army. The ELA."

"It sounds like one of those revolutionary movements from the seventies." His lip curls.

"Well ... It was a group decision. I'm sure we could—"

"Let us file that under 'future consideration.'" His smile returns along with the sparkle in his eye. "You have the research, the *Edison Data*, and you have a plan to acquire the *Chaac Equation*. Where do you keep this data? Where is the secure location?"

Betty recoils. He should know better than to ask such a sensitive question before they have an agreement in place. As charming as he is, trusting him could be a fatal mistake. The temptation *Chaac* represents could turn any honest man into a thief—or worse. People have killed in pursuit of this project—and hers is a critical piece. After carefully considering her answer, she says, "For security reasons, naturally, I cannot—"

She hears her name shouted from a distance. Locating the source, she sees the ELA's hacker, Logan Taylor, running toward her at full gallop, one arm waving madly. He shouts again.

His awkward, gangly frame reaches them. He takes a second to catch his breath, his hand held up to hold conversation. "Betty, Betty!" His breathing forces a pause. "It's Kevin. Kevin Winn ... Kevin was ... he was murdered last night."

CHAPTER 3

JACOB STEARNE

PLYWOOD FROM THE EAST-FACING WINDOW has peeled back far enough for the morning sun to smack my face like a fist. Unspooling my body from the fetal position in which I snatched a little shut-eye, I stretch, rub my eyes, and come face to face with a man in a toga who resembles Chris Rock. Mercury, a forgotten god left over from the collapse of Rome's pagan era, stands before me. The ridiculous little bronze wings on his silver helmet and a redundant pair on his sandals flap like hummingbird wings.

Go away, I tell him.

Mercury says, *How'm I gonna get a big-ass temple built in my honor when all I gots is a lazy muthafucka like you proselytizing for me?*

I say, *I just need a little more sleep, OK?*

Get yo ass up, homie. You done slept a hour already.

One more, I say. *That's all. One more hour.*

You don't want that, brotha, he says as a grin spreads across his face. *How you gonna get away from all the po-po on the street? From the color of your new threads, Ima guessing you need help running from the man—like always.*

Yeah, had a misunderstanding last night. I sneak up to the window and slink an eye to the warped plywood. Two cops stand on the cross street, asking citizens if they've seen a crazed American in a prison-orange jumpsuit.

I face Mercury and say, *I need a phone to call HQ so I can get lawyers, guns, and money. Where can I get a phone?*

Oh, dude. He turns his back on me. *You think us gods gonna smile on you and tell you shit when you act like you just done? I wake you up, save you from the cops, and right off you be asking for favors. Not a single thank-you. Not a word of worship. No adoration. You might as well be a ungrateful teenager telling your moms, I don't need you no more—but can I has the car keys tonight? Ya feel me?*

My psychiatrist thinks I suffer from PTSD-induced schizophrenia just because I see and talk to an ex-god. What does he know? He just wanted me on meds and out of his office with my wild stories. They aren't stories.

Mercury once had the biggest temple in Rome. He guided many an emperor in the ways of commerce and eloquence. He carried messages for the people. According to him, Julius was a nobody until they hooked up. Cicero was a dropout before he found Mercury. He was the one who clued Shakespeare in on all the Roman history. He believes if he makes me into a world-famous hero, I'll tell everyone about my religion. He thinks I can get him back into Prime Time, fill stadiums with worshippers, have people preaching his word on street corners with megaphones. He wants to get even with Jesus for kicking him and his pantheon to the curb. So, he helps me out now and then, gives me a heads-up when death lurks around the next corner.

It works.

But like all gods, he insists on being worshipped—constantly. Believe me, that gets old.

I must admit, there have been many times when he's saved my life. None of my brothers in arms ever argued with his divine intervention when taking enemy fire. In fact, in the heat of battle, they often begged me to summon his help. They didn't use ugly psychiatrist-words like "delusional" or "paraphrenia." They didn't tell me to take meds. They offered to sacrifice doves and goats if it would get them out of the line of fire. Dodging bullets will cure the most cynical of atheists.

The only thing that makes me question that he is the Roman god of eloquence is his insistence that the future of rhetoric lies in the voice of inner-city youth. He points to words that came from the African American community such as cool, jazz, hip, bad, bling, chill, funky, and the list goes on. He has a point. And he can channel Shakespeare, John F. Kennedy, or Cato the Elder if I call him on it.

Voices in the street drift up to me. The cops are coming.

I take a deep breath and mentally prepare to worship a figment of my imagination that produces physically verifiable results some would attribute to the actions of an immortal deity.

I'm sorry I didn't give thanks and praise, I tell Mercury. *If it weren't for your divine guidance and holy intervention, Riga's boys in blue would be pushing their muzzles into my sleeping face right now. You are the greatest. You are the best. You are my favorite ... um.*

I hear the scuffing of boots on the dusty floorboards a level below me.

Mercury says, *Holy Diana! You mortals distract easy.*

I'm in a two-story abandoned commercial building built when the Tsar still held sway in these parts. It smells of ancient dust and neglect. Riga was one strangle away from being deserted before they broke free from the Soviet dictatorship. Like a ghost town over a gold mine, prosperity flooded back, but every third block is a reminder of its past. My refuge is one of those reminders.

Mercury points to a corner of the ceiling, where I spy a chunk of fallen plaster revealing a small attic. The ceiling is low enough to jump to a crossbeam. I pull myself into a tight space and back away from the opening just as the voices enter the room below.

A dormer window gives me a slice of light.

The cops talk in bored tones and tromp across the room below me to the next one over. They'll need to come back this way to leave, so I hold my breath.

Beneath me, the plaster ceiling bows downward. My toes barely reach the nearest crossbeam on that end of my body. My elbows support my weight on another. I'll have to plank until the cops leave.

Then I smell the acrid scent of marijuana. The freaking officers chose this moment to smoke a joint. Great.

As quietly as possible, I reposition myself for better weight distribution. I wind up facing the dormer window. It gives me a fair view of the building's exit onto the street. I can wait here until I see the police leave. Perfect.

Across the narrow lane is a house with four windows facing me. In one of the windows is a woman. She's staring at me. Blankly. I'm not sure she can see me with the morning glare in the glass. Pushing her brown hair out of her eyes, she reveals a youthful, attractive face. No makeup. A tight, paper-thin t-shirt barely conceals her body. She waves.

Oh, she can see you alright, homes. Mercury cackles. *She can see you staring at her nipples.*

I am not. I … there's nowhere else to look at the moment.

Yeah, rrriiiggghhhttt. He punches my shoulder. *She'd be a bit young for you.*

Doesn't matter, I'm not interested. The girl's wave turns into a strange hand movement.

Oh, that's right! He cackles again. *You be all over that Betty Bardon business, huh?*

No. She's on my task list to locate and monitor.

Mercury says, *Yeah, you be monitoring that shit all night long, dawg.*

I am not going there with Betty. Um. This time. Yeah. It's strictly business.

I watch the girl do the strange wave again. She holds her hand up flat, palm facing me, thumb tucked in. Then she folds her four fingers over her thumb. She repeats the motion while staring into my eyes from thirty yards away.

I never studied sign language, but I know that sign. It means something. Something about danger. For her? Or me? Is she going to turn me in? No. She's trapping her thumb under her fingers. Because … damn. What is it? Is she the thumb? Meaning: she's trapped. Oh, right. It's the signal for abused women. It means she needs help.

Whazzat now? Mercury looks confused. *You think she needs help? Where'd you get that?*

I give her a thumbs-up. She looks relieved. Then I hold up a finger to wait. She looks perplexed.

I turn to Mercury, *Read about it in* Vogue. *It's for abuse victims to use during video calls. It became a thing in the pandemic when everyone was locked down. The isolation drove some people mad and domestic violence exploded.*

When did you start reading Vogue, *bro?* Mercury looks at me like I'm spoiled meat.

I skim it so I can converse with women about things that interest them. But I can't tell my used god that. His pantheon ruled back in the day when toxic masculinity was for wimps. Instead, I tell him, *The same day I met a god who tries to look more like an inner city rapper than any of the statues of him in Rome.*

Hey now, Mercury says. *We been over this a million times. As the Book-of-Myths y'all call a 'Holy Bible' says: the Creator done up man in his image. And where do anthropologists claim* homo sapiens *evolved theyselves right off the chimpanzee family tree?*

With a sigh, I reply the same way I always do: *Southeast Africa.*

He asks in a taunting voice, *And what kind of skin tone be the fashion choice in those parts?*

Then how come the Roman artists made all their statues look Italian?

How many black artists do you know? he asks.

Uh. I stutter a moment before coming up with, *That guy. The one who did the painting ... of the guy.*

Uh huh. Mercury slides in front of me. *I suppose you be talking about Kehinde Wiley and his portrait of the president? OK. And what color does Mr. Wiley use when he painting a god?*

Um, well, I dunno.

Y'all see god in the mirror, you never see god in someone else. And yet we be in everybody you meet. Every. Body.

The patrolmen shuffle through the room below me, still smoking their joint. They lumber down the stairs to ground level and kick at the sheet of plywood covering the exit. A few seconds later, I see them walking down the street.

Beyond the dormer window, the girl waves at me again. I nod back, crawl back to the hole, drop down, and head for the exit.

Oh, so you gonna be her hero now? Mercury asks. *Save the day for some hot young babe in the hopes she's gonna shower you with her affections in return?*

I say, *No. I figured out where I can steal a phone.*

CHAPTER 4

CAPTAIN REDGRAVE

CAPTAIN MARISA REDGRAVE'S BLOOD BOILS as she paces the office of Municipal Police Chief Dubra. The Chief looks like a parody of Winston Churchill with his pot-bellied privilege, while his assistant is as willowy as a reed. Both men wear their dress uniforms with all the medals they could find. She's glad she did the same. Tempering herself while considering everything from the briefing, she carefully considers her response. Muni police don't ask for help often. But this time, Chief Dubra went directly to the top to request assistance.

"Do I have this correctly?" she asks in Latvian. "Your officers arrested Jacob Stearne for murder at one this morning. Instead of notifying the American Embassy, they tried to transfer him downtown. At three this morning, before reaching his destination, they let him escape from—"

"They certainly did not 'let' him escape," Chief Dubra snorts.

"Oh? Is it now standard procedure to use an unmarked executive vehicle for jail transfers?" Her short auburn hair sweeps her collar when she snaps a look at the man. She crosses her arms over her single-breasted jacket. "Is it standard procedure to seat a prisoner directly behind the driver with no protective barrier between them with his wrists cuffed in front of him?"

"No, but—" the Chief's assistant starts to speak but stops and touches his fingers to his lips when Marisa fixes her steely gaze on him.

"At what time did your men identify him?" she asks.

"Right away," Chief Dubra says. "We're not stupid."

"Your men knew they had a battle-hardened veteran who now runs special operations for the American oligarch, Pia Sabel, and they put him in a car with only one officer?"

"They knew they had a man decorated by the President of France for stopping a massacre at a cathedral in Paris. They knew they had a man decorated by the Chancellor of Germany for saving three international finance ministers from—"

"Yes, yes, a hero. Or so the Sabel Security marketing department would have you believe. Like everyone else, I watched *Le Héros de Paris*. But don't forget what the American Army Rangers trained him to do: kill. Is there anyone in the world better at it than the Rangers? And Jacob Stearne was one of the best Rangers in history, making him—the best murderer in the world." She pauses a beat. "Remind me, Chief Dubra, on what charge did your men arrest him?"

Lifting his gaze to the ceiling, he turns away as he mutters, "Murder."

His assistant stage-whispers to his boss, "We don't need the English detective."

"My father may have been English," Marisa says, "but all he left me was my surname. I was born and raised here in Riga, same as you. You may address me as Captain Redgrave."

The assistant turns away, head bowed. The Chief's gaze works its way down to the floor, as far from her as he can keep it.

Marisa takes a deep breath, realizing she needs to get this meeting back on a cooperative level. Still, what they're doing chafes her to no end. In a softer voice, she says, "Tell me about the search."

The assistant points to the map resting on an easel next to the Chief's desk. "After the initial sweep of Old Town, we set up search quadrants and divided officers into groups of eight pairs—"

"What time was this?" she asks.

"At nine this morning."

"Six hours after losing him?"

The assistant shrugs.

She steams. "He could be in Helsinki, Stockholm, or Warsaw by now."

The Chief faces her. "We had sightings and reports. We had every reason to believe we would catch him at any moment."

"What reason?"

"Well, for one, uh, he was on foot," Chief Dubra says.

"And he was wearing our orange jumper," the assistant chimes in hopefully. "Very distinctive."

"Distinctive?" Marisa scoffs at the taller men. "Your plan was to spot him in a city where one of ten buildings is abandoned and boarded up? A man who once evaded the Taliban for a week without ever leaving their headquarters?"

The men look away in opposite directions from each other.

"And where are you now in your search?" she asks.

Chief Dubra straightens and faces her. "We have determined he is no longer in the city."

It's all Marisa can do not to shout at the man. She manages to get her next question out in a normal, if not slightly strained, tone of voice. "And what do you need from me?"

"Well, it's perfectly obvious," Dubra says. "We want you to search the rest of the country for him. He is now outside my jurisdiction."

Marisa holds his gaze for a long, uncomfortable beat. "I know what you are doing, Chief Dubra. It won't work." She wags an accusatory finger in his face. "I will not be your scapegoat for losing a murder suspect. Why? Because I will make sure everyone knows what I know: that Jacob Stearne has not left the city. He is here. Right under your nose. How do I know this? Because I read his profile. He operates like a ghost, using the late-night hours when your most junior staff are on duty, going where you least expect him, moving in directions that make no sense, staying close to you until you let your guard down. He once hid in the sewer of Brest, Belarus directly beneath police headquarters because no one wanted the disgusting task of looking there. He might be on the roof of this building. Maybe in the basement." She stops to take a breath. "Not only do I know this, but you do too."

"Are you shirking your duty?" Dubra's voice rises with outrage. "Are you refusing to search the countryside for this escaped suspect?"

"Oh, no, Chief Dubra. I am taking this assignment. You see, I know why you asked for me. You believe the case is hopeless. You believe he can't be found. And you don't want your men—and they are all men—to have that stain on their records." She points to the neat row of 5x7 portraits of his top lieutenants that stretches across one wall. "You asked for me because you wanted a woman to take the blame. You think women don't pursue serious careers in this department. You think I have nothing to lose by failing. But you're wrong. I will find him. As good as Jacob Stearne is at killing, I am better at apprehending the guilty."

The assistant's mouth falls open. She looks him up and down with contempt.

"Now, I am commandeering your search," she says as she takes her phone out of her jacket pocket. "We will scour the areas you've already searched because he will believe those areas are safe."

"What? I didn't give permission for you to—"

"Before I agreed to fix your problem, I told Interior Minister Anna Krasnova what tools I would need to succeed. She agreed with my assessment and gave me full authority to take control of any resources required." Marisa thrusts her phone toward Dubra. "Would you like to confirm her decision directly?"

CHAPTER 5

JACOB STEARNE

THE WOMAN WHO ANSWERS THE door wears a sheer teddy. She gives me a once-over that ends in a sneer at my orange fashion statement. Excessive make up gives her a tired look, as if this is the end of her shift, not early morning.

"Do you speak English?" I ask nicely.

She replies in Latvian with unmistakable rudeness and starts to slam the door.

Kicking it back open before it latches, I say, "There's a lady upstairs. I'd like to speak to her, see if she's OK."

The startled woman backs into the living area on my right where three more ladies with too much makeup and scanty negligees sit around a coffee table. Card game in progress. Cigarettes smolder in their fingers. Wisps of incense trails up from a tabletop statue. They look up quickly.

Mercury slides around me. *Awright! Homie, you done found the local chapter of Venus Libertina. Nice!*

I ask, *The what?*

Mercury shakes his head sadly. *One day you gonna read up on the gods that be saving your ass from Baghdad to Bogotá and understand the gods are multifaceted, like a kaleidoscope. Venus Libertina is the Venus of passion and pleasure. See? They even gotsa statue of Venus Callipyge.* Mercury looks disappointed in me because I'm confused. *Callipyge? Root word for the adjective callipygian? Aw. Look it up. Anyway. That be Latin for goddess with the nice ass. Back in the good ol' days, these would be professional acolytes of the goddess of desire. What y'all call sex workers.*

The coffee table's centerpiece is a two-foot Romanesque model in a tasteful pose with her toga pulled around front, exposing her shapely rear end.

I say, *Or traffickers, given that the woman upstairs signaled she's in trouble.*

The ladies playing cards are staring at me with shocked, pale faces.

I guess forcing my way in, looking like an escaped prisoner—which I am—is not the best introduction. I point up. "I just want to talk to the woman upstairs. Make sure she's OK."

"She OK," a deep male voice with a heavy accent says from the adjoining room. "You go now."

A short, burly man built like a fireplug steps out of the dark passage to my left.

"Great," I say. "I'd like to hear her say that."

He plants his stocky, bulldog frame in front of me. "I say you go now."

In a flash, I hook my left foot behind his ankle, push his opposite shoulder backward, and send him sprawling to the floor behind me. "Thanks, don't mind if I do—after I speak to the young lady."

I charge up the staircase at the back of the hall and march into the room where I saw her in the window.

She's staring at me with huge copper-hazel eyes. Her face is proportioned with what artists call the golden ratio, Mother Nature's pattern of perfection. Her light brown hair cascades down either side of a face twisted by pure fear. She's wearing leggings that fit like body paint. Some form of astrological tattoos run up the side of her neck: moons, stars, orbits. A sleeve of roses and patterns starts at her elbow and disappears under her flimsy shirt.

She's scared. I've seen this fear a hundred times before. Asking someone to save you is a great idea until it happens—then you face the reality that the Earth beneath your feet will quake into a hundred shards. You're about to leap into an unpredictable future with zero visibility and no way back. Instantly, a victim of unspeakable crimes will cling to the known over the unknown. I've tugged refugees away from ticking bombs and it's no easy task.

I ask softly, "Do you speak English?"

"I'm American. Connecticut." Her hands cover her mouth as if she misspoke. "Um. Oh. Symone, Symone with a Y."

"Nice to meet you, Symone-with-a-Y." I stick out a hand, low and unthreatening. "Jacob Stearne. You made the sign for—"

Symone gasps a split second before I feel the muzzle of a pistol touch my ear.

"You go now," the deep voice says again.

I turn slowly to face him with my hands open wide enough to appear unthreatening. "Sir, please take your finger out of the trigger guard and put the gun down. I don't want to hurt you."

"You go now." Maybe it's the only English phrase he knows.

"Last chance," I tell him. "Take your finger out of the trigger guard. If you don't, it'll break when I disarm you."

His fierce, dark face frowns in anger and resolve. The pistol's hammer is already cocked, a round is already chambered, the safety is engaged. He flicks the safety off with his thumb. His finger begins to tighten around the trigger. No more options.

With a lightning-fast flick, I shove the safety back on while wrenching the pistol barrel to the side. Trapped by the trigger guard, his finger is levered backward toward his wrist. We both hear the snap of tendons and muscle. He looks shocked. Before he can react, I give his shin a quick kick, more pain than damage, then slam my knee into his groin. As he doubles over forward, I smack his nose with my knee, sending him backwards in a heap. Works every time.

I check his pistol, a clean looking CZ75, the Czech answer to the Baretta. It sports a fifteen-round magazine, which I slide out and find full. I flick the safety back on.

Arms surround me from behind. I wind up preparing to send an elbow into my attacker's face when I realize I'm not being jumped. It's Symone and she's hugging me.

"Oh my god!" she shouts. "Really? You're Jacob Stearne? The Hero of Paris? The—"

"Don't believe the clickbait." I peel back one of her hands. "Do you need help?"

"Hell yeah!"

"Then let's go."

"Let me grab my things." She rips herself away from me and starts shoving gossamer threads of clothing into a backpack. She moves like a gymnast, a split second of mental preparation followed by explosive kinetic energy with a physical grace.

While she's busy, I take the clothes off sleeping beauty and change out of my incarcerated-casual look. His clothes are too small for me. The pants look like capris and won't button. The shirt makes me look like a gym rat in a crop top showing off my cannons. I opt to rock my dayglow apricot instead.

As I climb back into the jumpsuit, the woman who first answered the door barges in. She's yelling in a language other than Latvian and waving her phone. The one word I can identify is *politsiya*. In most European languages *police* sounds roughly the same. Something I don't want. At the same time, I'm not sure she does either. But then, I'm not sure about Latvia's stand on sex workers.

"Do you speak her language?" I ask Symone.

"No. That's how I got in this mess," she calls as she zips her backpack. "I thought we were talking about dancing. These guys are into extras."

The woman stops yelling, stamps her foot, and points at her pimp. The message is clear: I've damaged her collector and she's not happy.

I rummage through the man's pockets and find what I need most: a phone. I shove it in my pocket and yank out the man's wallet. It's full of euros, mostly hundreds and two hundreds. I take out a thousand euros and hand the wallet to the lady.

She takes the remaining money with suspicious fingertips and a curious sideways glance at me.

I pull the phone and point to the screen. "Are you in his contacts? I'll pay you back."

The man at my feet stirs. I stomp on his chest to hold him down.

The woman tilts her head, trying to understand what I'm telling her.

I do what most Americans do when confronted with a language

barrier: I repeat myself louder. "If you're in his contacts, I'll pay you back. Venmo?" Then I remember Venmo doesn't cross the Atlantic. "Xoom? Wise?"

Money is a concept she understands. She touches the screen, opens the Xoom app and points at the contacts. She says, "*Ya* Tatjana. *Tri tysyachi, three thousand.*"

"I'm only borrowing one thousand," I protest.

Someone knocks at the front door.

Tatjana pouts sarcastically. "Three thousand—*net politsii.*"

Which I think is Russian for *no police.* Plural.

Trust is not my favorite currency. I've survived battles in places the American public won't hear about before 2045 because I live by Stearne's Law: *Paranoia is the result of acute situational awareness.* And I've just become acutely aware of my situation.

"You're a formidable businesswoman, Tatjana. OK, three thousand euros. I'll send it in an hour."

Glee lights up her face and she sprints downstairs. I take my victim's hand, hold it firmly by the wrist, and pull his broken finger straight out before letting go. It snaps back into place. He inhales in shock, then realizes it's fixed. More or less. Painful beyond words, but it will heal. Bonus: no doctors. His sheet-white face looks at me with a mixture of awe, fear, and hatred.

Downstairs, the front door opens. Tatjana greets Riga's finest with a silky, seductive voice.

CHAPTER 6

BETTY BARDON

BETTY BARDON STRUGGLES WITH THE doorknob of the house she rented in Jurmala, Latvia. It feels impossibly heavy, as if it had turned to stone. Inside, members of the Electric Liberation Army, the group of young scientists and physicists she has assembled, await her leadership. But her mind is in two places at once. On one hand, she struggles with the shock and grief of losing one of her most ardent colleagues in a tragic murder.

On the other, she concentrates on the immediate need for financial support from Joe Rouleau. She's glad he offered to drive her back so she could deal with the tragedy. A wealthy man with emotional intelligence is exactly the kind of partner she needs.

A veil of guilt clouds her vision as she realizes how terrible it sounds to be distracted from the death of an associate, but it's true. While she mourns the loss of Kevin Winn, she funded this group out of her pocket. And that pocket is now empty. Her one chance to get financial aid from Pia Sabel imploded with her realization the billionaire would never turn over the *Chaac Project* to anyone else. Betty's options had dwindled quickly. Now she's close to making this happen. She cannot fail now.

Joe Rouleau reaches around her, twists the knob, and thrusts the door open for her. He gestures her ahead of him. His sad eyes drop with deference. She gives him an appreciative smile and steps inside. Logan Taylor follows them inside.

Kayla Clay, dressed like a '60s hippie in bell bottom jeans, rushes to her in tears. Pulling Logan in, Betty embraces them both. Chris Anrig, always in his gym clothes, and Francesca Bartoli, wearing a designer outfit, join them, completing the group hug. This is what's left of her army—four kids under twenty-five. She sighs as they break.

"Who would want to kill Kevin?" Kayla sobs.

Betty can think of several women, including herself, who might consider killing the young man. As much energy as he brought to the cause, she found his misogyny and narcissism exhausting. In the early stages, she had found it necessary to take on enthusiastic supporters instead of people with an adult level of maturity.

Francesca reminisces about Kevin's arrival in Riga: he'd brought chocolates for all. Logan adds how Kevin learned Wolfram programming to help him. Kayla announces she has composed a poem to commemorate their loss.

"In a deserted field the lonely sparrow lies," Kayla recites.

That's when Betty tunes out. She hears Joe rummaging in the kitchen. Drawers open and close, cabinets open and shut, a kettle nears the whistle stage. Is there a worse way to impress an investor? Have him arrive the morning after a murder? Things were going so well an hour ago.

"The police questioned me about some guy," Logan says after Kayla finishes. "They kept asking about a guy, thirties, buzzcut, buff, maybe on the tall side. I didn't see anyone at the townhouse before we left. I don't know who they were talking about."

A silence falls over them for several breaths. Then Chris says, "Kevin's parents called. They will arrive tomorrow to claim his body."

"I cannot believe we left Kevin behind," Kayla wails and breaks down. The others pat her back.

Betty winces. She hadn't considered counting heads when they left the townhouse. Do you have to do that with adults? A group of five feels the same as a group of six. Besides, they rarely went as a group. They often split up, going in different directions. She couldn't be expected to know Kevin's whereabouts at any given moment.

A scary thought grips her like a fist of ice squeezing her intestines: What if Kevin had been murdered while they were in the house? What if one of them was the murderer? She shakes the thought away. Too chilling to contemplate.

But what if an assassin was after them? What if this guy the police were asking about, the buzzcut-guy, should come to her house tonight to finish them off?

"We must stay together from now on," Betty says.

All eyes turn to her. Their faces slowly turn white. She has almost ten years on them, a lifetime of experience and wisdom in their eyes.

"You … You think we are in danger?" Chris asks.

"Oh my god!" Kayla shrieks, suddenly aware of Chris's implication.

Joe enters carrying a tray overflowing with cups, a tea kettle, scones, butter, and jam. Betty flinches at the sight of the scones. Days old, they might be hard as rocks. She'll dunk hers in the tea as if it were the custom.

Joe sets the tray on the coffee table with a flourish like a magician's assistant. He asks, "Why would you be in danger?"

Ignoring him, Francesca asks Betty, "Do you think that Chinese guy did this? You said we should keep watch for them. They are deadly, you said."

Joe turns to Betty, "Chinese guy? Deadly? You mentioned Pia Sabel. Who is this?"

"Deng Zhipeng," she says. "The Chinese internet billionaire is also interested. He's been dangerous in China, but not in other …"

Betty lets her words trail off because she doesn't know how to make it sound better. Deng is quite capable of killing for *Chaac.*

"Your project is most revolutionary," Joe says. He turns to the group. "Betty is right. It is best if you stay together at a time like this. There is comfort in numbers."

"We'll be fine," Chris Anrig says. "Probably a random thing. Mentally ill person, or robbery."

Betty is grateful for a calming voice. Chris, the Swiss artist and engineer, is built like a tank and fears nothing. The others look to him with questions in their eyes. Will he protect them? Is he as good with his fists as he is sculpting marble? She doesn't know; fighting never came up before.

The kids nod their heads. At least they believe in him.

What if Chris killed Kevin? There was the problem of Kayla. After

Betty spent several weeks seeking Pia Sabel's help, she'd returned to find Kayla in the center of a love triangle with Chris and Kevin—a motive for killing that dates to the beginning of time.

Joe pours tea and hands a cup to Francesca. She takes it and mumbles *grazie*. Joe offers the next cup to Betty.

In automatic mode, her fingers take the saucer and steady the cup while her gaze remains on Joe. She wants his investment, but now is not the time. She thinks about what she should do next: soothe and calm her people. How should she do that? A wake? A memorial of some kind?

She can't focus on a remembrance knowing that Joe Rouleau is about to leave. He might reschedule their discussion, but should she take that chance?

"We should do something," Francesca says.

"Like a eulogy?" Chris asks.

Francesca shrugs. Kayla nods. Chris stares at his teacup and tries to take a bite of his scone. It sounds like he's chewing on a rock.

None of them know about funerals. They don't know what's supposed to happen. Betty realizes they might not have been to one in their young lives. Betty's been to too many. She says, "His parents will arrange a funeral according to their customs. We don't want to interfere with that. However, we can hold a wake in his honor."

A collective exhale escapes the group as if they'd been holding their breath for some time. Betty senses a wave of relief sweep around the circle. She's done the right thing.

Logan takes a short call, then announces, "That was Captain Redgrave from the police. She will be by later to take our statements about last night. We are not to go anywhere."

Everyone nods, lowering their heads while they mentally review their movements. They want the police to have every bit of information that will lead to finding the killer.

Betty does too. She'll give a full account of everything she knows. Most things. She had taken the group to meet Joe Rouleau at the Airbnb he rented. After letting themselves in and waiting for half an hour, he called to apologize that he was stuck in Paris. He rescheduled. While she was talking to him, Kevin found the liquor cabinet and poured generous drinks for his ELA comrades. They decided to explore the four-story townhouse. After finishing her call, Betty discovered they were acting like college kids at a rager. She scrambled to get them out of there before anyone broke anything. Her best idea to round them up: *Let's go clubbing.*

Where and when Kevin went missing, she had no idea. Disappearing was Kevin's modus operandi. He often chased after women or discovered a party elsewhere and wandered away.

"Regretfully, I have an appointment I must keep, Betty Bardon," Joe whispers in her ear, disrupting her thoughts and sending a pleasant shiver down her spine.

"Oh, Joe, I'm so sorry." Betty slides her palm down his chest absent-mindedly before pulling it back quickly. "I mean. I'd like to talk to you more about—"

"No more talk. I have made my decision." He stares into her eyes.

Her heartbeat accelerates like a hotrod in a race. She should've left the kids to focus on Joe. He's her last best hope, and he's walking away. She scrambles through ideas to postpone his next sentence. Anything to buy time.

He doesn't give her the chance. He says, *"Grand-mère* relies on me to vet her trust's investments. When I do, I find poring over financials with accountants is like reading a novel: it's all fiction. Instead, I walk among the employees of a company. I talk to the people. Are they happy, are they dedicated, are they close?" He takes Betty's cup with one hand, holds her hand with his other. He sets the cup on the side table and pulls her close. "Your people are extraordinary. Not once in this discussion did anyone talk of running home. No one spoke of fleeing the danger. They are close, like a family. You have done well, Betty Bardon. You have something here worthy of my support."

He lets go of her hand and takes a few steps toward the door.

"Take your time with them." He nods toward her ELA. "Have a proper wake. Call me when you're ready to discuss the details." He shrugs, then smiles. "Electric Liberation Army. We must discuss this first."

CHAPTER 7

JACOB STEARNE

I WAS WRONG. GETTING SYMONE to leave her captors was not a problem. Prying Mercury out of the den of iniquity was damn near impossible.

He floats next to me as if he were reclined on a lounger, his little wings flapping up a breeze while he sips wine from a goblet. *Holy Vesta! Y' know what's wrong with Americans, homie? Y'all be founded by the Puritans, that's what. You gots to slow down and chill, baby. Relax and de-stress. Y'all too anxious. That's why white people don't move they shoulders when they dance. Ain't nothing wrong with having a little fun now and then. C'mon, let's go back. Tatjana'll show you how to let go of all that anger you got inside you.*

I don't have any anger inside me. I keep trying to figure out how to dial a phone with a Latvian-language screen. *I'm on a mission and I need to contact my team.*

"What team?" Symone asks.

"Do you know what the phone app looks like in Latvia?" I hold the phone between us.

We're halfway down an alley where we ate sandwiches for lunch crouched behind a discarded dining room set. It's a warm and beautiful sunny afternoon. If I had a pillow, I'd take a nap because I need one. I haven't slept more than an hour since London yesterday. Or was that the day before?

"Why not use the icon with a phone on it?" She points.

Like magic, it appears on the lower edge of the screen. I swear it wasn't there a second ago.

"Oh, they use a different color." I click it and dial the Sabel Security emergency number.

Symone doesn't wink at me exactly, just a twinkle that looks like a wink. Maybe it was a wink. I'm not good at reading females.

Just when Emma, my operations manager, answers, Symone grabs my face and plants an open-mouth kiss on me. With the scent of candy apple perfume wafting from her, she rolls over on top of me, shielding me from the street.

I hear Emma begin the standard line of questioning: Am I safe? Can I speak freely? Do I need extraction or a fire team?

Over Symone's shoulder, I see a squad car rolling by on the street. It passes us.

I break off just as Symone's tongue slithers across my lips to invade my space.

"Thanks," I say to Symone with a nod toward the street. "I appreciate the help."

She slides away, jumps to her feet, and claps her hands in front of her face as if she'd won a prize. "I can't believe it! I kissed Jacob Stearne!"

With a quick eye roll, I turn my attention back to Emma. "I got arrested last night and—"

"We know," Emma says with a hint of boredom. "You're supposed to be arraigned day after tomorrow. Legal is working on the response. We don't have a Riga branch, so we're Zooming in attorneys from Warsaw. Extraction or fight it out?"

"I'm staying," I say.

Behind me, Symone laughs, beside herself with joy.

"You'll need the standard package then?" Emma asks. "Automatic weapons? Anything big? Machine gun, grenade launcher, surface-to-air?"

"Pistol and darts are fine. The police here kill one tenth as many citizens per capita as the US so I should be safe. Oh, and clothes. Casual preferred."

"Maybe I should move to Latvia," Emma muses. "Where should I send everything?"

Good question. Does FedEx deliver to: suspicious-looking guy on the corner of a street I can't spell and a road I can't pronounce? That doesn't leave me a lot of options. While the cops might not be looking for me at the UPS store, the employees might call them about a guy in bright-freaking-orange asking for packages. That leaves me one option.

"Just send everything to that address I gave you last night." I think for a moment. It's the only safe address in Riga for me, hostile as it might become. "I'll be in touch if I need anything else."

"Right, it'll be there in an hour. Hang on, though. Ms. Sabel wants to talk to you."

My best friend, boss, and patroness is the last person I want to talk to. The closer we come to securing the *Chaac Project*, the weirder, more possessive she gets. She has an ugly fixation on this mission that scares me. I can't think of a good excuse to get out of it, so I tell Emma, "OK, put her on."

"Give me a minute. She just got out of surgery."

Surgery? But Emma's gone before I can ask what happened. Instead, my ear fills with Beethoven's Fifth Symphony. Hold music on steroids.

Symone throws her arms around me and looks up expectantly, waiting for a thank-you kiss.

"Uh, look," I say, "you're nice, and I appreciate the cover back there, but I'm not interested in—"

"Don't mood-poison me," Symone says. "I can't believe it's really you."

"OK, well, it is. So, I'm about to call an Uber … wait, they don't have them here. A Bolt, yeah, that's what they have. I'm about to call a Bolt. Where do you want me to drop you?"

"Drop?" She backs up, fire in her eyes. "What the fuck? You can't drop me. Are you one of those guys who treats women like trash? You just rushed in and saved me! That's got to mean something, right?"

"I'm not treating you like trash." I stare at her blankly. "I needed a phone. I figured I could steal one from whoever was holding you against your will." I shake the phone at her. "It worked. But I'm in the middle of something dangerous here—you don't want to get involved."

"I am involved! I just saved your ass from the police!" Her voice is way too loud. "And this is the thanks I get? 'Where can I fucking drop you?'"

Tell me about it, sister. Mercury glares at me as he sneaks an arm around her shoulder. *It's the same for us gods too. All y'all whiny little Earthlings pray and cry, 'save my baby; make me rich; wash my dishes; cure my cancer; don't let me go bald like my mama'—and then what do y'all do when we move mountains for you? Nothing. Not a Minerva-damn thing. Has you even sacrificed a rooster to me? I don't think so. And here you are, abandoning this poor, homeless thirst trap name a Symone.* He waves his hands at Symone as if she were on display at a jewelry store. *You should be ashamed, Jacob Stearne.*

Wash my dishes? I ask. *Do people really pray for you to wash dishes?*

Hard times, brother. He shakes his head and tosses his hands in the air. *A god's gotta do what a god's gotta do for a little adoration, y'know what I'm saying? Hold up! Izzat all you took away from what I just said?*

"Look, Symone, you're a good kid," I say, quickly realizing how patronizing I sound. "The job I have, the places I go, the things I have to do … you don't want to be there."

She tears up. "Where am I gonna go, huh? I'm not in Latvia because I ran away from my rich mom's mansion in the Hamptons. I'm alone. I got nothing. Nobody. Do you know how lonesome it is? No home, no family, no one caring if I live or die?"

Her eyes swell and fill with tears. Her nose reddens. I knew she needed to get out; I never stopped to think where she would go. I was focused on getting a phone. She senses my sympathetic reaction and throws her arms around me again.

"Just let me hang with you until I can get a place," her voice quakes. "I won't be any trouble; I swear to god. And I can help you. I know how to be useful in lots of ways."

The girl has no idea why helping me is dangerous. Unbidden, a memory of the love of my life explodes in my inner vision. Jenny Jenkins was trying to help me. I don't know if I'll ever recover from that incident. I say, "Things don't go well for people who help me."

She shakes her head, her eyes pleading.

"Jacob? Are you there?" It's Pia Sabel's voice on the phone.

"Yeah, yeah, I'm here." I hold up a hand to calm Symone and step away to focus on the call. "What surgery did you have? Are you OK?"

"Fine," Ms. Sabel says. "Well, that's not true. Broke my ankle. That's why I need to speak to you. Here, I'll send you a picture."

My phone dings. A photo of Ms. Sabel's leg fills my screen. From her knee to her big toe is a titanium scaffold big enough to build a skyscraper. Metal rods screwed into her bones rise out of her skin and connect to the rig. She looks like she's been attacked by an erector set gone mad.

I say, "Holy—"

"Looks worse than it is, but I won't be joining you in Riga."

I count my blessings. Not that I'm happy she's immobilized and in pain, but if she finds Betty Bardon before I accomplish my mission, there could be trouble. They have different world views. Betty believes in a world of equality. Like most uber-rich people, Ms. Sabel believes the world is hers. Literally.

Symone slides up next to me, disregarding my phone call, and says, "I'll only take a little while. I don't even have an OnlyFans page. If I can hang with you, and, y'know, borrow a laptop, I can get set up, take some pics, and start raking in some cash."

My gaze snaps to her with a hundred concerns. OnlyFans? Isn't that a semi-porn job? That's a crazy idea. There must be some other way she can make money. Maybe a legit job. Wait, she'd need to work for weeks before she'd have enough cash to be independent. I don't like that option either. There must be somewhere Symone can go.

"Listen up, Jacob," Ms. Sabel says in an impatient voice. "There's a nurse here with pain meds that'll make me loopy, so I've got to talk fast. Here's where we are: We thought we found the *Edison Data*, but it was a decoy. There's nothing on it but ten terabytes of a traffic cam in Chicago. Worse, Betty Bardon appeared on the *Today Show* yesterday. Did you catch it?"

"It's not big in Latvia."

"Right. Well, she announced she's leaving Hollywood to focus her career on cracking the equation for green energy. She used that term, 'equation.' She said no cost was too high to save the planet. We think it was a clever appeal meant to reach Rafael Tum. Rafael Tum has the

Chaac Equation. If she has the real *Edison Data,* and they collaborate, we could lose the whole project."

What she means is, they could beat her to the most important technology of the twenty-first century, wrecking her chance to become the richest person who ever lived. Even richer than Augustus Caesar, who Mercury tells me once controlled the equivalent of $4 trillion in today's currency. That would place her individual wealth as the third biggest economy in the world, squeezing ahead of Japan and just under China. She would leave Bezos and Musk in the weeds. As much as I admire her, no one should have that kind of money. Hell, there should be a 90% minimum tax on people who can afford to build their own spaceships.

Mercury says, *Never gonna happen, homes. Y'know why? Cuz people always see a fantasy of theyselves sitting on Caesar's throne, holding a thumb up or down. They don't see who they really be: the poor slob in the arena whose fate waits on Caesar's thumb.*

I look at him. Some truth in that.

"We can't let them get together," Ms. Sabel says. "That's your new, number-one objective: get the *Edison Data* from Betty Bardon. I can't stress this enough: number one priority, Jacob."

"I hear you," I respond. Hopefully, she won't hear what I'm not saying, which is, *I don't agree—but I hear you.*

"You know what we're looking for, right?" she asks. "It's an old-fashioned hard drive, 3.5 inch—"

"The size of a small paperback, yep. I know."

"Isaiah is in Monaco with Tania. They've been staking out Deng Zhipeng's yacht. They reported that Rafael Tum was there but hasn't been seen for a few days. They believe he gave the Chinese the slip and left town. I'm concerned he's meeting Betty. You must stop that from happening."

Symone wraps me up from behind and squeezes tight. At first, I can't tell if it's her over-enthusiastic-fan persona, or if I'm in danger again. I use the selfie camera on the phone to look down the alley behind me. The police car is back and it's slowing down. Two faces appear in the windows, staring at me. Symone is trying to cover me. It won't work.

I'm too tall.

"I hear you," I tell Ms. Sabel. "But I've got a bigger problem at the moment—staying out of jail. I'll be in touch."

I click off and bolt down the narrow cobblestones with Symone hot on my heels.

CHAPTER 8

CAPTAIN REDGRAVE

CAPTAIN MARISA REDGRAVE STANDS RAMROD straight on the top step in front of the Riga Municipal Police Department. Before her, two hundred patrol officers form a semicircle. They've had lunch, the sun is shining, and she has their undivided attention. The opportunity she's worked toward her entire career is here. This is her moment to shine or fade, and she is ready to go nova. Now is the time to take control, to make them understand who is in charge, leave no doubt, and no room for insubordination. She takes a sharp, deep breath, and thinks, *I've got this.*

She points a polished fingernail at the ground one step behind her right heel. Chief Dubra remains off to the side. She can feel his questioning gaze focused on the back of her head. She snaps her fingers and points again.

Chief Dubra steps into his assigned position.

Under her breath, she says, "Stay focused on a distant horizon and do not undermine a word that I say, Dubra."

He coughs, then forces himself to say, "Understood."

In a clear strong voice that echoes off the buildings across the street, Captain Redgrave says, "Believe me, I feel for you, gentlemen. I know from experience how annoying it is to be dragged from an operation only to be told by a stranger how to do the operation you were already doing, just so you can do it all over again. Well, today, I am that annoying stranger." She lets a wave of uncertain laughter circle the assembly. "I don't do this for amusement. I brought you in to address you in person to quell any rumor, to end any complacency, to ensure you are aware of the truth: we face a formidable foe. The notorious American, Jacob Stearne, escaped last night. Yes, I know what you're thinking—every European under fifty watched the dramatic series on French Netflix about him, *Le Héros de Paris*. We all imagined ourselves in the roles played by Timothée Chalamet and Mélanie Laurent, right?"

She allows another murmur to ripple through the ranks. Now they are loosened up, eager to hear more. She has connected with them. This is working. She can reset their expectations to reality.

"Don't let the magic of streaming cinema cloud your judgement," she says. "It is true, without so much as a table knife for a weapon, Jacob Stearne killed terrorists armed with automatic rifles—and he did it in less than sixty seconds. Yes, that saved the parishioners of *Église Saint-Sulpice*. But think for a moment what that same man could do to you when cornered. What could he do to your partner? Your friend? Your family?"

The crowd is silent. She allows each officer a moment to reflect on her statement. Confidence and pride rise in her chest. If she pulls this off, the minister will give her something big. Maybe even Dubra's job—since he isn't doing it.

"We must remember, Americans are not like us," she says calmly. "They are given to extreme violence, turning to deadly force at the slightest provocation." She bolsters her voice to accentuate her concern. "Jacob Stearne is capable of far greater violence than any other American. I say this, knowing my words are inflammatory, for one perfect reason: We will find him, and we will bring him to justice! We will not fail. But in the process, let us not hesitate to protect every Latvian from Stearne's deadly wrath." Now she rises to a full shout. "Do not question your authority to use deadly force. Do not allow one citizen nor one of your fellow officers to suffer so much as a paper cut from this savage American killer!"

Regaining her composure, she turns the details over to Dubra's assistant. The man explains how they will knock on every door, talk to every citizen, track down every vagrant to find someone who has seen a man in a bright orange coverall. With clothes like that, someone must have seen him. Listening to his weak voice, she knows she came across as the stronger leader, the obvious choice to run Riga.

When the assistant finishes with the assignments, she steps forward again.

"When we finish with the city center, we will move out to the resorts along the coast. We will cover a triangle from Kekava in the south, west to Jurmala, and up the coast to Carnikava. We will scour every rental and hotel, every room for rent. We cannot allow an American, no matter who plays him on TV, to commit murder on Latvian soil."

They give her a hearty round of applause which she savors for a moment. She has taken the first step. And it worked as she hoped. She can see it in their faces: renewed energy, revitalized dedication, a burning desire to please her. Pride radiates from her like the beam of a lighthouse.

She turns to Dubra. "They are your people. Give them the order to get to work."

He ducks from her gaze like a beaten dog before stepping forward.

While he speaks, Marisa sees the reporters she called earlier. She approaches them with a confident stride. Why TV shows always portray the police-media relationship as antagonistic, she never understood. When manipulated properly, the media can be a powerful tool.

"You will take turns for your exclusive interviews," she tells them. "Who is ready first?"

The hand of a young woman shoots up. Marisa nods to her and feels a triumphant smile spread across her face. She will need to get that under control; she must be serious for this solemn business. And it is a solemn business. Marisa Redgrave shall not rest until Latvia is free of this murderous American.

CHAPTER 9

JACOB STEARNE

THE ELEMENTS BATTLE EACH OTHER for supremacy. The sun warms the skin while an icy breeze blowing in off the Baltic chills it down. I can see why the ancients saw different gods for different elements, as if they were fighting over how you should dress.

Peering over the hedge, I see what I'm looking for: a small dark object falling out of the sky at roughly two hundred miles per hour.

Mercury leans over my shoulder and says, *Symone ain't no slouch in the cleverness business, dawg. That rug she threw over you saved your ass. Man like you should be nice to a girl like that.*

I say, *Yeah. And watch her suffer like Jenny?*

Mercury shrugs. *Humans. Always fretting about the small stuff. Y'all gonna die anyway, no need to get weird about it. Say, who's house izzat? I'm sensing danger. What's going down?*

I say, *I need a safe place for a day or two until I can figure out who killed that boy and offer him up to the police. Otherwise, they'll hang me before the lawyers get here.*

The falling object becomes clearer as it races toward the ground. It's what I expected: a carbon-fiber box with an aerodynamic shape for stable falling.

Symone follows my gaze and sees the package. "What is that?"

"A gift from the gods," I tell her. "In this case, the corporate gods of Sabel Security."

The box pops a chute at fifty feet, twenty feet late, and crashes hard onto the front porch of the Victorian dacha we've been watching for half an hour. The large clapboard house leans toward a large tree that leans into it, like drunk friends holding each other up.

I jump the hedge and sprint for the house. Symone does her best to keep up.

Just as I arrive, a stocky young man springs from the front door searching for the source of the loud crash. First thing he sees is the box half buried in the porch, surrounded by splintered wood and a collapsed parachute. As I arrive, he steps forward, positioning himself between my package and me. He moves like a Mastiff puppy, powerful but with muscular uncertainty.

"Stopp! Wer bist du?" he asks.

That much German I understand. *Stop! Who are you?* I stick out a hand and give him my politician's smile. "Stearne. Jacob Stearne. Sorry about the damage—I'll have it fixed right away."

He eyes me suspiciously before glancing behind me to see Symone trotting up the driveway.

"What is this? What is going on?" he asks in English with only a hint of German accent.

"Jacob?" Betty Bardon strides out of the house. She takes in the trunk-sized box, the damaged porch, and the remains of the parachute before turning her gaze back to me. Her voice rises in both pitch and volume as she asks, "What the hell are you doing here? And why are you wearing that?"

Seeing her again makes my heart stop beating. Suddenly, I remember how her breathtaking beauty makes men forget their own names. I take a deep, calming breath. I wasn't expecting to react like that.

Mercury turns to me, *You picked Betty's crib as your hideout? Dude, what have you been smoking? You done scorned this woman. Oh, you be toasted like a marshmallow now. Hopeless.*

I tell him, *I didn't actually scorn her. It was more like—*

"You think you can just show up at my door and ask for sanctuary?" Betty's voice rises another level of volume and intensity. "You had your chance. You chose Pia Sabel over me. You made your loyalties pretty clear that day, Mister. How dare you show up like this?"

My heart starts up again, racing this time. I haven't spoken yet and

I'm already out of control.

Her ice-blue eyes flash like lightning. Her mouthwatering figure hides under a suit fit for a banker, not a movie star.

The silk of her blouse trembles, giving away her racing heart. She's having the same reaction to me that I'm having to her. I take another deep, calming breath to pull myself together.

I say, "Can we discuss this inside, like—"

"Don't you talk to my man like that, lady!" Symone steps to my side, jutting out her chin, fists on her hips, and a scowl to scare the devil.

"Whoa. Hang on now." I twist to face her. "I am not your—"

"If you trust him—he's all yours," Betty snarls. She turns up her nose at the sight of Symone's diaphanous t-shirt.

The young man standing next to Betty is also taking in Symone's diaphanous t-shirt. He doesn't turn up his nose, though. Instead, his mouth slowly falls open. Two more faces appear in the doorway, watching us.

Betty faces me. "Underage, Jacob? Is that what you're in to?"

"Hey!" Symone yells. "I'm nineteen!" When we all turn to her with skeptical expressions, she adds, "In September."

A cab drops off a young woman carrying several bags of designer clothes. As she approaches with a curious look at our gathering, the young man standing next to me asks, "Did Papà release your credit card, Francesca?"

"For the funeral," the young lady replies with an Italian accent. "My money."

She squeezes past me and through the others, heading inside.

"Mind if we go in?" I ask again. "This fashion attracts the wrong kind of attention."

"That's a jailhouse jumper. Why would I want you inside? What have you done?" Betty leans in, a furious scowl on her face.

"He rescued me from sex traffickers, that's what!" Symone barks.

Betty snaps a judging scowl at the girl. "What?"

"A madam and her gorilla dragged me into her stable." She squeezes my arm and runs her hand up and down it. "Jacob got me out of there. Saved me."

Betty's expression changes in an instant. She was never a sex worker, but a circle of rich men abused her at an early age. She feels Symone's pain. She says, "Oh, you poor thing! What happened? Come inside and sit down. Would you like some tea?"

She reaches out, gives Symone a hug, turns them both toward the door, and waves several other onlookers out of her way.

When they cross the threshold, the young man on the porch and I face each other. I gesture at the package sticking out of the wood. "Um. I'll just grab this and, you know, follow them inside. If that's OK with you."

"Did you say 'Jacob Stearne'?" he asks. His stomach growls, causing him to blush. He forges ahead. "The Hero of Paris?"

"Well, I wouldn't say 'hero.' That was a couple years ago and more fate than—"

"Can we make a selfie?" He grins big.

While he hoists his phone into position, I push his hand down. "Not dressed like this. You'd be incriminating us both. So, uh, inside? Shall we?"

"Oh, *bitte,* sorry, yes, please, come in." He grabs the package by the handle and yanks it out of the floor while gesturing me forward. "Chris Anrig. It is a pleasure to meet you."

We shake hands and go inside.

The two other women in Betty's entourage sit on either side of Symone on the couch. My rescued companion regales them with the horrors of trafficking. The girl with the new clothes pulls tags off her haul as she listens. Another young man watches thoughtfully from the nearest seat. Chris drops my package at my feet and joins them.

Symone spins a yarn about someone bashing his way into a house where ten vicious mobsters held twenty women in chains as sex slaves. Apparently, her savior started a horrific fist fight that escalated to a knife fight before concluding in an epic gun battle the likes of which haven't been seen since James Bond died.

I'm as entranced as the others. I can't wait to find out who this guy is. While she holds us all spellbound, I open my box of goodies and change. It's relatively private since the women notice nothing but Symone's story and the men notice nothing but her t-shirt.

Emma is the best ops manager I've worked with. Everything I asked for sits in one box dropped from a passing airplane. Pistol, magazines, Sabel Darts, Sabel Vision, Sabel Monocular, Sabel phone, three new passports, a backpack. Even Sabel toothpaste. Everything except a second change of clothes. Only one day's worth, including underwear. There is a note at the bottom that reads, "Sorry about the clothes. Supply chain problems. More to come."

"Jacob," Betty calls from the kitchen, "give me a hand in here."

I find her washing teacups. I grab a towel and start drying them. A kettle sits over a flame on the stove.

"Is that true?" Betty asks, nodding over her shoulder at Symone's impromptu thriller.

"Her version contains a significant dose of hyperbole." Then I explain about Symone using the hand signal and my subsequent raid on an otherwise female-run brothel with one lone enforcer. "She says she came to Latvia as a dancer, but they expected something more."

"I know how that goes," Betty says. "Show up to read for a movie role and find yourself on the set of something very different. No reading required." She glances out at the living room. "Poor kid."

She pulls a box of teabags off the shelf and starts dropping them in cups. She's one tea bag short. "Sorry for exploding out there. You caught us at a bad time. One of our friends was murdered last night." She finishes the bags and fills a small pitcher halfway with milk. "So, what's your story? What were you arrested for?"

"Murder."

She freezes in place, the milk container hovering over the pitcher. She cranes over her shoulder to look at me. Color drains from her face.

With as much compassion as I can muster, I tell her, "They mistook me for whoever killed your friend, Kevin Winn."

She can't breathe for a beat. Then her breathing picks up, fast, shallow, and panicked.

I continue, "I came in yesterday morning to keep an eye on you and the Electric Light Army—"

"Liberation," she says. "Liberation Army. It's not a '70s rock band. No one gets it right. We might change the name."

"Whatever. Anyway, I followed you and your friends to a townhouse and watched while your squad got the party started."

"You were spying on me?" Fire lights up her eyes.

"You lied to me about the *Chaac Project*. You lied to me about the *Chaac Equation*. I came to figure out why. I discovered your, uhm, army, ELA, and that you had them in place long before you and I ever met. Something you conveniently forgot to mention."

Her eyes lower, her lips tremble. She searches for an excuse that will probably be a lie, so I talk over her.

"When you and the ELA left, I snuck in the back door. I wanted to see whose house it was, why you'd been there. Just as I walked into the kitchen, a man stumbled into the room, bleeding profusely from the neck. Someone had slit his throat. But they weren't professional about it. They slashed across his larynx the way they do in the movies. Only nicked his carotid artery. See, it's deeper in the neck than people realize."

"Whoever did it wasn't a professional—" her gaze rises to mine "—like you?"

"I know right where the jugular and carotid are. Everyone I've opened up bled out in seconds. Like I was saying, Kevin staggered into the room, still conscious, still mobile maybe sixty seconds after the fact. I figured I could save him. I heard someone fleeing the scene. I chose to save Kevin instead of pursuing the killer. That turned out to be a mistake because Kevin was unsavable. If I'd had a medkit with me, maybe I could've saved him. Maybe not. Hard to say. Anyway, the next thing I knew, there were four Latvian police drawing down on me."

"He, he … did he suffer?" Her voice is shaky.

"I'm not going to lie—he lived long enough to know what was happening. I doubt it was painful though. Blood loss to the brain makes you lose consciousness pretty quick."

"Do you know who did it?"

"No. I didn't see you and the others leaving. I heard you. I thought everyone left, but it could've been one of yours who stayed behind, it could've been someone who snuck in same time I did, could've been a homeless guy wandered in seconds after you left. I have no idea. Yet."

"Well, you can't stay here." She looks me over, noting I've changed clothes. She turns to the fridge to put the milk away. She opens the door. "You should turn yourself in. Let justice take its—"

"I'm staying right here." I close the fridge in front of her. "Locals have a tendency to hang foreigners, then go looking for whodunit. I don't want to be proved innocent posthumously. I'm going to figure it out and hand the killer over to them." I get nose-to-nose close to her. "And that killer could be one of you."

CHAPTER 10

JACOB STEARNE

BETTY AND I KNOW THERE are a lot of unscrupulous people chasing *Chaac*. For all I know, she could be the murderer. We both know I need her help, and she needs mine, although she doesn't want to admit it. We face off for a long, uncomfortable time, staring each other down. The next one to speak loses the game. I never lose.

"We need Jacob's help," Chris says leaning into the doorway. "In case the killer comes after the rest of us."

Betty gives Chris a steely glance that telegraphs how little she cares for her young associate's unsolicited opinion. Then she swings her ice-blue gaze back to me.

"This is merely my thinking on the matter." Chris holds up his hands in surrender. "Of course, I will abide by the wishes of the group."

She gestures for him to take the tea tray. While he comes forward, Betty and I resume our stare-down. He glances from her to me and back, takes the tray, turns, stops. Looking at Betty, he asks, "You do not say this before, about knowing Jacob Stearne. He has many skills that could help us."

"You heard what I said to him," she replies without breaking our staring contest. "He had a chance to join the right side of history. He chose Pia Sabel's leash."

Chris wisely decides to quit the debate and serve the tea. We hear him tell the others in the living room, "Betty is kicking out Jacob Stearne."

A mixed reaction follows. While their voices cross each other, I can make out conflicting sentiments. *He's a wanted man.* Another says, *What is she thinking? We need him.*

Symone's voice rises above the others, "You'd be fools to send him away. If he gets mad, he could kill all of you with his little finger."

Which doesn't help my cause. Someone leaps on her for threatening them. Someone else jumps to her aid. Their voices rise. My fate remains uncertain.

"If you don't leave," Betty says, "I'll have to call the police. Otherwise, I'll be an accessory. I can't take that risk when I'm this close to an important deal."

"You've made a deal with Rafael Tum?" I ask.

"Rafael?" She tilts her head and frowns, curious where I would get such a crazy idea. "No, I've found someone willing to fund the cause."

Dude, Mercury says, *you've been replaced. That be good and bad news at the same time.*

I say, *How can it be both?*

Mercury says, *The good news: she got over being scorned by you, so you don't have to worry none about her clawing your eyes out. The bad news gonna be who the new guy is. I'm betting he's handsome and good in bed. Meaning, you be moving on.*

I say, *He can't be better in bed than me. Women always come back for more. They need me.*

"I don't need you," Betty says sticking her chin out. "Or Pia Sabel for that matter. Joe Rouleau is enthusiastic about changing the world for the good of all humanity. He's a visionary, a man interested in creating history. He has unlimited resources at his fingertips. His organization can make the *Chaac Project* a reality. He makes things happen in industry, art, and media. He's educated and erudite. People from all over the world seek his wisdom. He's morally and physically strong. And he's a royal."

A beat of silence rests between us.

"You had me at royal," I scoff.

Another beat of silence.

I add, "You know who's looking for you? Mikhail Yeschenko and the Russians, Remmo Nidal on behalf of OPEC, and Deng Zhipeng for China. Seeing as how you're an hour's flight from Saint Petersburg, my money's on Yeschenko winning the race. And you're going to take him on with these kids?"

A hint of concern creases her face. We both know she's tangling with people willing to wipe out her little gang of idealists before breakfast tomorrow. She says, "They're brilliant in their fields."

"I take it Kevin Winn's field didn't include self-defense." The pain in her eyes tells me I went too far. "Sorry, that wasn't fair. What fields are we talking about?"

"Francesca Bartoli, thin girl with the long, dark hair is our data analytics specialist. I don't have her working yet because we still need the *Chaac Equation*. Then there's Chris Anrig, the muscular guy, heads our cybersecurity. He sweeps the place for bugs every day and thwarts hackers if we have any. Kayla Clay, the one with the big smile, is our cryptologist. Like Francesca, she'll be working hard once I have the *Equation*. And then there's Logan Taylor, the skinny guy with glasses, my hacker. He's proven useful several times already."

I nod rhythmically. "So, an untested data analyst, a cybersecurity amateur, an inexperienced cryptologist, and a hacker who doesn't have anything to hack. What will they do when Yeschenko's men—all former spetsnaz soldiers—put them in a chokehold headlock?"

"They're not 'untested,'" she snaps.

"They're fresh out of college. Young idealistic revolutionaries out to change the world. Which is all very well and good, but they're not in a nice, safe college anymore. They're in the real world where people like Yeschenko and Deng are willing to kill to preserve the status quo." I wait while she realizes I'm right. "I've seen the experts in these fields at Sabel Technologies, and they're twenty years older. Don't let the movie business fool you with the teenaged nerds who perform instant magic; there are people who have been doing this for decades and can predict which trick Logan or Kayla might try next. None of which helps with the chokehold."

Betty swallows hard and frowns as the danger she's facing becomes clearer.

"Betty! There you are." A man leans into the kitchen.

If he's the new guy, Mercury is right. He's handsome in that regal, debonair, fashion-savvy, rich, Euro-hunk kind of way that no one likes.

Betty would never fall for an overdressed pool boy like this guy.

"Joe," she says with a lilt in her voice. "How wonderful to see you again."

Wonderful? I look at her and see the pupils in her bright blue eyes dilating as she faces him. The new guy, Joe, rips his gaze from Betty long enough to look my way. But only for a glance; then he's back to full eye contact with Betty.

"Oh, um," Betty says, "this is Jacob." She steels her voice. "He was just leaving."

He ignores me and addresses her in crisp, studied English with a hint of a French accent. "I am sorry to drop in unannounced, but my rental is not yet available. I was unceremoniously ushered out. My first thought was to spend an hour or two with you discussing the terms of our investment. Then, I realize the events of last night must be quite distressing. Naturally, I could not impose. However, I hoped you would be my guest at dinner instead."

"Oh, what a kind and thoughtful invitation," Betty replies. "Regretfully, I can't leave the others at a time like this. They're quite upset."

"I meant the collective 'you.' Everyone is invited." He bows his head slightly.

While Betty thinks for a moment, Joe notices me and checks me up and down. We're about the same height and build, but there's no question about who would win a fight. I could take him down while handcuffed. With shackled feet. Wearing a blackout hood. In a straightjacket. Drunk.

"You look familiar. Have we met?" he asks.

"No."

Joe offers a hand, looking me in the eye. "Joe Rouleau. I am most pleased to meet you."

"Jacob Stearne." I give his hand a firm squeeze.

"Not *the* Jacob Stearne?" His eyes light up and he smiles. A charming smile. "Of *Le Héros de Paris* fame?"

"Sorry, the what fame?"

"*The Hero of Paris*," Betty says with a disgusted note in her voice. "It was a huge hit in Europe last season. A Netflix dramatization, eight episodes about your little escapade in Paris."

"First I've heard of it." A moment of clarity shines a light on the phrase both Symone and Chris used when meeting me. Come to think of it, I've heard the phrase used a few times before that as well. "Don't they need my permission or something?"

Betty rolls her eyes. "You're so trusting, Jacob. If you had even considered joining the Screen Actors Guild, you would never have so blithely signed your Sabel Security employment contract. You gave Pia Sabel and Sabel Industries the rights to your life story. In this case, the Sabel Entertainment division struck a deal with … ah, doesn't matter, you're done. You're just lucky they decided to call it *Le Héros* and not *Le Fou de Paris.*"

Joe barks a laugh, then stifles it.

Le Fou … I think that means the fool.

Back up a second. Did she say Ms. Sabel owns the TV rights to my life? When did that happen? And how do I get them back? Suddenly, I'm not so sure Ms. Sabel's my best friend. Questions about who I should trust go off like popcorn in my head.

"Betty," Joe admonishes her, "that was unkind. I am most certain Jacob Stearne is a good man." Joe eyes me again, this time with more aggression. "Although, on the news … well, they say things not so nice."

"What do you mean?" Betty asks. Without waiting for a reply, she pushes past him into the living room.

She turns on a TV, opens a browser, finds the local news station, and the post about me. But it's in Latvian. I see a woman in an official uniform spewing angry words as if she were on the hunt for Heinrich Himmler. Spittle flies from her lips when she says my name.

Francesca translates in German. Which doesn't help me but appears to help the others.

I steal a glance at the room. Symone is on my side. That's one. Betty is not. Of the rest, the woman I believe to be Kayla Clark pales in shock. Chris Anrig is shaking his head as if he's hearing blasphemy that oddly makes sense, like the Pope listening to Galileo explain celestial mechanics. Our interpreter stops interpreting to stare at me as if Stephen

King's worst villain has risen from the dead and stands before her. The other guy, Logan Taylor, squares his jaw and clenches his fists. He's refusing to believe what he hears.

If that French show made me look good, the cop-lady on TV is twisting it into a pretzel of evil. Her brass name plate reads "M. Redgrave." Not exactly Latvian for "Smith." But she sure hurls the language like a native.

Mercury says, *Hey homie, you got two out of seven on your side. Ima place a bet at the gods' casino that at least one of them is gonna call the hotline scrolling across that screen.*

I say, *Betting against me?*

Mercury says, *Just going with the odds, brother. Say, this Joe Rouleau fellow look more amused than concerned. He hasn't taken sides yet.*

Redgrave looks directly into the camera and finishes with a vicious snarl and a mean glare. She's calling for my head on a spike. She plans to have a parade with her in the lead hoisting that spike like a drum major's mace.

I've seen this speech a hundred times before, always given by colonels who thought they should have made general by now. Which is pretty much all of them. Taken at face value, it appears to be an impassioned appeal for public safety. But that's not what she's really doing. She's making a political speech, a power grab. I can work with that.

But it'll take a day or two. And that means I need a good hiding place.

Somehow, I have to find the *Edison Data* while dodging political infighting. And the Latvian police just tacked "dead-or-alive" onto my wanted poster.

When the video ends, all eyes turn to me. And I'm down to one out of seven on my side. Symone, bless her barely-legal heart, is still with me.

What are my options?

Making a run for it makes the most sense. Even if Betty gave me her blessing—which doesn't appear likely—all it would take is one traitor making a call to the cops and I'm toast.

I could take them all hostage. I once sequestered twelve heavily armed Taliban officers all by my lonesome. I did have to execute a few of their lieutenants before they became calm and docile enough to herd like sheep, though. I can't kill the lieutenants here; that would be bad manners.

"Well," says Joe Rouleau, capturing the attention of everyone in the room. "What shall we do with *Le Héros de Paris*?"

CHAPTER 11

BETTY BARDON

LEANING AGAINST THE LIVING ROOM wall, Betty Bardon crosses her arms and watches the group dynamic unfold. She considers her four companions as younger siblings. Joe leads the discussion like a professional facilitator. The kids look up to him because he's nearly forty and, at their tender age, they assume that implies wisdom.

Although, as she listens, she notes that he conducts himself in a mature and intelligent manner. He even takes the time to let each person express their feelings. It's gone well into the evening, nearly dark outside, and he's managed to keep everyone engaged and involved.

She wants to give thanks to whoever runs the universe for sending Joe. She needs his cash to pay rent and phone bills. Her mobile phone will be shut off in two days and the landlord promised to drop by tomorrow—with an ultimatum.

Logan already asked his parents for financial assistance but didn't look comfortable doing it again. If push comes to shove, she could always ask Francesca for some cash. The girl's everyday outfits cost as much as rent. Several times Francesca called Papà in Milan, then went shopping, returning with Dolce and Gabbana, Michael Kors, and Chloe Gosselin.

Betty still wears her movie wardrobes, which are rapidly dating her style.

Jacob heads upstairs after telling everyone they could speak more freely without him in the room. Though she finds it suspicious that he dialed his phone while walking away. Who is he calling? Pia Sabel. Must be. Live updates on Betty and her ELA. She should expect no less—that's what Sabel pays him to do.

She wonders why she ever expected him to join her. Like her kids, she'd been taken in by the Cannes-Hollywood version of Jacob Stearne. She had hoped that once he listened to her plan, to make the intellectual property for a super-efficient metacapacitor open source and free, he would join her and protect her from the likes of Yeschenko, Deng, and Remmo Nidal. She'd been wrong. He was Pia Sabel's lap dog. Anything else was a fantasy. He would take everything Betty worked on, every scrap of information she'd collected, and turn it over to Sabel in a heartbeat.

And to think she almost fell in love with the man.

An angry scoff escapes her, which causes everyone to glance her way for a beat. She shrugs a dismissive apology for the interruption.

No matter what the group decides, she knows she must get rid of Jacob before he discovers anything.

Naturally, Jacob left his young girlfriend behind on the couch. His proxy. The girl is probably spying on them, reporting any tidbits about the project that might escape in the conversation. Which makes her wonder about the trafficking story. Symone referred to Jacob as *my man*. Under what circumstances does a girl like that use that wording? She can only imagine what those two are doing.

While these thoughts cross her mind, Symone looks at her as if sensing her rising animosity. As the debate over Jacob's future rages on, the girl gets up and comes to stand next to Betty.

"You had your own run-in with sex traffickers?" Symone asks quietly.

Betty meets her gaze, remaining silent for a beat.

"Yes," she says. "Different situation. I'm glad you're here and safe. No matter what we decide about Jacob, you have a place here until you decide where you're going next."

"Oh, I know where I'm going. Anywhere Jacob goes."

Betty can't hide her surprise. "Oh. So you two are—"

"No. Nothing like that yet. It's just … Well, I'm a long way from America, I ain't got shit for cash, I don't speak the language, and—" she waves a hand at the others "—you guys couldn't take a squeaky toy from a puppy. Now you've got killers chasing you down. Yeah. I appreciate your sympathy, but it's smarter and safer to stick with Jacob."

"If you need airfare for a ride home—"

"Home? Where is that? I got no home." With a huff, Symone pushes off the wall and retakes her seat between Francesca and Kayla.

Betty regretted her words as soon as they left her mouth. She doesn't have airfare for herself, much less anyone else. She's relieved and saddened at the same time. Relieved she doesn't have to come through with a plane ticket. And saddened to hear Symone is scared and alone in a foreign land.

Betty feels Symone's fear. She's been there, frightened of every male she sees, trying to live her life while making herself invisible, flinching at every dark corner or loud noise. Unable to sleep. At least Betty had a home. Years of therapy helped, too. Earning her graduate degrees helped even more. Making enough money to carry pepper spray and install an alarm system improved her confidence. The fact that Symone has a long way to go and no support to get there pains Betty.

Thinking about danger brings her to Jacob's warning about Yeschenko and the others. Her plan had been to use Joe Rouleau's money for security. Would it be enough? Would Joe agree to the protection she needs?

She can rule out Kevin's death being a random encounter with a drug addict. Someone out there—the Chinese, the Russians, the Arabs—might not know where she keeps the *Edison Data*, but they know she has it.

It could've been Pia Sabel for that matter. While she believed Jacob when he said he didn't kill Kevin, he could be lying.

She hears her name called by Joe.

"Remmo Nidal?" he asks.

"Oh," she says, hoping to gloss this over quickly. "They're a sketchy security company out of Morocco. They do the dirty work for OPEC and, um … yeah, they can be dangerous."

"You do not mention this before?" he asks with heat in his voice.

She shrugs. What else can she say? She needs his capital—why would she tell him the downside risk isn't losing money but getting killed?

He restarts the discussion with the others. She goes back to thinking about how Kevin died and what steps she could've taken to prevent it. Lost in guilt, she doesn't notice the group breaking up until Joe touches her forearm.

"You said nothing," Joe says. "But it is well known you do not approve."

"He's a liability," she replies. "If they catch him, we go to jail with him."

"Yes, these thoughts were expressed."

"Did you reach a decision? Sorry, I've been distracted."

"You care about him?"

She catches his gaze, uncertain if that was jealousy or a rhetorical question. She breathes a beat before answering. "He saved my life. I owe him for that, but I won't let my gratitude endanger the ELA. What did they decide?"

"They didn't." He tilts his head, examining her. "They left it to you."

She sighs. "Well, if that's the case, you know what I think."

"True. But do you know what I think?" Joe asks, his inquiring stare bearing down on her hard enough to make her look away.

Bad manners, she realizes. She has no idea what he thinks. And she's about to ask him for rent money.

"You're right," she says. "I welcome your opinion."

He waves toward the kitchen for privacy. She leads the way. He backs her into a corner with a non-threatening, but territorial posture.

"Kayla reports you do not trust him. I sense this as well from your inflection when mentioning him. You told the others you gave him an ultimatum not long ago. That leads me to believe there is some history there, yes? Perhaps a lover's animosity colors your opinion?"

Betty can't meet his gaze. "The past doesn't matter."

She feels his judgmental look examining her face. After a long beat, he says, "*Qui vivra verra.* He who lives shall see. Until then, I ask you to set aside anything that happened in the past, even those things you say do not matter. He may prove quite useful to our plans."

Betty looks up quickly and asks, "How?"

"You told the others he chose Pia Sabel over you. He is here as her spy, no? We know this and can use this to our advantage. As Sun Tzu said, 'keep your enemies closer.' Why not keep him close?"

Betty bites her knuckle as the concept roils her stomach. Having Jacob and Joe close could cause problems in a number of ways. The last thing she needs is two strutting males marking her as their property.

She looks into the gold flakes in his deep brown eyes. "Keeping him close would be the same as surrendering to Pia Sabel. He will take everything—because he can."

"We can control him. Use him to our advantage."

"You're dreaming. *Le Héros de Paris* didn't begin to show the real Jacob Stearne. He is ruthless and brutal, capable of cold-blooded violence like you've never seen." She sees Joe flinch. "How do you expect to control him?"

A thoughtful look clouds his face. His eyes sweep the room checking for eavesdroppers before he leans conspiratorially close and whispers, "We blackmail him."

Betty gasps as several questions in her mind fight for priority. The question she can't bring herself to ask: what kind of moral compass does Joe Rouleau have?

He doesn't give her a chance. He shrugs and says, "Not a nice thing but pragmatic. There are many reasons to do this, chief among them are intelligence and economy. By controlling what he sees, we control what he reports. As for economy, we save a lot of money having a one-man army."

Joe's smile grows slowly as Betty feels herself warming to the idea.

"We control what he sees and hears?" she asks. He nods, letting her think through how it works. She says, "When we need privacy, we simply tell him the cops are coming. Clever."

Clever isn't the right word. Devious might be better. She's been devious, and she doesn't like it. Justifying her past actions was necessary for the greater good but it never sat well with her. Jacob was right: she had lied, obfuscated, and omitted more than she cared to admit. As much as she hated doing it, her distrust of Sabel and Stearne proved prescient. But where does one draw the line? And how risky is it to harbor a fugitive, especially one capable of bringing the Latvian army to her doorstep?

As distasteful as the method might be, Joe's right about needing Jacob's skills. When she makes the final trade to obtain the *Chaac Equation*, she'll need someone for protection. And Jacob *is* a whole lot of protection.

"You're right," she says. "It's not nice but it's pragmatic."

"I ordered dinner for you," Jacob's voice comes from the doorway. "It's being delivered. My way of saying thanks for the hospitality."

"Oh, you didn't need to—" Betty starts to say.

"Chris's stomach was growling," he says. "Your fridge is empty, and you're rationing milk. That adds up to: you're broke. Sabel Security is buying if you prefer it that way. So, thanks again. I'm out of here."

Jacob backs away.

"Wait," Betty says quickly. "We've decided to let you stay."

"Can't," Jacob says as his boots pound up the stairs. "Cops are outside massing for an assault front and back. Gotta run."

CHAPTER 12

JACOB STEARNE

I HAVE NO IDEA HOW I'm going to get out of this. I know how I got into it, though: I made the mistake of living up to my promises. I sent €3,000 to Tatjana plus the €1,000 for the cash I borrowed. No surprise, Tatjana realized she could add reward money to her haul by letting the cops know I had her guy's phone. They triangulated it—and now they're here.

If the gods really cared about me, one of them might've sent a message reminding me to ditch the phone in a passing pickup truck. This is why I'm an atheist.

I look both ways to make sure Mercury is nowhere near. Thinking things like that gets me into trouble. I don't see him, which means he's pissed at me about something, so I'll have to figure out an escape on my own.

From the attic's dormer window, I can see the assault team moving into position. The neighborhood is made up of six large lots. Each house sits in the middle of the lot with a main entrance on one road and a back door crossing a large yard to a smaller lane on the opposite side. There are three houses to the north and two on the south. The police have set up a command center on the main road beyond the southernmost house. Columns of officers snake up both sides of Betty's property like a python cozying up for a squeeze.

Mercury leans over my shoulder to say, *Sneaking out on Symone is just cruel, homie.*

I nearly jump out the window. There ought to be a law against gods sneaking up on people, scaring the daylights out of them.

Half the fun of being eternal is watching you fools suffer, Mercury says. *Just like you done to poor Symone. Why not take the girl with you, dawg?*

Keeping an eye on the cops, I answer, *And watch her get shot on the rooftops?*

Mercury says, *Shoulda taken that machine gun Emma offered you, then you could mow them all down from here.*

I respond, *That's your advice? Start a war with Latvia? They're part of the EU and NATO. If I won this evening, I'd lose by morning.*

Didn't say it was gonna be easy, home boy. Mercury shrugs. *Sure be fun watching you go out in a blaze of glory, though.*

Times like this make me want to go back on my meds.

I pull out my monocular and adjust it. It uses an invisible laser to heat the air at an adjustable distance, creating a mirage-like mirror. It lets me see around corners like an invisible periscope. It works great in wide open spaces. As I try to get a look at the police operations center, all I see are leaves, branches, and trees. I adjust it closer in. Directly below me, under the eaves, I find ten officers lined up with their shoulders pressed to the south wall. Half the men face the east, the other half face west. They're about to storm around the corner and enter both the front and back doors simultaneously. A smart plan.

Betting on the fact that most people don't look up, I ease out onto the shake roof. The smell of moss and eternally-damp shingles greets me. I close the window behind me, tossing a bit of dirt on it to cover any sign it had been opened in the last year. I work my way around to the huge birch reaching from Betty's house to the one just south.

Whispers of instructions from the squad leader float up to me from ground level. I hear a frightened waver in his cadence. That's normal in real life. If you're about to breach a fortress and you're not scared, you'll be the first to die.

A shingle gives way under my foot and slides into the gutter. I stop breathing. No sounds come from below. I wait and strain my ears until the only thing I can hear is my heart pumping blood through my veins.

Carefully easing the monocular out of my pocket, I use it to look over the edge. They're still focused on their mission, waiting for someone to give them a signal. Stretching the monocular farther out and over the roof's hip ridge, I see a lookout glassing the house from the street. He's the one who will give the order to go. He raises his binoculars, checking the roof.

I flatten against the steep shingles and hold my breath. I have an angle, and I'm around a corner from him, but anything tall enough to be seen over the ridgeline could give me away. I've no idea what he can see. My nose might alert him to my presence.

After a breathless minute, I sit up enough to check the lookout again. His binoculars are back on the front door. He didn't see me. Which means he'll be giving the order any second now. I have to be ready when he does.

The first birch branch I test is far too thin to hold my weight. Scootching as silently as possible, I move to the next. It's more promising but all it would take is a crack of the branch under my weight and ten men would lift their rifles to fire on full auto until half the tree fell to their feet.

Below me, in the attic, I hear Symone's voice calling out. "Jacob? Jacob, you up here?"

I turn to Mercury leaning on one elbow, enjoying the scene as if he were watching *Mission Impossible XXVII*, or whatever number they're on. I hold out a hand with a shrug, the visual version of, *Can you get her to shut up?*

Mercury says, *What izzat? Are you praying for the gods to help you out, homie?*

Beneath me, Symone's voice rises again. "Jacob? Where the hell did you get to? You damn well better not have bailed on me."

I say to Mercury, *If it's not too much to ask. Would you mind getting her to shut up so I can get out of here?*

Not too much to ask? Mercury looks disgusted. *What have you done for me? Any act of supplication? I don't think so. Huh-uhn. Not even one ceremony to honor the one true god who loves you and protects you in times of need. Not once. I saved your scrawny ass from the Taliban, Russian Spetsnaz, the IRS, ISIS, the—*

Yeah, yeah, yeah, I get it, I tell him. *I'll do whatever you want. But I need to live through this first, so I'll do it later. Just get me out of here.*

With a skeptical eye roll, he vanishes.

Below me, I hear Symone tromping downstairs, muttering mean things about me as she goes.

I test the branch and wait for the men below me to get their signal. The wait is short. Suddenly, the boots of ten heavily armed men pound the planks around the house. They batter the doors open and spill in front and back.

With that racket going on, I slide across the branch slicker than a drunk monkey.

When I get to the trunk, which is located on the neighboring property, I take inventory of my options. I could cross the tree to the house next door. But the neighboring roof doesn't have attic dormers and may not offer a way down. I could climb higher to avoid detection, which might work if I can hang onto branches all night without falling asleep, letting go, and falling to my death. I could shimmy down and try to sneak out. Dangerous as it is, that's my best option.

Then, something to the south catches my eye.

In the staging area, where the cops rallied before the assault, there are two personnel carriers and a communications van. Four officers stand at the van, looking in. Behind them, in the dark, a lone woman paces nervously, ten yards from the others, biting a knuckle.

It has to be the woman from the TV broadcast. What was her name? Redgrave. I can tell it's her because she ordered what she hopes will be a big, noisy bust. The trouble with giving orders like that is that you deliver them with utter confidence—while inside, you're sick with doubt. All injuries will be your fault. Any success will be claimed by your superiors. Any mistakes will end your career. Right now, her gut is roiling with acid.

Mercury leans over my shoulder. *Feeling sorry for her, yo? Go talk to her. Work things out like that therapist always be telling you.*

I say, *You're telling me to walk into the command post while ten heavily armed men are searching for me, adrenaline wiring them up like meth-heads? And you wonder why I don't believe in you.*

Dude, has I ever steered you wrong? Mercury slaps the back of my head. *Try thinking, bro. What's she doing out here, huh? What's she worried about?*

I say, *Same thing I am: getting out of this mess.*

My discarded deity has a point. There's only one way out of this for both of us.

I slide down the tree and sneak down the lane until I'm peering over a parked car. She's listening to the reports from the van, staring at the ground, still biting her knuckle. The men at the van are hyper-focused on the live feeds on their monitors.

I crouch-run close to her. When she takes another glance at the van, I step silently behind her.

With one quick move, I grab her left wrist and bring it around her front, holding her from behind tighter than a lover. When she instinctively reaches for her pistol, she finds my right hand already holding it down.

"Redgrave," I whisper tersely in her ear, "you wound your men up so tight, if you call for help, they'll gun us both down before they realize what they're doing. Friendly fire sucks."

Her body is so tense she feels like an icicle, frozen and ready to snap.

With a heavy accent, she whispers back, "Turn yourself over, let justice work. You not be harmed."

"That's not justice." Lifting her left hand with mine, I point to the command center. "That's a hunting party. I saw your performance on the local news. If your people don't accidentally kill me, the locals will come with torches and pitchforks to finish the job."

"I give you word."

"Yeah. Tell it to my heirs."

I have no idea where to go from here. In front of us, her men are still focused on the monitors in the van. I could keep her as a hostage, but to what end? Adrenaline charges through my body like lightning in my nervous system. "I didn't kill Kevin Winn."

"Is not my problem."

"You sure as hell made it mine with that speech."

I hear a car door open behind me. I can't turn without giving Redgrave a chance to run. I can only pray to Mercury it's not more cops.

"Jacob," Symone's voice floats from the car in a whisper-shout. "Quit screwing around. Let's go."

"I didn't do it and I can prove it," I tell Redgrave. "Your lead man wore a body camera. Look for the footprints."

It worked; I raised her curiosity. Redgrave twists in an effort to look at me, but I hold her tight.

"You're a good cop," I tell her. "You'll figure it out. What's your mobile number?"

She hesitates, then tells me. I repeat it out loud, she nods. I commit it to memory.

Then I pull her pistol out, eject the magazine with one hand, kick it across the pavement. She and I both know she won't alert her team to my presence until she's retrieved it. It would make her look bad. Which means she can't tell them I was here, held her hostage, and escaped. That would make her look worse.

"I'm going to find out who did it and call you," I tell her. "Until then, I gotta run."

I let go of her, turn, and fly as fast as my legs will carry me toward where I last heard Symone's voice. I'm five strides in before I realize the girl has stolen a freaking police car! I dive into the passenger seat. She hits the gas while I'm still dragging my feet in.

CHAPTER 13

JACOB STEARNE

THE DOOR SLAMS ON MY ankles. I'm not going to lie—the pain stings enough to make me bark. I get the door closed and snap on a seatbelt. I take in my environment. I'm sitting on Symone's backpack, my shoulder squeezed against a special laptop frame bolted to the console with an array of switches and buttons underneath it.

Symone swerves around the intersection, swinging wide into the oncoming lane after the turn.

"Do you know how to drive?" I ask.

"I'm learning."

She levels an innocent trash can and brushes a tree before hanging a left while holding the accelerator to the floor. Brakes are for losers. The back end slides hard onto the shoulder, dipping into the ditch. Miraculously, she recovers. But not before we tip up on two wheels and slam down hard.

Mercury leans between the seats. *I gotcha, homie. I can correct her driving tactics while you find us a way out of this.*

I say, *What do you mean?*

Mercury says, *She stole a cop car. Latvia be all modern with the technology bling. They gots that voodoo stuff in these cars tells HQ where they be. Every cop in the Baltics gonna be bearing down on your ass any minute now.*

I yell at Symone, "Pull over."

"How?"

"Take your right foot off the gas, put it on the other pedal and shove it down hard."

The tires shriek us to a stop while I do my best to keep my face from plowing through the dashboard. Dust swirls around us as I catch my breath.

Reaching across the laptop, I slam the gear selector to Park. "Get out."

"You're not leaving me!" She grips my arm, clinging for dear life, her face and voice pleading desperately.

"They're going to catch me and open fire. You don't want to be there."

"No!"

I don't have time to argue. I jump out, grab the Sabel Visor from my backpack, run to the driver's side, and rip open the door. My plan to pull her out and toss her on the road is foiled by the fact she has already scrambled across the console and is belting into the passenger seat. No time to argue.

Throwing it in gear, I power down the lane. No idea where I am.

I hand Symone my phone. "Find us the most expensive resort in Jurmala and book a room."

She gets to work while I push buttons on the console. First button I find is the siren which screams our location to everyone south of Stockholm. After switching it off, I find the lightbar. It lights up the neighborhood in case the deaf didn't get my location from the siren. Then I find what I'm looking for, the headlights. I switch them off.

We're driving in the dark.

Sabel Visors provide a patented blend of night vision, lidar, and thermal imaging. I'm driving in pitch black with a full view of the road ahead. It's marginally better than eyesight in daylight.

"Found one," Symone reports. "Lielupe—however you pronounce that—up the coast."

She maps it out and holds it where I can see it. Four minutes away. The downside: only two roads between here and there.

"Thanks," I tell her. "Make a reservation for tonight. Most expensive suite they have."

She thumbs out my instructions, then looks up sharply. "What's with this popup that says, 'Select Identity?'"

I try to remember which passports the cops took when they booked me. I'm pretty sure they have my UK passport with the Aberdeen address. "Scroll through until you find MacDonald."

"What is that, some kinda secret spy stuff?"

"Just book the room under MacDonald. Then book an Uber, I mean a Bolt to pick us up at the hotel in five minutes. Use a different identity."

She figures it out in seconds. "Wanna tell me what that identity thing is about?"

"This car has GPS. They know where we are and are looking for ways …" I realize we're driving across an overpass. Below us, at right angles to our travel, is a train track. "Hey, how late do the trains run in Riga?"

"How the hell would I know?" She crosses her arms and pouts. "Hold up. I do know. Tatjana told me I'd be Cinderella if I didn't catch the 11 PM train outta downtown."

I glance at the time: ten past. I crank the wheel, spin the car around, and go back to where the overpass began its rise from ground level. A service track leads off the main road toward the rails. I take it down to the steep embankment and park.

"OK, you stay here," I say. "Tell them I took you hostage."

She cowers in her seat looking like I was shoving hot branding irons at her.

Mercury leans between us. *Zat how you treat people, dude? Really? Izzat how you was raised? A woman rescues you in a car and you just dump her like your high school sweetheart when you went off to college?* Mercury waves a hand at Symone. *Ima get you outta this, bro, but you gotta take her with you.*

I lie, *I've got a plan. I'm good. I'm not getting her involved.*

Mercury says, *OK.*

We're silent for a beat. Which is unnerving when you're hanging out with a god.

Well, I say, *um, just out of curiosity, what were you thinking?*

Mercury looks me over with the all-knowing, all-seeing gaze of the gods. *I be thinking the Latvian railroad uses the old Russian scale, that*

1520 mm wide thing and the track of this here PO-lees car just happens to be ..."

Mercury loves drama. He makes me wait.

I say, *What? C'mon. Just tell me.*

1520 mm! Mercury grins big. *You get your tires lined up on those tracks and you can fly down the rails. Ain't nobody gonna follow you cuz they'll think you gone crazy.*

I say, *They already think that—and not without cause.*

Above us, on the overpass, flashing emergency lights fly by. They're close. Not a lot of options left. Dropping the car back into drive, I ease it over the tracks and work the steering wheel until I get all four tires on the rails. Leaning out of the door for a look, I discover the tires flop over both sides of the steel rails the way a middle-aged dad's stomach hangs over his belt. It fits. I can't believe it.

Neither can Symone. Her eyes have gone from wide with shock to popping out in horror. She might need surgery to get them back in. She asks, "What the hell are you doing?"

I press down on the gas. The tires grip the rails like they were made for this. I don't even need to steer. I tromp on the gas and away we go. Lights out and GPS reporting an impossible location to the authorities. That should keep Redgrave guessing for a while. We fly into the night, running dark.

"Are you insane?" Symone asks.

"That's what the doctors say."

We drive along in silence for a moment. Then I have to ask. "If you're really eighteen, how come you don't know how to drive?"

"Who's going to teach me, you?" Her voice has a nasty snarl to it.

"No parents then?"

"Know how all the kids on TV live in a nice suburban house with a yard and a dog and a white picket fence? I grew up sleeping on Mom's couch in her one-bedroom apartment. Used furniture. No idea who my dad is. Mom drinks. Her friends would come over, they'd all get plastered, then one of them would wind up pawing at me. I left when I was fifteen."

"Where'd you go?" I ask.

She sighs long enough to make me regret bringing it up. I decide not to press.

"I figured I was better off stripping," she says. "At least they ain't supposed to touch you in there. I made enough to rent a room with Crystal for a while. She was nice. I've been on my own since then. It's lonely." She sniffles and turns away. "Don't have to rely on anyone else."

I consider how her last sentence would be more accurate if she turned the words around: *Don't have anyone else to rely on.* A stab of empathy pains my soul. I've had that feeling a few times myself—most often because an officer's battle plan sucked.

Then something from her story hits me in the gut.

"You were a stripper at fifteen?" I can't hide my outrage. "Is that legal?"

"You must be one of them farm boys never goes to the clubs, huh?"

I try to answer but words don't come out of my mouth. In fact, I am a farm boy, and no, I don't care for those places. The whole thing feels pointless. I'm not saying I've never been. I was in the Army and platoons tend to visit clubs as a unit. Although I always voted to visit a bar with a dance floor and women with whom one might have a future, as fleeting and minimalist as it might be.

"Hell," she says, "as long as you got someone's ID, they'll let you dance for tips. You just gotta be ready to run if the bouncer at the front door presses the button."

I think about the men I know who like those clubs. I wonder if they know there's a good chance they're ogling an underage girl. There is an element of delusion involved once you've crossed the threshold. One of those convenient lies we tell ourselves. As if the real world stays outside and everything inside is morally sound: the girls are of legal age and they like you. The customers look around at the other patrons and nod to each other, silently asking: *Is this OK?* And they get an equally silent response: *It must be.* And that makes it so.

A few seconds later, a single, piercing headlight rounds a wide curve coming straight at us. I do the word problem from grade school: If the last train leaves downtown at eleven, when will it reach the outskirts?

Right about now. Apparently.

There are no exits from this track bed. The rails are dug below the surrounding terrain, leaving a steep embankment. There's a good chance the engineer at the controls won't be watching a protected stretch like this. This is the time when he would be catching up on TikTok. We're going sixty and he's going at least that for a combined 120 mph collision. The gap is closing fast.

I yank the wheel and bounce the car over the rails and onto the embankment. I know we can't go straight up, so I try going at an angle. We get clear of the tracks and ties but can't get upward traction, as the front end goes up, the back end drags us back down. The train bears down on us.

Opening the door on the uphill side, I step out, reach back in and grab Symone. She grabs her backpack with one hand, mine with the other, and scrambles out fast. We clamber up the embankment a foot or two before the impact.

The car spins over our heads like a two-ton frisbee and cartwheels down the track as the train races past unscathed. Crunching glass and steel, groans and screeches, banging and clanging, metal on metal continues down the rails with declining energy. After an eternity, everything is silent.

Symone and I keep climbing. We reach the top, where a line of trees separates the recessed train tracks from the city. We stagger to the pavement of a road and look around.

A quarter-mile to our right, the Lielupe Hotel is lit up in blue-and-white flashing police lights.

CHAPTER 14

JACOB STEARNE

"DAMN, THEY'RE AHEAD OF US," Symone says, her shoulders drooping with disappointment.

"All part of the plan, kid."

Except, the trouble with a plan is: things never go according to. The Bolt driver is on the wrong side of the entrance and the language barrier is killing me. I try but can't get across how he needs to look to his left to see me. The hotel's artful entrance is shaped like the number eight, designed to give guests a full view of two gardens. Maybe they were going for an infinity symbol, I don't know. I'm at the bottom of the eight, he's in the middle, the hotel's front door is at the top.

Off to one side of the entrance are three police cars, lights flashing. They appear to be figuring out how to cordon off the area without alarming the wealthy guests. Which was my plan: check in online, get them focused on the building, then catch the Bolt from nearby. They would never expect me to be a few yards from their containment perimeter. But that plan required a Bolt driver who speaks English. I didn't tell Symone to check that option on the app.

"Stay here," I tell Symone. "I'll get him, and we'll swing around to pick you up."

Her vice-like grip clamps my arm. Tears fill her eyes. "You're going to leave me."

"No." I stare at her a moment. From the way she's clinging, it's clear she has abandonment issues.

The story of her childhood fills my head. She's been abandoned by everyone she's ever known, both morally and physically. Rightly or wrongly, she dreamed up a fantasy about me the minute I appeared in her doorway. A fantasy that I would rescue her the way I rescued everyone in that TV show. From that, she figured I'd give her some stability in life. I didn't sign up for that.

At the same time, I can't turn her away.

I put both hands on her shoulders. "I swear, Symone. I will not leave you."

The tears crest her eye lids and drip down her cheeks. She nods, resigned to being left by the side of the road. Again.

I can't believe people bring kids into this world and then ditch them, but they do.

Without time to reassure her, I pat her cheek, realize that's condescending, and bolt for the Bolt.

Mercury flies alongside me. *You can just lie like that, homie? No sense of honor?*

I say, *I meant it. I'll figure something out.*

Dude, Mercury tosses his hands in the air, *you be about to run for your life and you out here making promises you can't keep to a nice girl who done saved your ass by stealing a police car.*

I stop at the Bolt, open the door, then stop. *Stealing the police car made things worse for us, not better. Grand theft auto, destruction of public property, fleeing the scene of an accident ... I don't know how many charges they'll throw at us.*

Mercury says, *In that case, you gonna need all the gods you can get.*

I answer, *If you're offering to help me—and not make things worse just to watch me squirm—I'd appreciate your help.* I shake my head. *I realize that's a big IF.*

You gonna need to perform some kinda sacrifice, prove you care as much about me as you expect me to care about you, Mercury says.

I hop in the Bolt. The driver looks over his shoulder. I smile. He doesn't. He says something in Latvian. I point at the Bolt app with an address I've no intention of going to but entered so the police will think they have me. He points at his dashboard screen and says something in Latvian again. I point to the circle, indicating that I'd like to get moving now, and thrust a finger in the direction of Symone.

He presses the gas abruptly. I'm shoved back into the seat while he makes the sweeping turn in the wrong direction. I lean over the headrest and see his dashboard screen.

My less-than-flattering mugshot fills one side of a news bulletin. He's heading straight for the cops.

I bail out and roll through twenty rose bushes. Thorns tear at my clothes, leaving a thousand tiny cuts in my skin and clothes. Getting to my feet, I see Symone running toward me.

I wave her in a diagonal direction, toward the opposite side of the hotel from the cops. The garden circle has small trees and large bushes. Between them, I catch glimpses of the Bolt driver talking to the cops and pointing at the spot where I jumped.

When I get closer to Symone, I say, "Remember when I told you things don't end well for people who hang with me? I won't leave you and I mean that, but you'd be better off running in the opposite direction. I'll find you later."

"Yeah," she says as she runs. "Heard that one from a bunch of people."

"OK," I say. "You've been warned."

"Where we going, anyway?"

"If you're the police, which way do you expect fugitives to run?" When she looks around, I add, "So we're going in the opposite direction."

She looks toward the cops as we near the end of the garden. We stop behind an evergreen and watch them through the branches. The pavement is wide open from here to the edge of the ten-story building. I point to our destination: a side door fifty yards around the corner from the grand entrance. She nods.

When the officers run down the lane away from the hotel, we run toward it. We round the corner, heading for the side entrance. I stop and listen. Feet slap the pavement going away from us. I want to celebrate my brilliant deception. We've just made a clean getaway.

Then a face leans around the hotel's wall. The face is under a police cap. The cop pulls out a whistle.

Not such a clean getaway.

Grabbing Symone, I shove her toward the door. We wrench it open as the whistle alerts half the city to our presence.

We wind up in a laundry. From there, we find a stairwell and start jogging up the steps.

Symone's in good shape. She keeps up and doesn't complain. If you're going to rescue someone from traffickers, people who don't bitch and moan are worth the effort.

We're three floors up when we hear the cops enter the concrete well below us. We keep pounding up. Unless you have a helicopter waiting for you, going up is usually a bad idea. They'll have you trapped on the roof.

I tap out a request for another Bolt. This time, to meet me at the back of the hotel.

We get to the roof and run to the edge.

"Why come up here?" Symone looks over and chokes. "What were you thinking?"

I grab my special rappelling rope. No thicker than garden twine, a weave of magic fibers stronger than steel and a thousand yards long spools out of my backpack. I loop the open end around a stout flagpole, attach the deceleration device, and walk to the edge.

"You weigh less than one-fifty, I take it," I say to Symone.

She looks at me, the thin wire running to the flagpole and back, the tiny steel buckle that will regulate our falling speed, and says, "Are you insane?"

"Asked and answered," I reply. I grab her around the waist. "Hold tight."

"WAIT!" Her breathing is panicked. "Have you tried this before?"

"As a matter of fact, I used a rig just like this to jump off a fifty-story building in Monaco with Betty Bardon last month." I step to the edge, dragging her with me. "This is only ten stories."

"This is how you date girls?"

"We're not dating. We're fleeing the—"

She jumps on me, wrapping her legs and arms around me so tight I can't breathe. "Just tell me it's gonna work."

I jump. She screams. I cover her mouth.

When we land, she puts her feet on the ground and looks up at me. "That was fun, scary-fun. I want to be like you: kicking ass, afraid of nothing and nobody."

"No, you don't," I say, uneasy with her description of me.

The rappelling system auto-rewinds the cord, dragging the free end up to the top, around the flagpole, and back down.

I spot the new Bolt twenty yards away. At the same time, I hear the sound of a large piece of steel wrenching and groaning like a falling tree. I look up in time to see the flagpole teetering high above us. A quick look at my wire shows flakes of metal imbedded in the abrasive-weave. Retrieving it caused it to hacksaw through the flagpole.

Grabbing Symone's hand, I run for the Bolt. The pole crashes to the ground behind us. When I look up at the roofline, I see faces wearing police caps. I wave and keep running.

This time, I have a €500 note ready when I get in. I hold it in front of the driver. He looks at the note, then at me, then back at the money. He sees the flashing blue-and-white lights on the other side of the building. He shrugs and sets his Bolt app to "inactive."

In accented English, he says, "Where to?"

CHAPTER 15

CAPTAIN REDGRAVE

CAPTAIN MARISA REDGRAVE LOOKS OVER the hotel parapet. Ten floors, forty meters. In the dark. How the hell did he do that?

Her blood boils. Three escapes in an hour. She had the stolen phone located and sent in a ten-man assault team. Seconds after her men breached the house, Stearne held her hostage. That's a story she will take to her grave. She shakes with resentment at the thought.

How dare he? Who does he think he is? She takes consolation in thinking he'll slip up soon and she'll be there to catch him. It'll be a cold day in hell before she lets that arrogant American win.

The team thinks Stearne was never at the house, that he planted the phone there to throw them off. The residents denied knowledge, and the phone had been found under the front stoop as if thrown there. The house held no other signs of Stearne's presence. The only thing odd they found was a hole in the porch. No one could explain it. And she can't tell them she knew damn well Stearne had been there. She can't even tell them about the woman's voice she heard calling his name. Nor can she tell anyone it was Stearne who stole the police cruiser.

Although she did berate the officer who went to watch the raid on the house and left his patrol car running.

Marisa crosses to where Lieutenant Krollis squats to examine the flagpole's base. He shines a light on the clean break. It looks as though someone used a professional saw.

"Why would he do this?" Krollis asks. "How does this help him get off the roof?"

"Did you find any ropes?"

"Nothing." Krollis rises. "My men said they saw him on the ground running with another person."

"Man or woman?"

"They couldn't tell. It was too dark on that side. We found no trace of them—and we even checked the beach for footprints."

Footprints. Again, footprints. What was it Stearne said about footprints?

"That is a good excuse for letting him get away, Lieutenant Krollis." Marisa runs a finger along the flagpole cut. She says, "He escaped custody with nothing more than a coverall, now he has rope." She points to the flagpole's base. "Kevlar rope can cut tree branches. He must have something like that, only stronger and more abrasive. That means he's getting help."

The lieutenant nods with admiration at her reasoning. "I must say, it is an honor to work with you, ma'am. If you do not have a personal liaison, I would be honored to act as your aide."

She looks him over. Flattery is suspicious but effective and she needs an assistant.

"The assault team reported an odd suitcase at the house," she says. "Have them bring it to me, Lieutenant Krollis."

"Yes, ma'am." He salutes and adds, "We are not so formal in the Riga Division, you may call me Kaspars."

"OK, Kaspars. You will call me Captain Redgrave." She looks at the lights of central Riga rising like steam above the trees of suburban Jurmala and wonders where Stearne would've gone.

Her phone rings, disturbing her thoughts. After a quick look at the caller, and a deep breath, she answers and says, "Minister Krasnova, how good of you to call. What can I do for you?"

"You can tell me you caught him."

"I will not lie to you, Minister. We have gotten close, but Stearne leapt from a ten-story building to evade us."

"Call me Anna. Only the men have to call me Minister."

"Thank you, Anna."

"I say that because you and I would like nothing more than to show up Dubra. The road for women in Latvia has been long and difficult. People like Dubra make it more so. This is why I sent you."

Marisa looks at her watch: well past midnight. "I understand, Minister—I mean, Anna. We have not done our best yet. We are learning about Stearne quickly now. He has gotten help, though I don't know from whom or how."

"It is good to hear you're gaining ground." Anna pauses long enough to deliver her message. "Dubra called me a few minutes ago. He wants his men back. We have waited decades for an opportunity of this magnitude, Marisa. Your press conference was brilliant, your marshaling of forces was professional, your execution of the search is perfect."

Anna leaves a long silence.

Marisa understands her and says, "But the results are not."

"This is unfortunate. I told Dubra to fuck off. He wasted an entire day losing the man, he cannot expect you to fix the problem in an evening while he sips martinis. He threatened to go to the same reporters you spoke to. He intends to give them a progress report. I ordered him not to speak publicly."

"How did he take it?"

"Not well. We should expect him to send someone else to the reporters. I doubt he will cast you in the best light."

Both women are silent a moment. Finally, Anna breaks the quiet. "You said Stearne is getting help? Whom do you suspect? Locals?"

Marisa considers telling Anna the whole story: that Stearne fears a lynch mob and promised to catch the real killer. Doing so would require her to expose her secret. A disaster, despite the sisterhood of women. She considers telling her of the woman's voice, the shadowy figure seen running from the hotel. Any of that will lead back to Stearne getting away from her.

Marisa takes a deep breath and says, "He had high-tech equipment when he made the leap from the hotel roof. I suspect the company he works for, Sabel Security, is helping him somehow. It is possible Pia Sabel would take a call from the Interior Minister. Perhaps she would encourage her employee to turn himself in."

"This is a good idea," Anna says. "But I will not call the woman who is friends with presidents and prime ministers just yet. We would need evidence of his reckless behavior. Video would be best. Have you any?"

"Not at this time," Marisa says as she thinks about the bodycam Stearne mentioned. He said something about footprints. Guilty people love to watch the police chase wild stories; it gives them the feeling of control over the events. But Stearne was specific. Something he wanted her to see.

She mutes her phone and calls out to the lieutenant, "Kaspars, get me the bodycam video from Stearne's arrest."

"Right away, Captain Redgrave."

Minister Krasnova expects results, not failure. She unmutes and concludes her call. "I promise you, Anna, I will not rest until the murderer has been apprehended."

CHAPTER 16

BETTY BARDON

Betty Bardon stands at the door to the Grand Hotel Kempinski Presidential Suite, her hand poised to knock. She retracts it and takes a deep breath. So many things bother her, she can't prioritize them. Jacob fled seconds before heavily armed soldiers stormed her house. Hours later, Jacob invited her to breakfast as if nothing had happened. Who does that?

He's a dangerous man, yet Joe Rouleau thinks they can blackmail him. That could backfire in so many ways, she doesn't want to contemplate them. She still hasn't worked up the nerve to ask Joe for money and the landlord will be there before lunchtime. Someone killed Kevin Winn, but Joe shows no concern. Is Joe blissfully ignorant or brilliantly cunning?

Turning to Joe, she says, "This is a bad—"

Jacob opens the door wearing a tan Henley, blue fashion-ripped jeans, and Bottega Veneta climbers. He looks like a Euro celebrity, as if Francesca has been giving him fashion tips. Not only that, but his lips look warm. His chest looks strong and broad, his arms inviting. As handsome and charming as Joe is, Betty finds a strong desire to rekindle what she and Jacob had in their brief Canadian tryst.

With an elegant gesture into his opulent suite, Jacob says, "Free breakfast is never a bad idea. Thank you for accepting my invitation."

He looks down the hall beyond her. She knows he's looking for the rest of the ELA.

"Just us," she says. "We want to talk to you first."

They enter a living room where Jacob's outfit from the day before lies scattered on the couch. She picks up the shirt to examine it. Joe leans over her shoulder. A thousand tiny tears and rips have shredded large swaths of the material. She asks, "What happened?"

"Turns out," Jacob says with a nonchalant wave of his hand, "rolling in rose bushes doesn't bring the bliss you might expect. But you gotta try it to know, right?"

She never knows when he's joking. Several small cuts are visible on his neck, ears, and hands. He gestures toward the dining room, through two glass doors.

"Mind if I use your toilet first?" she asks.

"What you really want to know," he says with an annoyed glance, "is if Symone slept in this suite last night. She did not. She has a room down the hall. Feel free to check the sheets for yourself, though." Jacob waves a hand in a big arc. "Right through there."

Joe Rouleau laughs and claps his hands. "I like you, Jacob Stearne. With you, there is no bullshit."

Betty's embarrassment is doubled by an even stronger desire to plant that kiss even after, or maybe because, he called her out. They'd had an instant rhythm and natural understanding of when to slow down, when to speed up, and when to stay on the breathless edge. She'd never had that kind of instant intimacy with anyone else.

But Jacob's superior tone of voice has pissed her off. She makes a show of making the trek through the suite to the bathroom. A giant tub stands in the center with a platter-sized rainforest showerhead hanging from the ceiling high overhead. Wet towels stained with small streaks of blood lie on the floor. Did he really roll in rose bushes?

She runs water in the sink and flushes the toilet to round out her story.

On her way out, she notices the sheets are pulled back frugally on one side of the oversized bed. The other side is as smooth as the maid left it. He did sleep alone. That doesn't rule out the couch or the pool-sized tub. Still, she tells herself, Symone is not here. Nor are her clothes or accessories.

In the dining room, she finds Jacob and Joe seated at one end of a formal table set for ten. A waiter stands at one end of the room behind a row of chafing dishes. Bacon and fresh baked bread scent the air.

The men are laughing while exchanging conspiratorial ain't-that-the-truth looks. No matter how much therapy she goes through, finding two handsome men laughing while she's entering a room makes her nervous. After her abuse at the hands of wealthy men, she has never shaken the idea that all men are sexual predators.

"Flash your tits and they give you money," Symone says from behind her.

Betty can't help but flinch.

"That's an effective method, but self-defeating," she replies. "We need to meet men on a level playing field so we can beat them at their game."

"OK, sister. Let me know when you get that going on." Symone sports a fashionable ensemble of fitted but not tight black pants and an opaque pale blue buttoned-up blouse. It's an outfit Betty has seen other women of Sabel Security wear. Not a uniform, it's a flattering-yet-professional statement. Not one she expected to see on Symone. The girl skirts around her and heads straight to the waiter. He lifts the lids on the chafing dishes for her.

One more glance at Symone's and Jacob's fashion statements and Betty recalls his operations manager, Emma, could deliver custom-made clothes and designer fashions in a matter of hours. That tells her he's still in direct touch with Sabel Security despite being Latvia's most wanted man. There are distinct advantages to working with Sabel.

Jacob rises and bows as Betty approaches. She might love to hate him, or vice versa, but he does have a gentleman's manners.

She moves close to Joe, who attempts to rise after seeing their host's formality. Pushing his shoulder down lightly, she takes the chair next to him.

"You invited us here for a reason," Joe says to Jacob.

"To thank you for not turning me in last night," Jacob replies. "I appreciate that. I'd like to come back and hang with you guys for a few days."

"Why?" Betty asks, staring at Symone. "So you can spy on us for Pia Sabel?"

She feels Joe's glare strike the side of her face like a slap. They talked about this. They were going to be friendly, not ruffle feathers, say little, listen a lot, see what he wants, stall, and make a rational decision after a private discussion. They need Jacob a lot more than Jacob needs them; they just don't want to appear desperate. Just now, she blew through the whole plan.

Couldn't be helped.

"I could do a better job spying on you from a distance." Jacob smirks. "Which is what I was doing for twenty-four hours before Kevin Winn was murdered. You had no idea."

His superior attitude rankles her again. With snark, she says, "Really?"

"I searched the place for the *Edison Data*."

"You couldn't have." She regrets letting her astonishment get the better of her. "We were there all day."

"And yet, I did. Chris is an engineer but would rather be an artist; Francesca owns more designer clothes than Pia Sabel; Kayla reads a library worth of books every ten days; and Logan plays racing games without end. Formula One, I think."

Betty chokes. He was in the house while they were there. Joe is right—they need that kind of skill. But must he flaunt his expertise, thus making it impossible for her to ask? She snarls, "You were going to steal my work?"

"The *Edison Data?* It's not yours. You ran the experiments and kept the logs—on Ms. Sabel's stolen formula."

Ownership is an argument she doesn't want to get into right now. If it's ever settled, it will require lawyers and court rooms. She folds her arms and huffs.

Jacob's face is blank as he changes gears. "Before you walked out on me a couple weeks ago, you heard Ms. Sabel talking about *Chaac*. You heard her psychopathy rising. She sent me here with an unlimited budget to find whatever you have and bring it back. Given her state of mind, do you think that's a healthy idea?"

Betty can't stop herself from looking shocked. He's right on all counts. Pia Sabel sounded like a child stealing a toy from another child, repeating "Mine!" over and over. But to hear that observation from Jacob Stearne, Sabel's best friend and most loyal employee, is incomprehensible.

"It is obvious," Joe says, "that we think the best course of action is to make it public. What are Ms. Sabel's intentions?"

"Same as every billionaire," Jacob says flatly. "Use it to rule the world."

Betty finds herself becoming cynical. He's lying. She knows it. But he's not a liar. If anything, he's too honest. And his words fit with his high moral standards. All that aside, bringing him into the ELA is a big risk. Besides, she's not sleeping with Joe Rouleau, but she should at least give him a chance. He is paying the bills, after all. Or will be soon.

Symone brings a steaming dish with the strong aroma of fresh dill to the table and sits next to Jacob.

"That smells delicious," Joe says. "What is it?"

"Something I can't pronounce," Symone says. "But he says it's the Latvian farmer's breakfast—potatoes and sausage baked in creamy scrambled eggs. Least it ain't porridge, the only thing Tatjana serves."

"I am suddenly ravenous," Joe announces.

Betty and the men rise, examine the buffet, and make their selections. Betty opts for rye bread and oatmeal, Joe takes the same dish Symone is having, and Jacob fills a plate with apple pancakes.

They eat in silence for a moment.

After a few bites, Betty says, "We could turn you in at any time. We could blackmail you."

Jacob stares at her until she turns back to her oatmeal. He says, "Threats don't become you."

Betty tries to meet his gaze but feels Joe's disapproving stare. Instead, she looks at Symone, who is keeping uncharacteristically quiet. The girl who defended Jacob at their first meeting appears more than subdued. Silenced.

Betty catches her eye and asks, "What do you think, Symone? Should I trust Jacob? Let him inside my inner sanctum?"

After a comprehensive examination that Betty assumes is the young girl's way of sizing up the competition, Symone looks around the table before coming back to Betty. "None of my business what you decide. If I got a vote, I like it here. My room's not as nice as this suite, but it's a helluva lot better than Tatjana's and a damn sight nicer'n yours."

Joe looks an unspoken question at Jacob.

Jacob holds his gaze for a long beat. "Something I learned from hanging with Ms. Sabel: the best hotels are also the most discreet. A first-class bellman will bring bodies in and out, and never mention it. Eventually, though, a smart cop is going to check registries. I've got a couple hours at the most before this place is burned."

"Why should we take you in?" Joe asks.

"Because Betty stashed a part of the *Chaac Project* called the *Edison Data* somewhere. And you need someone to protect you from all the evil bastards like Mikhail Yeschenko who will kill people like Kevin to get it."

This time, Betty's shock turns audible. Her gasp echoes in the room. Hearing Jacob refer to Kevin's murder so casually hurts. Joe touches her wrist with concern. Even Symone looks worried about her.

Jacob's cold stare tells her he blames her for Kevin's murder. Does he think she killed the boy? Or does he think her negligence led to his death?

Joe faces Jacob, "Mikhail who?"

"Yeschenko, Russian oligarch," Jacob says. "Biggest oil exporter in Europe before the Ukraine disaster. He cornered his market by murdering rivals with his team of Russian special forces veterans. If Betty handed him the *Edison Data*, he'd kill her because it's easier than saying thank-you. And if you're bankrolling the ELA, he'll kill you too because it's cheaper than repaying loans."

Joe turns slowly to Betty with irritation in his face and heat in his voice. "You did not mention this before. The Chinese, the Arabs, and now the Russians? Are there others you failed to mention?"

Betty feels Jacob's questioning glance going back and forth between her and Joe. Maybe she should've been more forthcoming about the risks.

"Don't worry," she says. "I have it under control."

CHAPTER 17

BETTY BARDON

BETTY FEELS THE HOT GLARES from both Joe and Jacob. They think they understand the problems Betty faces, but they don't. The men in the room assuming they know what's best makes her blood boil. Even more infuriating: their critical frowns. That drives the decision about what she must do. Like a dark and angry storm on the horizon, a plan forms that makes her future miserable and dangerous. Yet, it must be done, and only she can do it.

Turning to Joe, she whispers, "Sorry. I still have concerns about who pulls his strings. Give me a minute."

"May I speak to you privately?" she asks Jacob. With a glance out of the room, she rises and leads Jacob to the living room.

Joe squints his displeasure, then engages Symone in small talk.

Jacob starts to say something. Holding up a finger to silence him, Betty gathers her thoughts, but it doesn't do any good. Her thoughts are scattered like dust in a storm. She's never been this scared before. Her life feels like a vice crushing her from both sides with no way out. She decides to speak from her tormented heart. "This is difficult for me to say, Jacob, but I need your help."

"And you want me to believe it's because you're in love with me, not because you're going to give me the *Edison Data*."

She can't stop her eye-roll. "I need help, not bullshit like that."

"Same," he says with a dead-serious stare. "I told you I wanted to hang at your place. Now you're asking me to do it as your personal security guard. You haven't been honest with your Euro-boy about the risks. Obviously, you have a problem you haven't told me about. What do you want, Betty?"

Betty worries her fingers as her breakfast turns over inside her. "I'm pretty sure Yeschenko killed Kevin, and I'm afraid he'll kill more of my team. I need help, protection."

"What do you really want?" he asks.

She looks into his eyes as her annoyance rises. "Not you, if that's what you're thinking, Mister. Oh, I am so over you, I could—"

"Forget you and me," he states flatly. "You went on an adventure—it careened out of control. A boy died. What do you want now, Betty?"

Her gaze falls to the floor. He's right. She imagined making a few deals, working with Rafael Tum and the ELA kids on the project, and solving the riddle in a matter of months. That turned out to be total fantasy. The last thing she expected was Russian, Chinese, and OPEC mercenaries murdering people to get her data. But Jacob's is a legitimate question: What does she want?

She says, "To produce an open-source metacapacitor that can save humanity from extinction."

"Nice—if you're interviewing for Miss America. This is the real world. Right now, you're out of cash, you have no investors, you—"

"He's going to invest. We're going back to the dacha to finalize terms right now."

"No investor will give you money if there's no return on that investment. Open-source means no return. He's stringing you along." He places a hand on her shoulder until she meets his gaze again. "And you're stringing me along, too. You're asking me to risk my life for you. What's the return on my investment?"

"Well, I'm not giving you the *Edison Data* if that's what you're asking. Pia Sabel can kiss my—"

"We agree about her. I'm asking about your goal here. If I help you win, what does that look like? You know damn well you're not going to finish the project before any one of those factions wipes you out. I keep asking and you keep ducking the question: what do you want?"

The weight of the last twenty-four hours feels like a monster on her back. Mikhail Yeschenko, Deng Zhipeng, Remmo Nidal, Rafael Tum—

she underestimated all of them and now Kevin is dead. What does she want indeed.

"I want to get out of this alive." She falls into Jacobs arms, fighting tears. "I just need a few days. I have a plan. Trust me."

His arms circle her for a moment, filling her with a tenuous sense of security. Then he pulls back, looks her in the eye. "You know Stearne's Law. There's no 'trust me' allowed. What's your plan?"

Stearne's Law works both ways: should she trust him with her plan? Psychopaths are coming for her with relentless pressure. Betty realizes she's never been in this situation before. The last time she faced a world of danger, Jacob was in charge. He saved the day, again and again. She felt safe in his presence, with nothing to worry about. This time, it's all on her. She needs to think like a leader, take responsibility and give orders. The trouble with leadership is that she must give orders with utter confidence—while inside, she's sick with doubt.

What does she want? No more dead kids.

The only way that can happen is if Jacob is on board. What alternatives does she have? Bringing Jacob in was Joe's idea which implies Joe has no expertise that could defend the ELA. Chris Anrig promised to be their muscle, but he's just a boy. Symone was right about the lot of them: they couldn't take a squeaky toy from a puppy.

Taking a deep breath, she tells Jacob her plan. Every detail, including the ones she has to think up while explaining it. He asks a few thoughtful questions without revealing his position. She keeps talking, hoping he will talk her out of it, or have a better, simpler plan. He only listens.

When she finishes, he holds his chin, stares at the floor, and says nothing for a long time.

Finally, he looks up. "What are you, Betty Bardon? What is your expertise? Are you a soldier? A spy? Assassin? Machine gunner? Or a physicist and actress?"

"Those last two," she says with a resigned sigh.

"Don't lose sight of your strengths," he says. He lifts her chin with his knuckle. "Stay in your lane."

She doesn't know what that means. Her eyes search his. He offers nothing. He turns and heads back to the dining room to rejoin the conversation.

The anguish she feels tears at her insides like a chainsaw. An empty and frightened feeling creeps up her spine. He's right. She's way out of her league. Taking on this project against people like Sabel, Yeschenko, the Chinese, the Arabs … is crazy. But she must. She got the ELA kids into this mess. It's up to her to get them out. She'll have to find a way. With or without Jacob.

CHAPTER 18

JACOB STEARNE

THE ONLY THOUGHT CROSSING MY mind as I close the door behind them is: They are not on the same page. The looks they exchanged spoke volumes. If I asked them who was in charge, they would both say, "I am." Betty laid out her whole hopeless plan. Joe told me nothing of substance. I'll keep doing what I need to, and hope Betty doesn't get herself killed.

But one thing's for certain: she has the *Edison Data*. I confirmed that by making a statement and watching her choke. A good actress would've done a better job of hiding that fact. Worse, I'm not the only one to figure that out. Kevin Winn died because she has it. Why? Did he figure out where Betty hid it, and she killed him to keep the secret? Was he spying on her, met his handler there, and died for lack of results? Did he see something he wasn't supposed to see? Was it unrelated? A love triangle could also be a motive. The ELA had three young men and two young women.

Whatever the case, Betty's in trouble. Deep. I'm not sure I can help her. I'm not sure anyone can. That bothers me.

Before I leave the foyer, there's a knock on the door. I open it to find Joe Rouleau with a sheepish look on his face. Betty is at the end of the hall, waiting for the elevator.

He says quietly, "You are not given to bullshit, Jacob. For that reason, I thought we might discuss our mutual admiration of Betty Bardon like gentlemen. Let me be blunt—are you still interested in her?"

Before the words *Hell no!* leave my lips, I realize my advantage. I put a hand on his shoulder and squeeze. "You're not used to dating American women, Joe. They have this bizarre idea that they can date anyone they choose." I give him a sly grin and punch his shoulder. "May the best man win."

As I close the door, his face bunches with anger. He'll get over it.

I text Emma, asking for a full background check on Rouleau. She'll get back to me when she has something.

When I turn around, Symone stands in the foyer with one more blouse button unfastened than during breakfast. She blinks in a way she thinks is seductive.

"Did I do it right?" She steps up close and speaks with a pout. "I did what you told me. I kept my mouth shut like a good girl. Are you pleased?"

"Yes," I say. "Thank you."

She closes in another step, toe-to-toe. She starts to unbutton another button. I press two fingers to her clavicle and push her back a step.

"Don't go there," I say. "I'm not interested."

"Every man's interested in what I got." She looks me over. "Oh. Are you gay? I mean, it's OK if you are."

Mercury tilts his head at me. *I'm starting to wonder the same thing, dawg. You got a slab of tenderloin standing in front of you and you be turning it down? Whatcha doing—practicing for the Catholic priesthood or something?*

I say, *Things have changed since Rome. We don't objectify women the way you've been going on about Symone.*

Zat so? Mercury grins. *You been on Instagram lately? Who be objectifying whom for whose sake?*

I say, *That's different. Somehow. I don't know how. Anyway, we don't take advantage of people when they're in a bad place.*

"I'm not gay," I tell Symone, "and I'm not interested. I understand where you're coming from. You're used to a world where you exchange sex for favors, protection, help. I'm going to help you because it's the right thing to do. No need for anything else."

"Help me what?" Symone's voice takes a derisive tone. More accusatory and distrustful.

"Help you get somewhere safe, get a job, and get …" My voice trails off because my promise not to leave her last night was more reaction to her situation than rational thought.

"A job doing what?" Symone asks. "I got a career and I'm good at it."

"Look, I'll figure out what happens next after I get a thousand Latvian cops to stuff their pistols back in their holsters. Until then, think of me as your older brother."

"Definitely gay." She huffs, spins around and throws herself on the couch. She picks up the remote and turns on the TV.

I grab my torn clothes from last night off the couch and consider where I could find an incinerator. I don't need my DNA lying around where Redgrave can find it and plant it at the crime scene. The waiter wheels a cart full of dishes out toward the service entrance. Catching his eye, I hand him the clothes and €100. Like all good staff at high-end hotels, he understands the need to destroy evidence. He shoves the clothes into a chafing dish and wheels it out.

"Hey, big gay brother," Symone calls out. "You gotta see this."

Standing behind her, I see an official wearing a uniform similar to Redgrave's with a similar insignia. There are three emblems on his epaulet where Redgrave had four. And he doesn't have her stage presence.

Looking up the insignia on the Sabel Official Identification database, I discover the woman I embraced in the alley last night is a captain. The guy on TV is one rung down the ladder at lieutenant.

Symone has the English closed captions on. The man refers to Redgrave's search for the dangerous American being stalled. He commits to keeping Riga safe by adding a second search team led by himself. He promises the state and municipal teams will work together to ensure the maniac Stearne—previously considered a hero—will not murder any more Latvians. He fails to mention Kevin Winn was American. He finishes with an interesting point: Americans are known for one thing—mass shootings.

Nice.

One thing is clear: he's a lieutenant who's backhanding Redgrave's work. Only a fool would go after a superior officer without someone of higher rank to back him, so that means this guy speaks for Redgrave's rival. If these competing officials are going to use me as a pawn, they need to get in line like everybody else.

Mercury steps in front of the TV. *Ain't that sweet, yo? Now you gots two gangs of bloodthirsty civil servants looking to mow you down for they own TV ratings and career advancement. You be hitting the headlines now! You be Mister Big Time.*

I say, *Why do I have a feeling the gods are behind this? According to the Bible, God and Satan bet on whether Job would lose his faith if they destroyed his world. Then they did.*

Mercury says, *That Job-stuff ain't part of the one true religious pantheon, homie. You be backsliding into that Judeo-Christian mythology. Keep focused now. Show the gods some love, make a sacrifice, and maybe a god who cares will help you out some. Just axing for a little respect, yo.*

If I weren't hallucinating a fully-realized god with tiny wings and a toga, I'd conclude religion is an imaginary construct allowing humans to deal with the irrational and random absurdity of life.

Back in the real world, I wonder: What options do I have? Fight or flight. The map in my head shows me Helsinki, Stockholm, and Gdansk all under 300 miles away. I could summon a Sabel jet and cross the Baltic in thirty minutes. That's an option.

Of course, with the mood these Latvians are in, they'd shoot me out of the sky. NATO members have the best surface-to-air missiles. Even if I made it, those other nations are Interpol members and would turn the jet around before I landed, giving the Latvians a second shot with those missiles.

Flight is ruled out. What are my options on Fight?

I made a promise to Captain Redgrave to catch the real murderer. I have to figure this out. Just a little more pressure now. So, what next? Start with all possible suspects for killing Kevin Winn: anyone chasing the *Chaac Project*, which includes Russian mobsters led by Mikhail Yeschenko; the Chinese delegation led by Deng Zhipeng; the surviving ELA members, including Betty now that I think about it; and a possible random serial killer out looking for victims in Latvian beach cities.

Although that last one seems a stretch. The bottom line: I don't have a clue. Which means I need to find one.

I'm the victim of office politics—in a city the size of Tulsa, in a nation with the population of Nashville—and I need to visit a crime scene on the other side of town in broad daylight. I need help. Real-world help. I need Miguel Rodriguez, my oldest friend from the 75th Rangers. And I need Isaiah Reddick, the latest addition to our team. I need them both; I'll settle for either. But they're on assignment with Tania Cooper and she's still mad at me for something. I need a higher power on my side.

I dial Pia Sabel.

CHAPTER 19

JACOB STEARNE

EMMA COMES BACK ON THE phone. "OK Jacob, I found out why you can't get hold of Pia Sabel. You know how she had those titanium rods screwed into her leg and ankle bones and they were attached to a crossbar to hold them in place? Well, a new attorney had some papers he needed signed. He tripped and fell on top of that whole titanium-cage thing."

"Ohmigod," I say, wincing. "That must've hurt."

"I wonder where that attorney is working now. Anyway, Pia's back in surgery, on heavy pain meds, and will be mumbling lullabies until this time tomorrow. Even then, she won't be in shape to overrule Tania. Before you ask, I tried Tania again. She told me the same thing she told you: Isaiah and Miguel are on assignment under her command."

"Did you try—"

"Yes," Emma says. "That's why you've been on hold so long. The only person who outranks you and Tania is Jonelle Jackson and she said, and I quote, 'I'm not getting between those two children. Tell them to work it out for themselves.'"

"Great."

"Sorry, Jacob, you're on your own."

"Tell Tania, if she ever finds herself staring down five hundred cops—"

"Tell her yourself. If Ms. Jackson isn't getting between you two children, you can sure as hell count me out."

Looks like I won't be getting any earthly help, so I guess it's back to worshipping a down-on-his-luck god.

"She did leave a message for you," Emma says. "She said to tell you the one and only priority is getting the *Edison Data* and bringing it home."

"Yeah, she mentioned that a few times."

"Just the messenger."

We stay silent for a beat.

"We got a little background on Joe Rouleau," Emma says, breaking the pause. "His great-grandfather claimed to be next in line to the Russian throne. Tsars, Romanovs, that kind of thing. But his family hasn't had much luck reclaiming it for the last hundred years. His grandmother owns a ton of commercial real estate in Paris, Amsterdam, Brussels, and Zurich. He was a privileged rich kid, degree from Sorbonne, added a masters in art history, then he joined the *Armee de Terre*. We don't have much after that."

"Do we know where he was stationed?"

"Abu Dhabi was his last known, twelve years ago. He was in logistics."

"Logistics? No one does logistics for twelve years. Boring AF."

"In other news," Emma says, "I've got more clothes lined up and those stealth cameras you wanted. I sent them and some other goodies to your last known address, Betty Bardon's rental."

I thank her for her efforts and click off. Damn Tania anyway. We're both executing missions at the direction of the President of the United States, and she sees it as a competition instead of a collaboration. Well, two can play that game. If she needs any of my resources, she can forget it.

What resources izzat, homeboy? Mercury sits on the couch next to me and points at Symone, who is happily playing Angry Birds on her phone. *You got a terrific resource right there. Although Tania don't swing that way, so I don't see her requisitioning your stripper for a pole dance anytime soon.* Mercury looks around the room. *As a matter of fact, I don't see you gots any resources to trade at all.*

I say, *Maybe not right now, but ...*

I've no idea what resources I might stumble across that Tania would need.

Mercury says, *People always dreaming about beating they workplace rivals but we gods ain't gonna let that shit happen. Too easy. Worse'n that, yo, the boys in Riga-blue are at the front desk, going through the registrations.*

Leaping to my feet, I grab Symone and put Escape Plan D into action.

Fifteen minutes later, a Peppo's Pizza Delivery truck pulls up to the hotel's loading dock where I've been hiding behind the trash compactor. Symone puts a blindfold on the driver and shoves him in the van's cramped back.

She's wearing a Peppo's shirt unbuttoned over the modest shirt Emma provided. Somehow, the modest shirt has lost another button. I don't know if Emma sent Symone a push-up bra or if she made hers into one, but she's got some cleavage showing.

I climb aboard. In back are ten steaming pizzas on warming trays and a teenaged boy wearing the blindfold with a smile.

"Great work," I say as I climb in. "Did €500 do the trick?"

"No, so I let him squeeze my tits. We have the van for an hour."

I look over my shoulder at the delivery boy.

"Not him," Symone says, "the owner. The kid gets a squeeze when we're done."

"Don't do that." I palm my face. "I do not approve. I have plenty of cash. We can bribe our way—"

"You're riding across town in a van with no windows—just like you wanted. How about a little fucking gratitude instead of this judgment bullshit, huh?"

I don't have anything to say to that, so I take up a position behind the front seats where I won't be seen from the street.

Twenty minutes later—after many pointers on how to drive, when to brake, the speed at which you can take a corner without two wheels coming off the ground—we're in Jurmala, rolling slowly past the crime scene. I'm in back, using my monocular to periscope a view of the townhouse. It's one in a row of five next to another row of five. They sit across the street from upper-class dachas in a slowly gentrifying neighborhood. Some homes are new and beautiful; others could use a little gentrification. Four blocks north, a string of nightclubs front the beach.

A cop sits on the front stoop surrounded by fluttering yellow crime-scene tape. The cop looks bored and watches the van. Which blows our cover. We can only make one pass without drawing scrutiny.

Cruising through the alley behind the townhouses shows the backside boarded and taped up at ground level. I had checked out the rental listing online before going in the night of the murder. It's a simple layout, meant for summer renters. The ground floor is a living room with a powder room. A small deck off the second-floor kitchen has French doors. A new surveillance camera under a dome the size of a soup bowl has been fixed on the deck support. Third floor windows latch on the inside. The fourth floor is an attic-office without windows on this side.

Symone stops at the end of the alley. She says, "You're not going back in there, are you?"

"I have to find a clue about who killed Kevin."

"There's a cop outside," she says with attitude. "He goes in to take a piss and you're toast."

"Thanks. I can deal with situations like that just fine."

"I'll go in."

Mercury materializes next to the blindfolded boy. *She gots a point, bro. The sun is shining, the cops are waiting for you to make some moves. They gonna pounce on your ass in numbers ain't been seen since Scipio Africanus defeated that upstart Hannibal at the Battle of Zama, ending Carthage's reign of terror.*

The battle of what? I ask. *Never mind. You're telling me Captain Redgrave has this set up as a trap?*

And Betty's crib too, Mercury says. *So, you gotta be nice to my girl here.*

I say, *I can't trust a stripper. She takes her clothes off for cash. She'll sell me out in a minute.*

Mercury looks offended. *Where izzat anti-stripper attitude coming from, dawg? It's a respected branch of the oldest profession. And don't forget: you weren't so high and mighty about the girls at Noir Lounge when you was on leave in Qatar. You wasn't so picky about the ladies at the Maze Club in Bucharest. Or the—*

I was young back then. I didn't have my life riding on it, just a few crisp twenties.

Mercury, god of commerce, says, *Well, there ya go, homie. Pay the girl. She can help you.*

Help me how? I ask. *Flash her boobs?*

"Why are you so afraid of a little boob?" Symone asks. "Worried you'll get a hard-on that'll pop your zipper?" She changes her tone of voice to a news announcer. "Jacob Stearne, he ain't afraid of no Taliban, neo-Nazis, Russians, nobody—oh, but show him a nipple and he's gonna pass right out."

She laughs hysterically.

Ignoring her is the best move. I hope.

I can't ignore the boy in back, though. He gasped at the mention of my name like he'd come up for air after being underwater for three minutes. I'm glaring at him when I feel Symone's hand wrap around my bicep and tug.

In a pouty, baby-doll voice, she says, "Martins, you won't let Auntie Symone's secret out, will you?"

The boy obediently shakes his head no.

She continues, "You're not going to tell anyone about Auntie Symone chilling with the Hero of Paris, are you?"

He shakes his head with more energy.

She finishes with, "Now be a good little Martins and don't believe what those nasty police people are saying—or Auntie Symone won't be nice to you later."

He lets out a sigh of pure lust and smiles.

Damn, my gender is too easy.

But Mercury's right. This townhouse is a trap. Thanks to Redgrave and Netflix, everyone between Berlin and Saint Petersburg knows my face on sight. Doing my own footwork would be suicide.

Sensing my predicament, Symone says, "I want to help. Teach me what I need to do."

"No!" I look at her closely. She recoiled when I snapped at her. "It's too dangerous."

"I can do anything," she says. "Just teach me. Please? I want to be like you."

"You don't want to be like—"

She scowls and says, "You don't know what it's like. Every day, Jacob Stearne strides through the world fearing nothing because you can destroy anything. Not me. Any man out there can hurt me, take me, do what he wants. You don't know how that feels."

"You're right," I say. "I don't know your world view. That doesn't mean you should be like me. It's not a path that's easy or safe."

"I don't care," she says, her voice sinking in volume. "I'm sick of being scared all the time. I want to be a fearless, ass-kicking hero. I'm done being terrified of every guy who pushes me into a corner, every guy who follows me out of the club, every guy who tells me he's going to be real nice to me. Fuck that. Show me how you beat up guys and kick down doors."

She holds my gaze for a long silent moment. She's dead serious. I don't know what to say. Finally, I say, "I'm not on a mission to kick down doors. It's more of an espionage thing. Spy stuff. But I can't spy if they lock me up for murder. Thanks, but I'll figure something out."

She twists back to the steering wheel with a pout and folds her arms.

The trouble is: I don't have any options. Symone is the only assistant on my side right now. As I look around the van, I realize, she's done a pretty good job.

Turning back to Symone, I say, "I need you to pull around the block and drive through that alley once. You're getting a test."

"Why? What test?"

"Shhh … that's part of the test."

She does as I ask. In a couple minutes she has gone around the long way and has us back in the alley without passing the sentry cop a second time. Passed the first part of the test with that one.

As we trawl the alley, I lean between the front seats, keeping my face out of the light but getting a little view. I have her drop a Sabel Monitor the size of a small mobile phone out her window.

Pointing to the building, I say, "I want you to look at that townhouse and tell me what you see. How would you get in and what are the risks?"

Her eyes devour the scene. She takes in the whole unfenced backyard, scouring the features, doors, and windows. When she can't see anymore, she speeds up, then slows to a stop at the end of the alley.

She turns to me and says, "I'm not a thief, I'm not a spy. I have no idea what that was all about. Talk to me."

"First, you noticed the cheap wireless security camera someone put on the deck above the ground floor? Wasn't there two days ago. That's the cops monitoring the back yard. The door there is boarded to slow you down while the guys watching the camera send in troops."

"Why would they do that?" she asks. "Wait, you mean criminals really return to the scene of the crime like they say on TV? That's stupid."

"Captain Redgrave thinks I was after something in there and will come back to get it. She's expecting me."

"Ooh, being a fugitive's gotta suck," she says with a little snark.

"If you waltz in there, they'll know I sent you. So, we need to be clever. That monitor I had you drop on the ground will feed wireless data back to my ops team in Maryland. They'll hack the system and fake the feed. In real life, unlike the movies, that takes time. When it's set up, we can come back, climb to the deck, go in through the French doors."

That was how I got in the night of the murder. The lock was easy to break with a strong twist. The townhouse owner doesn't worry about security since any burglar worth his salt would break into the bigger houses across the street.

"You said 'we!'" Symone fast claps and giggles with excitement. "I'm working with Jacob Stearne! I can't wait to post this."

"Whoa! You're not posting anything. You do and Redgrave will lock us both up for life—if we live through the shootout. Have you posted anything?"

She faces me, her expression drained. "I'm out of data on my plan. And the guys at Betty's looked at me funny when I asked for the Wi-Fi password."

"Good. Don't post anything."

Decision time. Go it alone and take one huge risk? Or trust a stripper who turns nineteen in three months? Cops on the edge won't fall for her boobs and I'm not sure she has anything else in her bag of tricks. Symone could become collateral damage in a second.

CHAPTER 20

JACOB STEARNE

SYMONE DRIVES US BACK TO Betty's rental, where an obvious unmarked cop car waits at the end of the block. Taking a pizza, she hops out, crosses the street, walks up to the two men in the car, and talks to them. While bending at the waist. With her buttons undone.

They take the pizza with smiles.

She trots back to the van, rolls it down the driveway and around the back.

The three of us haul the remaining pizzas inside for the ELA people. I figured since I am one of them now, I should bring gifts. The two ELA women give Symone some side-eye with serious disapproving looks.

"Button up that shirt," I whisper. "You're making the competition nervous."

She starts to say something snippy but bites it back when she sees my face. I'm serious. She steps around me, facing Kayla and Francesca, and buttons up with exaggerated gestures. Then she turns up her nose and pushes young Martins ahead of her out the back door to the van. Assuming Martins is getting his promised reward, I decide not to watch. That way, I'm not condoning anything. It's one of those lies we tell ourselves when we silently ask: *Is this OK?* And we give ourselves an equally silent response: *It must be.* And that makes it so.

"Where is Betty?" I ask the women.

"With Kevin's parents," Francesca says.

"This came for you," Kayla says, holding out a package.

I tuck it under my arm, sling my backpack over one shoulder, and pound my way upstairs. As I pass the women's room, I notice the remnants of a shopping expedition on the floor. Designer clothes are strewn about, tags scattered nearby. For a moment, I wonder if I'm looking at Fashionista-Francesca's haul, but it's easy to tell the Italian's closet from Kayla's by the quantity of expensive clothes. These are basic fashions, which makes them Kayla's. Did she come into an inheritance, or is she upping her game because of her proximity to her wealthier roommate? Lying beside the pile is a box cutter with an extended—and potentially lethal—blade. Noting this, I head upstairs to the next level.

There's space in the attic, which is less accommodating than the Presidential Suite but offers an escape route should another assault team storm the building. I lay out my sleeping bag, inventory my gear, and think.

Getting into the murder site is not a problem. Getting out alive is a different story. Sending Symone to do it feels as abusive as the guys who put her on a stage at fifteen. What they did was immoral; what I'm contemplating is not—but it could be worse. It could be deadly.

I take in my attic home. Exposed rafters, unfinished floorboards, musty boxes, the smell of aged dust. If I don't do something, this will be my prison. That makes Symone my only option.

I hear Symone coming up the stairs, talking to Francesca as she comes. They part company at the floor below the attic, the bedroom floor.

Her irrepressible smile shines in the gloom. Stopping at the top of the steps, she leans against the newel post and crosses her arms. "Wanna tell me about this 'we' stuff you were talking about?"

"First, give me your phone." From her expression, you'd think I asked her to sacrifice her first born. I add, "I'm hiring you. You're now a contract worker for Sabel Security. Welcome aboard. You hand over that piece of crap and I'll give you a Sabel phone. Satellite uplink, totally secure, unlimited data, and no social media posts without Emma's approval."

I hold out a phone. It looks just like an iPhone, only thicker because of the extra security circuits. She stares at it while she thinks about the trade.

Her skeptical gaze eases for a beat, then returns. "What do you mean contract worker?"

"You'll be paid a per-day rate while you're helping me. It—"

"How much?"

"Three hundred a day, plus expenses."

"Forget that," she huffs. "I make a grand a day dancing and there's a club on the beach. I saw it. Ain't one Tatjana controls, neither."

"A grand a day works out to two hundred thousand a year," I tell her. "If you were making that, why are you carrying a five-year-old phone with a cracked screen and a limited data plan? Yeah, roll your eyes all you want—the math doesn't lie. You might've made a thousand one time, but not every night. The deal is: three hundred."

"Five."

I shake my head. I can't believe I'm haggling with a kid who's barely out of high school. Trouble is, I need her. Obviously, she gets that. It occurs to me that strippers are excellent capitalists. I say, "Three-fifty."

"Four-seventy-five plus tips."

"There are no tips," I tell her. "Four hundred. Final offer."

"Four-seventy-five." She crosses her arms under her boobs and squeezes her cleavage together.

"No," I say while straining to maintain eye contact. "Four hundred."

"OK, I'll split the difference with you: Four-seventy-five and you can have the tips."

"Fine," I say.

Mercury says, *The math don't lie, zat what you said? She just made the math lie and you swallowed it whole. She didn't split no difference and there weren't no tips to begin with.*

I say, *I knew what she was doing, I got tired of negotiating.*

Mercury says, *Oh, izzat what you're telling yourself?*

I'm still holding the Sabel phone out. "Before you sign the paperwork, which is on this phone, you should know what we're doing and why. We will be conducting what's called a black bag operation: breaking in to collect intelligence. As for why: there are several factions trying to corner the market on a new tech that will change the world. Betty is an expert in the field and some of these factions are targeting her to get an advantage."

"Yeah," she sniffs. "I heard what you guys were talking about at breakfast. Pia Sabel wants to rule the world. Betty and Joe want to give it to the public. Whatever 'it' is. But I get it. I'm down."

With our gazes locked, I quickly realize she's smart. Street smart. At the same time, I know what's underneath that crusty shell: a naïve little girl. I say, "There are a lot of dangers involved."

"I know," she says impatiently. "The cops might mistake me for you because we look so much alike—except I'm a foot shorter, a lot prettier, and not as flat-chested."

"It's no joke," I tell her. "Their brass convinced them I'm a vicious killer. When they go into a room expecting me, they'll shoot first and say, 'oops' later. They might even apologize to your corpse on the way to the morgue."

The smirk leaves her face. It's getting real. Good. I need her to be serious.

"You can't talk or flash your way in," I say in my drill-instructor voice. "The guy out front will have a list of authorized personnel and will require ID. Captain Redgrave will have put the fear of god into every person in uniform. They'll be on their game. That means you'll be going gray, blending into the neighborhood while sneaking in the back door on the second level. How are you at climbing silently?"

"Uh, did we say four-seventy-five?"

"We're not revisiting that. If you can't do it, or don't want to do it, I'll wait until HQ can get someone out here."

"No. No, I'm good. I can do this. Just tell me about that silent part."

"You know how you hated this outfit Emma sent for you?" I wave a hand at her clothes. "The shoes look like sneakers but fit like socks because they're special. They don't squeak on any surface, and they stick like glue when you climb. We have gloves to match. The pants you hated are made so they don't swish when you walk. That shirt has the same material."

Symone lifts an arm and feels the cloth. She rubs it against her ribs and nods when it makes no noise at all. "Sweet."

I fill her in on basic burglary techniques, only I call it "spy craft" to make it seem nicer. I demonstrate by moving silently from floor to floor making her mirror my moves. She's a quick study. Dancing keeps her balanced and in control of her limbs. While she's far from field-ready, she's better than I expected.

We sneak into the computer room, where we find Logan typing away on a laptop. We get out without Logan even looking around, which I consider a success. We make our way past Chris Anrig, who's working out in a spare room. We head downstairs. I show her how to walk on the outside edges of the treads to minimize squeaking staircases.

We get to the living room right when Betty walks in the front door. She takes one exhausted look at us then stares at Symone's cleavage. Out of the corner of my eye, I see the young woman has popped those pesky buttons again.

"What are you two doing?" Betty asks with a suspicious tone. "Joe let you join, but this is still my operation." She looks me up and down. "No matter what you bring to the table, you're still one big, huge liability." She side-eyes Symone. "And I don't recall giving you permission to bring your stripper."

She put a lot of emphasis in the first syllable of that last word.

"Wish I could say it's nice to see you too," Symone snaps. She crosses her arms and twists her back to us.

"Don't take it out on Symone." I step between them, facing Betty. "I take it things went badly with Kevin's parents?"

"As you might imagine." She blows out a breath. "They blame me. Said I lured him out here. They acted like we were lovers. I told them it was all about physics, at which Kevin excelled, but they weren't buying it. They pushed me out and told me not to contact them. Ever."

"I'm sorry."

"Yeah, sucks. No funeral, no closure for the ELA."

She watches Symone, who watches Francesca come downstairs with a shopping bag. Francesca says she's going out for a bit, then leaves. Symone wanders over to Kayla, reading in the other room.

Betty keeps her eyes on Symone while she asks me, "What are you two doing?"

"I hired her," I say. "Hey. Don't give me that look. I hired her to work. She's pretty good at doing what she's told. Don't give me that look either. It's not like that. There's nothing going on between us. At least, not as far as I'm concerned. She's going to be my eyes and ears outside this house. I need to figure out who killed Kevin before Redgrave and her rival in the police department find me."

Betty tilts her head and bats her lashes over those ice-blue eyes. "I could help you."

Her offer surprises me on several levels. She's a lot smarter than me. And significantly smarter than Symone. That should be a good thing, but smart people often consider themselves smarter than you in all areas. Which makes them difficult in circumstances like this one, where I have a lot more experience. Betty might know Quantum Electro-whatever it is, but how many times has she cheated death by holding her breath? If I tell Symone to hold her breath, she will do it without asking why. Betty would ask and that one spoken word in a silent room could get her killed.

As much as I'd like to work closely with Betty again—for more reasons than pissing off Joe—this is not the mission for a reunion. Those blue eyes are still staring into mine. Damn it. I really want to work closely with Betty again. Intellectually, I know it's a terrible idea. But … no way.

"You can't help," I tell her. "You're a suspect."

Betty's face turns red. She's building up a head of steam that will explode in a second.

I hold up a finger and say, "Everyone is a suspect until they're eliminated. I'll work to take you off my list first."

She accepts this and steps closer again, those eyes come up to mine with an invitation. "I didn't do it. You know I couldn't. Look at me, I'm a wreck."

"You're an actress." I pivot the conversation by asking, "Hey, what about this Joe Rouleau guy? What's he about?"

"He's funding the ELA. Well, that is, he will be. Soon."

"And he's handsome."

Her eyes wander the room before coming back to me. She starts to say she hadn't noticed, but realizes I'd call her on that one. She turns away and heads to the kitchen. "Still, I could be a bigger help to you than a stripper—even if you still suspect me of something so terrible."

Joe Rouleau opens the back door and steps in.

"A stripper?" He looks us both over with a good measure of disgust. "Surely you didn't bring your *putain* with you."

"She's no such thing!" Betty juts her chin at the man. "Symone is a dancer. Sex workers deserve the same respect as anyone else."

Joe puts his hands up in surrender. "Sorry, this was out of line for me to say. I came to discuss financial arrangements."

I lean against the cabinet with my best sultry look and say, "Let me know if you need help with 'finances,' Betty. I'm good at handling figures."

That earns me a scowl from Joe and a *not-now* glare from Betty. With a grin, I peel off the cabinetry and go in search of Symone.

She's showing Kayla how to twerk while Chris and Logan observe like Olympic judges.

Dragging her away, I hand her an earbud. "This has a camera in front. We'll be in contact the whole time you're going through the house. I'll see exactly what you see. To keep the noise down on your end, you give a thumbs up for yes and thumbs down for no."

"Got it." She pushes the earbud in and looks at the app on my phone. Immediately she gets the infinity mirror effect and looks away before she gets dizzy. She says, "OK, with you walking me through it, I can do this. We're gonna make a great team."

I'm reminded of how ill Redgrave looked after she sent in the assault team. She gave the order and immediately second-guessed herself to the point she couldn't watch anymore. That's how I caught her. It reassures me that Redgrave is a good cop thrust into a bad situation. She's honest. I can work with that. As a matter of fact, I should call her and give her an update.

At the same time, it makes me realize I'm in the same situation she in was last night. I'm sending someone into harm's way. Worse, I'm sending someone too green and naïve to know how dangerous it is. Symone is a living example of the Dunning-Kruger effect: a person's lack of specific skills in a certain area causes them to overestimate their competence. At least Redgrave sent in people who were trained.

My heart sinks. Symone's an amateur and I'm sending her into a dangerous place. This is a bad idea. Really bad.

CHAPTER 21

CAPTAIN REDGRAVE

CAPTAIN MARISA REDGRAVE STARES AT the carbon-fiber box on the floor next to her desk. For the nth time, she leans in to examine the scratches on the underside, the guidance wings, and the parachute still hanging from the opposite side. She can't believe what it looks like: a suitcase made to re-enter Earth's atmosphere from outer space. Or at least fall from 30,000 feet. What was in it? Who sent it? It had to have been weapons for Jacob Stearne, but nothing about it is traceable.

Marisa returns her attention to the bodycam video from the murder scene. The officer wearing it at the time, Ilja Tobers, has just charged into the foyer of the townhouse. One officer clears the room in front of Ilja. Another comes from the back, announcing the ground floor is all clear. One of the cops calls out in Latvian to see if anyone is in the house.

An urgent voice upstairs responds in English, but Marisa can't hear distinct words.

Ilja leads the others up the enclosed stairs to the next floor. The stairway opens into a dining room on the street side of the townhouse. Ilja crosses the room to a junction with another stairway leading up to the next floor. To his left through an archway is the kitchen.

A smooth pool of dark blood fills the space from the upper stairway to the kitchen's archway. Nearly two liters of what looks like thick, dark syrup covers an area larger than a body. As Ilja approaches the archway, a prone body becomes visible. Kevin Winn lies on his back, his legs wide, blocking the entire archway. On the far side of him, deeper in the kitchen, Jacob Stearne sits on his knees, applying pressure to Kevin's neck wound.

Stearne looks up and says, "I found him like this and tried to stop the bleeding."

Ilja and the other officers shout instructions in Latvian for Stearne to put his hands up and back away from the body. Stearne protests. The audio is garbled but she thinks he's saying if he takes his hands off Kevin's neck the boy will die. The officers either don't speak English or don't understand what Stearne is saying. They repeat their instructions and move in aggressively.

Looking sick, Stearne lifts his blood-soaked hands. A fountain of blood erupts from Kevin Winn's neck. Stearne puts his hands back on the wound. Whether it's to stop the bleeding or finish the job is not clear. His movements trigger a reaction from Ilja's partners.

Two officers tackle Stearne.

Marisa stops the video. Seventh time through and she still didn't see any footprints. Stearne was either in the middle of killing a man or trying to save his life. If he was murdering someone, why would Stearne want her to watch the video?

There was clearly a lack of communication on scene. None of the officers spoke English? It's taught in Riga's grade schools. Most young people in Latvia, as in much of Europe, can speak it as well as Marisa. They grew up on SpongeBob. In Marisa's experience, it's rural folk who don't have it available in school. Where does Chief Dubra get his recruits—the border towns near Belarus?

Her phone rings. The caller ID reads: Mikhail Yeschenko. She's heard the name in the news from time to time but can't imagine why he's calling her. Out of curiosity, she takes the call.

"Marisa," Yeschenko says. "I need an update on your investigation."

"Who are you?"

"You saw my name and you answered. You know who I am."

"What is your interest in this case?"

"I have many interests in Latvia and am welcomed at the highest levels. By the way, Minister Krasnova thinks highly of you. There is no need for concern; just tell me if you caught Jacob Stearne."

"This is an inappropriate call, Mr. Yeschenko. I will verify—"

"Just tell me if the raid at Betty Bardon's house netted anything of value."

"The EU has issued strong sanctions against you, Mr. Yeschenko. I will not speak to you again." Marisa clicks off.

Instantly, she texts Minister Krasnova, "Mikhail Yeschenko called me directly and dropped your name. Should I take his call?"

The reply is immediate. "Never. He is sanctioned. He must be working with someone inside Dubra's operation. Yeschenko brings the kind of corruption that could get Latvia kicked out of the EU. Remember, texting is not a secure communication."

Marisa sighs. Chief Dubra's mismanagement she expected. Laziness and political turf wars, she expected. Corruption? Especially involving one of Russia's most violent oligarchs? Her stomach tightens. Her anxiety quickly turns to rage. She fires off an email to Dubra that starts: *It has come to my attention that one or more of your people is in touch with* ... She types out a long rant for five minutes then stops. She leaves the email open. When she cools down in a few minutes, she'll review and edit before sending.

Her phone rings again. This time, it reads: Jacob Stearne.

Her heart stops at the sight of his name. Since she gave him her contact information, she must be careful about taking his call. She thinks up a plausible cover story about how the American got her number, then fires off a text to Lieutenant Krollis ordering him to trace her current call. Putting Stearne on speaker, she asks, "You are ready to turn yourself in, Jacob Stearne?"

"Not until you go on national TV to calm the hysteria you created." He leaves an unspoken beat. "I'm calling to offer you a better deal."

"This is not negotiation. You will not be harmed. I give my word."

"Yeah?" he says with attitude. "What about your pal? The one who tossed gasoline on the fire you lit? I didn't catch his name."

"His name is no matter. He is mouthpiece for Police Chief Dubra."

"So that's your rival, the Chief of Police? You aim high, Captain Redgrave. I noticed you're in a turf war with Chief Dubra that will make or break your career. I'm calling to help you."

"Help yourself—turn yourself in. If not, we find you soon enough. You know it is matter of time."

"Oh, are you tracing the call?" His snarky attitude comes across like sandpaper on a rash. "Let me save you the trouble. You'll pinpoint a spot in the desert about eighty kilometers northeast of Riverside, California. That's where Sabel Satellite uplinks geo-locate all calls unless I click a different setting. It's where we keep our main array of satellite dishes. So, are you interested in my offer?"

Marisa's first instinct is not to believe a word he says. Criminals love to burn police hours. He's done it before with the footprints. "Why do I believe you when you lie about footprints?"

"You're better than that, Captain. Look again. It's not about the footprints that you see. To make Dubra's theory work, what footprints do you need?"

"No need for footprints. You were there. With the bloody hands."

"OK, you're slower than I thought. You want to beat Dubra because your career depends on it. I want to beat Dubra because my life depends on it. We're allies. When you figure out the footprints, think about this: what's better than catching Jacob Stearne?"

"Go ahead, mansplain," she says with snark of her own.

"Catching the real killer—the one Chief Dubra missed." Stearne clicks off.

Marisa wants to hurl her phone across the room. The arrogance of Americans! His superiority! How dare he accuse her of being slow. He's lying.

Wait a minute.

Why would he call her and risk discovery just to lie? Because he's a psychopath. If there is one thing she owes her country, it's to bring Stearne to justice. Now.

Lieutenant Krollis calls next.

She picks up and says, "What?"

"We have his location," Krollis says, "Somehow, he escaped us. He's in the California desert—"

"Let me guess, about eighty kilometers northeast of Riverside, California. No, lieutenant, that is where Sabel Industries routes all their calls. It's where their satellite dishes are located. Everyone knows that."

She clicks off, tosses her phone on her desk, and runs her fingers through her hair. "Damn."

After giving herself a moment to steam in resentment, she decides not to review her nasty email to Chief Dubra. She makes sure Minister Anna Krasnova is copied on it and clicks "send."

CHAPTER 22

JACOB STEARNE

I'M SITTING IN THE ATTIC, my laptop in front of me, my phone propped up on my backpack. Midafternoon sunlight filters through tree branches, barely reaching me through the window. The universal smell of ancient dust is the same in Latvia as back home. I'm about to run Symone on our mission. I've been part of a thousand dangerous missions, but this is the first one with an innocent, untrained life at stake. My stomach's tight.

Emma tells me how the Sabel Tech team hijacked the original feed from the police security cameras at the murder scene. They're posting it to my laptop, scrubbing people like Symone from the frames, then sending it on to the Riga police monitors. We control what they see. There are two cameras, which is an oddly small number since Redgrave is counting on my return. Her rival, Dubra, must be slow-walking resources to her and giving them to the other guy. Works to my advantage for now.

The cop on sentry duty is gone from the front steps. He disappeared between the time Symone and I rolled by and when my techs stole the camera feeds. We don't know if he went inside or left the area. That's a huge problem.

Logan nicely offered to drive Symone anywhere she needed to go in his rented VW Golf. Errands, she told him. He didn't care, just fawned over her, and held the car door open for her. Symone had gone radio silent—against my wishes—while they drove there. She just now put the earbud in and connected with me.

The video feed comes through in hi res. She's walking down the alley behind the row of townhouses. I have her turn her head left and right so I can see the area. The alley is one-sided. The townhouses are separated from an apartment building by a stand of trees. One townhouse on the end appears occupied, while the other four are listed on Airbnb as available with only the murder scene rented this week. That's ideal for Symone's approach.

She scales the ground-floor supports and reaches the second-floor deck in three seconds flat. Dancing keeps her fit and nimble. "Nicely done," I tell her. Next, she tries the kitchen door. It opens easily. Not surprising since I broke the lock, but I'd think the police would have fixed that before now.

Unless it's a trap. Our planned excuse is Symone will pretend to be a YouTube personality doing a live feed. It might work. If they don't look too closely.

"Ease into the room," I tell her. "Keep your breathing steady. You're doing fine. No sudden moves, take each step—"

"OK, Dad," she whispers. "We went over this a million times."

Somehow, I'd forgotten how much fun it is to work with teenagers. I grit my teeth and pray to Mercury that the missing cop isn't inside. Her spoken words could echo in the empty house.

The kitchen is a simple layout: sink and counter on the right, oven and fridge facing her, table and chairs on her left. The floors are light-colored ash.

In the archway to the dining room lies a dark stain covering an area roughly the size of a king-sized bedspread. Symone stands perfectly still after realizing what caused the stain: Kevin Winn's blood. It's been cleaned up but not scoured. Scattered on the floor and into the next room are photographer's markers. The crime scene investigators aren't finished. That's a problem.

I hear Symone's breathing pick up a notch. My monitor shows a spike in her heart rate.

"Try not to think about it," I tell her.

Her breathing becomes shorter, more ragged. Her heart rate screams into high gear.

"Hey, Symone, it's OK. It is exactly what you think: blood. A man was killed there last night. We already knew that. They cleaned up the evidence and left a stain. You're going to be fine."

"How old was he?" she asks with a trembling voice.

"Kevin? I don't know. Early twenties, I think. But don't speak—there could be cop in the building." Her heart rate drops a little, not enough. "Are you OK? You can leave if you want. Remember, thumbs up or down for an answer."

The camera doesn't move and she doesn't answer. She's frozen in place and panicking. Thirty seconds goes by. Then another thirty.

"Symone, are you with me?" I ask. "Would you like to come back?"

No answer. Heartbeat drops a little more. I hear her trying to control her breathing.

Being frozen like this could be a disaster if anyone comes in. That does it for me.

"Hey, Symone, I'm sorry. This was a bad idea. I want you to tiptoe back to the door and leave. First, we have to get your breathing under—"

"No." Her answer comes short and fast. "I got this."

She doesn't but pointing that out would be counterproductive. She'd argue.

I say, "OK, last reminder: use hand signals, don't speak." I wait until she gives me a thumbs up. "Now. We're going to take a long, deep breath through our noses for four seconds, then hold it for seven, then exhale slowly over eight seconds. I'll count it out."

Following my instructions, we go through the panic-attack protocol four times. I keep pace with her. We're working together. Her vital signs return to near-normal. It's time to distract her from the death scene. "You're doing great, Symone. Now, show me the countertops. Move slowly so the camera doesn't jiggle."

We move through the kitchen drawers and cabinets then out toward the dining room. In the hallway on her left, two open archways lead to the stairwells. One goes up, and the other down, both obscured by thin walls.

In the dining room, more photographer's markers stand next to four glasses on one end of the table. Some have traces of liquid; all have been dusted for fingerprints. On the sideboard are four bottles of liquor. The

ELA kids had a party with the owner's booze before they left.

I guide her to the stairs leading down. She gasps and freezes.

"Did I hear a toilet flushing?" I ask.

Symone's gloved hand gives me a thumbs-up in the camera. She finally remembered to gesture and maintain silence. I'm proud of her. Now we know where the sentry is. Calming her, I have her move to the other stairway, the one that leads up. I have her hold there, waiting and listening. Either the cop will come up, or he'll go outside.

While she waits, I see where Kevin's blood spray hit the wall at the back of the stairwell. That tells me he faced his killer on the steps. He was looking up; maybe he heard an unexpected noise and leaned in to check. The killer was coming down, which explains the sloppy slash across Kevin's neck: a bad angle. Kevin then turned and staggered away from his assailant. The instant I saw him, I called out, announcing my presence. The killer, already on the stairs, fled upwards. My attention went to saving Kevin.

The first two stairway treads have blood on them. On the third is a roughly triangular bloody print. I tell Symone to put her hand next to it for scale. It's about the size of her palm. No prints on the other treads. Symone points across the camera's view toward the other stairway.

"Is he coming up?" I ask and get a thumbs-up in reply. Her heart rate spikes. "Slowly. Keep your feet on the outside edges of the treads. Don't panic."

She gives me another thumbs-up. Then she rushes quietly.

"Stop," I tell her. "You need to check the next level before going up there. Someone might be waiting there."

She gives me a thumbs-up and proceeds to the archway opening onto the upper floor. She scans the third floor from ground level before going the rest of the way. It's a short hall with bedroom doors on either end and a bathroom in the middle. Then she gestures in the camera pointing down and slightly back.

"He's going to the kitchen?" I ask and get a thumbs-up. I have her proceed to the bedroom at the front of the house—opposite from the kitchen—where the floorboards are less likely to squeak over his head.

The room has a queen bed, the sheets smooth and unruffled. More markers lie in odd places where the crime scene people might've found hair or fiber evidence. Symone sweeps the room. Tucked under the bed is a single shoe with a red sole. A stiletto heel, satin in a purplish shade of blue. Louboutin, or a knock-off. Expensive in either case. A marker stands next to it.

I have her pull the shoe out and hold her hand next to it for scale. The discolored toe section is roughly the size of the triangular blood stain on the third tread. Blood stains mar the welt just above the sole. She replaces it exactly where she found it.

Next we stop at the top of the stairway and listen. The cop downstairs is opening and closing the back door.

"Don't be alarmed," I tell Symone. "He heard something. He isn't sure what, but he's on high alert and knows the back door is not secure. He'll call it in. At some point in the next few minutes, we'll have an opportunity to leave. When it comes, we need to be quick. Cautiously quick. Until then, keep calm and keep working."

We hear a two-way radio squawk followed by the officer doing exactly what I expected. I think. He's talking in Latvian, but he's calm and even in tone. My guess is he's saying, *Backdoor is not secure; get someone out here to fix it. I'm going to look around.*

And that means he's going to be coming upstairs shortly. Telling Symone this might spook her. Not telling her might cause her to freak out when she realizes what's going on. That's a big risk. I feel the question tie my stomach in a knot. I don't want to tell her, much less admit it to myself, but our little YouTuber story might not work. If the cop is hearing noises, he might be clearing each floor with a drawn pistol. If he's well trained and calm, we don't have a problem. But most cops don't get the training they need or deserve. Untrained cops are nervous, and nervous cops are trigger happy. That could be a big problem.

"Take a peek in that bathroom," I tell her. "Take as few steps as possible. We don't want creaking wood."

She moves down the hall and leans in the doorway. With a good sweep, I can see the sink has markers in the basin and on the floor. Next, I have her move to the back bedroom. It's empty and pristine. No markers, no evidence. She repositions to the next stairwell, the one leading up to the top floor. According to the Airbnb listing, there is an attic-office upstairs. Unusable space made semi-usable to enhance the listing.

When she hears the cop coming up from below, she heads up to the next level. Her heart rate is hitting the maximum. I fear another freakout coming.

"Take it easy, Symone. You're doing great. I'm with you. Nothing bad is going to happen."

We run through the breathing exercise again and it works a little better this time. She resumes her mission, heading up to the attic.

She remembers to stop before reaching the top of the steps. She scans the room. It's large, open, with angled sides. On one end is a dormer window. In the middle is a door in the wall. It looks out of place. Positioned where it is, it could only lead to the townhouse next door. Symone points to the door, silently asking permission to check it out.

"Turn the knob slowly and quietly," I tell her. "If it opens, great. If not, forget it."

What I don't tell her makes my stomach do backflips: If Redgrave set a trap, that door would be where she plans to spring it. My heart leaps into my mouth when the knob turns easily in her hand. It opens to a brick wall. Symone lets out a disappointed huff.

I wonder why the owner put a door there. It could've been a single owner of both townhouses using it to expand. Or two friendly families giving their kids play space. In either case, the properties change hands and the new owners closed it up. No way to know. I stop thinking about it because I'm more worried about Symone.

"Where is the cop?" I ask.

She crosses to the top of the steps and points down. Through the earbud, I hear the cop tromping his way up.

CHAPTER 23

JACOB STEARNE

SYMONE SITS ON THE ROOF just to the side of the dormer, right where I told her. We have her breathing under control, and it's a warm summer day. She hears the sentry cop inside shuffling around just inches from her. If he sticks his head out the window and looks around, he'll see her. I tell her not to move a muscle—she might creak the rafters.

We hear his radio squawking again. He replies, then his footsteps retreat from the dormer area.

"That means his locksmith is coming," I tell Symone. "He'll be going downstairs to meet them."

"I heard him," she says in a whisper. "He clunks when he walks. What do I do? Anyone on the street can see me. Jacob, I'm scared."

I guide her to the roof ridge, then two townhouses over. If someone spots her there, we'll make up a story. At least she won't be at the crime scene. I have her slowly pan the neighborhood.

The feed my hackers stole from the Latvian police shows me a minivan pulling up out front. It has a lock and key painted on the side along with text that must be Latvian for mobile locksmith. The sentry warmly greets the middle-aged woman climbing out.

As they turn back toward the townhouse, the sentry stops and takes inventory of the upper levels. He remains stopped long enough for the locksmith to turn back asking him if he's OK. There's no audio on the police feed, but he points to the top floor dormer and says something. Then he shrugs and they go inside.

Turning my attention back to Symone's camera, I spot our way out. I say, "Did you get Logan's phone number?"

"Why? Jealous?"

"If he's close by, he can get you down. What's the answer: yes or no?"

"Yes," she admits sheepishly.

Why am I not surprised? I have her call him, tell him to steal the beat-up frisbee in the yard behind the townhouses, toss it on the roof next to her, then get the broken ladder lying at the end of the alley. It's about four feet short, but if he's clever about it, he can get her down.

She calls him and he readily agrees to help, except that he's at a coffee shop several blocks away.

"You don't mind the attention he pays me, do you?" she asks after the details are settled and Logan is on his way.

"I'm only interested in a working relationship with you, Symone."

"Are you just telling yourself that? Sure sounds like it."

"We've been over this."

"I hear you talking, but I've seen your eyes—"

"Keep it professional," I snap.

When a woman unbuttons her blouse, a man notices. I'm human. I'm also on the verge of being sent to a Latvian prison for the rest of my life. My eyes might go where Mother Nature sends them, but my mind is focused on my freedom. At least, I try.

"Logan talked a lot," she says. "Men do that. They like to talk to me. Is that OK?"

"Symone, I told you I'm not interested in you."

"He talked about the night of the murder. Do you want to know what he said?"

Unclenching my fist, I answer her with a lot of tension in my voice, "Yes, Symone. I'd very much like to know what he said."

"Then stop being so mean to me." She pauses. "OK?"

I bite my lip hard to keep from swearing at her to get on with it. She's like Mercury in many ways. I take a breath and sweeten my voice. "OK, I'd appreciate it if you would tell me what he told you."

"He said a bunch of them left the townhouse and stood outside waiting for Kevin. See, Kevin's always late. First one to wave a fifty at a dancer, last one to put it in her g-string; you know the kind. Well, anyway, Logan said Betty went back inside for something. So Logan was talking to Kayla Clay. You know, I think he has a thing for Kayla. Did you notice?"

She waits a beat as if she's expecting me to answer.

"I don't care. What else did he say?"

"Do you think Kayla would get all weird if I … you know, talked to Logan more?"

"I don't know. What did he say?"

"You said you were going to stop being mean."

My frustration at getting a simple story out of her is about to explode in a torrent of foul language when Mercury materializes in front of me.

Mercury says, *Hey now, brotha, you know what she wants you to say.*

I say, *Doesn't matter what she wants. I want to know what Logan said.*

Mercury says, *She wants you to tell her Kayla doesn't matter cuz YOU don't want her putting the moves on that boy. If'n you tell her that, then she gonna tell you what Logan said. If you want something from a woman, you gotta do what she wants first. Everybody knows zat. Aight? So boom.*

"I don't care what Kayla thinks," I tell Symone. "I would appreciate it if you didn't put the moves on Logan." Symone lets out a satisfied sigh, so I add, "Or any of the ELA people for that matter. We have to keep a professional distance."

Symone says, "Logan left his jacket in the house. It was a warm night, but it gets chilly if you're out late, so he brought a jacket. He tries to hide it but he's like a nerd, y'know? So he ran back, found it on the ground floor, didn't see Betty or Kevin, and went back outside to hang with the others. Now he feels guilty because if he'd gone to check on them, he might've stopped the murderer. You know what I think? I think he's telling me Betty Bardon—that really, really old actress?—is the killer. And I think he's right. I mean, who else could've done it? No one else was in there."

She sounds so sincere, it pains me to crush her enthusiasm. Still, it must be done.

"Before you find a rope and a tree to hang Betty," I say, "there's something you should know about investigating crimes: people lie. Sometimes it's to avoid suspicion, sometimes it's to cover negligence, sometimes to deceive themselves. We all lie, especially to ourselves. And then there's a disappointing fact: the guilty always try to throw shade on someone else. It could've been Logan. Maybe he was jealous of Kevin."

"Yeah, huh?" she says. "I can see that. He's a quiet one. Say, they're a weird bunch, didya notice? I mean Kayla always dressing like fifty years ago; and Chris with those gym-T's—well, at least he's buffed for it; and Francesca with the expensive-as-hell clothes, what's with that? Is she rich or something? And Logan—"

"Sorry, I don't follow fashion."

She's quiet a moment, as if she's disappointed in me.

"Hey," Symone says a moment later, "here comes the frisbee."

A saucer flies onto the roof. She scrambles for it, then looks over the edge. The ladder comes up shorter than I expected. Whether she's daring, or completely underestimating the danger, I'm not sure, but she dangles over the edge until Logan wraps up her legs and guides her down.

He gets her to the ground when we hear a shout. It's the sentry-cop standing fifty feet away. He's yelling at them in Latvian.

"Got my frisbee, mister," Symone calls out in a nasty voice and holds up the disc. With extra snarl, she adds, "Is that OK?"

Sometimes that teenage voice comes in handy. The cop waves them off and goes back inside. I breathe again, she's clean.

Two minutes later, she gets in the car with Logan—and turns off the communication. She's trying to make me jealous. I've forgotten the games teenagers play.

I'm just glad she got out of there alive. I feel relief wash over me like a cool wave on a hot day at the beach.

I take notes about the many obvious clues she found. As much as I hate to admit it, our partnership worked well. Quite well. But, after witnessing her panic attack, I realize: I can never do that again. We were lucky the guy didn't hear her hyperventilating.

Now it's time for a cautious celebration. I go downstairs to the kitchen where I find Betty, in a bright, floral print sundress with a carefully harnessed halter top, stirring a pitcher of iced tea. She offers me a glass. If I didn't know better, I'd say Betty's fashion statement had been influenced by Symone's constant display of cleavage. Although, while Symone works hard to create cleavage, half the women in Hollywood still hate Betty for showing up to the Oscars with her natural beauty popping out of a plunging neckline a few years ago.

Thanking her, I take the glass and guzzle most of it in one go. The tension of putting Symone at risk made me forget I'm thirsty and starving.

"How are the budget negotiations coming?" I ask while she refills my glass.

She frowns and stares blankly at the counter. After a long beat, she says, "He's detail-oriented. Needs to know everything. It's almost invasive."

"That's how investors are. Nothing new there, so that's not what you're really worried about. Your concern is because he wants to know where you hid the *Edison Data*."

She looks up sharply. Answer enough.

While she stares at me, Symone bursts through the back door and jumps on me. Her legs wrap around my body, her arms around my neck. She plants a big, wet kiss intended for my lips. Just in time, I turn so she smacks my cheek.

"I can't believe we pulled it off!" She yells with enthusiastic abandon. "I gotta tell you, I was so scared the whole time—I get horny when I get scared—and that guy was right there, about to catch me! But we were working together, like totally in synch. With you it was, oh god, it was— it was like you were right inside me!"

CHAPTER 24

BETTY BARDON

BETTY SLAMS HER ICED TEA down so hard it splashes. The bang reverberates through the kitchen. Logan stands in the backdoor, his mouth agape. Kayla and Chris pop in from the living room side in time to see Symone all over Jacob.

How dare she? Her legs are wrapped around his tight butt, her arms circle his strong neck. Her body clings to his beefy shoulders. She tries to kiss him again. A public spectacle that infuriates Betty until her anger snaps like a pencil.

She turns and stalks out, getting halfway down the hall before remembering the tea. She'd left the meeting with Joe to get them both drinks; she can't return without them. Indignant, she tromps back to the counter, picks up the pitcher and two glasses, glares at Jacob—who gives her a this-isn't-what-it-looks-like side glance—and storms out all over again.

In the dining room, Joe Rouleau looks up from his laptop with a warm smile that she likes a lot better than one of Jacob's smirks. He says, "*Thé glacé maison*, I mean, tea with ice, sorry, how do you say it?"

"Iced tea," she says. The gold flecks in his brown eyes practically glow in the dimly lit room. The indirect sunlight from the two windows on one wall make him look like a film noir hero from Hollywood's golden age. His good looks are only overshadowed by his charm. A much more refined man than Jacob Stearne.

"What made so much noise in there?" he asks.

"Jacob's little—" Betty searches for a better word than slut "—friend ran an errand for him only to return with a vivid and salacious imagination about what took place. If we believe Jacob."

Joe studies her for a stretch, then takes the glass she holds out for him. "Yes, it was ill mannered of him to bring her into the house. With whom does she sleep?"

Betty hasn't thought that through yet. Kayla and Francesca share a room with two beds. Chris and Kevin are sharing a room. *Were* sharing. Logan has a room of his own. That means Chris and Logan would have to move in together, even though Logan contributed some personal wealth to the cause in exchange for a room of his own. For the computer equipment he needed, he said. The only other option for the girl is to stay in the attic with Jacob. That is not going to happen.

She'll worry about that later. Right now, she needs to get her hands on the Rouleau family fortune. The landlord is due any minute and she's short several thousand euros.

"You will let nature take the course, yes?" Joe asks.

"What do you mean?"

"Jacob and Symone, they share a room. This is less trouble for everyone and no need for sneaking around in the night."

"Jacob's not interested in her," Betty snaps. She looks away, scouring the corner of the room with her gaze. "He shouldn't be, that is. She's too young."

"She is of legal age, no?" Joe says as he observes her every move. "And Jacob is that kind of man if I am not mistaken. His eyes betray his words." He places a gentle hand on her wrist. "If what you say is true, you no longer have feelings for Jacob Stearne, then it is not for you to stand in their way. Keep your mind focused on the goal: *Chaac*."

Betty steals a glance at Joe to see if his words are intentionally ironic. Jacob isn't the only male in the house checking out Symone's every move to see what she might reveal next. Their eyes follow her like magnets. Men.

"Yes, you're right," she says. "I don't care what Jacob does." She breathes, smooths her dress, then meets his gaze. "Now, about the investment. We have an immediate need and then—"

"The discussion moved beyond the short-term cash flow problem. We had discussed the *Edison Data*. It is the only piece of the puzzle in your possession now, is this correct?"

"Well, yes. I assure you I have access to it when needed. Right now—"

"Were it my decision," Joe says while tipping a pen on end, only to turn it over and tip up the other end, "I would take the word of such a beautiful woman without hesitation. However, the French government and the EU require strict adherence to due diligence requirements. There must be proof of assets."

Betty inhales deeply through her nose, realizing that doing so suggests displeasure. She doesn't care. She is displeased. The *Edison Data* is her only asset and her only bargaining chip. To reveal the location of it would be the same as turning it over—which could be the end of her involvement. Plenty of honest men would become common thieves to get hold of it. She had hoped Joe would respect her need for security.

"As you know, it is a physical thing: a large hard drive. It's over ten terabytes of data from the years of my experiments for the Russians. It's a blueprint of failures. Having that information will save years of R&D for anyone who has access to the *Chaac Project* and the *Chaac Equation*. I can't let anyone know where it is because too many people want to steal it."

His heart-warming smile glows at her. "Surely you would not accuse me of attempting to steal your most prized possession."

"Well, no," she says quickly. "That's not the problem. I've read about Mikhail Yeschenko and his operators. They track people, they follow people, they bug houses." She waves a hand at the room. "We could be bugged right now. Chris sweeps the place every day, but we're not sure if the Russians have equipment we can't detect."

"This is why we have Jacob Stearne," Joe says. "Put him to work. Make him earn his rent. I hired him to do this."

Betty considers pointing out that Joe has not yet invested a dime in the operation, making his "hire" a decision only in his mind. Saying so won't help her pay bills. Or endear herself to the man. And she needs his investment. It's not just rent, food, and utilities for the next few weeks. To gather the other pieces of the project, she'll need large amounts of cash. Readily accessible cash.

"Jacob is problematic," she says. "We would be fools to trust him. No matter what he says, he works for Pia Sabel. They're as close as siblings. Closer. I don't believe him for a minute. Sabel is a bigger threat than Yeschenko with one major upside: she won't have us killed. Yeschenko, on the other hand, has unlimited resources and will stop at nothing to get the *Edison Data*. Jacob is one man; Yeschenko has a hundred. I cannot simply show you the *Data*."

"Betty." He tsks. "I cannot tell *Grand-mère*'s attorneys I failed to verify a simple asset in accordance with French law." Joe throws his hands up in frustration. "I cannot do as you wish. We are at an impasse."

He rises and goes to the window.

Most Hollywood actors played a game of importance, fluffing themselves up to be big stars with a blockbuster coming out next summer. They tended to live with four to six other daydreaming actors and screenwriters hot bunking a two-bedroom apartment. With his insistence on seeing the *Data* firsthand, Betty begins to wonder if Joe Rouleau is like one of those actors. Does he have access to investment capital? A watch, expensive clothes are nice props, but what other evidence had she seen? If he's a poser, what options does she have?

As she watches him, she sees the landlord crossing the backyard heading for the kitchen door. Her heart implodes. If she believed in a higher power, she would pray for deliverance.

Joe stands perfectly still, unflinching, uncaring. For a moment, she considers testing him by stepping behind him, putting her arms around his trim, fit body, and asking him in that voice no man has ever refused. She could do it with ease. Once upon a time, she had been Symone's age and wielded her gifts like a weapon in the battle of the sexes. She won every skirmish.

But she doesn't play those games anymore. He might have serious money, and if he does, she will chase this deal on merits, not a mattress.

Unfortunately, merits won't solve her immediate problem.

"There's a reason I can't show you the *Edison Data*," she says with a resigned huff. "It's in a safety deposit box in New York."

He looks over his shoulder at her, a frown on his face. "This should have been said earlier. We can go there and verify it. It will be safe in an American bank—even if we are followed."

"There is a problem." She folds her arms across her chest. "Opening it requires two signatures: mine—and Kevin Winn's."

After staring at each other for a few beats, a knock on the open door breaks their deadlock.

"Hey, just so you know," Jacob says while leaning in, "some rude guy stopped by demanding rent. I paid him for you. Least I could do since I'm a fugitive endangering everyone. And I'm starving, so Symone's going around getting everyone's dinner order. My treat."

"Thank you," she replies.

He starts to leave the room. Then he stops and raises a finger as he turns back.

"Hey, we didn't discuss it," Jacob says brightly, "but I'm putting Symone in your room, Betty. You have a king-sized bed and a large couch, and anywhere else could cause problems." Jacob's gaze bounces from Betty to Joe and back. "Oh, were you two ..."

Jacob's finger wiggles back and forth between her and Joe.

"No," she snaps with too much heat. "Joe's going back to his place after dinner."

Joe looks at her with astonishment sliding into disappointment.

"Zat so?" Jacob stifles a grin and asks, "Where is your place, Joe?"

"Unfortunately," he says with a sigh, "the rental where Kevin was killed."

CHAPTER 25

JACOB STEARNE

"Wait, what?" My mouth falls open. I check Betty for confirmation, then back to Joe. "You rented that place? Have the police interviewed you about it?"

"No need. My intention was to meet Betty there that night. That's why she and her people were there. Regretfully, I was delayed in Paris. I flew in yesterday morning."

"That's right," Betty says. "In our original arrangement, we were to arrive before him, find the key, let ourselves in, and wait for him. The flights from Paris are often delayed. We got there and waited half an hour when he called."

"Are the crime scene people done?" I ask.

"Not yet," Joe replies. "They offered me a hotel. I must call them soon to make arrangements."

I toss this around in my head for a moment. If he wasn't in town, he can't be a suspect. That doesn't mean I don't suspect him of something. I just haven't found a crime to pin on him yet. Give me time.

I walk out of the dining room—leaving Joe to make his best case for spending the night with Betty—and type a text to Emma asking her to find out who owns the Airbnb Joe Rouleau rented. Why didn't anyone mention it was Joe's rental?

Mercury blocks the hallway in front of me. *Cuz you be the prime suspect, homie. Why they gonna tell you anything? And that ain't even what you should be worried about.*

I stare at him and wait a beat. He's going to make me work for it. I say, *Since you're my favorite, best-looking, most awesome god—or figment of my imagination—would you please tell me what I should be worried about?*

Mercury says, *Gonna stick with that snippy-ass attitude, huh bro? You been spending too much time with Symone, boy. But Ima let that shit slide cuz we be vibin' here. Check it: you ever wonder why Betty ain't right behind you asking who killed that kid? Usually, people wanna know whodunit when a white kid bites it. Wazzat all about?*

Joe brushes by me in the narrow hall. He stops a stride away and says, "Thank you for the dinner offer, Jacob. It is most kind. Regretfully, I must depart."

"No prob," I say and watch him leave.

Symone comes up the hall, her eyes fixed over my shoulder, which tells me Betty is behind me. The younger lady leans to one side, scowling at Betty—who uses my shoulder as a shield. I snap my fingers in Symone's line of sight and guide her gaze to me. She softens a good deal when she faces me.

"No one can make up their mind," she says, "so I'm ordering Italian, family style—if that's OK. What do I do, just use the card on this phone, like Apple Pay or something?"

"Technically, it's Sabel Pay," I answer. "Just make sure you know which ID you've selected so it matches the credit card."

"You gave her a credit card?" Betty's voice has a high-pitched squeal of outrage in it.

Before I can answer, Symone leans around me to ask Betty, "Did you kill that kid? You were the only one there, you had to a done it. And you're just gonna let these Latvian cops hunt down my man like a dog?"

Gently but firmly grabbing my employee's shoulders, I turn her around toward the front door. "I'm not your man, OK? But I am starving-hungry, so if you wouldn't mind ..."

Symone looks over her shoulder with a smile and a wink, "Gotcha covered, *Big Boy*. I'll be right back."

She trots down the hall and calls out, "Which one of you big strong men wants to drive?"

I face Betty, intending to follow up on Symone's blunt question about committing murder.

She speaks first, "'Big boy?' You don't have to explain your girl, Jacob. It's fine. You can do what you want. I'm over you. So over."

I watch her ice-blue eyes show no emotion at all for a long, breathless moment before I reply. "You're quite an actress."

"I mean it. I don't feel—"

"So we're both going to lie about it?" I ask.

Her mouth opens to issue a rebuttal that never comes. Her lips quiver, then close. She takes a deep breath and says, "I think that's best."

"Is that how you handle Kevin's murder?" I ask.

Betty staggers back a step. "How dare you! I didn't … I want you to leave."

"I just paid the rent," I remind her. "Answer a couple questions for me. Why didn't you tell me Kevin was killed in Joe's rental? How do you spend most of an afternoon talking numbers with Joe instead of helping me find the killer?"

"You don't understand," she says, tears forming in her eyes. "I told you, I'm under a lot of pressure here. There are things happening … You're in danger. It would be better if you left Latvia. Tonight. For your own safety."

Only a fool would fall for an actress's tearful plea. I've played that fool too many times. Yet there is something in her voice that makes me believe her. Her skin vibrates with fear even as her gaze sweeps the floor unwilling to meet mine.

"You said you had a plan," I say. "You need me."

"Well. Yes. That's true. But the options keep getting worse."

"Remember what I told you: stay in your lane."

"I'm trying." Her tear-filled eyes rise to mine. "I'm not sure you grasp what's going on here. It's worse than you think."

"You do care about me," I say.

"I don't want anything bad to happen to you. That's all." Her hands squeeze my arms. "You're right, I am lying to myself. No matter how much I try not to, I still care about you. But you're still grieving Jenny. I'm wasting my time—and knowing that hurts, Jacob."

Like getting hit by a wave at the beach, images of Jenny crash into my mind. Jenny's legs tangled in mine as we lie on the couch reading books on a quiet Sunday morning. Jenny standing next to me after Lt. Hale's funeral when I fumbled the engagement ring at her feet. Jenny running out of the cave carrying the bomb while I remained chained to the wall, unable to stop the inevitable. Pain jolts through me like lightning bolts. Betty's right, I'm not over Jenny.

"I get it," I say. "I'm not good company. But I couldn't get out of Latvia if I had to. The city is locked down tight."

"You escaped from Morocco with the entire Moroccan army chasing you."

"Where did you hear that?"

"It was in *Le Héros de Paris.*"

"I gotta watch that thing, find out what else I've done. In real life, it was two cop cars and a harbor patrol." I scoff. "Whole army. Jesus, Hollywood."

Her eyes search mine. She says, "Forget them. They're not the problem."

"Oh, I know what the problem is, Betty. It's what Symone was talking about. She helped me piece together a timeline that places you in the townhouse—alone—very close to the time of the murder."

Betty leans back as if I'd slapped her. She can't speak, she's dumbfounded. Whether it's an act or genuine outrage at my accusation is hard to tell.

"Most of your group left the townhouse together," I say. "Everyone gathered at the corner waiting for Kevin. Then you went back inside. You said you want my help, so take me through what happened next."

She blushes, takes another step back, her eyes flashing with bitterness. "Alright, if you want to know. Not that I owe you any explanations. As you've figured out, I'm out of funds. Strapped. The others wanted to go clubbing. In the past, I've always paid for the first round or two. Morale builder. It's become kind of expected. Trouble was, I had €20 left to my name. I'd noticed some cash in the kitchen. I went back to see if there was any more. I was desperate."

Her blush darkens. She turns away to hide it.

"You were going to steal from an Airbnb?" I ask. "Never mind. Let me guess—there wasn't more than a euro or two in the kitchen. And Kevin was there."

"No," she says. "I didn't want anyone to catch me, so I looked around first. He should've been there. He wasn't on the ground floor, and he wasn't on the kitchen level either. I tiptoed up the stairs to the bedrooms—no Kevin. I figured I'd missed him, that he'd gone outside. Then I heard someone on the top floor. There was nothing up there but an old desk, so I figured it was Kevin. I went back to the kitchen, looked around, like you said, there was nothing but a few euros. I went to the ground floor and found Logan and Kayla coming out of the bathroom together—"

"Logan and Kayla?"

"I didn't ask. There are six—were—six of us. They're young; relationships are fluid; I don't judge. Anyway, the three of us walked out together."

Mercury stepped between us. *Dude, now who's doing the lying? Was it Logan? Or did Symone relay the story right? Or is Betty talking allat whoopty woo just to throw you off?*

I say, *I don't know. Help me out here.*

Mercury says, *Help you out? Say, where izzat sacrifice at anyhow?*

I say, *What kind of sacrifice? Oh, right. Something with a rooster. Well, I haven't found one yet. Soon as I do, I swear to Ceres, I'll get right on it. By the way, what is a rooster sacrifice anyway? I mean. I don't have to actually kill it or anything, do I?*

Mercury shakes his head with disappointment and vanishes. Guess I'll have to figure this out for myself. Which beats getting arrested in Latvia for animal cruelty. That would get used against me in my murder trial: *… and he killed a rooster!*

"I'll verify that with Logan and Kayla," I tell Betty. "None of that adds up to why you're worried about me. You know I can handle myself."

She huffs and fidgets. "OK, then. Here it is. Joe doesn't know I speak Russian. During one of our breaks, when I left the room, he put someone on speakerphone, and they spoke in Russian. I was just coming back in, stopped in the hall." She lets out a frustrated sigh. "I didn't catch the whole thing, but the other person said, 'I play Stearne like a chess game. Everything he's done since he came to Riga is a move I planned for him. He will get Rafael to bring the *Chaac Equation*. I will leave him no option.'"

CHAPTER 26

JACOB STEARNE

WE STARE AT EACH OTHER while I process the cryptic quote. Sounds like something Mikhail Yeschenko would say, no doubt about it. Especially since it was in Russian and he's usually ahead of everyone else by several moves. Then there's Joe's claim to the throne of the Tsars. Not that it worked out so well for the last guy. Doesn't mean Yeschenko is above putting delusions of grandeur in someone's head: *The Winter Palace rightfully belongs to you.* Is Joe dumb enough to fall for that kind of manipulation?

Still, Betty's concerns are misplaced. I give her a been-there-whupped-that shrug. Betty worries her fingers; her brow knits with concern. Her posture shows she's accepted that I'm staying in Riga and she resigns herself to losing this argument with a sigh.

I get the feeling she is genuinely worried about me. More than ever before.

"Well then." Betty flips her hair back over her shoulders. "If you'll excuse me, I need to make room for your little friend since you insist on foisting her on me."

With that, she swishes her sundress out of the room and stomps up the stairs.

Symone's impeccable timing has her arriving seconds later with two guys bearing pans of Italian pastas, meats, and salads. Kayla and Francesca set the food out in the dining room.

Symone nods her head toward the hallway. I take the hint and meet her. She holds up her phone and shows me a picture of a dark-haired man wearing a long coat. He's staring directly into the lens and doesn't appear pleased to have his picture taken.

"This guy was following me," Symone whispers angrily.

"Are you sure?"

"Any woman knows when she's being followed by a creeper. This guy wasn't creeping though, he was following like a killer. He thought I was going inside the restaurant for dinner, looked freaked when I popped out and snapped this."

"Send it to Emma. Ask her to run it through facial recognition."

"I did a Google image thing. Got nothing."

I stare at her blankly until she catches my drift.

"OK," she says, "I'll send it to Emma. She has superpowers?"

"Better than superpowers—she can access Sabel Technologies. They do facial recognition for twenty-three governments."

Symone's mouth forms a silent, *Oh.*

Kayla and Francesca announce that dinner is ready. Everyone looks at me as if I'm the guest of honor. I spent too much time on army bases with ten thousand hungry and ill-mannered soldiers to let others go first. I take a plate and fill it quickly.

Chris and Logan follow me. When they reach the end of the line, they take their plates and bolt upstairs to play a video game.

I sit at the table with three young women. Francesca perches her Gucci sunglasses at the crown of her hair. Kayla's tie-dye t-shirt has a spot of sauce; which makes me wonder what happened to her designer clothes. Symone's blouse has dropped a button again. It's amazing that thing stays on at all. A lacy black push-up bra peeks from inside. Where the hell did she get that?

I never asked Emma to send lingerie in the packages. Then I recall giving Symone a Sabel phone with several emergency numbers on it, including Emma's. Apparently, Symone is one clever and resourceful girl. I text Emma an instruction to send Symone only modest clothing from now on.

Emma responds instantly, "A woman needs certain things. Try not to worry about it."

Great.

Since we have phones, I surreptitiously type out a short instruction to Symone. I tell her that I will be asking questions of Kayla and Francesca and that she is to listen and take notes on what we learn. I end it with, "You can debrief me later when we're alone."

I can tell when she's read it because a smile stretches across her face.

Mercury takes the empty chair between us. *You dawg. You d-a-w-g, dawg. 'When we're alone!' Symone's lapping that up. You gonna be hitting that young thing after all! I'm proud of you.*

I say, *I will not be hitting anyone in Eastern Europe in the foreseeable future. Nothing good would come of it. I only added that 'alone' bit to make sure she takes me seriously and keeps her mouth shut.*

Holy Diana, you is a manipulator, Mercury says. *You leading her on like that? Dude, you is foetorem extremae latrinae.*

I say, *C'mon, you know I never got the hang of Latin.*

Mercury says, *You are the stench of a low-life latrine. You smell like shit, bro.*

Nice, I say.

"Sure is," Symone says. "Did you try the garlic bread?"

"Kayla, if you hadn't joined Betty, what would you be doing?" I ask to ease into a conversation.

"Graduate school, if I could afford it." She breaks off a chunk of garlic bread and dips it in her sauce. "I'd love to have a PhD in poetry."

Symone and Francesca check Kayla to see if she's joking. She's not.

"Let me guess," I say. "Your parents won't help with that one because it will never earn back?"

"They couldn't even if they wanted to. We're from Manchester." I must be looking confused, because she follows that with, "We're not rich. They can barely afford to send me books."

We eat in silence for a few chews. Then I ask the same of Francesca.

"Ehm." She takes a thoughtful beat. "I could follow Betty to work on quantum electrodynamics. Or fashion. I prefer the career in fashion, but Papà does not pay for that."

"He'd pay for grad school in physics?" I ask.

"Truthfully, he is not approving of what I do now. He is executive for Olio Completo, oil company. They talk big about green energy, but they make money from crude." She side-eyes Kayla. "I pursue my dreams my own way."

"Very independent of you," I say right after she takes a mouthful of pasta. "Would you please take me through what happened the night of Kevin's murder? From when you were waiting for Kevin on the sidewalk."

She holds up a finger while she finishes chewing. Kayla watches her closely.

"Sì, but, em, no one waits for Kevin." Francesca's Italian accent thickens. "We waited for Betty. Kevin went back inside to see what was taking her so long. Then Kayla went in to use the toilet. Chris and I talked—"

"No," Kayla says. "I used the loo at the club, later. I stayed on the sidewalk with Chris and Logan."

"*Sbagliata*! Wrong." Francesca waves a finger like a scolding schoolteacher. "I walked ahead. You went with Logan. Looking for his jacket, you said."

"Yeah, alright, Logan asked me to help him, but I didn't go in for the loo."

"Betty told me you and he came out of the bathroom together," I say.

"Eeww." Kayla looks sick. "Not with Logan. In the loo? No way. I went in to help him look, yeah. But we found it straight off."

"Did you hear anything?" I ask.

"What d'you mean, like Kevin being killed?" Kayla swallows hard, trying not to be sick.

"No, I mean, footsteps in the kitchen or on the stairs."

"Nothing like that. We were only in there two seconds." Kayla looks at each of us. "I'm not going into any dark rooms with that boy, right? Not long enough for one of you lot to start talking about us."

I feel Symone staring at me. She can't wait to discuss the stories. I give her a glance that tells her she's doing great and to keep doing great by not talking. Quiet is not her strength.

"So Kevin left with you guys at the beginning?" I ask Francesca. "He was on the sidewalk with you?"

"No," Kayla says.

At the same time, Francesca says, "Sì."

"No, he wasn't." Kayla glares at Francesca. "How would you know who was with us, anyway? You weren't even … you had your nose in Chris's chest the whole time."

"No, no, no." Francesca waves her finger again. "Chris is the *narcisista*, em, narcissist, sì? Always pumping iron, as if muscle makes the man. You are liking Chris, not me. Don't put your *fantasia* on me!"

"Me?" Kayla nearly lifts out of her seat. "I'm not the one fawning over—"

"Symone's right," I bellow in my best baritone. "The garlic bread is to die for."

I catch Symone smirking at me. She picks up the plate and offers the bread to the others. With a shrewdness I never expected from her, she redirects their conversation to getting Chris and Logan wardrobe upgrades. Neither young man has the fashion sense the ladies want to see.

After mopping up my pasta, I head upstairs. I lay out my gear for my operations later tonight: Sabel Visor; climbing gear; plenty of weapons, both lethal and not-so-much; and listening devices. My video surveillance system pulls up quickly on my laptop, showing me the police cameras from the murder site. All quiet.

An intra-company text comes in from someone I've never heard of before, a Dr. Franklin. When I click on his bio, it says he's the psychologist for the People's Success and Creativity Department. After a few head-scratching seconds, I figure that must be what they're calling Human Resources these days. I text the psych, "Busy. What's this about? Can it wait?"

He texts back right away, "Important. Re: Blackworthy."

That can wait. He's texting the wrong guy; I'm not on the Blackworthy mission. I stuff the phone back in my pocket.

Symone runs up the stairs and stops at the top. Her blouse has one remaining button still on the job. She leans back on the banister and says, "We're alone. Are you ready to *debrief* now? Is that what we're going to call it?"

I've had enough of the teen-vamp. I dive into drill sergeant mode.

"Straighten up, button those buttons up to your clavicle. You're working for Sabel Security now. When you work for us, human lives are on the line. Tonight, it's going to be my life. Take it seriously."

She stands ramrod straight and does up her buttons with lightning speed. When she finishes, she looks up with tears in her eyes and races across the attic to throw her arms around me.

"I'm sorry," she sobs. "I'm sorry, I'm sorry, I'm sorry. I just want you to like me. Enough so you'll want me to stick around. You know? And I don't want you going anywhere. I don't want you risking anything. Just stay here where it's safe. Please."

Her emotion is over the top, even for her. This is the girl who, an hour ago, called me big boy, and asked Chris and Logan which one wanted to drive. I'm no expert on bipolar disorder. Is this what's called rapid cycling? If she's not bipolar, this is different, more basic. She's been abandoned in a big, scary, cold, uncaring world. I peel her off me and push her back.

"Let's respect spaces, OK?" I ask gently.

She sniffles, nods, and pulls out her shirttail to blow her nose.

"Now," I say softly, "I value your opinion on this matter. What did you think of Francesca and Kayla's stories?"

Her still-wet eyes flash. "Liars!"

CHAPTER 27

JACOB STEARNE

THE SUN FINALLY SETS AFTER 10 PM. I work best at night and, this far north, darkness comes in a short window. I suit up with my gear and head downstairs.

Betty is dressed for serious business. She wears a designer power-dress with accentuated shoulders, shiny black shoes, and dark stockings. An Art Deco hairbow, large and glittery, adorns her hair. She searches the foyer closet like a madwoman, then suddenly turns around and says, "Has anyone seen my cape?"

Blank stares answer her. She slams the closet closed and turns to Logan, asking to borrow his car in a snippy tone. When he hands over the keys, she flies out of the house to a destination that is, apparently, none of anyone's business.

Whatever she's doing, it's eating her up with anger judging from her fast stride and the back door slammed in her wake. I think about the cause of her irritation for a moment. A few possibilities revolving around either the handsome Mr. Rouleau or the pert Symone come to mind. But even that doesn't explain the level of tension.

The only other vehicle in the ELA belongs to Chris Anrig. He jumps at the chance to drive me wherever I need to go. I don't explain the mission, and he doesn't ask. That *Le Héros de Paris* thing is working for me.

Symone checks in on my earbud and reports she sees all the video feeds and has solid audio, just like I did when our roles were reversed. She's excited and worried about me at the same time. I'm not sure what to make of her.

When Chris pulls onto the street, a pair of headlights fire up and swing in behind us at a distance. I explain our need to run an anti-surveillance route and direct Chris to take four righthand turns followed by four lefts, going fast on one block and excruciatingly slow on the next. He's excited about the tradecraft. His eyes are wide open, his breathing is deep and strained, but he's handling it. And loving that he's handling it.

I ask my standard icebreaker. "Chris, if you hadn't joined Betty, what would you be doing with your life?"

"Studying Anna Weyant," he says.

"OK, I'll bite. Who is she?"

"Only the greatest artist of our generation." He glances at me as if I'm a Neanderthal. "You have not seen her paintings? So elegant, harsh, and yet always playful. I saw her at Blum & Poe last spring. Amazing. What I would give for one of her works."

"Are they expensive?"

"€1.6 million for *Falling Woman*." He laughs. "Only two million out of my price range. But one day. Perhaps."

"I can trust you to be honest with me, right?" I ask.

"*Ja*. Sure."

"Whose idea was it to make up a story about the night Kevin was killed?"

"What?" He nearly breaks his neck looking at me.

I point to the road to get his eyes back on it. In my ear, I hear Symone give a revelatory *Oh shit* sigh. I hadn't filled her in on why none of the stories matched up.

"When I go into the field with a legend," I tell him, "I rehearse it with one of my buddies. I have them drill me on details, do their best to trip me up, lie to me, make me lie to them. We spend hours doing this because our lives depend on it. But you and your ELA friends spent, I'm guessing, five minutes planning a lie about who went into the townhouse and who stayed on the street. I can tell, because you have the same general concept, but you guys never worked out the details. You're all over the map."

"Uh." Chris stays silent for a long time.

In my ear, Symone whispers, "Smack him around! Make him tell you."

"Were you all together when you left the house, including Kevin?" I ask.

"No. Kevin was not there."

"Who went back inside first?"

He hesitates, glances at me, faces the road again. He's not going to say.

"OK, tell me this. When you first stopped on the sidewalk, before anyone went anywhere, who was with you?"

"All of us," he chokes. "Betty, Kayla, Logan. Me."

"Francesca?"

"She went ahead, I think. We met her at the end of the block."

"Who went inside?" I ask.

He clamps his mouth shut.

"Never mind," I tell Chris and Symone. "I get it: you don't want to rat out your friends. It doesn't matter—I already figured out what happened. But Chris, when the cops come, don't lie to them. They'll throw you in jail and not even the Swiss ambassador will get you out. Tell them the truth."

He swallows hard and concentrates on driving. Sweat beads on his forehead.

The car we were trying to lose follows us around every corner and matches our speed.

In my ear, Symone starts begging me to tell her. I text her to stop talking. She does.

Emma buzzes me. I conference her in with Symone.

"Got a hit on your mystery man following Symone," Emma says. "Remmo Nidal operator out of Tangiers by the name of Hakim Haddadi. Not someone we know much about, so we expect he's low-level muscle. But that's not the interesting part. Bring up that photo and zoom in on the car behind the guy."

I bring up Symone's picture on my phone and zoom as instructed. Five yards behind the Remmo agent, his parked car waits. In the passenger seat, grainy but distinct, is the face of Rafael Tum, the former Guatemalan revolutionary turned professor who ran off with the *Chaac Equation*. The old man saved my life a couple times, and I returned the favor. We're even. But since his disappearance, I'm not sure what he's up to, good or bad.

I scour the picture's background, in and around the car. What's missing are the husband-and-wife duo of Eli and Amit Sofer, Mossad agents, known to have been working with Rafael at the time he dropped off the grid. I thought they were working as a triumvirate on this project, going everywhere together. Where are they and why does Rafael have a Remmo Nidal bodyguard instead of the Sofers?

And the big question: why is he following Symone?

"Who is that guy?" Symone asks.

"Someone I need to talk to," I tell her.

"Why is he in the car with the evil-looking dude?"

"I don't know yet."

Emma changes the subject with a polite cough. "One other thing. Dr. Franklin from People's Success wants you to call, Jacob. It's urgent—and confidential. Like emergency urgent."

CHAPTER 28

JACOB STEARNE

THANKING THE LADIES, I DROP Emma and Symone off the comms link and look up Dr. Franklin's number on the company directory. While I do that, I explain to Chris what we're going to do next: another bit of tradecraft, spy stuff. He's excited about his role.

Spotting an airline bottle of rum in the cupholder, I grab it, I stuff it in my shirt, and dial the People's Success doctor.

While it's ringing, I tell Chris to make a right into a tight alley. I instruct him to go around the block slowly and come back to pick me up. As he slows into the alley, I pop open the door and roll out.

The good doctor connects at the exact moment I'm flinging myself onto the ground. He hears my *oof.*

"Jacob, are you all right?" he asks. "The video feed is panning too fast. By the way, these calls are always video calls, but I'm seeing what looks like a helmet-cam. Why is that?"

"In the middle of an operation here," I answer as I leap to my feet. "What's so urgent, Doc?"

"Oh, well. It's about Ms. Blackworthy. Is she with you at the—"

I pull my tactical knife and flatten against the alley wall close to the corner.

"Whoa!" Dr. Franklin says. "Is that a knife?"

"Yeah. Like I said, I'm in the middle of an op. But I don't know a Blackworthy. Talk to me, what's up?"

"Ah, yes, it's Blackworthy, spelled like it sounds, and first name, Symone with a y. Middle initial—"

"Gotcha, Symone. OK, what about her?"

The car following us takes the corner into the alley too fast to spot me. I lash out with the knife and slash his tire. At the same instant, the driver sees me. He slams on the brakes. He wants to rumble.

Perfect.

"We urge you to be cautious with her," Franklin says. "We take our employees' mental health seriously and—"

I run to the car as the driver opens the door. He's twisting in his seat, getting ready for the confrontation. As expected, it's Hakim Haddadi, Symone's admirer. There's a reason I attacked him from this spot—it makes his position untenable while mine is going at full gallop. His left shoulder tangles in the seatbelt, slowing his movement and forcing him to lean out of the car.

Haddadi puts up one hand and says, "No, no, monsieur ..."

I've got him exactly where I want him.

"—uh, well," Franklin is still talking, "we are concerned about her state of mind. She should not be subjected to any extreme violence or violence of any—"

At that moment, I launch my full bodyweight into the driver's face, leading with my knee. My victim's head slams between the door frame and the body's A-pillar. It sounds like a watermelon cracking open. He's out cold.

"Whoa. Whoa. Whoa! Jacob. What was that?" Franklin asks.

"Extreme violence." I'm panting from the exertion. I check the guy over, take his pistol—a Walther PP with suppressor—and stuff it in my belt.

Grabbing the driver by the lapels, I toss him back in the driver's seat and slam my elbow into his throat. That gives me the time to look around.

The car is empty. No Rafael Tum.

I stab Haddadi with a Sabel Dart and check his pockets, which are empty, then pour Chris's rum on him. I slam the door closed.

In my ear, I hear Dr. Franklin hyperventilating. Something he said at the beginning replays in my mind. "Wait, did you say this was a video call? That means you just saw all that?"

"Did you … I just witnessed a murd … You killed that man!"

"Calm down, Doc. Deep breaths. Slow exhales. He's not dead. Sabel Darts inject a small dose of Inland Taipan snake venom that produces flaccid paralysis. That's followed by a strong dose of sleep medication that keeps him out for a few hours. I poured the booze on him so the cops will toss him in the drunk tank for the night. Keeps him out of my hair for a while."

There's a long pause. I hear him doing the deep breaths.

"OK, OK, I get it," Franklin says while still breathing heavy. "I've never seen an operation … That's clever. You're really—"

"Yeah, I'm good at what I do, Doc. What was that you were saying about Symone?"

"Right. Well, keep her away from operations like yours. She shouldn't be anywhere near you."

"Why is that?" I ask.

"I can't tell you. There are confidentiality issues at play here. I can tell you this: her mental health is at risk. You need to get her as far away from the … well, the things you do, like what I just saw you do … I still can't believe it … you could've killed that … ah, where was I? Oh yes, she can't handle that kind of stress. So you need to transfer her duties to another department."

I look into the black night sky. I remember her shaking with fear about being deserted. Her tears were real. I remember my promise not to leave her. Promises you make to abandoned and abused teenagers, the kids society would rather forget about, aren't promises you can walk away from.

"That ain't gonna happen, doc."

Chris comes around the corner and stops the car in the alley. I hold up a finger, asking him to wait a second.

"Well, it has to happen," Franklin says. "I know you're famous for breaking rules and Ms. Sabel lets you get away with it all the time. But. This isn't an optional rule. This is—"

"What's wrong with her?"

"I can't tell you that. As I said—and you are well aware—there are confidentiality—"

"Listen up, Doc. My patience is exhausted, and I hate rules, especially when they're thrown in my face." I switch the video from my earbud forward-cam to my phone. The guy is in a suit and tie sitting in an office in Washington DC, forty-five hundred miles away. He's soft and gray, never faced down a terrorist in his life. I feel my volume rising with my rage as I speak. "Right now, my life is hanging by a thread and Symone Blackworthy is holding the other end of that fucking thread! Whatever problem she has, I need to know—and you need to tell me. Right now! Because if you don't, I'm going to jump down this goddamn phone and rip out your fucking throat!"

His face pops with surprise and fear.

"OK, OK, OK," he shouts holding up his hands. "She's a Sandy Hook survivor. She was in third grade when twenty kids were shot to death in the room two doors down from her. All survivors of school shootings have PTSD to some degree, Jacob. They all handle it differently. Some self-medicate, some get counseling, others live in abject and debilitating fear. A few are fine and well-adjusted. But just imagine what Symone went through—the terror, the sleepless nights, the jolt of pain at loud noises, the distrust of people in authority. Nothing in her life felt stable after that. She trusts no one. Every day she feels like a mouse in an open field with a thousand starving hawks circling in the air overhead ready to swoop down at any second.

"On top of that," Franklin continues, "Symone left school in tenth grade. There's no record that she took part in any counseling. That's a sign that she's deeply troubled by her experience. She could act out in any of a thousand ways. She could be unreliable, excessively sexualized, jumpy, given to emotional extremes. There are lots of ramifications. Jacob, she needs psychological help—she should not be around you … or anything like what I just saw."

For several beats, I can't breathe. For some reason, that story deeply affects me. When the air comes back to me, I hear myself asking a stupid question. "How do you know so much about survivors?"

"It's not me personally, it's the profession. There are studies. Unfortunately, we know a lot about them because there are now over 250,000 school shooting survivors in America. It is a uniquely American problem. No other country has shootings on this scale—not even close. One thing you should know about those survivors, Jacob: none of them just shrugged it off."

"Why did she attach herself to me, then? She knows about me, she knows I live a violent life, watched some show called, um—"

"*Le Héros de Paris?* Excellent series. Loved it. Well, if she saw that, then met you, she believes you can protect her. Like a personal bodyguard. But that's also a dangerous fixation for her. She sees you as a messianic figure." He says nothing for a beat. Then continues, "So, you can see why you need to transfer her—"

"Not happening. Gotta go." I click off.

Standing in a barren alley in Riga, Latvia, I stare blankly at Chris Anrig, who waits patiently in the car. I collect my thoughts. Symone, a Sandy Hook survivor, who I sent into harm's way and talked out of a panic attack when she saw a bloodstain the size of a bedspread, is now my eyes and ears on what could be a horribly violent operation. This was a bad idea. Really bad.

What's the right thing to do?

I click her connection back on. "Hey, Symone. You there?"

CHAPTER 29

JACOB STEARNE

CHRIS DRIVES ME TO THE townhouse where Kevin was murdered. No sentry outside this late at night, but two floors are lit up inside. I'm not registering any warm bodies in there, but that might be the heavy insulation they use here blocking any possible heat signatures.

Chris drops me off two blocks away. I walk back through trees and alleys to the string of townhouses. The murder scene is opposite me. The ladder Symone and Logan used earlier today is still in place. I climb to where it's short of the top.

I leap to the eave of the roof, then do a strong pull-up, barely catch the edge, and pull.

Mercury looks down from above, leaning into my space. *Damn, homie, you picked the perfect woman for your mission: one of the few people on Earth be more damaged than you. Wazzat all about, anyhow?*

I say, *Hanging from a roof by eight fingers in a country that has a shoot-on-sight order for me is not the ideal place for a Socratic circle. Could you back up, gimme some room to get up there?*

My favorite god scootches over on the shingles and waits while I pull my chest up, then swing a leg into place and roll the rest of the way onto the steep roof.

You let her fall hard for you, Mercury says. *Now you gotta take responsibility for her.*

Hey! I say. *I didn't let her do anything. I've been pushing her away. Maybe Franklin's right, she should be in a nice, safe office somewhere. I should trust his expertise.*

Mercury says, *You saying the honorable thing be transferring her ass to another department?*

I say, *She's got abandonment issues. She needs a stable life somewhere safe. That's not me.*

Mercury stares at me. *She got abandonment issues—so you gonna abandon her? Howzat honorable? C'mon now, this ain't no time to go quitting on your girlfriend. Forget about that doctor—break all the rules and get moving.*

I say, *The doctor knows these things. Who am I to argue about her mental health?*

My head snaps back and forth after saying those words. Mercury's gone.

I hold my head in my hands. I am insane. I'm sitting on a rooftop thousands of miles from home doing mental gymnastics to wriggle out of a promise using the delusion of a deity as my advisor. The fact is: Franklin said Symone needed to be as far from me and my brutal life as possible. The other fact is: I made a promise to her and breaking it would crush her. Possibly forever. I don't have any answers.

I make my way along the roof ridge and turn the comms back on.

"What happened?" Symone's voice sounds desperate.

"Nothing," I answer. "Bumped the mute button. Did you see anything in video feeds from the Latvian cops?"

"All clear. But I think someone's inside. Gotta be, right?"

"That's what I'm thinking."

I crawl to the townhouse next door to the murder scene. Taking care not to creak the rafters, I make my way to the dormer window in the attic. I risk a peek inside. Night vision and thermal show me an empty space. I cut the glass out and quietly let myself in.

It's not what I expected. The same size as the other attic, this one is not a finished space. Bare wood boards form a rough floor. Exposed insulation lies between open beams. One feature is exactly what I expected: a false wall has been placed against the wall shared with the murder site.

"What is that?" Symone asks. "Is that the back of the door from when I was there?"

I pull a handle on the left and a ten-foot section of wall swings in toward me, revealing a door into the crime scene. The back side, which faces the crime scene, is covered with the brick Symone saw when she was here. If the cops opened the door from the crime scene side, it would appear the doorway has been bricked up for years.

I close it and start downstairs in this neighboring townhouse.

"What are you doing?" Symone's voice is desperate again. "We don't know anything about that place. Someone could be down there."

"I'm sure there is," I reply via text. "I'm going to flush him out. If I go through the fake door, he could come up behind me."

"OK." Her voice is shaky.

I text more, "Can't talk. Trust me. Your job is to keep an eye on the video feeds and let me know if anyone shows up."

"Right. Sorry."

I sneak down the stairway. A wall hides my existence from anyone on this floor, but my thermal imaging works fine. There's no insulation between rooms. I see a heat signature in one of the bedrooms. The figure is seated and bent over. I take the last step to the floor. The wood beneath my feet groans like an old man.

The thermal image of the man rises from his chair with alarm. His posture looks like he's leading with a pistol.

I back up the steps and flatten against the wall.

My adversary is good: he circles the stairway entrance in a clearing maneuver. He won't be easy. His pistol appears in the entry. The sight sends Symone into a shrieking fit, since she sees what I see through the video cam.

I jump to a squatting position on the landing directly in front of him, which catches him off guard. The man's arms hold the pistol at full extension, aimed up the stairs. He tries to bring it down to shoot me, but I'm below his waist. Leading with a Sabel Dart, I rise quickly off my haunches, my shoulders shoving his elbows, and his pistol, upward while my dart lands in his neck.

He collapses to the floor.

Short and thick, he's built like a fireplug and sports a large, thick mustache like a medieval Cossack. I pat him down and add his pistol to my growing collection. He's heavily armed with knives, an ankle-pistol, and a detonator. No sign of what it detonates, but I assume he's wired the building to prevent detection. No ID. I snap a picture of him and send it to Emma for facial recognition.

For a moment, I wonder if I'm looking at the man who killed Kevin Winn. But the Cossack has Russian military tattoos on his forearm. Which means he's a pro. A pro wouldn't mess up a throat-slashing. He's not the assassin.

I stand perfectly still and listen for more enemies in the townhouse.

I can't hear anything because Symone is still freaking out through the comm link. I pull my earbud and stuff it in my pocket. Then I send her a text telling her to calm down so I can maintain situational awareness. I don't wait for an answer. I move to the next stairway down and listen.

Nothing shows up in the thermal image. I hear nothing. I'm pretty sure I'm clear. I don't want to risk going down another level and I don't want an adversary coming up behind me. I deploy a volumetric sensor. If anything larger than an owl enters the room, I'll get an alert.

For that to work, I'll need to have my earbud back in. I text Symone, asking if she's calm enough for me to use the comms. She texts a meek "yes."

Returning to the room where the Cossack had been working, I check it out. A monitor hooked to a laptop displays the feeds from four cameras in the building next door. A blinking light shows me everything is being recorded on the laptop. I connect a USB cable to my phone to install a little spyware. Twenty seconds later, it's done.

Onscreen, I see the cop-sentry eating cookies in the crime-scene kitchen. It's a different guy from the afternoon, heavier and older. Paging through a few screens with the cursor, I find four cameras in the crime scene townhouse, one on each floor.

Symone's voice whispers, "What's wrong with that keyboard?"

She has a keen eye. Under each of the Latin alphabet characters are symbols in different colors.

"Good call," I tell her. "It's a Cyrillic keyboard. Russian."

I go back to the attic, open the door to the crime scene townhouse, and enter the attic-office. Checking the floor below as best I can with thermal imaging, I determine all systems are go for descending one more level.

I make it to the bedroom that Symone had scoped out earlier on her adventure. The bed is still made, the markers still in place, nothing touched. But the shoe with the red sole is gone.

I hear the sentry climbing the stairs.

Stepping out to the landing, I stab him with a Sabel Dart. I catch him before he rolls down the stairs. With some effort, I pull him up and lay him out in the hall. In my earbud, I hear Symone hyperventilating. I've explained the darts to her. She knows this is a non-violent solution to the problem. But something triggered a panic attack. It must be the weight of the whole experience. I'm not sure how to handle that.

Mercury says, *Sure, you do, homie. All you gotta do is the same thing men have been doing for ten thousand years when women go all emotional: Ignore her.*

That is SO misogynistic. I can see why the Romans fled your temple for the Christians, I tell him. *Why don't you help me out here?*

Misogynist? Mercury clutches his heart as if wounded. *Moi? I be the least misogynist god you know.*

You have two thousand years of gender studies to catch up on, I say. *We don't burn witches anymore. Tell me something useful. I need to find a clue to who killed Kevin Winn.*

Burning witches wasn't my thang, homie. Mercury looks sad. *That be your so-called-Christians. Somebody own some land you want to get yo hands on, call they a witch and boom, the land go up for sale soon as the smoke clears. Speaking of smoke clearing, that Cossack and Redgrave be waiting on you to come round here. Think about it, bro, what they think you looking for?*

I say, *They think I'm looking for evidence. But I need more than that. Something even more fundamental than finding Kevin's killer—finding the reason Kevin was killed. Betty and her crew came here to meet Joe Rouleau, but the meeting was called off. The group left, and Betty came back inside. Why?*

It strikes me like a frying pan in the face: dead drop. It's so obvious now. Spies hand off secrets to their handlers by leaving the secrets in a public place. Like a country club storeroom, a hollowed tree, or an unused mailbox—all fall under the classification of dead drop.

Betty told me she went back into the townhouse alone. It could have been to drop the *Edison Data* for someone. Could Kevin have walked in on her stashing it and she had to kill him? Possible, but way out of character for Betty. It's possible Kevin knew what was up and waited to see who would retrieve it. That could get him killed, especially if he was young, idealistic, and imagined he was saving the day. This is all speculation at this point. I have nothing to go on.

Who would she leave it for? Not Joe, because she's telling him she still has it. She knows everyone is after her. If I were hiding it, I would put it in the last place Joe would look: in his own house. Betty might have thought of that. What I need to figure out is: Where would an actress leave a valuable hard drive?

Symone comes back to operational status and checks in. "Sorry, sorry. I'm good now. I'm OK."

After bringing her up to date on my thinking, I make a methodical search of the townhouse. Betty mentioned searching the kitchen for cash. Liars stick close to the truth to make their lie easier. I search there first. Nothing obvious. Moving to the great room, I check the dining room. Nothing. Moving to the couch and side chairs, the cushions also yield nothing.

Then I notice the TV has a DVR attached. A hard drive is tucked in back and connected with a USB cable. I pull it out, cable and all, and stare at it. Definitely an old-style hard drive about the size of a small paperback. This could be it. I connect it to my phone and start uploading the contents for Emma to have analyzed.

Making a hasty exit back the way I came, I stop in the alley and wait for Chris. While I wait, I call Captain Marisa Redgrave.

CHAPTER 30

CAPTAIN REDGRAVE

CAPTAIN MARISA REDGRAVE STANDS AT attention in front of Interior Minister Anna Krasnova's desk. The sharp-boned face of the minister is lemon-sour, like a prosecutor making a case for the death penalty. Her high-fashion pantsuit bears wrinkles from the long day. Standing behind her right shoulder smirks Police Chief Dubra. Marisa knew she was in trouble when she received the minister's summons in the middle of the night. Dubra's presence means it's worse than she thought.

Marisa keeps her eyes on the shelf behind the minister while the woman rants. On the shelf are the minister's many diplomas and a few books, mostly history and administration. On the left is a picture of faculty from the University of Latvia, with Anna Krasnova dead center. An inscription on the frame reads: Our favorite dean. The sentiment is doubtful given that everyone looks like they're there under duress. Marisa knows how they feel. The largest picture on the shelf shows the minister and Prime Minister, shaking hands and smiling like politicians. On the sides are a few pictures of her family, mom and dad, no husband or children.

Minister Krasnova, no longer Anna, is wrapping up her lengthy diatribe. "You know better than to send an email to everyone in the department making charges and threats without substantiation. This is not the USA—we don't do that. This is an embarrassment for the department and for you."

"I most humbly apologize, Minister Kras—"

"How dare you publicly shame a fellow officer when you have made no more progress than he?"

"I am sorry, Minister. I let the call from Mikhail Yeschenko rattle me—"

"Make one more mistake, and I take you off this case."

"Understood, Madam Minister."

"That is all. You are both dismissed."

Dubra marches to Marisa's side and gestures to the door.

"Wait," the minister says. "There is one last thing."

Minister Krasnova rises, plants her fists on the desk, and leans toward them. "The American Secretary of State called me to have the search for Jacob Stearne dialed down."

Marisa is too stunned to speak. She should have expected Jacob Stearne's popularity to gain him powerful help. Instead, she treated Stearne as a common criminal when he's an uncommon criminal. Having the American Secretary of State call is proof of just how uncommon. She steals a glance at Dubra, who is also stunned. At least they're on even ground.

"I assured him," the Minister says, "we will not harm his precious hero. I also assured him we will prosecute the man for any and all crimes he committed. To appease the American gods—and the $400 million in foreign aid they give us—I put a hold on all charges except for the destruction of a police car."

No one speaks for a moment.

"That is all," the Minister says. She picks up a pen and begins filling out a form.

Marisa can see it's a disciplinary report but can't see the name at the top. She turns on her heel and marches out of the office ahead of Dubra.

Lieutenant Krollis leaps to his feet from a chair in the hall and salutes them both. Smarting from her spanking, she has no desire to acknowledge him.

She strides ahead, hoping to leave both men behind so she can catch Stearne and charge him with something. But what? Stealing an official vehicle? At least the minister left her that paltry scrap.

Dubra tries to catch up with her, waddling like a watermelon with toothpick legs, no doubt to bask in the glory of his little victory. She picks up her pace, quickly leaving him behind, and makes the marble staircase knowing full well Dubra will opt for the elevator.

When she rounds on the third-floor landing, her phone rings. A quick glance shows it's Jacob Stearne. She looks up and down the hall to make sure she's alone. Falling back against a wall, she lets out an exasperated sigh and answers in English. "You are turning in yourself?"

"Did you take the shoe from the crime scene, or was that Dubra?"

Marisa gasps. In one short question, Jacob Stearne has turned her nightmare-night into a living hell. How does he know about the evidence? How does he know what was taken? He's deeper in this investigation than she or Dubra. That is not good.

"You are now there?" she asks. "We have man at the house. If you do not turn yourself in, we find you. I have entire town of Jurmala surrounded in five minutes—"

"I asked you a simple question and you threaten to re-enact the Normandy invasion? Who has the shoe—you or Dubra?"

"How do you know that shoe? What are you doing, Jacob Stearne?"

"I told you. I'm trying to find the real killer so you can make Dubra look bad. Did you figure out the footprints?"

"You make fool of me. Make me, how you say, spin my wheels? I look at video many times, no footprints."

"Exactly," Stearne says.

Marisa is about to curse him when, suddenly, the video begins to make sense. She sees the smooth pool of blood filling the archway into the kitchen. Beyond the blood lies Kevin Winn. Beyond Winn kneels Jacob Stearne in the middle of the kitchen on the far side of Winn. Stearne is right: no footprints.

She says, "If you are killer, there should be the footprints? Is that it? His throat is cut at stairs, he staggers to kitchen. You are on far side of body when camera gets there. There are no footprints. Had you been killer, you would have stepped in blood."

"See? I knew you were smart."

Marisa holds the phone close to her ear and checks again for anyone eavesdropping.

Decision time: Talk to him or send in the army? After the tongue-lashing she just got, mobilizing the troops to find a man wanted for nothing more than vehicular destruction would hasten her demotion. But negotiating with him? After everything she said to the press? Tough call.

"Why me?" she asks. "Why you are not calling Dubra?"

"You know why."

"I know nothing of sort. Wait. Wait. I see. Because I am assigned to case after murder, you trust me. You think Dubra is corrupt or incompetent. Tell me why you think this."

"You know why."

She has ideas but nothing concrete. There's no way she will tell a stranger what she suspects. She has no idea who Stearne would tell or what he might do with any information she gives him. That raises the question: What does Stearne know? Why is he so cryptic?

None of which matters. With her career hanging by a thread, she has to trust him. She asks, "What do you want?"

"I want you to find Kevin Winn's killer and get Dubra out of office."

"Why?"

"You know why."

"Stop saying that. Answer me."

"You answer me first. Who has the shoe, you or Dubra?"

"It is in lab. Under my protection—they are honest."

"Good. Meet me at Betty Bardon's rental in twenty minutes. Oh, and don't bring a SWAT team, just you, an aide—and one pair of handcuffs."

"You are turning yourself in?"

"No, I'm leading you to evidence. You'll discover enough for a big, fancy press conference by tomorrow."

"Wait, Stearne," she says with too much of a pleading voice. "Who was the woman? The one who stole the car and helped you escape?"

There is a moment of hesitation, letting her know she struck a nerve. Then he regains his composure and says, "Twenty minutes."

CHAPTER 31

JACOB STEARNE

IT'S NEARLY MIDNIGHT WHEN CHRIS drops me two blocks from Betty's house. He then executes the series of anti-surveillance maneuvers I'd taught him. First, he pulls into the driveway, gets Kayla to go with him, and pulls back out. They drive around the block, pull in the back yard, leave again, and drive around a few blocks. As he comes by me, I give him an all-clear sign. No one is following him. The one Remmo Nidal car we disabled appears to be the only one out there tonight.

Using a tree at the end of the block for cover, I keep watch for observers on foot.

While I look, I try to consider the clues from the townhouse. Easiest to analyze is the Cossack and his Russian-language laptop. While there are many Russian speakers in the country, I sense this is Mikhail Yeschenko at work. My biggest worry: did he get a clear picture of Symone? Was his Cossack recording when she was in there? I have to apply Stearne's Law: *Paranoia is the result of acute situational awareness.* And that means: Yeschenko's people must have video of Symone.

In addition, a Remmo Nidal operative with Rafael Tum followed Symone. Why would they follow her? Even if they know who she is, that she's staying with Betty's ELA crowd, and that she runs errands for me, what makes her a person of interest to them? Leverage? That's bad for Symone. Something about Rafael Tum in a car following Symone tingles the nerves in my neck. I need to think on that more.

But none of these people suddenly showed up this morning. They must have been watching Betty for days. The fact that they haven't killed her and left town indicates she still has the *Edison Data*. And they haven't killed me either, which indicates they think I might discover it. They might be right if that hard drive checks out. But she's playing a dangerous game. She knew the bears she was poking when she decided to pursue *Chaac* on her own without Ms. Sabel's help.

Symone didn't sign up for this. She wanted to get out of a brothel. And I showed up, framed by Hollywood fiction, and fell into the role of savior in her imagination. I'm no savior. My chosen profession is dangerous to her and her mental health. I heard her panicked reactions to my acts of violence. It dredged up the horror of her youth. What kind of hell had she lived through at the age of eight?

For a moment, I think about what my third-grade experience was like. Rainbows and unicorns. Nothing bad happened. No nuclear drills like my parents. No active-shooter drills like today's kids. No one stormed the classroom next door and shot twenty first-graders to death with an assault rifle. I didn't hear the screams of children over the hammering bangs of a semi-automatic weapon pounding out their lives.

Franklin is right. She doesn't belong anywhere near me. And that brings up a secondary thought: Did I hear him right? The US has 250,000 school-shooting survivors? I feel sick.

Because I'm in silent mode, Emma texts me her update. It reads, "Recent items: 1) Cossack in the townhouse is former spetsnaz operator Maksim Zaika, currently employed by a Russian oil export company owned by Mikhail Yeschenko. 2) USB drive is all porn; last accessed three weeks ago. Most likely left by previous guest. Several techs offered to investigate for a full report. I gave them the go ahead but told them not to bother with a report. They're happy. 3) Joe Rouleau flew from Paris to Riga twice on Air France. Once the day before the murder, and again the next morning. He is not listed on any manifest going back to Paris. Lastly, his Airbnb is owned by an investment firm with no connection to anyone we're tracking."

I think through them in order. I already ruled out the Cossack as the killer. But his background confirms what I've thought: Yeschenko is involved. That's not good. I should've realized the USB drive was too easy to find. The *Edison Data* could still be somewhere in that house. I need to find that drive. Joe's travel? Easily explained: either he had a body double make one trip for him, or he came out here on public airlines and flew back on a private jet in between. In either case, why?

I text her a thank you.

She texts back, "One other thing. Dr. Franklin took advantage of Ms. Sabel being on heavy pain medication and had someone put a transfer in front of her. She signed it, so it's official: Symone has been transferred to the Customer Service department. Also, you have an Employee Conflict Mediation session scheduled tomorrow. It appears you threatened a fellow employee. My money's on that being Franklin."

I text back. "OK."

"'OK' doesn't sound like you," she texts. "'Fuck him' sounds like you. We'll talk when you're free."

Conflict Mediation? Clamping my jaw tight to keep from screaming my many frustrations, I stow my phone. The reason you never find me at headquarters: backstabbing bureaucratic office politics.

I clear my head. I've got real work to do.

Movement at a hedge twenty yards in front of me brings me back to the present and reminds me of who I was looking for. He's showing up right about where I expected. He's using night vision to scope out Betty's house. I creep up to the figure dressed in black crouching next to a hedge.

I tap him on the shoulder and ask, "What's with the ninja outfit, Joe?"

He jumps a foot sideways with wide, white eyes. "Oh. Jacob. You startle me."

"Yeah, I do that to people," I say. "I have a question for you, though. Why did you take two commercial flights into Riga but none back to Paris?"

He twitches a smile. "I cancel the first flight. We discussed this."

"The airline manifest verifies you on both flights."

He backs up another step. He looks like he's thinking, *How am I gonna lie my way out of this one?*

CHAPTER 32

JACOB STEARNE

I STEP INTO JOE'S PERSONAL space. "Why not come inside instead of standing out here in the cold? Captain Redgrave is on her way over."

With that, I turn and stride to the house. He hesitates, then jogs to catch up.

"Jacob, whatever you think—"

"Save it." I keep marching. "You're not my biggest problem."

Opening the door, I usher Joe in first. I get a conversation started about the promise of the *Chaac Project* with Kayla, Logan, and Joe before slipping away to sprint upstairs.

Symone won't be happy about the transfer; that much I know. I made a promise. She'll throw that in my face. It doesn't matter. I can't destroy what's left of her emotional well-being for the sake of a promise made before I understood her trauma. Her mental health must come first.

Proceeding to my attic retreat, I find Symone lying on my sleeping bag, the laptop and phone still in mission mode beside her. She's sobbing into my pillow.

I pull her up to a sitting position and sit next to her. She falls into my shoulder. Instinctively, my arm circles her and I hold her for a long time. Whole minutes pass while I think of how I'm going to say what I need to say. Nothing comes to mind because, no matter what it is, I lack the courage to say it. Her whole body is shaking. I can rip the band aid off or peel it back slowly. I opt for slow.

"Want to talk about it?" I ask gently.

Instead of answering, she shakes her head violently and sobs into the pillow again. I let her go for five more minutes, squeezing her tight with my arm. I'm aware tears are the sign of an emotional transition. Soldiers have no immunity from them. Sometimes, after a horrific firefight, a soldier will break down in sobs of gratitude when transitioning to safety. What worries me is the lack of finality in Symone's. They seem endless.

"The danger I was in—it overwhelmed you?" I ask.

She nods vigorously. Her sobbing picks up.

I know what happened. She held it together while we were connected on the comms link but inside, her psyche was shredding. I don't know how to put that back together. I'm out of my league here. Taking down terrorists? No problem. Helping a young woman recover from trauma? No idea.

Mercury takes a knee in front of me. In an unusually soft voice, he says, *You was right, homes. She deserves someone better'n you. This ain't a time where you ax yourself if this be OK, then tell yourself it must be—cuz that won't make it so.*

I say, *I don't know what to do.*

He puts a hand on my shoulder. *You know someone who does, brotha. Give Franklin a call. Make nice.*

I nod at him. For once, he's giving me advice I can accept. But that's a tough call. I want to strangle the man, not ask for his help.

Like magic, a distraction appears: I hear Captain Redgrave's voice entering the house at ground level.

"I've got to go," I tell Symone. She grabs me, pulling hard. I tell her, "I'll be right back. I just have to clear my name with the cops. Then I won't be on the run."

This helps. Her grip recedes a little. Very little, but it's a start.

"I already made a deal with them. They're not going to arrest me," I hope out loud. "I promise I will be right back."

She lets go, sniffles, and looks at me with big, tear-filled eyes. In her sad and hollow gaze, I see eighteen years of loneliness turning into cold, prickly needles of fear.

My mind flashes on Jenny running out of the cave carrying the bomb. She wanted to be the hero for once. A bright white light obliterates her silhouette. Everyone around me dies. Mostly the bad guys. But all too often, the innocent. My heart feels like fine crystal shattered on concrete.

I don't know how to help her.

Extricating my shoulder, I drop down the stairs quickly and find everyone except Betty talking in the living room. The ELA gang is in the middle of denying my existence when I prove them liars, which doesn't make my entrance appreciated.

"Captain Redgrave," I hold my arms wide. "We meet again. It's been too long."

I notice her face tighten up with fury while the young lieutenant standing next to her looks confused. Apparently, she still hasn't told anyone about meeting me. Guess I'm her back-door man.

"Start searching here. Move upstairs one room at a time. When you find it, you will know what it is, what it means, and who it belongs to. But, it won't be enough evidence for a conviction. It will be enough for you to make your enemies look bad, your press conference look promising, and the haste of others to put me in jail look amateurish."

She thinks this over with a finger pressed to her lips and a cold, hard stare driving through me.

The ELA gang stares with open mouths at our interaction. I like being full of surprises.

Joe faces me aggressively, fists clenched. "What is the meaning of this, Jacob? You invited the police here? You are the wanted man, no?"

"Marisa comes in search of the truth," I tell him. "If you're innocent of the crime, you have nothing to worry about."

"You will address me as Captain Redgrave," she says.

I laugh.

Looking over the man Marisa brought with her. His name tag reads: K. Krollis. His rank appears to be lieutenant.

Joe isn't done. He faces Marisa and asks, "Do you have the search warrant?"

"She doesn't need one," I answer. "I paid rent on this place, and she has my permission to search for any evidence Kevin Winn's murderer may have left here."

Angered and powerless against my logic, Joe steps back.

"You have planted evidence here," Marisa concludes.

"When you find it, you will know it wasn't planted. Quite the opposite, in fact. That's why I'm not leading you to it. Because, honestly, I don't know where it is."

"You know what it is," she says eyeing me suspiciously. "You asked about the shoe."

I shrug. "It could belong to anyone."

While she doesn't like my answer, her gaze begins sweeping the room.

"One other thing before you start," I say. "There is a Russian sleeping in the townhouse next to the crime scene. He has a laptop that's been recording the inside of the crime scene with hidden cameras, possibly for a couple days. I hope and pray it recorded everything, including the murder. It may be the conclusive evidence you need. You should send someone over there right away to make sure your team collects the evidence and arrests the Russian before someone else does."

Marisa's eyes widen. She shoots a glance at her assistant, Krollis, who pulls his police radio and dispatches officers to the scene with urgency in his voice.

I hold up a finger. "If you'll excuse me a moment, I have a delicate personal matter that needs my attention."

Stepping into the downstairs bathroom and closing the door for privacy, I dial Dr. Franklin.

"Jacob," he answers with a sniff, "I'm just sitting down to dinner with my family. This is an inappropriate time to call, especially since you know we have a mediation—"

"Just add it to the list for your conflict party!" I snarl too loudly. "Listen up, Franklin. I just spent ten minutes holding a young woman in the middle of a nervous breakdown. I couldn't say anything because I didn't have any idea what to say. That's not because I'm stupid. It's because Ms. Blackworthy's problems are not my area of expertise. I'm good at what I do. I have killed our nation's enemies with my bare hands. I have jumped out of jets doing five hundred miles an hour from six miles up to land on top of terrorists. I have run through hailstorms of enemy fire to save children. What I don't know how to do is tell an eighteen-year-old that I lied to her. I promised I'd personally keep her safe. I've learned something tonight, Franklin. You were right in the beginning: I can't keep her safe. Mental health is a foreign language to me. That means my promise was a lie. I don't know how to tell her that. But you do. That's your area of expertise. So tell your family you'll be late for dinner because you're going to call Symone Blackworthy and explain how she's getting transferred to Customer Service. Make her believe it's a good thing. Make sure she loves the idea. Do it right now."

CHAPTER 33

BETTY BARDON

BETTY BARDON'S HEELS CLACK ACROSS the cold marble of the Grand Hotel Kempinski in Old Town Riga. At the beginning of this long day, she met Jacob in this same hotel. Now she crosses the lobby again, just before midnight for a completely different purpose. A thousand needles of fear spear her brain. Her gaze darts across the floor and into the corners, avoiding eye contact with anyone. In the seating area, three men are embroiled in a vehement debate, their words clanging like dishes in a cheap diner. When she strides by, their voices subside and their eyes follow her. The elevator doors clump shut behind her. The carriage lifts her to her fate in the penthouse suite.

She checks herself in the elevator's mirror, adjusts her hairclip, and straightens her jacket. Her skin vibrates with panic, but her lipstick looks fine. If someone had predicted she would do this tonight, she would've argued it an impossible fate. Now, she sees no way out. A badger of anguish tries to claw its way out of her stomach.

Jacob's words provide some level of comfort: *Stay in your lane.* She can do this. She must.

A burly, red-bearded guard, his hands clasped behind his back, waits in the hall with a poisonous stare. She raises her hands to let Red Beard pat her down. Once he's satisfied, he opens the door and gestures her in. Hesitating as if she were entering the last circle of hell, she steps over the threshold leaving behind the ashes of her pride and honor.

In the suite's living room, Mikhail Yeschenko looks up. He snaps his fingers and the two men talking to him quickly retreat to the room next door. Wearing a pristine suit, bright yellow tie, and shiny shoes, he spreads his arms wide and smiles a reptilian grin. "Betty, you become more gorgeous every time I see you."

An instinctive, self-preserving, and ultimately fake giggle escapes her. It's a sound she's bubbled up plenty of times for men. She can't believe she's doing it for a murderous bastard like him. He embraces her and kisses both cheeks. She pats his shoulder and politely pushes back. The subtlety of physical interactions is a Hollywood art form, one she has studied, practiced, and mastered. The casting couch did not disappear with Harvey Weinstein's conviction.

"A drink?" Yeschenko offers.

"Martini, please."

He smiles and snaps his fingers. A man she hadn't noticed at the far end of the room perks up. With a quick and silent glance, Yeschenko gives orders. The man disappears through a side door.

Yeschenko asks, "Where did you dig up that pathetic Frenchman?"

Caught off guard that he knows about Joe, she offers nothing more than a raised brow. "He's the scion of an old family with deep pockets."

Yeschenko motions to facing loveseats. He takes one while she takes the other.

"Fairy tales," he scoffs. "Do you know who he really is?"

"Careful, he might be your next Tsar."

Yeschenko laughs immediately and heartily. When his mirth rolls to an end, he asks, "What do you know about Joe Rouleau?"

"He wants to join the ELA." Betty tries hard not to fidget. "We haven't decided."

"We? Those ducklings who follow you around like a mother hen make the decision? Or is it you who has not decided?"

"We haven't finished the background checks."

He harumphs his disbelief. "You did not turn Jacob Stearne over to the police. Why?"

"I've come to make a deal, Mikhail." She waits to see his reaction. Blank. "My first demand: You must leave my friends alone."

"Answer my question." His beady eyes narrow to a withering gaze.

As important as her demands may be, Yeschenko holds all the cards in this game. She says, "I determined he could be useful to me. I plan to strike a deal with Rafael Tum for the *Chaac Equation*. To make that work, I'll need Jacob to make sure Rafael lives up to his part of the bargain."

"Make a deal with the old guerrilla? Or is he going by professor now?" Yeschenko holds up a hand. "No matter, he is untrustworthy—and you have no leverage. This is why you come to me."

The nearly invisible bartender appears at her elbow with a chilled martini, then hands a drink to Yeschenko. The oligarch's gaze never leaves hers.

She asks, "Why did you kill Kevin Winn?"

"This is the new normal for Americans: unsubstantiated allegations?" He scowls and waves a dismissive hand. "I did not kill your boy. All Westerners are alike in this, assume the Russian is a psychopath. No respect. I meet with American businessmen, and they treat me like peasant. I am successful, industry titan, more money than Pia Sabel. Yet, she thinks me inferior. She will not act so high and mighty when it is I who has *Chaac*."

He huffs, taking in the room while he resets after his rant.

Betty takes a sip of her martini. Vodka. She reminds herself that when ordering from Russians, specify gin.

He sets his drink on the coffee table between them and leans back, feet apart, arm over the sofa back. Confident and unafraid. "You lie about Stearne."

She pauses to look at her drink while she thinks. "If you didn't kill Kevin, who did?"

"You're afraid of Stearne." Yeschenko sips his drink. "It is because he sees through you. Yet you want me to believe you can manipulate him into robbing Rafael Tum. They are friends, no?"

"Who killed Kevin?"

"Enough of this!" he yells, his face flashing red as he leans forward aggressively. Then he calms, resumes his relaxed posture, and shrugs. "Have you not watched news? The police say Stearne."

Betty shakes her head. "There's no way. Jacob is not—"

"You try my patience, Betty," he says. "You come here to make deal, yet you insult me with accusations and ignore my questions. This is offensive. Tell me what you offer."

He resettles himself, adjusts his pant leg, sips his martini, and waits.

"I can bring you the *Edison Data* and the *Chaac Equation* in a few days. What I ask in return is—"

"You ask nothing. First, let us examine where you are." Yeschenko leans forward, rubbing his hands together as if examining a chessboard on the table between them. "Joe is wealthy, handsome, charming, and has some claim to royal blood. What woman in your desperate state could refuse his advances? You need him, yet you move Jacob Stearne into your attic and send Joe Rouleau into the night to fend for himself. Why is this?"

Covering her shock and sharp breath with a sip of her martini, Betty's mind spins through a thousand answers. Before she can think up something better, she finds herself blurting, "Because I suspect Joe works for you."

"Ah, finally, the truth." Yeschenko leans back. "Does it not feel good, Betty?"

Instead of answering, she swallows the rest of her martini like a shot.

"You are afraid of Stearne," Yeschenko says, "yet you bring him into your house instead of making deal with 'scion of an old family.' Do you know what this tells me? It tells me two things: First, you have determined Monsieur Rouleau is not who he pretends to be. You won't believe me, but I assure you there are no pretty boys like Joe in my employ. They are too lazy, expecting much and doing little. Second, you believe you can make a deal with me, and that Jacob Stearne can get you out of it afterward. Now tell me, do you really think one man can stop me from getting what belongs to me?"

"That's not … I," she stammers into silence. This is not going the way she planned. She must get it back under control. "I keep Stearne close because I believe he stole the *Edison Data* from me."

It might not have wrested control in her favor, but the great Yeschenko looks like someone kicked him in the balls.

"WHAT? How could you let this happen?" He's on his feet, shaking a fist at her. "You have one hard drive keeping you alive. Without that, what good are you?"

She tosses up her hands. "I'm not 100 percent sure what happened. If he stole it, Sabel would've sent a jet to pick him up by now. But he's still here. He says he wants to join the ELA, that he's done with Sabel, that she's gone crazy. I don't believe him, yet he is here, and my data is gone. For that matter, Joe is still here—and you are still here. Either of you would've left the minute you got your hands on it. That means: It hasn't gone far. Maybe whoever has it doesn't know what it is. That means I can get it back."

"This is why you come to me?" He doesn't wait for an answer, he turns his back, scratching his chin.

In his silence, Betty's thoughts involuntarily turn to Kevin Winn. Despite his denial, Yeschenko is the kind of man who could kill a young, eager kid. Or order it done. Working with the Russian is a nightmare. She shivers. As frightening as the situation is, she has no alternatives.

"What puzzles me," Yeschenko says, facing her, "is what you came here to offer?"

"The *Edison Data* is retrievable. The *Chaac Equation* is within reach. What no one else has is my expertise. I offer you my cooperation to bring the entire project together."

Yeschenko retakes his seat, staring through her as he moves. He picks up his martini, sips, and sets it back down. "You may be of use, I agree. Few are as familiar with it as you. Let us pretend you can retrieve your work. Then how do you deal with Professor Tum?"

"I have an arrangement to meet him soon. That is why I need Jacob Stearne. He can steal the *Equation*. No, Jacob is no friend of the old man. Rafael tricked him last outing and he's still pissed. Besides, you have been playing him like a chess game since he arrived. Leave him no option, and he'll take care of Rafael for us. But first, I need something from you."

Yeschenko doesn't move, doesn't blink, doesn't speak.

"I need," she begins, regretting the desperation in her voice, "your promise not to hurt anyone in the ELA. I know what you will do to me, but don't hurt—"

"I said I did not kill that boy!" Yeschenko shouts, his face red. His words shake the walls. "I will not hear any more of this whining. For all I know, it was one of you!"

Once again, his personality shifts in an instant. He calmly continues, "Your knowledge is of value, your idea to manipulate Jacob might work, but you do not possess the most important element of your bargain: the *Edison Data.* On top of that, I cannot shake the feeling you expect Jacob Stearne to save you in the end. This makes it difficult to trust you."

He rises, offers Betty a hand up, signaling the end of the meeting.

She takes it and faces him. Never before has she been face to face with such a malevolent man. He exudes evil. But she has no other choice. Her team may not appreciate it when they find out, but this is the only path. If she does this right, lives will be saved. If she blows it … she can't let herself think about that.

Yeschenko walks her to the door, opens it, and holds it while blocking her exit. He tugs her hand and holds it firmly.

He says, "I accept your offer. You will find and produce both the *Data* and the *Equation.* Use whatever means necessary. You will apply your expertise to resolving the metacapacitor. You will be handsomely rewarded." He hesitates, squeezing her hand and peering into her eyes. "However, you must understand one fundamental element about working with me: Jacob will not kill you and your precious ELA while you sleep. I, on the other hand, will not hesitate."

CHAPTER 34

JACOB STEARNE

FROM THE BOTTOM OF THE attic stairs, I hear Symone talking on the phone. I can't make out the words, but after making a lot of single-syllable replies, she becomes engaged in conversation. That's a good sign. Franklin better be good at what he does. The girl deserves more out of life than what she's been given these last ten years.

Marisa searches one bedroom for evidence while Krollis searches another.

Taking a seat on the bottom steps on the bedroom level, I wait for the inevitable. Emotions in this house are about to explode.

Joe and Chris come up from below with Kayla on their heels.

"What are you doing?" Chris asks. "Do you think Kevin's killer is one of us?"

With my eyes fixed on Joe, I answer, "What is better, finding the killer among your friends—or not finding the killer?"

Chris and Kayla look at each other like a pair doomed for the gallows.

With a shout of excitement, Krollis runs into the hall holding a switchblade in his gloved hand. Marisa joins him, looks it over, holds an evidence bag for Krollis to drop it in.

"Who belongs to this?" she asks.

"It is mine," Chris says. "But I never used it. I bought it for fun. I swear." He pleads with his eyes and open palms to Marisa's cold glare.

She pulls out a pocket-black light, shines it on the knife. Dark ink stains the inside, the sign of blood before luminol is sprayed on it. She gives Chris an expectant look and waits a scary moment for an answer.

"If that is blood," he says with a quaking voice, "it is mine. I cut myself playing with it. Stupid but …"

"We see soon," she says and drops it in an evidence bag. She goes back to work.

A few moments later, I hear Marisa call Krollis from the primary bedroom. Her lieutenant runs from across the hall to join her. We see the flash of phone camera lights. Chris and Kayla glance at each other again, this time dejected. Their heads drop into their hands. Logan and Francesca join us, see the sadness on their friends' faces, then freeze.

Marisa comes out holding a plastic evidence bag with one Louboutin shoe, satin in a purplish shade of blue with a red sole. The way she holds it makes everyone aware it is evidence in the murder of Kevin Winn. The others collectively gulp.

Marisa's face darkens, her eyes narrow to slits. She says, "Now you are ready to turn yourself in, Jacob Stearne?"

I toss a glance, directing her attention to the ELA kids lining my end of the hall. I answer, "This proves I didn't do it. There was only one print on the stairs."

Outside, we hear a car pull into the back yard and up to the kitchen door. The only person missing from this evening's festivities is Betty Bardon. Her minions look in the direction of the parking area, hoping she can bring sense to this nightmare.

Marisa holds the bag high and inhales a deep breath in preparation for a long, loud shout at me—but stops. Her gaze falls on the evidence bag with Chris's switchblade in Krollis's hand. Her expression gives her thinking away; her mind is working like a Swiss watch. Several pieces of the puzzle are coming together for her. She lowers the evidence to her side, looks at each of Betty's kids, then back at me. Holding my gaze, she reads my mind. The shoe proves nothing, yet at the same time, everything.

With a tight nod, she agrees to my terms. We have an understanding.

"Who is this shoe belonging?" Marisa asks the gathered ELA members.

All of them look away in different directions. In several languages they mutter, "I dunno."

"Will one of you tell the truth," I say.

"It belongs to Betty Bardon," the Italian reluctantly answers. Then she looks up quickly and adds, "Is this proof? Does this mean she is Kevin's killer?"

All faces snap to look at her, the accusation making sense. Then they face the police, waiting for the answer and fearing what it might be.

Downstairs, the kitchen door opens and closes. On our landing, no one speaks. Everyone listens. The house is eerily silent. We hear Betty pour a glass of something and clink ice into it.

Marisa pushes past the kids and storms to the stairs. Krollis starts to follow but the five of us beat him to it.

We spill into the living room like a flood. Betty stands in the kitchen archway with a puzzled look on her face.

Marisa marches up to her holding the shoe between them. "Betty Bardon, this is your shoe?"

After a quick glance, she answers, "Yes." She cocks her head, puzzled.

"I place you in custody pending official questioning in murder of Kevin Winn."

"What?" Betty's single-syllable question ricochets around the room. She looks to the rest of us.

Lieutenant Krollis grabs her arms. The kids turn to me as if they're witnessing another murder in their tribe, one orchestrated by me. As her wrists are pulled forward in front of her and cuffs clinked on them, she inventories the others, looking for the one who betrayed her.

"It's just for questioning," I explain. "Because she has a passport and could flee the jurisdiction, they bring her in and hold her." I turn to Betty. "Don't say anything without an attorney present."

"You did this!" Betty screams at me, her ice-blue eyes flash as anger turns to rage. "I hate you!"

Krollis marches her to the door and out to his car. Marisa stays to observe us for a moment.

"What have you done, Jacob?" Joe looks as hurt as Betty's soldiers.

"The only thing I did was let the authorities into the house, Joe. But you can do something. You could go with them to the police station and throw her bail. Or you could arrange a lawyer for her." I wait a beat while he silently glares at me. "But you won't."

Joe looks away. The others watch him with a hint of confusion that quickly turns to disappointment.

"It's a jolt to all of us," I tell them. "Francesca, all your clothes are fancy designer stuff. Are you sure that shoe isn't one of yours?"

I may as well have doused the young Italian with a bucket of ice water from the look of her. "Louboutin? *Fuori moda!* Ehm, so twenty-teens."

Turning to the others, I say, "I don't know what this means for Betty. We still have a mission and the resources to accomplish it. Let's keep our heads clear and bring the *Chaac Project* to the public. For Kevin."

My rallying cry doesn't move them.

Krollis returns, curious about the mood. He stands next to Marisa and nods toward the exit. She holds up a finger to stall him, wanting to listen a little longer.

Logan looks me over with pure hatred. "You brought them here. You told them it was here. You set her up!"

Holding up my palms, I reply, "I never touched that shoe, nor did I set foot in Betty's room."

None of them look at me. Their arms are crossed tight across their chests; their gazes fall in different directions from each other. Two world-shattering catastrophes in two consecutive days. It hurts.

Francesca explodes in Italian. I don't know the language, but I can tell she's blaming Chris for having a switchblade. Kayla joins the fray, telling them she, too, has a knife. Which turns out to be a bad idea: Krollis runs to her room and retrieves it. Shouting erupts in German and Italian. Judging by the body language, Kayla and Chris are giving excuses for their weapons. In the end, they plan to rely on forensics to prove their blades were not used in the murder.

Marisa turns to me with a pair of handcuffs. "You are ready now, Mr. Stearne?"

"What? Me?" I point at the shoe still in her other hand. "You just cleared me."

"There is warrant for your arrest charging you for destruction of public property and stealing car."

It takes me a minute to follow her logic. Then I remember what seems like years ago: The cop car I left demolished on the train track. I tell her, "Sabel Security will replace the police car with a brand new one exactly like it. Since it was destroyed while I was trying to survive your misplaced manhunt, I think that's fair. If you arrest me, I will withdraw my offer to save the taxpayers of Latvia a large amount of money for something that is ultimately your fault—but I will be sure to withdraw that offer in public."

If she could bite me and get away with it, she would. Marisa knows I have her cornered. The court of public opinion will be on my side. Still, she's nice, she's smart, and she needs a way out. I add, "When I have solid proof, I will help you expose Dubra's incompetence. That won't carry the same weight if you throw me in jail."

Her interest in tearing me apart doubles, yet logic prevails. She crosses close to me and softly asks, "You have evidence Dubra, how do you say, rushes to judgment?"

"You already have the evidence." I wait for her curiosity to rise. "Work the timeline."

She squints at me. Her desire to tear me limb-from-limb in the public square still seethes behind her eyes, yet she knows I was right about the footprints and the shoe. Reluctant resignation softens her face. Without another word, she rushes out and slams the door behind her.

The argument subsides. Joe and four disillusioned, heartbroken twenty-ish faces stare at me. Without looking away, Chris says something in German. The others nod their agreement. I don't speak German, but I catch the drift.

They don't like me anymore.

Before I can sway them, a noise catches our collective attention. Symone's backpack falls down the stairs followed by her heavy tromping boots. Tears, channeled into dark streams of wet makeup, line her cheeks. She pounds her way to me and pushes a petulant face up at mine.

"I knew you were a liar!" she shouts. "I knew it when you offered to drop me somewhere like I was a piece of trash stuck to your shoe. You've been trying to get rid of me since we met." Her clenched fists beat on my chest. "You're nobody's hero. You're a lying little bitch. Well, FUCK YOU! I'm not *transferring to customer service*. I quit!"

CHAPTER 35

JACOB STEARNE

SINCE THE ELA GANG HAS grown understandably hostile, I figure it's time to move again. I gather our backpacks and leave two Sabel Darts on the kitchen counter. I'm confident there is one person in this house who will know what they are and use them if needed.

Grabbing Symone's forearm, I sneak her and our gear out the back door to the Bolt waiting down the street.

I don't make promises I can't keep, and that means I'm going to protect Symone whether she likes it or not. That also means I can't let her quit. She tries wrestling out of my grip. I pull harder, open the car door, and toss her in. I slide in next to her. The driver starts off.

I text a quick note to Franklin, "Add this to our conflict mediation: You suck!"

Probably a bad idea but pressing "send" sure feels good.

"You can't quit," I say to Symone. "I need your help."

"Too bad." She crosses her arms and scowls.

In the mirror, the driver checks us out. He doesn't need to speak English to know something's wrong in our relationship. I give him a soldier stare, the one that says: death-comes-to-those-who-look-at-me. He turns his gaze back to the road.

"You're not transferring to customer service," I tell her.

"That Franklin guy said it was a done deal. No discussion."

"Don't worry about him," I say. "I'll have him overridden by morning. He made a mistake, that's all."

"He said customer service was more dignified than stripping." She watches me closely.

"He has a good point about dign—"

"Don't you start. I like my job. I'm good at it. You think sitting in some soulless cube farm with no windows getting slobbered over by an old, married-with-kids fat guy they call a manager—who doesn't even put a twenty in my shirt when he drools down it—is dignified? Not. And for what? I make more on a noon shift than I would working a month for your random billionaire who couldn't care less if I dropped dead at his feet."

"Her feet," I answer. "Pia Sabel owns the place. She's twenty-eight and used to be a world-class athlete. She cares."

"Well, ain't that nice," she scoffs and turns to the window. "Is she the one you were bad-mouthing at breakfast this morning? Wait. Was that yesterday? Hey, what time is it? Two in the morning. Yeah, that was breakfast yesterday. I'm hungry."

Aw, that's sweet, homie. Mercury leans between the front seats. *You got that hero-worship syndrome so bad you be begging your local Venus Libertina for adoration.*

What hero-worship thing? I ask.

You don't remember when your personal witch doctor axed you how come you enjoy killing people so much?

I say, *Dr. Harrison is a Harvard-educated psychiatrist not a witch doctor.*

Says you, Mercury says.

I say, *Anyway, I don't recall him phrasing anything like 'enjoy killing.'*

Facts! He looks at me like he just realized I have Alzheimer's, then he relaxes. *Well, what he mighta axed you was what makes you want everybody worshipping you as a hero? And then, come to find out, it was cuz yo mama and daddy liked your big sister mo better.*

That much is true. I ask, *What's that got to do with this?*

Dude! You gots no adoration going on right now. You be hitting on this here sweet thing because nobody worships you. Those ELA people hate you. Joe hates you. And none of them stand up to how much Betty Bardon hates you. Do we need to talk about Redgrave and Dubra? Then you done burned Symone to where she don't want to be around you no more. She was all over you a hour ago, dawg. So now you be begging. That's a sure-fire case a hero-worship syndrome. Boy, you got problems.

And talking to a long-lost supernatural being would be the biggest problem.

Something about the terms he uses—like adoration and worship—sound more like he's talking about himself than me. To be fair, I do like it better when everyone likes me. I suppose it might be the same for the immortal crowd.

See now? Mercury says. *I can fix it for you. You be one rooster sacrifice away from having everybody love you again, homie.*

So that's where this is headed. I had a feeling.

Haven't seen one lately, I answer. *What's with gods and sacrifices anyway?*

Mercury curls a lip. *Brotha, you be asking for favors all day and night. All we want is a little respect, know what I'm saying? Like all them Hindus, praying to Lakshmi for wealth but never do nothing for her. Just like you, always axing me to do you a solid, then you act like I'm a figment of yo imagination. Disrespectful.*

We have this conversation every day yet this time it feels different. I understand how he must feel. I say, *I'm sorry. I've never told you how much I appreciate everything you've done for me.*

"You're welcome." Symone uncrosses her arms and meets my gaze. "So, what's the deal? Why do you need my help?"

I have no idea how she could help. Mentioning an operation was just to keep her from running away. I think through a few things I need to do but the potential for gunfights loom in each scenario.

"I have a squad I've worked with for years, but they're all tied up. You did well earlier, and there's more stuff like that I need to do. So, I need your help."

"You mean like spy stuff? Sneaking around? Or do you mean like shooting people?"

"I'm not going to lie: I'm a danger-magnet. Remember when I told you things don't turn out well for people who hang with me? That's what I meant."

"That's OK."

"You froze." I toss my hands up. "Freezing in the middle of an operation could get us both killed."

"I'll get over it. It's just …" She turns away.

"Yeah, that's a problem. We can figure something out. Maybe I'll only involve you in the sneaking-around stuff. Lower risk operations."

She nods. We ride a mile in silence. Then she says, "Six hundred."

"Six hundred what? Oh. Your daily rate? OK. Fine."

"Seven hundred."

"We just said six."

"Yeah, but you caved too easy. Seven hundred or I get out at the next stoplight."

"If I say yes, then you do the same thing again. Holy Neptune. OK, I'm skipping the next round, eight hundred or go ahead and get out." I wave at the street.

"Done. But it's not just about money, Jacob." She leans to me. "You know about me. That damn Franklin told you why I freak out at loud noises. I want to know about you. It's only fair. What do your demons look like?"

Mercury squeezes in behind me and whispers in my ear, *Oh yeah, homie, you got demons. She be thinking what Socrates said, 'an unexamined life ain't worth living.' She wants to examine your life.*

I say, *What do I tell her? She's fragile.*

Mercury says, *You could start with your first deployment, when you was eighteen and that guy you was pals with got shot in the face with a RPG by one of your own. Friendly fire woke you up real fast and still haunts you. That's a 'no,' huh? Too much? Y'all bunch a wimps. Fine. Hows about that time—*

You're not helping here, I answer. *Everybody knows war is hell.*

Mercury says, *Then tell her what Dr. Harrison said.*

"I'm not a hero," I tell Symone. "I'm a kid whose parents didn't love him. They loved my sister because she loved farming. I excelled at everything. I did it to get their attention, but I couldn't love farming. Too boring. I never felt like I earned their approval. Since they were pacifists, I joined the Army as my form of rebellion. They definitely didn't approve of that. I've been desperately seeking the approval of others ever since. What you think of as heroic is what my psychiatrist calls dysregulated behavior. Where sane people would seek a therapist to talk through their issues, I crave the attention I get from death-defying deeds."

She stares at me blankly for six blocks. It gets uncomfortable. Finally, she says, "That's the saddest pile of bullshit I've ever heard. Who do you sell that crap to? Do they believe it?"

"It came out in long discussions with my psychiatrist."

She laughs. "You sure she wasn't one of the other inmates?"

"Dr. Harrison is a Harvard-educated psychiatrist."

"Yeah, the ones with the fanciest degrees are the easiest to snow."

"Hey! You asked for my story. I didn't expect you to make fun of it."

"C'mon, who do you think you're talking to? I'm a stripper. The new girls always come in making some kinda excuse about why they were forced into the business. I mean, sure, some of them have mean boyfriends and some of them might've been abused by that uncle. But most of them want to be there because it's a kick. It's a high like nothing else—all those men admiring you, telling you they'll sell their soul to the devil if you run away with them. Telling you their family means nothing to them cause you're so beautiful. Yeah, a real kick. Then, after a while, you hear the same BS so much, it don't mean anything."

She sighs and shifts in her seat. We travel in silence for a few blocks.

"So," she says, "you crave attention by doing dangerous stuff, huh?" She reaches out and takes my hand in both of hers. "Like storming the Paris church where a hundred terrorists waited to ambush you?"

"Hundred? Ambush? What?" I twist to look at her. "Did you get that from the TV show?"

She nods and mimics a karate chop. "It was so cool."

"Freaking Hollywood." I sigh. "It was two guys with automatic weapons. I did take them down with my bare hands, though. Did they show that?"

She looks confused. "What about the guided-grappling hook and the computerized boomerang?"

Now I'm confused. "How do you computerize a boomerang? What

good would that … never mind. Forget that show."

She turns to the window for a few blocks as the driver eases our way into Old Town Riga. Dark and narrow buildings shun us as we pass under the disapproving tower of a fifteenth century basilica. She says quietly, "I've heard that dysregulated stuff before."

I stay quiet, waiting to see if she wants to say more. Her silence says a lot. We both seek attention, each for our own reasons. Maybe everyone does in their own way.

We pull into the alley behind the Grand Hotel Kempinski, where the night manager waits next to the trash compactor.

"We're not good enough for the front door?" Symone asks.

"Yeschenko's set up in the penthouse suite. He has a man in the lobby, and he monitors all the security cameras. Our people in DC spoofed his video feeds, but we can't fool the bodyguards."

The manager takes us back to the Presidential Suite. This time, Symone has a connected room. I'm beginning to trust her.

I hand the manager enough euros to out-bid Yeschenko. I thank him for his loyalty. I'm hoping the Latvian distrust of all things Russian will tip his scales in my favor, otherwise he could sell my location in thirty seconds. Stearne's Law rises after he leaves. I step into the hall and place a couple volumetric sensors in strategic locations—just in case.

Symone throws her hands in the air, spins in a circle, and says, "I love this place. I could get used to living large like this. I'm ordering room service." She picks up the hotel phone. "So tell me about this mission you have for me. What do I gotta do?"

"First, we have to figure out how to work together. I'm not a psychologist. I don't know how to help you. That's why I called Franklin—but that didn't go well. When we work an op, I can't have you freaking out, freezing up, or anything. Now that I know why stress makes you panic, I can try to avoid involving you in those situations. But what do we do when they come up?"

"I dunno." She shrugs, cradling the receiver under her chin. "Hey, back in the car, when we were talking about my pay, did you say, 'Holy *Neptune?*'"

CHAPTER 36

JACOB STEARNE

WHEN YOU BOOK THE PRESIDENTIAL Suite—and a sanctioned pariah from Russia is in the Penthouse Suite—they keep the kitchen open all night. Symone orders a hot fudge sundae. I hold up two fingers while she's on the phone and she orders a second one for me. Just because she's a stripper doesn't mean she doesn't have good ideas.

Going old-school, I find a piece of paper and a pen to jot down my priority list. First thing I need to do is to find a way to work with Symone that keeps her level. I write that down.

Mercury leans across the table. *Why izzat number one, homie? What about show your favorite god some love?*

I look at him, scratch out number one, and write down: "find rooster."

I say to him, *Happy?*

About as happy as Betty Bardon, he says. *I be happy when you keep your promises, bro. You know what else you gotta do? You gotta get that Chaac Equation outta that old guerrilla, Rafael Tum. Then you gotta get Betty outta jail. Then you gotta—*

Why do I have to spring her? I ask.

When you gets your grubby little hands on the Edison Data and the Chaac Equation, whatcha gonna do with it? You gonna take it back to Pia-Caesar-Sabel?

I pause for a moment in thought. Then I answer, *I don't know.*

I'm feeling a bit unmoored. I'm spending Ms. Sabel's money like a drunken sailor, so I should be loyal to her. President Williams asked me to come back with the whole thing for the sake of the nation, so I should be loyal to him. I promised Joe Rouleau and the ELA I'd be loyal to them. Something's gotta give.

"Do you think Betty did it?" Symone asks.

"Evidence points that way."

"She doesn't seem like the kind."

"What if I told you that two weeks ago, she tried to take a pistol out of my hand so she could shoot the man who molested her?" I catch her gaze until she realizes this is my area of expertise.

Symone's mouth drops open. "Wait, is that why she was so nice to me? I asked her about traffickers, but she didn't want to talk about it. Did she kill the guy?"

"I shot him instead. Saved her the nightmares."

A waiter brings in a tray with two hot fudge sundaes and an array of toppings on the side. My mouth is watering by the time he lays out everything in front of us. Symone wolfs down a couple spoonsful before I sign the check.

"So," she says while still slurping hot fudge, "you gonna find out who killed Kevin Winn then?"

Instead of answering, I toss buttered pecans on my double-scoop and take a bite. It's been a long time since I indulged in a hot fudge sundae. Too long.

My spoon slips greedily through calories and cholesterol while half the attempted load falls back into the bowl. As the fudge melts into an ice cream orgy in my mouth, I contemplate how to answer her. It's not an easy question for someone young to grasp.

I say, "What they get off that Cossack's laptop from the townhouse might tell us who did it. Depending on when they started recording, it might show the actual murder. If it's Betty, then we know. If the guy we found is the real killer, he probably erased it. And then, there's the possibility of a deep fake. So, I'm putting the hunt for Kevin's killer at the bottom of my priority list for now."

The sundae is great. I dive in for more. And more. Then I dump the rest of the pecans on top.

Symone prefers the pistachios. Like me, she's dumped the small bowl of nuts in her mix. She's swirling the fudge and ice cream. With her mouth full, she says, "What's on your list?"

I look at the paper next to me. "Secure the *Edison Data*."

She points her spoon at me before scooping more as she says, "Did you search the ELA house for it?"

"Naturally."

She squints as the icy dessert melting in her mouth causes her to pout. After swallowing, she says, "You searched the place. Is that when you planted the shoe?"

"I didn't plant the shoe," I say. "There was no shoe when I searched. Someone, maybe Betty, put the shoe there later."

"Something about that doesn't add up. No woman is going to walk around with one shoe."

"I'm aware." I down another couple bites before going on. "Some women bring an extra pair in case they need to kick up the wardrobe a notch. There could've been a spare pair in her bag and one dropped. I don't know yet. But next up: I need to find and secure the *Edison Data*."

"How you gonna do that?" Symone asks.

"I'll go to the jail and ask Betty where she hid it."

Symone shovels another huge scoop in her mouth and answers me with wide eyes, as if to say, *she's going to tell you?*

"Then I need to trade that to Rafael Tum for the *Chaac Equation*." I shovel a scoop of my own. "They planned to swap, giving them both two-thirds of the project. Rafael doesn't mind because he knows Betty is underfunded and will never get off the ground, while he plans to sell to the highest bidder and let them deal with Betty."

Symone says, "Is that the guy who was with the other guy? The stalker?"

"Tail," I explain while chocolate runs down my chin. I wipe it off with the pristine white linen napkin provided. "Stalkers in your world, tail in mine. Spy stuff."

She nods while holding an overladen spoon dripping fudge. As the load moves toward her mouth, a dollop lands on her chest. I point to it. She figures out what I'm saying, whips her shirt off, runs to her bathroom, splashes water on it, hangs it to dry, and comes back. Her lacy push-up bra is definitely eye-candy.

I get up, pull a t-shirt from my pack and hand it to her.

"What's the matter—can't finish your dessert with boobs in your face?" she asks. She puts the t-shirt on the table as if it were a used napkin.

"Can't afford it," I answer. "I'm not going to be that guy who drools without paying."

She laughs.

I take another spoonful of glop dripping with sugar and saturated fats. Then stop mid-shovel. I drop my spoon back in the bowl and lean back, thinking out loud. "That's a good question. Why was that guy following you into the restaurant?"

Mercury waves a hand in front of my eyes. *You got a downright infantile preoccupation with bosoms, you know dat, dawg? You're staring.*

I answer, *I'm thinking. When did you start using the word bosoms?*

Since I invented it eight hundred years ago. Yeah, you be thinking about bosoms alright, when you should be thinking about Joe Rouleau and Mikhail Yeschenko and Rafael Tum not to mention staying true to Betty Bardon.

Absently, I reply, *Yeah, how are they wrapped up in Kevin's murder?*

Keep thinking, homes, Mercury says. *Who you leaving out in that lineup?*

After watching me stare at her, she quickly dons my t-shirt, which reads, *US Army: Keeping heaven packed with fresh souls since 1775,* and tongues a dollop of chocolate rolling off her lip. She says, "I give up. Why?"

Her question breaks my stare and takes me a few seconds to figure out. "Why was he following you? Or, was he following someone else? Who drove you to pick up the food?"

"Chris and Logan."

"Both of them?" I ask.

"I can handle two guys."

"Let's keep it professional. What I meant was, the guy could've been following—"

"I am being professional. I can dance for two guys at the same time.

Happens all the time."

"Stay on topic, Symone. Hakim Haddadi, the Remmo Nidal guy, could've been following one of the ELA guys."

"Nope." She scrapes the bottom of her bowl for the last dregs of sweetness. "I knew those guys would feel bad about me paying for dinner, so I told them both to wait in the car. You know, avoid that whole schtick men do: pretending they're going to pick up the check but oh-I-musta-dropped-my-wallet-somewhere thing. When there's two of them, it gets extra awkward. So I went in by myself and that's when I saw your Remmo-Creeper following me. I know how to handle creepers: whip out the phone and live stream them. Only you got Emma filtering all my posts, so I could only record him."

I stare at her with a new appreciation as the concept forms in my head. I must have an odd expression on my face because she tilts her head to the side as if I were turning Martian before her eyes. She points at my bowl. "You gonna finish that?"

I push the bowl toward her, still staring. The concept is becoming clearer and clearer in my head. Like a timelapse of beach fog burning off. I see it now.

Symone grabs my bowl and spoons out the last.

"I need you to bail that guy out of jail," I say with a distant voice.

"Hadaddi? Are you fucking kidding me?"

My meditation clarified, I sit up straight and tell her, "He wanted you to be the cut-out. That is, to set up a meeting with me without Yeschenko finding out, he would do it through you. They've been watching that house since we first arrived. They know you and I are together … in a manner of speaking. He didn't approach the guys in the car, so he wasn't interested in them. To keep a covert tail on you, he didn't need to follow you into the restaurant. He wouldn't have—unless he wanted to give you a message for me."

"Then why did he back off?"

"In espionage, getting recorded is a bad thing. Getting live-streamed would be worse. His instincts made him abort his mission."

"Huh." Her single word response serves as a punctuation mark to my statement. "So now you want me to bail him out?"

"Right." I explain about setting him up for the drunk tank.

"Why me?" she asks. "Why not you?"

"Because we need a cut-out. The players watch each other. They know me, they know the ELA people, and that means they'll follow me—which would spoil the meeting. But you're not on the cast list. You aren't supposed to be here. Rafael Tum would notice anyone out of place. He told Haddadi to contact you. The Russians are watching me, not you. That is, as long as you keep your shirt buttoned up like a schoolteacher."

"That's what you want me to do," she says. "Is it dangerous?"

"It'll be like the break-in, I'll be watching and communicating. If anything looks suspicious, I'll call it off."

"OK."

The ease with which she accepts her mission makes me rethink this whole mess. What if someone confronts her? What if she freezes? I'll be nearby, but not close enough to step in front of a bullet. This is another bad idea. Really bad. I must stop using her just because she's naïve and willing. On the other hand, this is a simple task. The other guys won't be watching a precinct lockup. There won't be any danger. She'll be fine.

CHAPTER 37

CAPTAIN REDGRAVE

CAPTAIN MARISA REDGRAVE UNLOCKS THE door, pushes it open, then motions Betty Bardon into the dark room. When they're both inside, Marisa locks the front door and throws the bolt. She closes the curtains before turning on a light by the couch. Pointing to the sofa, she orders Betty to sit.

"What is this?" Betty asks, tossing her hair over her shoulder. "What's going on?"

"You watched *Le Héros?*"

"Sure. Everybody did." Betty looks around. "Except Americans."

"No Americans?"

"They don't watch movies with subtitles. Too much work." Betty scoffs. "This is your house, isn't it? Why are we here? Why didn't you take me to the police station?"

"In that show, they say about Stearne's Law. Does he really say that?"

"Paranoia is the result of acute situational awareness? Yeah, until you get sick of it."

"This is why I use my house for your detention. The more I become aware of my situation, the more paranoid I become."

Betty holds her wrists up in front of her with a silent request to be released.

"No." Marisa paces the small rug in front of the sofa.

"I didn't kill Kevin. I would never ... I don't know what Jacob told you, but I didn't do it. You have to know that."

Marisa slices the air with her hand. "Silence. I must think."

Her head races with thoughts, all of them starting with: why? Why are Americans swarming her city? Why is an American actress in Latvia instead of Hollywood? Why did Mikhail Yeschenko take an interest in Jacob Stearne? The stream of questions turns into a raging flood.

After pacing for nearly a full minute, she turns to Betty and asks, "You have love for Jacob Stearne?"

Betty's mouth falls open. "I, well, not anymore. Not after tonight."

Marisa rolls her hand, demanding more.

"We gave it a shot a couple weeks ago." Betty's gaze wanders around the room. "It felt special, like we really had something. We were working together, and we connected. Really connected—in Banff, Canada, of all places. After all, he's kinda handsome, he can be charming, and then there's the hero angle. So we hooked up for one special, magical … Well. Then, after he saved my life, I left but he didn't come with me. He chose Pia Sabel over me."

"He has the affairs with Pia Sabel?"

"No," Betty says. "At least, I don't think so. I'm sorry, I should've said he chose Sabel Security. He chose his career over me."

Marisa examines Betty Bardon and sees no signs of deception, no hesitation in answering, only fear of being arrested. Betty's hair hangs in her downcast face. She waves her hands and says, "Jacob Stearne does not point at shoe and say, 'See, she did it.' Why not? Why does he not accuse you?"

"Because I didn't do it."

"Your Russian friend does it for you?" As soon as she asks, Marisa sees the signs of deception. Betty's face pales, sweat breaks out on her forehead.

"Russian?" Betty glances at her briefly. "What do you mean? Mikhail?"

That answer jolts Marisa. She has learned not to push someone into a lie. It's better to change the subject and come back at it after the suspect lowers her guard. She takes the chair next to Betty. "Why you have come to Latvia?"

Again, deceptive signs litter Betty's face. "I want an attorney present before I answer any more questions."

"You are not arrested. Not yet. No need with attorney. But, tell me this: was Kevin Winn killed instead of you?"

Betty turns another shade whiter. "I want that attorney now."

"Yes, yes, we go to station, meet attorney, then questions. If you wish. Did I tell you: Mikhail Yeschenko has supporters, ehm, allies, inside Riga Municipal Police?"

Betty curls herself into a near fetal position and replies meekly, "No."

"This is why I ask about Stearne's Law." Marisa runs her fingers through her hair to relieve some of the tension in her head. "No one know you are in my house. You are safe. Do you want to tell me about Russians?"

Betty begins to tremble. "No."

"Why did Jacob Stearne know about shoe?"

"I don't know. I don't know why my shoes are such a big deal."

"Where is other shoe?"

"I don't know. Why are you asking me these questions? I said I want a lawyer."

"How do you know Mikhail Yeschenko?"

Betty grabs a red velvet pillow and holds it defensively against her chest. Crumbling further into a ball, she closes her eyes.

"I have problem," Marisa confides in Betty. "Someone kills Kevin Winn. I want to find that person. You and Jacob Stearne do not care about Kevin Winn. Not much. You chase something else. Mikhail Yeschenko also chase something else. What? What do you hide from me?"

Betty whimpers.

A text comes in from Kaspars Krollis: "Pulling up to your place now."

She texts back, "I'll be out in a second." Rising, she looks back at Betty. "What about Maksim Zaika?"

Betty looks up with red eyes filled with tears. "Who?"

"The Russian in townhouse next door to crime scene, has Cossack mustache."

"Oh, my god," Betty says. She buries her face in her pillow, crying.

"There were … Russians?"

Marisa is getting nothing from the American. In disgust, she walks away. Pausing at the front door to think a moment, she can't piece any of this together. She unbolts and unlocks the door. She steps out to the driveway and marches toward Lieutenant Krollis. She calls out while approaching him, "Did you get anything?"

He holds up a laptop in one hand, "Nothing. Sorry, it ran a self-destruct routine."

He holds out the computer.

She never sees the baton whooshing through the air—but she feels it crash on her skull.

CHAPTER 38

JACOB STEARNE

WE'RE IN THAT SHADOWY HOUR before dawn when the world is asleep and the cobblestones are silent. Soon, the sun will attempt an ambush with daggers of light, but for now, it's dark, overcast, and foggy. Buildings of unforgiving stone crowd us into narrow streets to watch us like sentinels. Not even stray dogs prowl tonight.

Symone and I reach a street corner two blocks from the police station. She's looking professional again after I used the blow drier to fix her blouse. The fudge stain didn't come out completely, but it's hardly noticeable.

I double-check the video feed coming from her earbud, and double-check the streets around us, and double-check with Emma that our Latvian translator is on the comm link, and double-check that Symone knows what to do when she gets there.

"Stop it," she shoves me. "You weren't this worried about me before, and this deal is easier. So knock it off."

"Hmm." I double-check the mini-drone I have circling the block. I remember being a teenager and bristling at parental-reminders.

"I'm going in," Symone says as she starts walking down the block.

I pick out a recessed doorway where I can see the station. My phone shows both Symone's live feed and the drone. She walks up the steps, enters the lobby, and from there, our Latvian translator reads her the signage over the comm link. The place is empty. After a couple turns, she finds someone half-asleep at a desk.

The man startles and jumps to his feet. Symone plays our interpreter on her phone as if it were an app. The man tells her to follow him. He leads her back to the front door where he goes behind a desk and starts typing on a keyboard. He reports they are not holding anyone in the cells who was brought in tonight.

Emma and the translator provide the name of the Remmo Nidal agent, Hakim Haddadi. He types away.

"Yes, he was here earlier. Slept two hours before we got his name," our translator reports. "Then his friend bailed him out."

"I'm his girlfriend," Symone says, affecting a voice like a jealous lover. "He asked me to bail him out. Who came for him? Huh?"

The man behind the desk recoils and shakes his head.

"You telling me some other bitch came for him?" Symone shrieks. Her acting is impeccable. Maybe Betty could get her a job in Hollywood. The man looks shaken. Our translator keeps a steadier voice that does little to calm the man at the desk.

He clacks away, stares at the screen, then twists it for Symone to see. It reads: Amit Sofer.

"Holy Jupiter," I say. Which is followed by silence on my team.

"Someone you know?" Emma asks after a beat.

"Yeah, known associate of Rafael Tum. I've dealt with her and her husband Eli before. Symone, when they release people, they should leave an address. Can you get that out of him?"

She asks. He shakes his head, no.

My video feed comes from her earbud, giving me a view from her eye level of where she's looking. The view swivels away from the desk, she looks down, her hands start undoing the top two buttons.

"Don't do that, Symone," I say. "It's not—"

Emma interrupts me. "Let the girl do what she's gotta do."

When Symone turns her cleavage to the officer, he clutches imaginary pearls and rolls his eyes to the heavens.

I finish my sentence, "—not going to work. He's gay. Whip out that €500 I gave you."

A second later, he's staring at the money the way a starving man stares at a steak. After a quick look around the room, he snatches it, jots something on a sticky note, and hands it to Symone.

She thanks him and leaves.

When she's clear, Emma's voice breaks the silence. "How did you know the guy was gay, Jacob?"

"Yeah, you sure know how to spot 'em," Symone says.

"You spend a year on a base in the desert with ten thousand men, average age of twenty-one, and you learn some things about people. That—and the fact he never checked out Symone."

While she crosses the street, I recheck my drone feed. A shadow fifty yards behind her flits like a bat in the night. My danger meter spikes. The shadow is closing on her at a pace that could overtake her before she reaches me.

I whisper in our comm link, "Pick up your pace a notch. Don't run—I want to see if that's a pedestrian or a tail behind you."

Symone does exactly what I ask without hesitation.

The shadow's pace remains steady. The guy could be an early riser or he could be a damn good covert operator. Stearne's Law kicks in. Amit Sofer springs the Remmo agent, and a shadow follows Symone from the station. What a coincidence. As good as Symone is, things are getting too dicey for an amateur with panic issues.

"Brush contact," I tell Symone. "Hand off the sticky note as you pass by me, then keep going straight to the hotel."

"No."

"I need you to control the drone, watch my back."

"I'm coming with you. I don't know anything about drones."

"It's not a discussion. You go back, run the drone from my laptop."

"He needs your help," Emma chimes in. "I'll show you how to work the drone."

In the comm link, Symone sounds like she's crying. As she passes by my doorway, she slaps the sticky note on my shoulder. Never gives me a glance, just keeps striding down the lane with her head down.

I move the drone to check the street behind her. I see a second shadow, twenty yards behind the first. Definitely a hostile tail. The two could be working a tag-team to avoid detection.

Scanning the address into my phone, I discover my destination is two blocks past the police station, down an alley. A sleazy old hotel. The kind that rents by the hour. That sounds like Rafael Tum. The former Che Guevara-wannabe never minds when Sabel Security foots the bill for a swanky resort, but on his own, anything dryer than his old jungle bivouac is the Ritz to him.

The first tail passes me. I stick out my foot, hook his ankle, and throw him against the wall.

He's scared to death. The smell of flour and yeast permeates his clothes. I feel it on my fingers. Even the best spy couldn't get that much detail right on short notice. He's a baker working the early shift. I apologize, dust him off, send him on his way.

The second tail saw my little altercation and has turned around. I set a good pace to catch up to him. The guy looks over his shoulder, then picks up his stride. He's older, gray, somewhat fit, and nervous. He glances over his shoulder again. Amateur.

He stops at the lane where I'm headed. He tries to look casual, like he's waiting for a bus. Only they don't start running for two more hours. The guy looks vaguely familiar, but I can't quite place him.

Behind me, I hear something clatter in the street. A second later, Emma comes on the comm link with Symone whispering apologies in the background. Emma says, "We had a little mishap with the drone."

"No problem," I answer quietly, "I've got someone who'll cover me."

Stepping up to the guy on the corner, I shove him to the wall behind him and slam my forearm under his chin, choking him. "Why are you following—"

Then I recognize the guy.

"Hey, you're that writer," I say. "That guy who writes those books about me. You're Seeley James."

He can't breathe, so he can't answer. He shakes his head, no. Then realizes lying to me is a mistake. He nods, yes.

I ask, "Why are you following me?" I release his windpipe just enough for him to answer.

He says, "Research for accurate books. You Sabel people never return my calls, so—"

Shoving my forearm back into his throat, I cut him off. "Yeah? Did you make a lot of money writing all that bullshit about me for Netflix?"

He squawks, "Nothing … to do with …"

I lighten up on choking him.

"They stole my work!" He gulps a breath. "Didn't pay me a dime. Plagiarized my whole book, *Death & Conspiracy*, then they changed everything."

I squint at him. "How can it be plagiarism if they changed everything?"

"Yeah. My lawyer told me I gotta work on that before I can file a suit. I'll come up with something. But they stole everything I—"

I shove my arm back into his windpipe. "Don't care. It's time you earned your keep. Hold this." I give him a panic button that sounds off in my comm link. "If you see anyone come down this alley, you press this button."

"OK," he says and swallows hard. He's white as a sheet and shaking like a leaf.

"If you run off," I tell him, "I'll hunt you down and break your typing fingers."

Happy that I finally found a good use for a lazy writer, I pat his shoulder and walk down the lane. It's dark and wet. Dew is forming. The hotel itself has one lone bulb burning in the lobby. A guy sleeps in a chair behind the front desk, his feet up on the counter.

Kicking his knees, I shove him aside and start typing on his computer. I have no idea what I'm typing because it's all in Latvian, but the guy pops up quickly and pulls my shoulder.

When I turn to face him, I press my pistol into his chest. "I'm looking for a guy. Came in here about an hour or two ago. Might've had a woman with him. Take me to his room."

I give him a minute to pee his pants, then I turn him and shove him toward the stairs. It's not the kind of place to have elevators. We go up three flights and down to the end of the hall. He opens the door with a passkey.

We don't need to turn the light on. Spreadeagled on the floor lies Hakim Haddadi, formerly of Remmo Nidal, his head cracked open and half his brains on the carpet. Beyond him, the window leading to a fire escape is open, the dingy curtains fluttering as if someone just left.

I turn to the manager and tell him, "His reservation is cancelled."

The alarm in my comm link shrieks like a wounded animal.

CHAPTER 39

JACOB STEARNE

BACKING AWAY FROM THE MURDER scene, I ask the manager to show me an unoccupied room. He says they're all occupied. I grab his master key, unlock the door directly across the hall. I then make him call the police and have him wait until they arrive. He does as he's told.

Stepping into the commandeered room, I see it has a tiny bathroom next to the door forming a short hallway; the space beyond is filled with a bed. No desk, no bureau, no luggage rack, no space. In the bed are two men and a woman, all naked, tangled, and slowly waking up. They rub their eyes and gasp one at a time as they find me pointing a pistol just over their heads and holding a finger to my lips, shh.

Tromping feet pound their way up the stairway from the floor below. Judging by the noise, I'm guessing four men. Heavy men.

Once I have the attention of all three occupants of the bed, I point to the small hallway formed in the junction of the bathroom and front door. They don't understand. I curl a finger and point, then wave the barrel around. I'm careful not to endanger them. After all, they're only pawns in my game.

One by one, they get out of bed, still naked, and squeeze into the hall. I line them up and start to push the girl to her knees. Then I think about rampant homophobia among Russian gangsters and push one of the guys to his knees in front of the other two. They shiver with fear.

Outside the door, I hear the Russians shouting at the manager. They just found the dead Remmo agent. I hear the word *policija* batted around. By tone of voice, I'm figuring the manager told them he'd called the police and the Russians aren't happy about it. One of them goes in to check on Hadaddi; the others fan out down the hall.

As I expected, one of them opens the door to my hiding place. The first thing he sees is the threesome with one man on his knees. He shouts, *"Pediki!"* which I believe is a rude slur. There is a moment in which the Russian considers whether he wants to go in the room for a full inspection.

I'm standing behind the threesome and around the corner, pistol at the ready. If it comes to a shootout, one against four gives me slim odds for survival. I hold my fire.

While he's thinking, Emma comes on the comm link and says, "Sorry, Jacob, but your she-devil has gone and done something rash." When I don't answer, she understands I'm in a tense situation and continues. "She remembered the man at the station saying no one was booked into jail last night. She went back to inquire about Betty. For an extra €500, he told her Betty Bardon was never booked into the system. We'll talk later."

The Russian says something to the threesome that ends with a derisive laugh. They don't answer.

In my earbud, Symone's voice comes on, "Jacob, I'm on my way to you now. Be there in three minutes."

Outside the room, a different Russian voice shouts something. The one in my room answers. Suddenly, there is a rush to Haddadi's room. The door to my room closes.

I hear more shouting, followed by tromping down the stairs.

Moving to the window, I pull back the curtain a quarter inch. I tell Symone, "Wherever you are, stop. Call an Uber and stare at your phone, look impatient."

"Uber? You mean Bolt?" She pauses. "Why?"

"Do it," I snarl.

"Hey, there's a guy on the corner wearing a big, long raincoat. Is that why you sound stressed? Is he a bad guy? You know what else? There's an old guy lying on the ground. I think the big guy hurt him."

I sense the braver of the three orgiasts pick up an object and sneak toward me. I point my pistol behind me, without taking my eyes off the street below. Whoever was brave enough to attempt sneaking up on me is no longer brave. A shoe drops to the floor. His swallow is audible.

Outside is a man in a dark duster. Russians love to hide AK-107s under them. Three of the guys who were in the building run out below me, heading for their lookout. There's one more guy somewhere. Probably the fire escape, but I can't be sure.

"Do what I told you," I say to Symone in my drill-sergeant voice. "I'll explain later."

I turn to the brave libertine. He covers his privates and trembles. Courage often collapses at the sight of a muzzle.

None of them speak English, so I wave the gun around to make my point. The two cowards get back in bed. At my insistence, the brave-for-three-seconds guy goes into the hall, still naked and cupping his Johnson, to scout for Russians. He goes to the stairway, looks down, does a second check, then waves me over.

The manager stands in Haddadi's doorway. I hand him a €500 note and tell him I was never here, but the Russians were. He nods.

Scanning the alley outside the lobby with my monocular, I see the Russians have left the area. The writer is up on one elbow, clawing at the sky for help. He'll be fine.

I make a mad dash to Symone, who has the Bolt waiting. As soon as I'm in, we take off. The driver never says a word, which raises my curiosity. I ask Symone, "What address did you give him?"

"Captain Redgrave's home," she says. "If no one's there, I have that other guy's address too. Krollis something. I figure if they didn't book her, they took her somewhere else, because Logan said they didn't bring her back."

I look her over. "Smart. Very smart. Thank you for taking the initiative."

She beams with pride.

I lean back in the seat.

Mercury squeezes between us. *What I be telling you, dawg? She ain't just a hottie. She's a thinker and a doer.*

I say, *She's also a liability. As smart and impressive as she is, Yeschenko's men aren't dumb, they'll find their way to Redgrave's too.*

We may be walking into a firefight. And that means Symone can't come with me.

Whoa now, Mercury says. *Don't be harshing on my princess. Even your Holy Bible claims Satan gots friends but ain't nobody got Symone's back. Say, you ever notice how little kids have them big eyes and red lips and innocent faces? Tellus Mater—she's the goddess y'all call Mother Nature nowadays—makes kids cute like that so the tribe won't leave them behind. When they get older, they ain't so cute anymore. Some of them teenagers get downright ornery. So Tellus Mater gave them the instinct to be useful to the tribe. That kinda negates the tribe wanting to toss them off a cliff when they start getting mouthy with facts about how stupid and mean all y'all adults are.*

I say, *And?*

Mercury raises his chin and turns away. *And Symone wanna be useful so's you don't go leaving her behind or tossing her over a cliff. Right now, you gonna see how hard it is to refuse Symone's 'usefulness.'*

"Haddadi was murdered," I tell her. "Minutes before I got there. Yeschenko's goons showed up seconds behind me. That means there's a good chance they're going to get to Redgrave's before us. You won't be safe there. I need you to go back to—"

She dives into my chest, sobbing. "I can't … it's worse. The waiting." She snivels and uses my shirt for a tissue. "I can't take it. I'd rather be with you. I won't freeze. I promise. I won't. I won't."

CHAPTER 40

JOE ROULEAU

JOE ROULEAU WATCHES LOGAN'S FINGERS clatter across the keyboard like a machine. Behind him, Chris, Kayla, and Francesca are equally mesmerized. Code scrolls by in several windows too fast to read. Logan's eyes scan from one window to the next. Finally, he spots what he was looking for. He pauses, staring at one window. He closes several others, slams some of his Red Bull, then returns to clacking away on the keys.

Joe looks at the others. They shrug back at him. When Logan finds something, they silently say to each other, he'll tell us.

Finally, Logan stops. His finger traces a line in a corner of his screen. He copies the text, opens a browser to a language translator, and pastes the line there. Slapping his thighs, he spins his chair to face his colleagues, and says, "This is why Symone asked me if Betty came back here: No woman was booked into jail anywhere in Latvia last night. The only person booked was released an hour ago—and found dead in a hotel a few minutes ago."

"Stearne did this!" Francesca shouts.

"You saw those cops pull her out of here," Chris says. "Stop blaming Jacob."

Kayla rolls her eyes. "You think the sun shines out of his—"

"We must keep focused," Joe says with his hands raised. He puts one on Logan's shoulder. "Nice work. Can you check the VDD? Perhaps Captain Redgrave works with the secret service. In Latvian, it's *Valsts drošības dienests.*"

Joe feels all eyes turn to him. He meets their questioning gaze. "I had to deal with them for a visa."

"Inside Schengen Area?" Francesca asks, a frown forming on her brow. "No passports or visas between here and France."

"This was for a business proposal two years ago," Joe says. "Visas are required for business."

Logan is already typing away like a madman. He says, "The VDD uses the same routers. Let's pray they left the same back door open."

As he begins typing, Joe notices Chris, Kayla, and Francesca hold hands and close their eyes.

Ten seconds later, Logan jumps up and says, "YES!" He pumps a fist in the air. Settling back down, he resumes his high-speed keying. Then, "No Betty Bardon. No people brought in for days … wait a minute." He looks up at Joe. "They interviewed you two days ago."

Joe shrugs. "The business deal is ongoing. When I came to Riga, I checked on my visa. Still good."

"OK," Kayla says with doubt trimming her voice. "Where is Betty then?"

Everyone checks everyone else in the circle. No one has any answers.

"It is that Jacob Stearne," Francesca says again. "Only the fools trust him."

"How much of the TV show was accurate anyone might guess," Joe offers, "but when it happened, he was quite respected in Paris. Why not trust him?"

"He plants the shoe!"

A murmur of agreement escapes the others.

Joe says, "Stearne and Redgrave know something about the shoe they have not shared with us. I noticed them looking at each other without speaking."

"One shoe," Francesca says as if that explains everything. "No woman has only the one shoe in closet. She lost one at murder scene."

"She wore Prada flats that night," Kayla says.

"Maybe," Joe says. "This is what Redgrave and Stearne have not—"

Downstairs, the front door crashes in. Many boots rush into the house, Russian voices bark out calls and responses.

Joe checks the alarm on the faces of the others. He catches their gaze and shakes his head. Resistance will not work. He holds up his hands and nods for the others to do the same.

Seconds later, three Russians in tactical gear charge into the room with assault rifles. One of the girls screams. For a moment, their world freezes.

In Russian, Joe asks, "Who is in charge?"

Using their weapons, the Russians push the kids next to Joe. They keep their hands up and squeeze together until the soldiers are satisfied. A fourth man enters the room with a spool of cord.

"No!" Joe shouts. "We will cooperate. Take what you want."

One of the soldiers holds up a hand to stop the others. Addressing Joe with a thick accent, he says, "We want *Edison Data*."

"So do we. Regretfully, it is not here."

The man presses the barrel of his rifle to Kayla's temple. The young woman closes her eyes hard and trembles head to toe. Her companions turn pale and quiver.

The Russian racks the slide and turns to Joe. "Five of you. One dies each time I ask a question and don't get an answer I like."

"Then start with me," Joe says. "As the most recent to join the group, I would be least likely to know. To leave me to the finish would be foolish."

The Russian moves his muzzle to Joe. "As you say. Now, where is it?"

Joe looks to the others. "Is anyone aware of Betty's plans?"

Looking sick, they shake their heads, no.

"Betty told me she locked it in a bank in New York City," Joe says. In unison, the others look at him, confused. Joe continues, "It did not strike me as a good place, inaccessible and distant. Can anyone confirm this is true?"

The Russian moves his rifle from Joe to Chris, checks the beads of sweat on his forehead, watches him quake for a moment. Then he moves to Francesca and does the same. He follows with the others. Kayla begins to cry softly. When he gets to Logan on the end, he sniffs. "One of you will die then."

He returns to Joe and presses the barrel under the Frenchman's chin.

"Wait!" Logan says. He pulls out his phone. "There is someone we can ask. She might know."

CHAPTER 41

JACOB STEARNE

SUNRISE WAS AN HOUR AGO, not that the heavy iron clouds hanging low enough to brush my hair let any light reach the ground. Fog darkens everything another notch. The driver swings into the lane leading to the home of Captain Marisa Redgrave and rolls slowly past her address without stopping, as instructed.

A dark red picket fence protects Marisa's property from the street. An official car with the interior light on and an open door waits in the driveway, its headlights shining on half the clapboard house.

A figure crawls on hands and knees across the dirt yard.

"We have to help him," Symone says, opening her door.

I grab her hand and tell the driver, "Go around the block. Drop us up the street."

Symone relaxes back into her seat. "You think it's a trap? Oh, right. Stearne's Law."

We get out a block away and make our way back. At Marisa's lane, I park Symone at a bushy lilac tree and tell her to be my lookout.

At the gate, I see the figure who had been crawling around on all fours is now lying flat on the ground. My Sabel Visor shows me one heat source inside. As I get closer, I notice the man on the ground is in uniform.

When I feel for a pulse, he jerks away and tries to look at me. It's Lieutenant Krollis with a red welt over his right eye.

He gets to his hands and knees, squinting at me. "Jacob Stearne? Why?"

"I didn't do this; I'm here to help." I pull his shoulder and get him to his feet.

Hearing footsteps behind me, I spin around with my Glock raised and aimed—at Symone. "You were supposed to—"

"I got scared." She keeps coming toward me.

"You're not doing me any good here." I look around, hoping we're safe. Whoever whacked Krollis left him staggering around, which is a fair indicator they've left the area. "Take this guy inside, get him a glass of water and a Tylenol. I mean, Paracetamol."

Symone helps Krollis to the door while I check out the car. The engine is warm, not hot. A laptop lies under a bush that frames the front door. The yard is half dirt and half grass, with a walkway. Nothing about the few footprints in the mud strikes me as conclusive. I peer around the side of the house and use my monocular to see around the back. Nothing.

Stepping inside, I find Symone has Krollis parked in the kitchen while she opens and closes cabinets. She finds glasses and pours him a drink from a filtered pitcher.

In the living room, a trail of muddy footprints leads to Marisa, who sits on the couch. She staggered back inside. She has her head in her hands; blood drips from the left side of her forehead. Symone brings me a glass of water, the Paracetamol, and a wet towel. I sit next to Marisa and hand her two pills and the water. She looks at them as if I were handing her dead mice. Her gaze rises to me with a question.

"You have a serious concussion, Marisa. Take these. It'll help with the confusion." I turn to Symone. "Hand me that trash can, quick."

Symone brings it to me. I get it under Marisa's face just before she retches her guts out. Three big heaves, then she stops. She still has the water in one hand and the pills in the other. She looks up at me.

Symone kneels in front of us, looking first concerned for Marisa then disgusted at the scent of vomit.

I tell them both, "Nausea. Common side effect of a concussion. Symone, call an ambulance. Marisa, do you remember anything?"

She shakes her head slowly and winces as if that singular motion were painful. She pukes again.

Symone holds the can while I daub at her wound. It's nasty but not as bad as it looks. Foreheads bleed a lot. As soon as I get the blood soaked into the towel, more oozes out.

"Ice?" I ask Symone.

Setting the can down, she runs to the kitchen and finds ice. Krollis follows her back. He stands awkwardly watching us. I wrap the cubes in the bloody towel and hold it to Marisa's head. She leans away. I pull her back.

"You should sit over there, Krollis," I tell him, nodding at a chair facing the sofa.

When he takes the seat, I offer him the trash can. He shakes it off. I ask him, "You dropped Betty and Marisa here, then went for the laptop?"

"Ja," he says in an absent voice. His eyes look dull and unsteady. "Oh. Laptop?"

"The one under the bushes."

His eyes flash with recognition, his body tenses, then relaxes. "I remember now. The laptop self-destructed."

"Symone, grab that laptop under the bush by the front door, bring it in, hook it up to your phone, and tell Emma you need the tech team. She'll take it from there."

She nods and runs out. I'm starting to like having her around. It's not as good as having seasoned veterans like Miguel or Isaiah with me, but she's handy at times.

"Laptop," Marisa says. She faces me. A wave of nausea twists her face before receding. She repeats, "Laptop."

"I thought you'd take Betty Bardon to jail, Marisa. Why did you bring her here?"

"Mik … Mik." She huffs. "Yeschenko is everywhere."

"You figured this was safer, which it should've been, but his insiders know where you live and found you. They took Betty?"

She looks around the room as if realizing for the first time what's missing. She looks back at me, suddenly pale and terrified. It's bad enough realizing you've been betrayed, but when you realize how systemic the betrayal is, you panic.

Just past her elbow, I see a red velvet pillow. The top ridge is damp, the pile all brushed in one direction. In another direction, someone has deliberately written K-R. Another letter might have been there, maybe a few more, but Marisa's elbow has rubbed out the rest.

Symone is in the kitchen, following directions from Emma. The tech team will work some magic. With any luck, we'll have some interesting answers in a few hours.

"Hey, Jacob," Symone says, her voice wavering. She brings her phone and laptop to me. "I just got a text from Logan. Check it."

She hands me her phone. The text reads, "Russians are going to kill us. We need to give them *Edison Data*. Where is it?"

"Isn't that what got Kevin killed?" she asks. "The *Edison Data*?"

Krollis, looking less confused by the moment, points at the laptop. "This is wiped. Self-destructed. They tried."

I wave him off. "Thanks, we're just confirming."

"You can't let Logan and them get killed," Symone says. "What do we do?"

"What makes you think it isn't a trap?" I ask. "He could be in league with the Russians and is trying to get us to tell him. Maybe Joe's holding a gun to his head. Maybe he's going rogue. He could be the one who killed Kevin—he was the first to lie about what they were doing that night."

"You have to tell them. You know where it is, right?"

Symone looks like an accident victim going into shock: she's sweating, breathing fast, and wringing her hands. The prospect of people she knows dying is triggering memories of Sandy Hook. I try to calm her.

When she starts stress-breathing, I slip the phone from her hand.

I text out the address where I want the ELA gang to go and press send. I need a code that the Russians won't understand but the right person will. When I come up with an idea, I have to remember where I'd seen it and what it looks like visually, because I don't speak French. After a moment of trying to remember how to add diacritical marks in a phone, I add another line, "*Partout où nécessité fait loi.*"

"What's that mean?" Symone asks.

"Literally translated, it means, *Everywhere where necessity do law*. I think. In practice, it means, *do what you must*. Or *the ends will justify the means.* Something like that."

She stares at me with a strange expression. "They're going to be alright, aren't they?"

"Look, Symone," I say as I squeeze her arm, "there's something you gotta understand about the business I'm in. Things don't always go well. In fact, you have to prepare for the worst—that way, whatever happens will seem better. The Russians have no reason to kill those kids. If they do, it will only complicate their mission. But that doesn't mean they won't. And there's nothing we can do about it either way. If they do hurt those kids, I'll kill every one of them. But that doesn't save their lives right now."

She swallows hard, forcing down her revulsion and trying desperately to pump up her resolve. There's a good chance she's going to freeze up on me.

I say, "This is why I wanted you to stay at the hotel. That way—"

"So I'd have to deal with that shit alone? Is that better? More dignified? Fuck you. I'm fine."

She's anything but. Her skin looks like grey plastic. Beads of sweat trickle down her temple. She wipes them away with her sleeve.

"We have to get there before the other guys."

"I'm fine." She stares at me, her lips clamped together so hard they tremble. "I won't freak out. I swear."

What should I do? Send her to the hotel where she can flip out by herself, or bring her with me where she can flip out in person?

I turn to Krollis. "How are you feeling? Up for a drive?"

CHAPTER 42

JACOB STEARNE

KROLLIS PILOTS HIS CAR TO the street in front of his house and parks in a light rain. It's a small, weathered bungalow with a corrugated tin roof. Not terribly prosperous. Symone and I hop out and follow him inside. Because daylight has yet to break through, he turns on the lights and waves his hands around.

He says, "This is it."

"We need to ambush them," I tell him. The place smells like someone used baking soda to cover up mold smells. "Which won't be easy since they're Spetsnaz veterans. Show me the best spots to hide."

Symone trails behind me like a frightened puppy. If I knew what to do with her, I would do it.

I figure we have fifteen minutes before the Russians arrive. We'll need to make use of every second.

Emma signals me through my comm link. "I have Ross Klebb on the line. Your Employee Conflict Mediation has been moved up to right now."

I tell her, "This is a bad—"

"No time is a good time," a man's voice says blandly. "I'm Ross Klebb, mediator for your mediation. Emma, you may drop off now. I also have Dr. Franklin on the line. Say hello, doctor."

Franklin's now familiar voice says, "Hello."

I pull my phone out and look at the video feed. Franklin looks extra smug, like he just called "check" in an international chess championship. Klebb looks like Hollywood's idea of a balding bureaucrat with zero emotion in his expression.

I'm not sure what's going down, but I have a sick feeling in my gut that this time, I may be in trouble. I yelled at someone one too many times.

So they fire me. So what?

My stomach twists an extra knot at the thought. I make ten times as much as I ever made in the Army and a lot more than anyone I know. Plus, I get to fly on private jets and rent five-star hotel suites on Ms. Sabel's dime. Not to mention, I get to kill people and get away with it. Extreme job satisfaction with loads of money is hard to replace.

I stuff the phone back in my pocket.

"Look guys," I say, "this is a terrible time. I'm about to host a surprise party for an unknown number of Russian—"

"We don't have a choice in the matter, Jacob," Klebb says in an authoritative monotone. "Ms. Sabel changed the schedule. She should be joining—"

"Is everyone on?" Ms. Sabel asks.

"Yes," we answer in unison.

I catch Symone's gaze and hold out four perimeter sensors. She takes them with vague recognition. I mouth the words, *Call Emma for instructions. Plant these outside.*

She mouths back, *What?*

Pulling my earbud out, I tell her what I need her to do. Her reaction is part fear and part gratitude at having something useful to do.

When I screw my earbud back in, Ms. Sabel's voice is raised in anger. "…listened to all seventy-three seconds of what Jacob said to you on the call in question. I could not believe you were getting your panties in a bunch over something an operator—under stress and in the middle of an important mission—said to you, Franklin. Did you think his threat to 'jump down this phone' was realistic since he was 4,358 miles away on a satellite link? No. Of course not. I am appalled that any of my employees would waste valuable company resources for a mediation over something so petty. But there is a reason you did it, and, since you're the psychologist, would you like to explain to the group why you insisted on this meeting?"

Sometimes, company conference calls can be interesting. I pull my phone back out to catch the video in progress. Ms. Sabel lies in a hospital bed, with a nurse's call button draped over the side railing. Franklin's expression has changed to something a lot like Symone's when she got scared, only he isn't in a life-or-death situation. He looks like a guppy, his mouth opening and closing in silence.

"I'll explain it to you then," Ms. Sabel says. "Since you couldn't possibly believe Jacob would make good on his threat physically, we know you had a different motive. Is it possible you were ashamed at how easily you caved and breached Ms. Blackworthy's confidentiality? And that precipitated blaming Jacob. Could that be the reason you insisted on this meeting?"

Again, Franklin does his guppy imitation.

"When I was on the Women's National Soccer Team," Ms. Sabel continues, "I got yelled at and threatened physically by coaches, teammates, competitors, fans, and strangers. They found a bomb at our hotel in Chile. They threw rocks at us in Armenia. Successful people take their jobs seriously and that creates a lot of passionate discussions. If I have employees who can't handle another employee blowing up, whether it's called for or not, I'm going to assign them to the National Team's security detail—where you will learn about stress."

There are days when I like working for Ms. Sabel.

I find an attic access panel in the back hall that leads to an unfinished attic space. It's not an ideal ambush spot because there's nothing above to hold my weight. I close the panel and keep looking. Two bedrooms, a shared bathroom, a kitchen with a dining area, and a living room. Not much.

"Klebb," Ms. Sabel says, "are you paid by the meeting? You're not. You know why? Because I don't want unnecessary mediations. Your first responsibility is to challenge the employees and assess if the reasons for calling the session are real or imagined."

"Yes, ma'am." Klebb's voice remains flat.

Opening the back door in the kitchen, I check the back yard. Symone is planting a sensor at the back, six feet away from me, at an apartment building's back wall. It marks the end of Krollis's property—no need for a fence. On either side, his neighbors have fences, one chain link, the other wood slats.

"Dr. Franklin," Ms. Sabel says, "I'm holding you personally responsible for Ms. Blackworthy's mental health. And Jacob, you're in charge of bringing her back safely so Dr. Franklin can begin treatment as soon as possible. You're also responsible for fixing your relationship with Franklin and making sure Symone trusts him."

"Wait a second," I pull my phone out to look at the video feed. Klebb—nothing. Franklin looks as shocked as I feel. "How am I supposed to make Symone trust this guy when even I don't trust—"

"You fucked up your relationship with him, you fix it."

There has never been a lot of arguing with Pia Sabel, so I fold. "OK."

"Franklin and Klebb," she says, "you are dismissed. Drop off this call."

Their respective screens blink out.

Ms. Sabel's face fills my screen. She looks at me and sighs. "You took on a huge responsibility engaging Ms. Blackworthy, Jacob. I'm proud of you. And mystified."

"You and me both."

I pause as I check out what I thought was a pantry. It's the door to the basement with stairs leading to a dark abyss below. Cold air, laden with the bitter moldy smell of dank places drifts up. No light switch.

I tell Ms. Sabel, "I can't get back to the States just yet, and I'm not sure how to keep Symone safe until then. I'd put her on a plane right now, but she breaks down in tears when I suggest we stand more than ten feet apart."

"Have you tried making her face her fears?" Ms. Sabel asks. "Maybe she has more guts than you give her credit for."

I consider telling her about how Symone freezes, but the girl comes in the kitchen door. She waves as she reaches past me to get another sensor off the counter. She looks calm now, which is odd because Armageddon is getting closer by the second. Maybe having a simple task was the key to unwinding her. I note that for later.

"That's a good idea," I tell Ms. Sabel. "I'll teach her the 40 percent rule. I've got to go. Get well soon."

She signs off with a wave.

"What's the 40 percent rule?" Symone asks.

"Your mind tries to preserve your body's resources by making you want to shut down when you reach 40 percent of your capability. Whether that's muscle endurance or stress levels, your mind tries to reserve 60 percent for later. If your body can run ten miles, your mind tells you to stop at four. If you try, you can push yourself 60 percent harder than you think."

"You don't have to worry about me," she says. "I'm fine. I won't let you down."

A quick examination of her tells me she means it. I've seen plenty of guys steel themselves before battle only to shit their pants when they see tracer rounds coming at them in the first violent blast of war. Nothing I can do about it now.

Symone goes out the back door, heading for the side yard.

"Hey, Krollis!" I yell.

"Ja?" He asks quietly from three feet away.

"Oh, there you are. What's down here?" I point at the basement stairs.

"Furnace, old stuff, jams."

"Show me."

He leads me down a rickety staircase of wooden slats laid on a stair stringer without benefit of nails or glue. No handrail. When we get to the bottom, he turns his flashlight to the right. I slide my Sabel Visor on but his light beam flares it, so I push it up to my forehead. His beam lights up a brand-new furnace, a stack of dusty boxes, and a plank shelf with a few homemade jams.

"Is there an exterior exit?" I ask.

Krollis shines his light behind me. When I turn, I see Betty Bardon standing in the corner. She's been trashed since I saw her last. Her hair is a mess, wet and loose hanging in her face; her designer power-dress with accentuated shoulders is wrinkled; the black shoes muddy; her face tired and sad. She says, "Hello, Jacob."

She turns and runs up a wooden ladder, shoving aside storm doors and bursting into the side yard. I give chase, getting up two rungs on the ladder when I see her on the ground outside, running. She grabs Symone by the hand and runs toward the street.

That's when I realize my mistake.

The all-too familiar feel of a cold rifle barrel touches the back of my neck. A Heckler & Koch MP7 automatic rifle is racked, I can tell by the sound. Only then do I remember what I failed to notice at Marisa's house: Krollis didn't puke—he didn't have a concussion. And the K-R on the pillow was the first two letters of KROLLIS.

CHAPTER 43

BETTY BARDON

THE RAIN COMES DOWN HARDER as Betty grabs Symone's hand and pulls. "We have to go."

Symone yanks back with surprising strength and says, "Where did you come from? Where is Jacob?"

The cellar doors slams shut behind them with a bang.

There is no time to lose, no time to explain. She tightens her grip and pulls the young woman harder. Symone digs in her heels.

"We have to go!" Betty shouts.

"I don't go anywhere without Jacob," Symone shouts back.

"We don't have time. He's been caught. But don't worry, he'll get out of it like he always does. We have to run. Right now."

Rain drips from Symone's hair. The girl looks cold and clammy, her eyes wide with fear. She's shaking her head back and forth violently.

"Symone, come on," Betty says and tugs again.

"I'd rather be caught with Jacob than go anywhere with you."

Betty freezes and lets go of Symone's hand. "You think I'm going to hurt you? Do something bad?"

"I don't know." Tears well in Symone's eyes. "I'm not cut out for this shit."

A car stops on the street in front of the house, forty feet from them.

Betty grabs Symone's arm and pulls more forcefully. Symone gives in and they make it to a line of boxwoods big enough to hide behind. Shoving the girl into a small gap in the hedge, Betty cowers in front. Symone is shivering. Betty puts an arm around her, stretching her raincoat to cover the girl.

Four car doors slam. Men bark orders in Russian and march to the house.

"We don't have a chance," Betty whispers to herself.

"You ratted out Jacob," Symone hisses. "You knew he would come here."

Krollis meets the Russians at the front door. He speaks in Russian and gestures to the property. A second car pulls up; four more doors open and slam.

Betty attempts to push deeper into the hedge. Symone's breathing is rapid and shallow. Betty squeezes her shoulder, trying to reassure her. She feels Symone rising, which will reveal their hiding place. She has to get ahead of this girl.

"Found her," Betty calls out. "She's over here."

Pulling Symone's arm, she drags her into the yard, then looks back. Symone's eyes become erupting volcanoes of fury, her emotion skyrocket into pure hatred.

Four armed men jog to them, grab their arms, and drag them toward the front door.

Lightning strikes nearby, cracking the sky. The rain comes down harder. Mikhail Yeschenko doffs his hat and uses it to gesture the way inside.

The goons shove them into the living room and tighten their grip. They maneuver the women to face their leader.

"You are quite the disappointment, Betty Bardon," Yeschenko says. He tosses his hat to Krollis, then shrugs out of his trench coat and hands that off as well. "You had a job to do."

"Your idiot arrested me," she nods at Krollis as she speaks. "I never had a chance."

It takes Betty a split second to realize the wad of spit that just hit her cheek came from Symone. Since the men won't release their grip, she shoulders it off.

Yeschenko cranes over his shoulder at Krollis, who stands back two paces.

"I had no choice, sir," he says. "Redgrave."

Yeschenko nods knowingly before returning his gaze to the women. "That captain is a bigger problem than I was told. You'll have to take care of her."

"I've put her in the hospital, sir." Krollis smiles. "She won't be any trouble for a few days."

"Well done."

Yeschenko crosses to Symone. He looks her over, salaciously licking his lips. "You must be Elton John's tiny dancer The sexy free spirit referred to in his—"

"Who the fuck is Elton John?"

Yeschenko looks like he's been slapped. Then he laughs. While looking Symone over, he says, "Well, this is a first. Jacob Stearne has taken up with a brainless slut. A far cry from you, my dear Betty." Yeschenko turns to Betty. "Are you not jealous?"

Betty fights the rising bile Yeschenko's words produce in her throat. "Tell them to let go of me."

Yeschenko produces a titanium baton, flicks it to extended length, and nods at his men. They release Betty from their grip.

"Afraid of me?" Betty nods at the baton.

"In case your friend tries to spit on me." He flicks a glance at Symone. "I give lessons in manners—free."

Yeschenko turns his back on them to face Krollis. "And where is our guest of honor?"

"This way, sir." Krollis nods toward the kitchen.

"Time to prove your value, Betty," Yeschenko says over his shoulder.

They troop down the creaking stairway into the darkness. Krollis hits a switch that lights up the corner where Jacob is bound in manacles and chains. He's splayed like the letter X. Betty can't stop a gasp from escaping.

Symone howls like a wounded animal and falls to her knees. The goons lift her back to her feet.

"Betty tells me you have the *Edison Data,*" Yeschenko says as he lifts Jacob's chin. "Where is it?"

"A gentleman would never call a lady a liar," Jacob says. "But something must've gotten mixed up in translation. I don't have it."

Yeschenko appraises him for a minute. Then examines Betty with a cynical eye. He slams Jacob's gut with his baton. "You must be under the misguided impression you two are still working together." After another thump of the baton, he turns to Betty, "Tell him."

Wincing at the Russian's violence, she considers the path she's chosen. Not only is it the right thing to do, it's the only thing she can do. It was and is the right decision. *Stay in your lane*, Jacob had told her. That's what she's doing. He might not like the way she drives that lane, but he offered no alternatives.

"You had your chance, Jacob." Betty feels irritation rising like volcanic heat in her body. "You chose Sabel over me. Ever since that day, you've meant nothing to me."

Relishing her chance to vent uninterrupted, she struts toward him. Her mouth curves into a vicious sneer as she summons a white-hot hatred of the men controlling her life.

"The chase for *Chaac* becomes more and more brutal every day. Remmo Nidal and Deng Zhipeng are breathing down my neck. Losing Kevin was too …" Her voice catches. She breathes and wills herself to continue. "Reality beats idealism every time. As much as I'd like to make it public, the lives of my people are more important. Safety has forced me to abandon the open-source concept. Since you and Sabel don't understand how deadly this race has become, I've chosen sides."

Betty feels stronger now that she's laid it out there. Her voice rises in strength and volume. She continues, "Mikhail Yeschenko has the determination, the men, and the resources to make *Chaac* a reality. And what do you have? A stripper. You treat this like it's just another adventure—another Paris. Well, I've got news for you: It's not. Mikhail understands that. He brought the power to succeed with him: men with unwavering loyalty and the stomach to do whatever is necessary to succeed. You—well, you don't stand a chance."

CHAPTER 44

JACOB STEARNE

WHOO-WEE, THAT WAS SOME SPEECH. Mercury steps out of the basement shadows, his eyes still on Betty. *Sometimes it just don't pay to get out of bed in the morning, am I right, homie?*

Yeah, I answer, *except, I would've had to go to bed in the first place.*

Not you, idjit. Me! He tosses up his hands, exasperated, then nods at my chains. *After all I done for you, you throw it down the drain cuz you can't be bothered to worship me with respect. Oh well. I wish I could say it's been nice knowing you.*

Hold up, I say. *How is this my fault? Where were you when Krollis was trapping me in my own ambush?*

Dawg, he says, *you was talking to a woman. You can't never hear me when you're talking to a woman. As a matter of fact, no man has ever heard god talking to him when he be talking to a woman. I told JFK to duck, but he was too busy bragging to his wife about how the crowds adored him. I told Benedict Arnold not to listen to his girl about switching sides, but did he listen to me? And don't get me started on Mark Antony, the original Mister P-Whipped Hisself.*

My patience grows thin. *What are you talking about? I didn't say anything to Betty.*

Mercury says, *Betty? Ah, dude, no. I be talking about Pia-Caesar-Sabel and Symone-the-Hottie. You was talking to one and checking out the other when you shoulda been listening to the one true god. Felt good to hear Pia-Caesar-Sabel ripping ol' Doc Franklin a new one though, didn't it? Felt so good, you didn't see me waving my arms and yelling in your ear. Didn't hear a thing, did ya?*

I say, *OK, I'm listening now. What? How do I get out of this? I'll do the sacrifice thing soon as I get out.*

Mercury smiles big. *Now that's what I like to hear: empty fuckin' promises from a desperate and doomed sinner. Never gets old. Just thirteen seconds ago, a woman in Seattle was pleading for divine intervention when she heard her husband come in the front door while her lover was riding her like—*

I say, *I swear to Juno, I'll really do it. I'll find a … I don't know how to do a sacrifice. But I'll look it up. I'll figure it out! I swear. Just get me out of this.*

Mercury taps a finger to his chin. *OK.*

OK? Great.

That was too easy, but I rattle my chains anyway.

You know that ain't how it works, fool. I don't reach into the physical world and set you free. Not when I can watch them torture you first.

He fades into the dark, laughing as he goes.

Betty is staring at me with a cold, unwavering gaze. Her hair is a bedraggled mess, her dress soaked with rain. She looks miserable. Something about her messy hair tingles my brain. There's something wrong about that but what it is doesn't come to me.

"But you flatter me," Mikhail Yeschenko says to her. He claps slowly and beams with pride at Betty. "I appreciate that because it's all true. I am the only one who can protect you."

Symone begins wailing.

"Don't worry, little girl," Yeschenko says to her. "I am not going to kill your hero." He turns back to me. "Many times I have passed on the opportunity to kill you. Do you know why, Mr. Stearne?"

I reply, "Let me guess—is this about your mom?"

Yeschenko answers by slamming the baton in my breadbasket. Being a smartass has a downside.

"I don't need to kill you," Yeschenko says. "Because you're doing it yourself. You weep and moan over the loss of poor Jenny Jenkins. She died because of you. But she isn't the only lover you've lost, is she Jacob? You've lost so many who can keep count?"

He turns slowly to face Symone, whose face is melting.

He says, "Oh, did he not tell you, little girl?"

Symone's tear-filled gazes rises to mine.

"Your Superman never told you how many women have gone to their great reward because of him?" Yeschenko lifts her chin with his knuckle. "Did you think he was your knight in shining armor? He is—if you have a death wish."

He examines her for a moment. She doesn't look at him; she's a dejected heap. He returns to me and gives me another taste of his baton, this time across the privates, sharp and painful. Extremely painful.

Despite the agony careening through my nervous system, I hear Yeschenko continue. "You're just a miserable serial killer who donned a uniform. The Army loved that about you, didn't they?" Yeschenko grins and gestures broadly. "Your exploits were legend. Then the Army found out how crazy you are. A madman about to go off the rails. An inevitable liability.

"And what did you do when the Army didn't love you anymore? Ran to Sabel Security. Pia Sabel has taken advantage of your madness for years. She plies you with jets, and toys, and guns, and then turns you loose to fight her battles for her. Without her, you're a criminal. Without you, she's nothing."

I tug at my chains, eager to beat the crap out of him despite the fact there is a good deal of truth in all that. Too much truth. Why have I been loyal to her? Because she pays me well? Is my soul for sale? I've always thought it was because she's the good guy, but lately, I'm not so sure.

Betty's glaring at me with abject hatred. Symone appears heartbroken to learn her hero has feet of clay. Well, I never asked anyone to worship me. I never told anyone I could save them or help them. People have their own expectations, often conjured out of daydreams—or unauthorized docudramas. I never wanted to be anyone's hero. I just want to do my job.

On that score, Yeschenko is right: I kill people. People who have been identified as bad for the future of civilization. People who can only be stopped by death. People like Mikhail Yeschenko. Although, killing him seems too good for him. He should be locked up for the rest of his life in a Latvian prison. That's the best way to crush his soul.

He lifts my chin with his baton. "You're a pathetic child, Jacob Stearne. You used to save the world for the glory of it. Job satisfaction. Then you watched Jenny die in your place. Now all you want is to go out in a blaze of self-loathing. I don't need to kill you. All I need to do is make you watch this."

He turns to Betty, and holds up what look like Sabel Darts, one yellow and the other black and white. She puts the black and white one in a pocket in her dress.

"This is Inland Taipan snake venom," Yeschenko says, waving the yellow one. He pulls Symone's arm out, stretching her in front of him. "Sound familiar? I recreated your famous Sabel Darts, but I used a lot more venom and no sleep medication. The result is flaccid paralysis leading to an excruciating and slow death. They tell me it's about twelve to fourteen hours of psychological agony for a woman the size of Symone."

My protégé's eyes blow open. She screams and writhes like a captured snake.

"All you have to do, Jacob," Yeschenko says in a voice loud enough to overpower Symone's screams, "is retrieve the *Edison Data* you stole, and get the *Chaac Equation* from Rafael Tum before your little girlfriend dies. Bring them to me in time and we will give her the antidote."

He pauses a moment to let me think about it while Betty pulls out the black-and-white injector to show it's the antidote, then tucks it away again.

And I do think about it. My mind races through questions: Why does he think I stole the *Edison Data*? Oh, right, he believed what Betty told him. Why threaten Symone? Does he think I'll do it to save her? Yeah. Truth is: he called my bluff on that one. I will move heaven and Earth to save the poor girl.

None of this makes sense to Symone. With her arm bared she looks more exposed than she ever imagined. Her eyes plead with me to save her from the poison.

Manacled to beams, there is nothing I can do to stop Betty. I wrench my wrists and ankles producing nothing more than rattling chains. I'm powerless.

Yeschenko hands over the yellow injector. "Betty, will you do the honors, please?"

Betty steps in front of Symone and raises it like a psycho about to stab a woman in a shower. Symone shrieks with the fervor of an eight-year-old hearing the children two doors down slaughtered by a madman who had unfettered access to automatic rifles.

Betty pivots on her heel, takes two quick steps, and slams the injector into my neck.

CHAPTER 45

JOE ROULEAU

JOE ROULEAU CATCHES PIECES OF their captor's conversations. Something about Lieutenant Krollis and an urgent need for all four of them to leave right away. As the Russians tromp downstairs without another word, the ELA members turn to Joe for answers. He can only shrug, temporarily stunned.

They've been spared—but he has no idea why and that makes it feel wrong. Leaving without killing them or taking them hostage means the Russians consider them meaningless—which can only be true if they have something better. They have the *Edison Data*, or are close to retrieving it, so they no longer care about the ELA.

He works over his next course of action in his head. How close were they to dying just now? Kevin Winn is already dead, proving the Russians are serious. Joe reviews the soldiers' expressions as they left. They were not jubilant. That indicates they have a lead on the missing data. They haven't taken possession of it yet.

What should he and the ELA people do?

They could clear out or stay put. If they choose the latter, can they defend the house? Not against those soldiers. Could they go into hiding? While ruminating over these questions, he sees Kayla posting something on Instagram. So, no hiding. Spring a trap? Again, not against the Russians he saw tonight.

He feels the group's attention focused on him, waiting for direction.

"We have to find the *Edison Data*," he announces. "If they come back, we would have a bargaining chip. If they don't come back, we haven't lost anything and can start working on the project. Where would she hide it?"

Their mouths drop open.

"You said it was in New York," Chris says.

"That is what she told me. I do not believe it, because how could she work on the project without it? Surely, she told you something about it. Something you held back from the Russians. Tell me what it is."

They look at each other, back and forth several times.

"What is it?" Joe asks. "What did she tell you?"

"That we should never know, so we could never tell," Kayla answers. "Safety."

"Safe?" Joe is incredulous. "Those men were going to kill us all and they didn't care if we knew or not."

Their shoulders drop. Their heads hang like wet rags on their shoulders.

"You are willing to die rather than divulge the hiding place? Because that is what almost happened—and might well happen anyway." He observes them closely to see if they understand how Betty's method left them vulnerable. "Did she give you a clue? Anything?"

"I don't even know what it is," Logan says. The others nod their agreement.

"She told me it is an old-fashioned hard drive," Joe says, "about the size of two iPhones, maybe a little thicker, made of metal with computer connections along one side."

Logan pulls apart a USB drive next to his main computer and extracts a 3.5" hard drive. He waves it at the others. "This kind of hard drive."

Joe feels his patience with them slipping. He notices a hint of distrust in their continuing glances. He says, "Listen, people, if we are committed to making *Chaac* a reality, we must consider one horrible possibility: we may have to proceed without Betty Bardon."

"What do you mean?" Francesca demands.

"I would never believe it, but she could be guilty of Kevin's murder. Or she could be kidnapped or coerced into something. It is equally possible she has sold us out. We do not know. Our first priority should be to find the *Edison Data*. With it, we have a bargaining chip should we need it. Without it, we have nothing. No *Chaac Project*, no future."

The tide begins to turn in their expressions. Far from resolute, their improving collective countenance shows in their posture. They stand straighter, hold their heads a little higher.

Joe says, "Take a moment to recall why we joined Betty in this endeavor. Nothing less is at stake than the future of humanity. The issue is not whether we can harness green energy into a useful replacement for fossil fuels—but more importantly, who shall own that future. Should it belong to the people? Or should it belong to Mikhail Yeschenko? Does the future belong to those willing to fight for freedom, or shall we become slaves of the rich? We know the answer. This is no time for whimpering and handwringing. This is no time for cowardice or desertion. This is the time to forget our fears and fight selflessly for our future. For the future of our mothers and fathers, friends, and lovers—in fact for everyone."

All four of them are stunned. They've leaned back away from him.

Chris is the first to change his mien. He steps forward and reaches to shake Joe's hand. "What you say is true. This is the time to push hard. I am with you."

One by one, the others follow suit. He shakes their hands and thanks them.

"Let's tear this house apart," Joe says. "We start in the attic and work our way to the basement."

They race up the narrow stairs and begin searching in boxes and under loose floorboards. Walls are tapped for hollow hiding places. Bricks are tested. Window frames checked. When they exhaust every conceivable place in the attic, they troop down to the bedrooms, checking each stair tread as they go.

When they reach Betty's room, Joe's phone rings. The caller ID reads Mikhail Yeschenko. He tries to shield the screen before he answers but can't be certain if Francesca saw it or not.

Yeschenko is ranting at full volume before Joe can properly answer the call. He steps into the hall for privacy.

"Calm down, Mikhail," he says. "I cannot understand you."

While he listens to Yeschenko continue the tirade, Francesca leans against the nearest door frame to eavesdrop. He quickly grasps the oligarch's demands. Still listening, he thinks about his options. Logan, Kayla, Francesca, and Chris are good kids but are no match for the forces aligned against them. Joe reassures Yeschenko in Russian and clicks off.

"Yeschenko has your number?" Francesca asks.

"He can find yours in minutes too, should he so desire."

"What did he want of you?"

Joe ushers her into the room where their entrance draws the attention of the others. He announces, "I am afraid Betty Bardon has raised the ire of Mikhail Yeschenko. That puts us all in danger. I have offered myself in Betty's place as Yeschenko's hostage."

CHAPTER 46

JACOB STEARNE

Everyone in the room is shocked. Especially me. But I can't do anything about it because the snake venom's flaccid paralysis is overwhelming. All the muscles in my body go slack. I sink as low as the manacles will allow. I can't hold my head up. I see only a cement floor. My mind is still working, which is the horror of death by this venom. You know it's coming and there's nothing you can do about it.

Around me I hear Symone wailing before Yeschenko's baton strikes Betty. The Russian is screaming at her. She just trashed his plans, and he's pissed.

I try ticking off the reasons she jabbed me instead of Symone in my head: She doesn't want Symone to die; a nice thought but I doubt it. It could be her way of breaking up with me. Although, killing an ex is a bit harsh, even for her. Maybe she has the *Edison Data* somewhere nearby and doesn't want me to find it. That doesn't work either because I would still need to find Rafael Tum, which will be difficult since our go between, Hakim Haddadi, is dead. Maybe she knows I'd ignore Yeschenko's demands and instead, spend the time killing his men and freeing the girl. She incapacitated me to spare the Russian.

Now that I think about it, Yeschenko knows that, too. To rely on me to get the two missing pieces, he would need enough men to overwhelm me in the final showdown. That tells me he has more men in the vicinity than the four I saw. I could take down four, but more than that is fantasy, no matter what Hollywood comes up with. Not even with a computerized boomerang. Troop strength is a constant battle in the intelligence world, and I have no intelligence on him. Now I'm worried. How many men does Yeschenko have in Latvia? His confidence tells me: lots. Nothing I can do as a limp noodle chained in Krollis's basement.

Feeling bad for even thinking it, I wish Betty had jabbed Symone instead. That way I'd be on my way to dispatching the Russians right now. At least the ones I can find, and that way I could at least go out in a blaze of glory. Hanging from shackles like this is embarrassing.

Humility looks good on you, bro. Mercury says.

Facing the floor, the only part of my derelict deity I can see are a pair of bronze wings on sandal-clad feet.

You happy? I ask him. *I'm hanging by my wrists.*

Now see that? That's what I be talking about. He leans down to look at my face. He shakes his head sadly and stands straight again. *You got a bad attitude, homie. You think I enjoy watching you get tortured? Well, OK, I gotta admit, the look on your face was worth the price of admission—but that's not what this is all about.*

I say, *I'm sorry I never got around to the sacrifice thing. I'll get on that, soon as I get out of here.*

Nah, ain't that neither. It's about virtue, boy. It's always about Roman values: virtue, honor, and gravitas. I'm not seeing that here.

I would shake my head but none of my muscles are responding. *I've got all that gravitas and ... stuff.*

Zat so? Mercury adds a measure of snark to his voice. *Who you working for then? Betty Bardon? The Electric Looney Army? Pia-Caesar-Sabel? Mikhail Yeschenko? Rafael Tum?*

He's got me there. I'm not committed. I know I'm not working for the Russian. And I doubt Rafael Tum has an offer worth listening to. Betty's little speech marked the end of her altruistic endeavor. That leaves one good alternative. *Ms. Sabel. I'm working for Ms. Sabel. Now, can you get me out of this?*

Silence.

Even though it's a bad idea, I can't stop myself from asking, *Where is god when you need him? I mean, if there is a god, how did he let the Holocaust happen?*

Mercury says, *The gods didn't let that happen, all y'all mortals did.*

Where was your ancestors when that was going down? Making rude jokes about Jews and Blacks, that's where. Not where they shoulda been: standing up. Slavery, Manifest Destiny, invasions, nuclear bombs—that ain't god's work. Ain't no god nowhere tell y'all to do that shit. Don't blame us. So that brings up the question you trying to avoid—who you standing up for today?

We've had this exchange before, and I know what he means. All theologies expect humans to take responsibility for their situation while all humans conveniently hold their deities responsible. Nonetheless, how am I responsible for getting dosed with poison? And how in the name of Venus am I supposed to get out of it?

A flurry of noises fills the basement. I can guess several of them. Betty takes a beating from Yeschenko. Symone gets manacled. Since there aren't that many support beams down here, I'm guessing they're leaving the women on the floor. From the sound of chains stretching to their limit, I guess they've been cuffed at the wrists and ankles and a connecting chain keeps them from standing upright. It's considered torture, but that wouldn't bother Yeschenko any. I hear some thrashing syncopated to Symone's outburst of sobs and epithets.

I hear Yeschenko start a conversation in Russian with the name *Dzhozef*, Russian for Joseph. Is he talking to my favorite Frenchman, Joe Rouleau? Yeschenko tromps upstairs, pouring Russian into his phone. Four pairs of boots follow him. The lights go out. Overhead, we hear the boots heading away from the basement door.

"Symone?" Betty's voice in the dark.

"Fuck you."

I wish my voice would work—I'd like to second Symone's motion—but flaccid paralysis includes the voice box. The only reason my lungs are working is due to Sabel Security's safety procedures that have us inoculated against the venom. Our scientists watched the *Princess Bride* and understood the valuable life lesson of Iocane powder. That, and the company doesn't want someone like me accidentally darting himself; it could be embarrassing. But the dosage I'm protected against is a lot lower than what Yeschenko has in his little Inland Taipan martini.

"It was the only thing I could think of to save you," Betty says.

"I'd rather die."

"I'm sorry you got caught up in all this."

"Don't talk to me."

A long silence follows. My mind wanders to strange things like, who's taking care of my dog? Did I water my weeds before I left home?

I'm not sure how long those thoughts occupied my mind. Could've been quite a while. I hear boots coming back down the stairs along with the sounds of dragging chains. Two sets of chains, meaning two people. Russians give orders in their dialect, then pound their way back upstairs.

"Who's there?" Betty asks.

"Francesca," she answers.

"And Chris Anrig," he says.

With her voice wavering, Betty asks, "How did you get here?"

"Stupid Joe," Francesca snarls.

"What do you mean?"

"He had a plan," Chris says. "He was to offer himself as hostage in your place."

"What? Why?"

"He said that way you could get the *Edison Data* and give it to Yeschenko. He thinks that's the only way we get out of this alive."

"Oh, my god!" Betty's shriek fills the house. "I can't believe it."

I try to speak. I desperately want to explain what's going on here. They don't get it.

"Believe it, yes," Francesca says. "I do not trust this man, so I tell him I go in your place. Not him. And Chris joins too. At last minute, we push Joe in car, Logan drives him away, and we come inside."

Predictably, the Russians saw the kids' offer to exchange two for one as generous and accepted—but didn't release Betty. Why? Because these kids may be smart but they're naïve, and Yeschenko preys on naïve. He lied to get them in, then slapped them in chains. They should've listened to Joe.

I make a huge effort to say something and get out only a single syllable. More of a grunt than a statement. No one notices.

"Where is Joe now?" Betty asks.

"Logan and Kayla drive him away," Francesca says. "None of us trust him. You must tell us where *Edison Data* is or they kill us all."

"It's Betty you shouldn't trust!" Symone shouts.

I can't make out who says what next because they're all talking at once. Francesca complicates matters by berating Symone in Italian. Chris defends Betty.

Betty's voice out lasts the other two. She's saying, "… you ungrateful little shit." There is a moment of silence. Betty follows up with, "Sorry. I, I didn't mean that."

I try again. Really hard this time. Two syllables grunted. That's progress. It's like being in a nightmare where you're calling for help but you don't have a mouth.

"How did Joe know I'm a hostage," Betty asks, her voice calm again, "or think he could take my place?"

"He gets call from Yeschenko and—"

"Yeschenko called him directly?" Betty asks.

"Is what I think too! Right away, something is rotten in Deutschland."

"Denmark," Chris says. "Rotten in Denmark."

"Germans. Same thing."

With a massive effort, I get out another syllable. I realize I can blink. I could blink out Morse code. That would be better than trying to talk. But do any of them know Morse code? Would they realize that's what I'm doing? Back to trying to talk. I get out another grunt.

Chains scurry across the concrete in my direction. Symone's face appears in my view. She's crawled across the cement and is twisting her body to look at me.

Now is the time to push that extra 60 percent reserve. I struggle and manage, "Trick."

The others begin talking, asking what she's doing.

She yells at them, "Shut the fuck up. He's trying to say something." She looks back at me. "Did you say, 'trick?'"

It worked. A little bit. This is worth the effort. I muster every ounce of strength I have and say, "Lis-ten-ing."

Symone's face scrunches up. She gets closer on her bound hands and knees. Her face is now directly under mine. She says, "Listening? Like, they're listening to us?"

CHAPTER 47

CAPTAIN REDGRAVE

THE DOCTOR'S EXAMINATION OF MARISA Redgrave frustrates her. He shines a light in her eyes and says, "Hmm." He asks her to touch her nose with her fingertip. When she touches her cheek instead, he says, "Mmm hmmm." He says something to the nurse about the Glasgow Coma Scale, but Marisa can't hear him for the ringing in her ears.

Her mind wanders to Jacob Stearne. He seemed helpful at her house. Why? She realizes there is a blank in her memory. She was in her house asking Betty Bardon questions. The next thing she remembers is vomiting in a trash can held by Jacob Stearne. What happened?

"Did you hear me?" the doctor asks.

"Sorry."

"Did your mind wander?"

"Wonder?"

"Mmm hmm."

And then he flashes the penlight in her eye again. First one, then the other.

Stearne did this to her. He hit her over the head and kidnapped Betty Bardon. No. That doesn't make sense. She arrested Betty at his insistence; why would he hit her over the head later? What was it he wanted? When they were at Betty's house, she had Betty's shoe, and Stearne insisted it was evidence when it was hardly a clue. She understood him at the time but now she can't remember. What was it he implied about the shoe? Was it an excuse to have her deliver Betty to him? Was it a plot on his part to make Marisa complicit in his scheme?

What the hell is that bastard up to?

"Count backwards from 100," the doctor says.

"Ninety-nine, ninety … um. Ninety-eight. Ninety-one. No. Wait."

"Hmm."

He pokes her knee with something sharp. Maybe. She can't tell because no part of her body moved in response. She hears herself say, "Ow." Her leg jerks.

"Mmm hmm." The doctor rises and turns to the nurse. "Glasgow eleven, maybe twelve. Let's call it eleven to be safe. Overnight."

He leaves and the nurse follows.

Thirty seconds later, the words she wanted to say come out. "Doctor, what is it?"

They're both gone. Her fists clench the sheets. She needs to get out of here, but she lies down. She needs to find Jacob Stearne and beat the story out of him. There's something he's hiding. Something about the timeline. What did he say about the timeline? The shoe wasn't conclusive, but the timeline has answers. Why does she think this?

An old episode of Eurovision plays on the TV on the wall. The noise gives her a headache; the brightness is overwhelming. The remote hangs by the bed. She slaps at it until she gets it in her hand. Why isn't there an OFF button on these stupid things? Then she sees it, the I/O international symbol. Her brain is not working at full speed. That much she understands now.

Finally, the racket ends. The screen goes black. She closes her eyes. She just needs a little rest.

"Knock, knock." Dubra's voice.

Marisa opens one eye. Riga's Chief of Police steps in and closes the door behind him. She throws the remote at him. Tethered, because it also has the nurse's call button and the bed controls, it falls over the bedrail near her elbow.

"You dropped this," Dubra hands it back to her. When she doesn't reach for it, he drapes it over the rail.

Giving her a compassionate once-over, he says, "It breaks my heart to see our angel hurt like this. You have proven to be a feisty little thing, haven't you? You certainly are no stay-at-home mom. How are you doing? What is the doctor's diagnosis?"

Several phrases come and go without finding their way to her tongue. The doctor said overnight, which she hopes doesn't mean what it sounds like. Not that she would ever tell Dubra. Instead, the words that finally spill out are, "Fuck off."

"Come, now. I didn't know you were given to emotional outbursts like other women. I'll ignore that and chalk it up to your condition. I am interested in your recuperation. Genuinely, my dear."

He pulls up a chair and places it near her. He doesn't sit.

"Fine." She feels a sense of accomplishment with that one word even if she couldn't muster a retort for his casual denigration. "I'm fine."

"I understand these things are harder for women," he says with a smile. "I want to make sure you have all the support you need for a full recovery. I'll be sure to give you twice the time off than the doctor prescribes. What can I get you?"

"Perp," the English word, is all she can say.

A wave of nausea comes and goes. She can't tell if it's from the concussion or Dubra's presence.

"What's that? Never mind. Are you married? To a man that is. Oh, no, I remember: you're alone. No matter. I'll assign a patrolman to check on you every hour after you're released." He frowns. "Perpetrator. Perp. Is that it? What the Americans always say in their movies. Ah, yes, I see. When I asked what I could get you, you wanted me to get the perp. Clever. Try not to worry your pretty head about it, Marisa. We have competent people combing the scene now. I'm sure we'll catch him in no time."

"The investigation," she says without the rest of her question formed in her mind. "I found the … I found the … damn." She clenches the sheets again. "Shoe! I found Betty's shoe."

"Isn't that nice." He pats her arm. "I'm sure she'll be happy to hear that. Riga's finest officer doing her best detective work in the case of the missing shoe."

He rests his forearms on the back of the chair and grins down at her.

If she had her service weapon handy, she would shoot the son of a bitch. Then she'd go hunting for Stearne.

"Well." Dubra rises and pats the chair. "I must be off. I have a great deal more work to do now. This unnecessary parallel investigation has taken on a life of its own and must be completed. To streamline things, I've put Lieutenant Kaspar Krollis in charge of finding Jacob Stearne."

"No." This time she has the rest of her sentence ready but stops herself. She changes course. "No, you are too kind, Chief Dubra."

"It is nothing."

"It is kind of … stopping by like this. In your busy day. I appreciate … concern."

He smiles like a kid given a candy bar. "Your health is most important. Rest up."

She gives him a royal wave, which is all she can muster. He smiles and leaves.

It takes three grabs to get the call button into her hand. Marisa can't tell if Dubra wound it around the rail on purpose or if her own lack of coordination is to blame. She pushes the call button several times, then drops it. It takes her a minute to get the side railing down. When her feet reach the floor, a wave of dizziness hits her. She holds onto the bedframe until it passes. A nurse stands at the door, shaking her head with disapproval.

"Leaving," she tells the nurse.

"The doctor said you're to remain—"

"I don't care. Where are … where …"

"Your clothes?"

Marisa nods and waves the nurse in. With a reluctant smile, the nurse digs into a cabinet and produces a thick plastic bag. Marisa pokes through it, finds what she's after, and gets dressed. Halfway through, she fights another wave of nausea followed by more dizziness.

"Are you alright?" the nurse asks, taking her by the arm.

"Men … Man problem. Tell no one …" Again, her fists clench the bedrail.

"A man did this to you?" the nurse asks. "And you don't want him to find you. Oh, you poor thing. No problem. I won't check you out—I'll tell people you're in the toilet. That won't work long, though, maybe through the afternoon."

"Thank you." Marisa pushes her aside and tries to tie her shoes. It doesn't go well. She drops the laces inside and shoves her feet in on top of them. Close enough. She rises and takes two strides toward the door.

Holding out a laptop, the nurse says, "The EMTs said the 'sexy-girl' wanted you to have this. I don't know who they mean by that—they were all men—so …"

Marisa knows exactly who they meant: Jacob Stearne's girlfriend. It might be a crude description, but it's effective. She takes the laptop, looks it over, can't decide why she needs it, but drops it into the plastic bag just in case. She heads for the door.

"Wait!" The nurse quick-steps in front of her, holding out her shirt.

Marisa glances at the shirt then at herself. A lot of skin shows underneath her uniform jacket, which is buttoned strategically just below where her bra should be. She glances at the mirror on the wall. Why should Jacob's girlfriend be the only sexy-girl out there? She grabs the shirt, shoves it in the plastic bag, and heads down the corridor. Her first objective: Find Jacob Stearne and beat the crap out of him until he explains everything.

CHAPTER 48

BETTY BARDON

BY THE FAINT LIGHT GLOWING from a small window, Betty sees Symone crawling toward her. At least, she thinks that's what's going on. All she can see is a faint lump of the girl. She can see more of Francesca and Chris, vague shapes anyway, though faces and expressions are still obscured in darkness.

Symone crawls directly to her, almost in her lap.

"What did he say?" Betty asks the girl.

"Nothing. Just noises."

"I'm sorry, I couldn't think of any other—"

"Shut up! I don't believe you anyway." Symone huffs. "You killed Kevin, we all know it. That's what that shoe was all about. You left the other shoe at the scene of the crime."

"I wasn't wearing heels that night," Betty says. "Tell her, Chris."

"I do not know your shoes," he answers.

"She wore the flats," Francesca says. "Black Prada knockoffs."

"Those are real," Betty says, then instantly regrets her pettiness. "Besides, who walks out of the house with one shoe on? And we went to a club afterwards."

"Did you take a pair of shoes with you?" Symone asks. "Ones for dancing? By the way, that story you guys made up about who went back in the house was bullshit. Jacob figured that out and called Chris on it. Whose idea was it to get your stories straight?"

No one speaks for a long time. Betty can hear the others breathing in a way that sounds like they're about to say something, then stop. There is some loyalty left in them.

"Yeah, no one say anything," Symone says. "We all know it was Betty. For an actress, you're a terrible liar. And you turned me over to these Russians."

"She would not do that," Chris says.

"She did." Symone turns to Betty. "Tell them, bitch. Tell them how you grabbed me by the arm and pulled me to the front of the house."

"Yes, but to hide from them."

"Oh, you call that hiding? You stood up and shouted to them. You turned me in. Why would you do that?"

"*Che cosa*?" Francesca asks. *What?*

"Symone was standing up," Betty says. "She was going to run. They might have shot us. I did it to protect us."

"I was not standing up. It was raining, my knees were in mud. You wouldn't believe it, guys. She called out to them and told them she found me. As if she'd get a reward or something."

Betty can't see their faces, but she can feel their questioning stares as if they carried the intensity of cattle prods.

"And that's not all," Symone continues. "She told Jacob that she chose to work with the Russian dude. Said it was because—"

"That's enough, Symone!"

"—she can't keep you guys safe. She said Jacob didn't have the guts for it. She said—"

"Enough! That's not … I only said what I had to say. I was trying to keep us alive. It was—"

"Oh yeah? When that creepy guy said, 'Tell him,' you spilled it out like you'd written it down somewhere. That wasn't something you made up. You meant it."

"What does she say, Betty?" Francesca asks. "Why do you say this speech?"

"I had to, OK? It was all—"

"She's vibing up with the Russian guy from now on," Symone snarls. "Said she didn't like the Chinese or those Remmo people neither."

"This is true?" Chris asks.

Betty blurts, "No! No! Let me explain!"

No one speaks for a moment. Betty takes a deep breath. "Mikhail Yeschenko contacted me and threatened to kill each one of us, one at a time, unless I gave him the data. This was right after Kevin was murdered, so I thought he did it. He says he didn't, but I don't believe him. And … then I told him what he wanted to hear."

Symone shoves her. "That ain't the half of it, is it? What else was in your bullshit, huh? What else did you *have to* tell him?"

"What do you mean?" Betty resists pushing back. "That's it."

"No, you told him Jacob had the Edison-thing. That was a lie! You have what that Russian guy wants and you won't give it up. It's gotta be back at your house."

"Wait," Chris says. "You told Symone where you hid the *Edison Data*?"

"No, no. Please, everyone calm down a minute." Betty tries to hold up her hands but only rattles her chains. "We have an important mission. These are high stakes. We have some formidable enemies who we must deal with. Keep in mind what we're trying to do: Save the whole world."

Silence for a couple beats.

"You're doing a lousy job," Symone says. "We're locked down here and Jacob is dying. What good do you think you're doing? This isn't saving the world; this is getting everyone killed. Why not just give that guy whatever the hell it is and get us out of here?"

"I can't. Jacob has—"

"I've been with Jacob every step of the way, lady. He doesn't have anything that belongs to you."

"Yes," Francesca says. "Joe says this also. You risk our lives for this project. I came for the science—we do no science. Where is *Edison Data*?"

Another beat of quiet passes.

"All this is true," Chris says. "It might be time to quit."

Betty's heart rate skyrockets. She can't panic now. Everything she fought for, everything she's worked so hard to get, is slipping from her grasp. These next few hours are critical to her success or failure. Either she lets them lose their will, or she pulls them together.

"Over the next few hours," she says, "Yeschenko will do everything in his power to break us. If we stand up to him and win this, we can take on anyone. And then we can finish the work we came here to do: make the history-changing metacapacitor. But if we fail, then everyone comes under the bootheel of one oligarch or another. Whether it's Yeschenko, the Chinese, or Sabel, it doesn't matter. They will become so rich, they will control every nation in the EU and the Americas. We would sink into the abyss of a new Dark Age made more sinister by their monopoly on our science. That's why we have to summon the courage, and bear any burden, so that a thousand years from now, people will know this was when we stood up and did the right thing."

The next silence stretches far too long. After a minute, Symone slow claps, the rattle of her chains mocking Betty's words. Betty feels the tide has turned. Everyone is aligned against her: Yeschenko, Symone, probably Jacob, and worst of all, her own people.

"Tell us," Francesca says, "where is *Edison Data*? Give it up. We know you have it. No more risking our lives."

Boots stomp across the floor above them. The basement door opens, the light flips on, several men tromp down the stairs.

Betty blinks in the glaring light to see Symone staring at her from half an inch away. She backs up. Symone follows.

"You bitch!" Symone leaps on her, struggling, shoving, and pushing.

Betty tries to fight back but Symone is on top of her. Oddly, the girl isn't hitting her or trying to strangle her. She's wrestling.

Two big Russians pull them apart and stand them up.

Their short chains keep them from standing straight. They're hunched over, half squatting like chimpanzees. Symone has a mischievous grin.

Yeschenko arrives and casually crosses to Betty. He looks her over with a smug face and nods at one of his henchmen. Her chains are unlocked.

"You hold out on me, Betty." Yeschenko says. He grabs a fistful of her hair and yanks it hard. "You told me Jacob held the data, but it was you all along. How dare you lie to me!"

CHAPTER 49

JACOB STEARNE

IF I HAD CONTROL OVER my body, and the scene wasn't so tragic, I'd laugh. Brilliant physicist Betty Bardon outsmarted by a stripper. Funniest of all: Betty has no idea what Symone just did. I wish I could hold my head up because I'd love to see the look on their faces right now.

What I can tell from the sounds around me: Chris and Francesca are backing away; several Russians have moved in; Symone and Betty have been separated; and Yeschenko is having Betty's cuffs removed. Some discussion between Betty and Yeschenko continues in Russian. She's pleading her case. Betty and Yeschenko rush upstairs. They take the guards with them.

I hear the boots tramping across the floor overhead. We hear car doors slam and engines fire up and cars drive away. I can't be certain, but I think they left only two guards at the house. That will prove to be their fatal mistake if Symone did what I think she did.

My three companions remain silent for a long time. After three minutes of quiet, Symone can't wait any longer to see if the Russians will forget about us. She crawls back to me.

She falls on the floor in my field of view. She decides to lay there a moment. "Did I do the right thing?"

I want to kiss her, hug her, lift her on my shoulders and parade her around the city. All I can muster is, "Yes." It sounds more like a small sneeze.

She smiles. "What do I do now?"

Trying to breathe with venom coursing through your veins is tough, but somehow I manage to get enough air for two words, "Jab. Skin."

Scooting around on her back to get in position, she lifts my trouser leg and stabs me with the black and white autoinjector she stole from Betty's pocket when she feigned a fight. If Yeschenko was telling the truth, it's the antidote.

She expects me to pop right up. I hope for the same but I'm feeling only a tingle. My ankle isn't the best place for an injection because it will take longer for the medicine to make its way to where it's needed in my head.

"Are you OK?" she asks.

Another herculean effort produces, "Time."

Four words and I'm exhausted. My eyes close. I'm not sure I can open them again.

It occurs to me that Yeschenko may have lied about having an antidote. It could be a placebo for all I know. He only offered it to force my participation. He's not part of any pharmaceutical company and that calls into question what kind of testing he's done for dosage. For all I know, his medical researcher may have said, "Close enough," and had another shot of vodka.

I try to open my eyes and only get one of them. The other still stings from having been open too long. It might be progress; I'm not sure. I try wiggling a finger. Inconclusive. My wrists have been holding my body weight against wide metal cuffs and are now sound asleep. Or amputated. Again, I'm not sure.

One thing I am sure of: If I don't lift my head soon, I'll suffocate. My windpipe is kinked. It's like breathing through a cocktail straw.

"What did you do?" Francesca asks.

"Nothing," Symone says. She stabs her fingers upward, then at her ear. "They're listening."

"What?" Chris asks.

"Forget it," I say in a whisper.

Symone snaps her gaze back to me. "You spoke! You said something!"

"Shh…"

"OK."

She's right—I did say something, though I can't replace the breath it took to say it. I'm fading. The world around me is dark and getting darker. It takes all my strength to inhale and even then it's not enough to replace what I've expended. I'm suffocating slowly.

"Someone comes," Francesca says.

I'm used to reading sounds like a book. On the clandestine battlefield, knowing which way a distant boot-crunch on gravel is moving can save your life. Among the sounds coming from the floor above, I can tell the first series of steps followed by a thud is an attack. A body drops to the floor. The second set of noises is more of a struggle. The attacker lost the element of surprise, and his second challenger is putting up a fight. It sounds like an all-out brawl. If I could, I would cross my fingers for the good guy to win the fight.

"What is going on up there?" Francesca asks.

"Shh…" I say loud enough for all three of them to hear. That's progress. I smile inwardly—maybe this antidote is going to work after all. Then the reality sets in: I can't breathe.

We hear a loud bang, metallic. To my trained ear, it sounds like someone has been thrown against a refrigerator and the machine rocked back on its feet before slamming back down. Now the fighters come closer to the basement door. Slugs and oofs and bodies crashing into the cabinetry. Then a last thud, then silence.

We hear heavy breathing. Life-and-death struggles expend a good deal of energy in a short burst. Whoever is up there, they're exhausted. After gaining his breath, the winner begins searching the house. I hear his footsteps pounding frantically across the floorboards overhead. He's running from room to room.

"Yell," I tell Symone. Again, I struggle to replace the breath I've lost.

Symone doesn't yell, she shrieks in an ear-splitting soprano with the volume of a train whistle. If she underwent training, she'd be a shoo-in for the Metropolitan Opera. It's hard to tell if she's screaming a word or just making noise, but it's effective. The boots overhead make frantic moves back toward us.

As I recall, the basement door was not obvious at first glance. I think our savior is figuring that out for himself. Symone keeps up her wail, stops to take a breath as deep as a near-drowning victim, then goes back at it.

The basement door opens. Heavy steps tromp down the stairs. A blue-white flashlight beam sweeps across the room, landing first on Francesca and then on Chris, before arcing across the concrete to find Symone. Lastly, it lands on me.

That's it. I can no longer see. My air is gone. I'm fading into oblivion. I'm a dead man.

In a voice freighted with alarm, Joe Rouleau shouts, "*Mon Dieu!* Jacob, are you alright?"

My senses fade. I can't feel my skin. Joe rushes to me, wraps his arms around my chest, and lifts me. Pressing me against him, he jostles me until my chin hooks over his shoulder.

We look like Tango partners in a passionate embrace. But my trachea opens. I gulp air, making a disgusting noise.

"This is how the Romans tortured people," Joe says. "His weight cuts off his air."

The kids crawl toward me, horrified now that they realize they were watching me die, not recover. Symone is crying again. Francesca joins her.

"Chris," Joe calls over his shoulder, "help me. He is heavy."

"I am chained."

"*Merde,*" he says. "Keys are in my pocket. Hold on." He whispers in my ear, "Forgive me, Jacob."

He lowers me to where my air passage cuts off again. He rushes to the others and frees them from their shackles. Running back to me, he resumes our funny-looking but life-saving position. This time, Chris gets behind me and lifts.

Francesca unlocks my feet but can't reach my wrists.

"I'm not tall enough," Symone tells Joe. "I'll hold him up, you reach his hands."

With surprising strength, she picks up my weight using her legs while Joe releases my wrists. With two snaps, my arms fall to my sides. I immediately slump over Symone's shoulders. As she topples over backward under my weight, Francesca shoves her shoulder in, and the two of them prop me up until Joe and Chris can lower me to the floor.

I lie on my back, my body responding in barely perceptible movements while Symone tells Joe about the venom and the antidote. Then all eyes turn to me.

CHAPTER 50

JACOB STEARNE

"I'LL BE—" I STRUGGLE TO distribute oxygen through my bloodstream to my limbs "—fine."

My words were weak. The mood in the room is downbeat. It's possible they didn't hear me. They crouch on their knees, surrounding me with concerned expressions. The four of them think I'm dead. Chris chews his fingernails; Symone's tears fall on my shoulder.

I'm not sure if I'm breathing. Joe starts CPR with chest compressions, at least a hundred a minute. After three rounds of this, I feel my lungs take a big gulp of air all on their own. I blink. They notice me blinking and collectively give a reserved sigh of relief.

I take a couple deep breaths. "Thanks."

After hearing me speak with a stronger voice, they give an unreserved sigh and sit back on their heels.

"Upstairs?" I ask.

"Two men," he answers. "I used the Sabel Darts you left me at Betty's house."

"Russian or …" I run out of air for a second. This time it comes back quicker. "Latvian police?"

"Russians. I checked the rest of the house. No others."

"Check again."

His face twists wondering why I'm asking, then he understands. He says, "This is Stearne's Law?"

He laughs but we all see paranoia creep up his spine. He visibly shivers and re-assesses the basement. Twitching a glance upstairs, he then peers into the surrounding dark shadows. He stands, his movements quicker and slightly panicked.

"I will take Francesca and Chris," he says. "We will have another look around."

When they leave, Symone lies next to me on her back and holds her phone where I can see it. "I've been looking through their social media posts."

She starts swiping around so fast, I have no idea what she's showing me. Then she stops and zooms in. Kayla on a crowded dance floor in a nightclub. Her t-shirt reads, *Will teach quantum physics for food.* The closest dancer to her is the Cossack, Maksim Zaika.

Symone explains, "This is Logan's Instagram from the night before their friend died. That's the Russian dude, the Cossack, right? I can't tell if Kayla's dancing with him or near him. Then there's this."

She thumbs through posts like a demon possessed. She stops on one that takes me a minute to realize what I'm seeing. The account is called @francescamadness, as in Francesca Bartoli. Symone shows me a video of a different club, on a different night. On the dance floor, Kayla grinds on Chris. Logan tugs Francesca's hand while asking her to dance, but it's hard to tell with the dance music blaring. Just as she stops recording, Symone pauses the video and zooms in. Leaning against one end of the bar is Hakim Haddadi talking to Kevin Winn. Betty stands on the far side of Kevin, signaling a bartender. Whether the two men are discussing something serious, or Haddadi is making small talk is impossible to tell. The video ends.

"Back … it up." My voice is getting better but it's still exhausting.

Symone does as I ask. I see what caught my eye, the brass rail and raised platform of a VIP section. I say, "Bottle service."

In the clubs Ms. Sabel goes to, the VIP treatment starts at $10 thousand. Latvia is not London, LA, or New York, still, I'm thinking it's at least a thousand if not two or three.

Symone pulls her phone back and examines it closely. After flipping through a few other videos and pictures she shows me another one with a bottle of Dom Pérignon on the table as Francesca pans to the dance floor. Logan is leaning over the VIP rail, pouring Ketel One into the glass of a random girl. He's flirting, but she takes the free drink, turns and disappears into the crowd. Francesca's voice hits the video with a laugh, saying, "*Negato!*" *Denied.*

"Yeah," Symone says. "Logan and Francesca are the rich kids."

Even so, I find it odd they would pour drinks for strangers while leaving their friends to struggle at the bar with the rabble.

Symone then scrolls through a bunch of posts by both Francesca and Kayla. Without speaking, she points out every provocative-for-a-physics-nerd Francesca posts. Kayla tries to mimic virtually all of them on her account. Francesca gets a thousand likes for every photo, but Kayla gets ten.

That's all the Instagram I can take in one sitting. My strength comes back a little. I raise a hand, then the other. My legs respond as well. Symone gives me a smile.

We sit silently listening to the feet going back and forth on the floorboards above us. They're conducting an extensive search.

I try sitting up. I don't quite make it. I'm on one elbow fighting dizziness. "Water?"

"Oh, right!" Symone bolts up the stairs with the enthusiasm of the young.

Joe comes down with a glass a minute later.

I manage to sit up and down the glass in one long gulp. I hand the glass back.

"You are looking much improved, Jacob," he says.

"I'm getting there." We're alone for a moment, making this the best time to work things out between us. "What does the DGSE want with Betty Bardon?"

He isn't amazed that I figured out his employer: France's version of the CIA. He dealt with that when I left him the Sabel Darts. What he struggles with now is what degree of honesty he should apply. He chews the inside of his cheek a minute before answering. "The *Chaac Project* does not belong only to the USA."

"It doesn't belong to the USA at all. It was developed by Pia Sabel's natural father. She is the sole owner of any intellectual property."

"Technically, this may be so. Realistically, should it not belong to

NATO at least? Should America not share it with its allies?"

"Again, America doesn't own it. At the moment, neither does Pia Sabel. Worse, too many people have died over this—and we don't even know if it works. There is one thing we agree on, though, and I'm counting on you to be a gentleman about it."

"Oh?"

"It should never belong to an autocracy," I tell him. "I'm sure you have your directive, as I have mine. Let's set those aside for now and get it back."

"What's DGSE?" Symone asks from the stairs. The sneaky kid crept down the boards without either of us noticing.

She comes into the room, kneels behind me, and starts massaging my shoulders. Part of me wants to put an end to the intimacy because I know she will take it too far. The other part of me realizes it's helping my recovery.

"An intelligence agency of little importance," Joe replies. He turns to me. "How did you know?"

"*Grand-mère's* money is in commercial real estate—an asset-rich, cash-poor industry—which means you never had access to working capital you could give Betty. That's why I paid the bills in the beginning—to spare you the embarrassment. When I copped the Presidential Suite at the hotel, you were unfamiliar with the discretion of the staff at high end hotels, which tells me you have zero access to your family money. Then there was the matter of your military service. Logistics in Abu Dhabi? Nice legend, but you forgot one thing: No one could do logistics for twelve years without either becoming a raging alcoholic or a suicide."

He tosses a bashful smile to the side. "True. I will update my CV when I return. Perhaps diversity trainer. No one asks about them. We are agreed then: we work together. What do you feel is our next move?"

Symone digs her fingers in deep and goes to the bottom of my shoulder blades. It's working. I look up at Joe. "I'm recovering, but my brain is still a bit slow. Give me a few minutes to parse out what happened here, then I'll have a plan."

"I will look after my victims. Just now, I find they had restricted airways as well. It was not my intention to kill them." He heads upstairs.

When we're alone, Symone does what I was hoping she wouldn't: slides her hands around my chest and holds me like a lover.

I'm about to ask her nicely to let go when she hisses in my ear. "Why are you just sitting here? We need to get moving."

"I was poisoned. I need a minute."

"What are you afraid of?"

"Um, dying. It's not my preferred milieu." I twist to look at her. "A little compassion here?"

"No. You're afraid of disappointing people. Like your parents or the Army. And now you think you're down, but you're just at forty percent. You're letting yourself quit. If you don't get going now, you will disappoint everyone."

I take two deep breaths. "I'd like to think people would find it more disappointing if I died."

"People use that against you. They know you hate to fall short, so they put you in these situations to control you. Like that Russian guy. He's playing you like a first-time stripper." She squeezes my shoulder. "Either you get off your ass and save Betty Bardon or I'm telling everyone your whiny story about how your mama didn't love you enough."

Her words throw me. "Hey! I told you that in confidence. I trusted you."

"And I trusted you to be a stand-up guy. Instead, I found you chained up like a drunk the girls at the club rolled for the fun of it."

Mercury claps his hands and stomps a foot. *Whoa, she told you, huh, homie? Rolled like a drunk. She gotta point there. You mighta taken down heavily armed terrorists with the help of your favorite god, but you ignored me and what happened? You went down so easy, this girl saying strippers coulda done it.*

Thank you, I say. *Your divine inspiration is worth every penny I paid for it.*

Well now, that's the point, ain't it? You ain't paid shit. No sacrifice, no worship, no adoration. I move mountains and you think it's all for free.

OK! I get it, sacrifice. Jesus Christ—

Don't bring him into it. His people walk for miles on their knees! All I'm asking for—

Fine! Leave me alone.

"Oh no, you don't," Symone says. "I'm not leaving until you act like the guy who saved Paris."

"I didn't 'save Paris.' It was just one church with about two hundred parishioners who were about to get slaughtered."

I hold my head in my hands. There's nothing worse than everyone having unrealistic expectations. At the same time, I do hate disappointing people. But not like she's thinking. I hate disappointing myself. I can do this. I can get up and get moving. If I don't, all these kids, including Symone, might die.

Pulling out of Symone's grip, I spin around and face her. "I thought you hated Betty. Why do you want to save her all of a sudden?"

"I wanna know why she lied to them. She told them you had the thingy. The Edison thingy. I …" Her lips tremble as her face fills with regret. "I told them she has it and they took her out of here fast. I think they're gonna kill her."

Symone makes a good point. Betty told them I had it to keep them from searching her. That means she had it recently. She wore a wide dress with at least one pocket, but those hard drives are bulky and made of steel.

After picturing her with her disheveled hair hanging in her face, it comes to me. I know what she did with it. Maybe. There's something I need to know first. I ask, "Where's Logan?"

CHAPTER 51

CAPTAIN REDGRAVE

Captain Marisa Redgrave watches the Bolt driver in front of her as if she were watching a movie. Her mind is working better but still not working well. She knows that. Understands it. Must deal with it somehow.

First thing she has to figure out is, who tried to kill her? Because that's what it was: attempted murder. According to procedure, she should leave it to Dubra, which she would do if he weren't totally incompetent. Or is he corrupt? The alternative procedure would be to call Minister Krasnova. That would be career suicide. She's on her own.

Why does Jacob Stearne tell her everything in riddles? She can't get a read on that man. First time she met him, he could've brought her career to an end. Instead, he gave her a riddle about the footprints. But he'd been right about that. Next, he claimed he wanted to take down Dubra and put her in charge. Why? Because he thinks she's controllable. He plans to manipulate her. Well, he already did that. That stupid thing about the shoe is what got her head bashed. No, that's not right. Why did she get hit in the head? She'll remember that later. Stearne is definitely manipulating her. No doubt the timeline was a manipulation as well. What timeline was he talking about? Stearne comes to town, an American boy is killed, Stearne is found with blood on his hands— simple timeline.

The shoe. Why did she utter only half a sentence about the shoe to Dubra? Marisa cringes as she recalls the incident. Should've kept her mouth shut. Now he thinks he's right about women: trivial, emotional, incompetent. DAMN!

"Sorry, ma'am?" the Bolt driver asks.

"Not you," she says. "I received an upsetting text."

"OK."

She looks him over from the back. Is he Russian? Does he work for Yeschenko? And that brings up another question: why are the Russians running around Riga, inquiring about murder investigations? Impossible to stop them—one in four Latvians is an ethnic Russian. They're all over the place and have shifting loyalties.

Nothing about this case makes sense. No wonder Dubra called the Minister and asked for help. He knew it was a career-bomb. One that just blew up in her face.

The driver pulls onto her street. She sees two black Mercedes G-wagons parked in the street. They look heavy and sit low, as if they're armored.

"Keep going." She taps the driver's shoulder. "I changed my mind."

He drives by without attracting attention.

Marisa leans back into her seat, hiding behind the C-pillar as they roll slowly past a vigilant bodyguard. Krollis's car sits in her driveway. Instantly, she realizes he's the bastard who hit her. He's Yeschenko's insider. She should've seen it coming when he told her it was an honor to work with her. He knew nothing about her at the time, only that she needed help. And he made himself oh-so useful. Clever bastard.

"Where to?" the driver asks.

"Anywhere. The beach. Don't worry, I'll pay."

He accelerates gently.

She wonders why she said the beach. It's raining and chilly. Sleep is what she needs, but this case will get away from her if she closes her eyes for one minute. Dubra is useless; Krollis is a traitor. Is Dubra giving Krollis orders? Who can she trust? No one.

Stearne's Law is real. If she could get some answers out of that damned American comic book character, she might figure this out. Where is he? Where can she find him?

Marisa wants to scream her frustrations again, but her phone rings. Jacob Stearne.

"Where are you?" she says before he has a chance.

"On my way to find you," he replies. "Are you at home?"

"My house filled with Russians."

"Yeschenko?"

"I think yes."

"And Krollis?"

"That *dupsis!* Yes."

"You should go somewhere you've never been before."

"How do I know a place to go if I never went?" That isn't the question she wanted to ask, but it's all her scrambled brain could get out.

"How about the Hotel Daina?" the driver asks, craning over his shoulder.

"What kind of place is it?"

"Nice, modest. It's where the Swedes go when they come here."

"Any Russians?"

"No, they stay at the Baltic Beach."

That place she knows. Bougey as they come, perfect for the Russians. She says, "Take me to the Daina."

On her phone, she hears Jacob say, "I heard that. I'll find it. I need to make a quick stop at your house, then I'll be right there. Do you have the laptop?"

"What laptop?" As soon as she asks, she remembers the nurse and squeezes the plastic bag. It's in there. "Yes, I have laptop."

"Good," he says, "I'll be there as soon as I can."

He clicks off. Marisa watches her country passing by outside the car window. It's not unlike her career passing by. Should she trust Stearne? No. But what else does she have to work with? Only then does she realize the question she should've asked Stearne: Why did you ask about the laptop?

The driver swings into the hotel's entrance. Thanking him, she staggers out with her plastic bag, up the steps, and into the lobby. A quick look around reminds her it's a beach hotel; no one stirs before noon—an hour away. The restaurant is closed but workers inside scurry to prepare lunch. A kiosk serves coffee in the corner.

Marisa gets a cup and takes it to a sofa with a view of the front door and an exit nearby. Setting her coffee down, she pulls out the laptop. Krollis said it self-destructed, whatever that means. But Stearne's sexy-girl wanted her to have it, and Stearne wanted to make sure she had it. Why? She opens it and presses the button.

A blank screen comes up with the Microsoft logo and big swirling animated letters announcing, "Welcome to Windows 11." A second flashy animation replaces the first screen and announces, "User identity confirmed."

Marisa sits up straight. Who identified what? She sees two blinking lights on either side of the onboard camera. Should she shut this down?

She's about to slam the lid when the screen clears and a woman in profile appears. It's a live shot of an attractive middle-aged woman wearing a Pan-African head wrap in black, green, gold, and red. She types away on a keyboard. The woman side-eyes Marisa, as if she just noticed her sitting there.

Appearing pleasantly surprised, the woman turns to the camera with a warm and engaging smile, as if they were long lost friends. "Well, hello Captain Redgrave! How nice to meet you at last. My name is Emma."

CHAPTER 52

JACOB STEARNE

I FLAG DOWN LOGAN, WHO'S circling the house with Kayla. They've been worried sick, uncertain about what to do next. They hop out and a flurry of I-thought-you-were-dead embraces follows in the light rain. After everyone hugs everyone else, they turn to me. Symone scowls at me impatiently.

I say, "Guys, I'm going to take down Mikhail Yeschenko and rescue Betty. I need you to go back to the house and wait until I get—"

"I'm going with you," Chris says with confidence. "For Betty."

"Me too," Kayla says, jutting her chin.

The other three agree, talking over each other. Joe shrugs as if to say, *we shouldn't endanger them but we need their help.*

I hold up a hand. "People, these Russians aren't playing around. They'll kill you."

"You can include us in your plans," Symone says, "or we can follow you around."

"We are ready," Logan says. The others nod along. "Oligarchs are the reason we joined this cause. We must keep it out of their hands."

"And I will ask Betty why she kills Kevin," Francesca says. A group argument about Betty's guilt or innocence erupts.

I step away from the crowd and make a short call to Captain Redgrave without anyone else hearing.

The good news is, she's safe. The bad news is, she's operating at a disadvantage thanks to the concussion.

When I finish with Marisa, I pull Logan out of the scrum and ask him,

"Those new hard drives, the electronic ones—how big are they?"

"About the size of your finger only much thinner," he replies.

"I mean capacity." I inhale the scent of Latvian mud and drizzle as my senses begin returning to normal.

"Oh, that depends. Do you mean the PCIe NVMe M.2 Gen 4 type?"

"Was that English?"

"Yeah. Universal technology abbreviations. Never mind. Are you asking about the ones as big as a small book, or the ones the size of a name badge at Best Buy?"

"The name badge kind."

"Those are usually one or two terabytes. Oh, there are new ones going up to eight terabytes—big bucks though."

"How big bucks?"

"Like €2,000 or so, each."

I thank him and push him toward Symone as Joe comes over to me.

"What was that about?" the Frenchman asks.

I check out my new frenemy. We're after the same thing, working for different masters. Right now everything's cool, but when I find the *Edison Data*, we'll be rivals. And now he's curious.

"I'm trying to figure out what we're looking for," I tell him. "It's an old-fashioned hard drive, the big, bulky, spinny kind. The new sleek ones don't hold enough data. We're looking for over ten terabytes of data."

He nods. "Where is it?"

"It might be at the home of Marisa Redgrave."

"The woman who ordered you shot on sight?"

"Women take a shine to me—eventually. She'll come around."

I watch Symone and the four twenty-ish kids in their heated debate about Betty's guilt and wonder how they'll survive taking on heavily armed Russians. I give a loud whistle. "If you're coming with me, I'll expect you to keep that energy under control."

We pack seven people into Logan's Golf. Chris and I are the biggest guys, so we get the front seats, with Chris driving. The rest put the back seats down flat and pack in like sardines. Half a block later, Symone realizes my lap is empty and moves in with one arm around my neck and her butt wiggling into place.

"Professional," I say in her ear. "Keep it professional."

"I am a professional," she whispers in an ear-tickling, husky, and wet reply. Her butt wiggles again.

Chris stops three blocks shy of the destination. Four of us climb out and stretch our cramped limbs. I send Logan, Chris, and Symone on a mission down Marisa's street. Since someone crashed my drone, my options are limited. This time, Logan, our Formula One wannabe, drives.

Symone's earbud camera shows me the layout: One Russian on guard out front, another in the back yard, one inside the front door, and the fourth at the back door. Impenetrable defense.

I slip around some tree trunks to get my own view of things. Using a combination of my monocular and my Sabel Visor, I get a look deeper inside. Betty faces Yeschenko and Krollis. They appear to be arguing. The couch pillows are all over the floor.

Checking my supplies, I show Joe that three Sabel Darts and a pistol remain. He waves off the weapon and holds up a collapsible baton of his own.

I deploy Francesca and Kayla to the corners of Marisa's block. Joe and I take up positions in the alley. Then I give Symone the signal.

Logan drives slowly down Marisa's lane. Symone leans out the window and shouts the Russian phrase I taught her, "*Tolerast mudak!* We escaped! Your buddies are bleeding, and we have the *Edison* thing, so fuck you!"

You can't beat teenagers for nasty inflection. The Russian phrase literally means *tolerant asshole,* which sounds odd but calling someone *tolerant* is a homophobic slur in Putin's Russia.

We can see the guards reacting as a group. The man in back covers his earpiece to hear better. He faces the side yard, preparing to back up his buddy. I'm on him with a dart before he processes the sound of my footsteps. The man at the back door sees me crossing his field of view and steps out.

Joe's baton comes down hard. The guard falls face down.

Together, we creep in through the kitchen. As I suspected, the others, including Yeschenko, Krollis, and Betty, have exited the front, thinking their boys would secure the building until their return. We hear the slamming doors of G-wagons out front. They sling muddy gravel from the lane as they chase Logan.

"They're after us," Symone says in the comm link.

"Stay on the route we planned," I tell her.

"We've got his phone on the dashboard. Map's all lit up."

Logan plays a lot of racing games and claims to be proficient in the real world as well. I can only hope he performs as well as he boasts.

"We've got five minutes," I tell Joe. "Less if they get close enough to figure out I'm not in the car."

We start searching the house despite it being obvious Yeschenko already searched it. We split up. I keep looking until we're far enough apart I can get out.

"I'm going to check the bushes out front," I call out to him.

When he acknowledges, I go straight to Krollis's car to check the back seat. Before I open the door, I check that Joe can't see me. The last thing I need is to find the damn thing and have the Frenchman take it away from me.

Inside, nothing but empty footwells. I slide my hand in between the seatbacks and the back bench. That's where I touch it with just my fingertips. With a second effort, I feel it slide deeper under the seat, out of reach. I try to make my fingers skinny, hoping to slide overtop and pull it back. Instead, it slips even farther down.

My hand is wedged in as far as I can get it. I'll have to remove the bench seat.

Pulling my hand out, I check the seat's construction and how it fits in the car. The first thing I find is Joe's leg. He's standing next to me.

"My English is fair, but I could swear that is a bush." He points at a boxwood. "And this is an automobile."

"Had a thought," I lie. "There's something down there. Can't say for sure, but I need to take the seat out."

Through the comm link, Symone tells me, "One of them is heading back. There were two G-wagons; now there's only one."

I tell Joe, "We have a minute left." There are four plastic-lined holes in the bench. I stick a finger in one of them and feel a latch of some kind. "I need a metal hook or something."

Joe pulls a Swiss Army knife out of his pocket and extends the multipurpose hook next to a well-used corkscrew. I take it and dig around until I hear a pop. The first plastic retainer comes free.

In seconds I release the other three. More shoving and pushing back and forth is required before the bench seat comes loose. I toss it out of the car and see exactly what I'm looking for: Betty's Art Deco hairbow. The reason her hair was a mess: she stashed the hairbow in the back seat when Krollis captured her.

"This is not the hard drive," Joe says.

A moment of truth for me. If I show him, we will be adversaries from now on. If I lie to him, I will have lied to the man who saved my life. There's only one path to take. I turn the hairbow over.

Like me, and most field operators, Joe is no techno-geek, but when he sees two obvious looking computer things stuck to the underside, he knows what it is.

He catches my gaze, confused. "This is not what we expect? Is it the *Edison Data?*"

"Can't be sure." I slide it in my pocket. "If it is, Betty has everyone looking for the larger mechanical kind. Quantum electrodynamics physicists tend to be clever like that. Anyway. We need to run."

After we put Krollis's car back together, I ask Joe to summon a Bolt to pick us up a few blocks away.

While he's preoccupied, I call President Williams on the president's personal mobile phone. Noon here is around 5 AM there.

He picks up with a groggy voice. "Jacob, do you have it?"

"Yes and no. It's not secure. I'm working on that and hope to have it locked up shortly. We have a different problem, though: the French have a man here and he's helping me."

"Helping you? That's not good."

"Could you ask President Macron to have him recalled immediately?"

"Uh, that is a big ask, Jacob. Could you just eliminate him?"

I pull my phone from my ear to make sure I dialed the President of the United States and not a dictator of an unstable country. Confirmed: POTUS. "Do you mean eliminate him as in: eliminate him? That would be a bit harsh, sir."

"Oh. Yeah. See what you mean. Scratch that. I'll see what I can do."

I click off just as the Bolt arrives. It's a good thing the president saw things my way. It would be rude to kill a man who just brought me back from the dead.

Joe opens the door for me with a friendly flourish. He asks, "Who did you call?"

"The President of the United States," I answer with a grin.

"Sure." He claps me on the back with a laugh, and climbs in.

Seconds later, we scoop up Kayla and round the next block. Francesca stands watch outside an apartment building. As she climbs in, one of the Russian G-wagons passes us in the opposite direction. They slam on the brakes and begin backing up.

Extending my last €500 note to the driver, I say, "Lose them."

CHAPTER 53

BETTY BARDON

BETTY BARDON STRUGGLES TO FIND comfort in the middle seat. Squeezed between a bodyguard and Mikhail Yeschenko, she rides a hump a child would complain about. Her feet straddle the driveshaft tunnel beneath her. Her hands are folded neatly between her knees.

"I've lost them," the driver says, peeking down a side street.

"No matter," Yeschenko replies. "Let Krollis and the others find them. We have what we need. Let's get back to Alexi at the hotel."

The driver wheels the heavy SUV around a corner and drives at a normal speed back toward Old Town. They pass the Lutheran Cathedral, through narrow, wandering cobblestone lanes to a small hotel. The car stops. A guard gets out and opens the door.

Betty follows Yeschenko and his man through the rain into the cozy lobby of a boutique hotel. The creaking elevator takes an excruciatingly long time to reach the fourth floor. No one speaks. A guard opens the door to a suite. Inside, two men labor at workstations with large screens. Several windows filled with code remain open on the monitors.

Yeschenko hands Betty's hard drive to Alexi, who plugs it in and begins working.

With a gesture to a bay window at the far end of the room, Yeschenko ushers her to the quiet place. When she faces him, his fists clench, his face reddens, the veins on his neck pulse. His savage sneer takes him beyond fury and hate to a psychopathic and murderous rage.

Through clenched teeth, he hisses, "You're alive because you're a brilliant physicist, Betty. But my patience wears thin. Too many times you have told me one thing and done another. While you may be the best authority on the *Chaac Project*, there are many other quantum electrodynamics experts out there. Some who are not as difficult. You told me what I wanted to hear. That pleased me—for a time. Now I wonder if you are committed to working with me or if you are doing nothing more than what you must to keep your precious college kids alive until Jacob Stearne can save you. Well, if a savior is who you wait for, where is he?"

Yeschenko spreads his arms wide, palms up, twisting left and right.

"I meant what I told Jacob," she says. "By killing Kevin Winn, you proved I cannot keep—"

"I told you this is a lie! I did not kill your boy." His shout draws the attention of his men. He glances at them and waves them back to work. Facing Betty again, he lowers his voice. "He who accuses is often the one who is guilty. Is this not so?"

He moves in close to her face, anger rising from him like steam.

"How can anyone think that of me?" she asks. "No. I meant only that … you have threatened my people and I fear that threat. The others—Deng, Sabel, and the rest—they are equally dangerous. I need your resources, I need your ruthlessness, I need your protection to complete the project."

He steps to the side, examining her like an artwork. In Hollywood, objectification is part of an audition. The way Yeschenko does it, she feels his eyes rip the flesh from her body to expose her bones.

"We lie to ourselves when we must," he says quietly. "You lie as if you're reading a script. Have you scripted your speech to make me believe it, Betty Bardon?"

"No. I swear, I really—"

"Then why not join me? Why not commit to my cause?"

"But I have joined you. I'm here, right now. I gave you the *Edison Data*."

He grabs a fistful of her hair and yanks her face down to his elbow. He growls, "You were supposed to poison the girl."

She struggles to relieve the pain in her awkward position. There is only one way—sink to her knees. When she does, he twists her head sideways, forcing her to look up at him.

"I'll be honest." A tear escapes the corner of her eye. Her nose swells. "I fear you."

"There is nothing to fear when you do as you are told."

How many times have men told her that? Threats have always accompanied the easy rationalization, *if you do what I say, I'll stop hurting you.* She was fifteen when Mr. Griffith seduced her into the world of rich men. Ever since, she's struggled to distance herself from them. As if being born beautiful forced her into a life as a prized possession. Bought, sold, traded. And now, once again a rich and powerful man owns her.

"Be honest with me, Betty." Using her hair as leverage, he twists her head to the right and left. "What makes you fear me?"

"You're an oligarch," she says. "You use money as a weapon to procure souls in your service. You alternate between angel and demon with no reason, no rules. You're guided by nothing more than your whims. Dangerous whims. You're dangerous not because you are powerful but because you are miserable."

He pulls her hair down, forcing her face up, her chin to his thigh, and looks down at her as if examining a bug. After a beat, he shoves her face into the arm of the chair next to her. "You have an outdated world view."

Betty pulls her feet beneath her and begins to stand. He shoves her, banging her head hard against the chair. "Stay on your knees."

Hatred and fear churn her insides like a cauldron of boiling anxiety. She slumps to an awkward position, her feet tucked beneath her, her hands on the floor.

"You don't see it, do you?" Yeschenko asks. "The days of democracy are over. The little American experiment failed. It had a good run, but now it's done. Democracies are being dismantled. The voting rights you once enjoyed have been whittled away. The liberties you cherish are being dissolved. Your reproductive decisions have been ruled into oblivion. Your vaunted free press? The largest news source in America is owned by a foreign family who trumpets any ideological whim that suits their fancy, no matter how divisive.

"But this is nothing new. The little people are always dominated by the strong. Tribal chieftains, pharaohs, emperors, kings, dictators—they were not elected." He spits the last word out as if it tastes bad. "The people who rule the world seize the power they want. They hold onto it with an iron fist. That is happening today. Not just in Russia and China, but in your beloved USA. Elon Musk, Bill Gates, Pia Sabel, Peter Thiel—these people control your life. Do you fear them?"

"There's a difference," she says. "You kill people."

Yeschenko laughs, first in an amused burst, then with gusto. "And your boyfriend, Jacob Stearne, does he not kill people? Many more than I, that I can assure you. When you contemplate the people he's killed, first you ask yourself, *Is this OK?* You see him idolized on television. And then you answer yourself, *It must be.* And that makes it so, does it not? Surely his victims deserved it. They needed to be stopped. Oh, young lady, lying to yourself is natural. Everyone does it. It's how we get by. The fact is, Jacob Stearne once murdered people for the US Army, and now he murders people for Pia Sabel. On whose orders does he act? Is that what makes him more palatable than me—that his assassinations are the whims of a woman?"

"No, I ..." Confused by the sense that he might be right about Jacob, she has nothing to say. She is just a pawn. At the whim of Sabel or Yeschenko or Deng, what difference does it make?

"It's time to pick a side, Betty." Yeschenko brushes her leg with the toe of his shoe. "And mean it."

Nausea turns her stomach like a storm-tossed boat. Where is it written that Betty Bardon has no choice in life? Why bother living if she has no control over her own destiny? What are the choices? Sabel versus Yeschenko?

To choose Sabel brings back the question he asked at the beginning of his statement: Where is Jacob Stearne? No matter what she expected of Jacob in the beginning, the fact that he thinks she killed Kevin Winn will stop him from helping her. Where does that leave her?

With no one to turn to but Mikhail Yeschenko.

"Sir?" Alexi calls from the far side of the room. He holds the hard drive up. "It's encrypted. We have no tools to crack it."

After a stunned beat, Yeschenko turns back to her and kicks her.

"Encrypted? You encrypted it?"

"No," she says. "The university encrypted it at the insistence of your comrades in the Russian Federation. They never decrypted it before they sold it last year. It was a security measure to ensure they got paid. The winning bidder got the keys. Too bad you didn't bid enough at the time."

"They didn't let me," he snarls. "Superstitious fools! They thought it was cursed. They wanted rid of it." He stands over her, his fists clenching and unclenching. "Where is the key? How do we get it decrypted?"

"I don't know." She blinks up at him. "The guy I stole it from didn't return my calls when I asked—because Jacob Stearne killed him. Aren't you the all-powerful lord and master? Can't you figure it out?"

Yeschenko's outrage boils over to where she can see murder in his eyes.

He brings himself back under control, though his body still trembles with rage. "And without me, what was your plan?"

"To trick Jacob Stearne into figuring it out."

"How would that work? He's no genius." He grabs her by the hair again and pulls her to her feet. "Before you answer, remember: if you don't care about your life, at least care about Francesca, Chris, Kayla, and Logan."

Betty draws a deep, sad breath. Francesca, whose biggest crime was fawning over brand names; Chris, whose only fault is his enthusiasm; Logan, who loves racing; Kayla, who might hack the encryption if given the chance—did they deserve being drawn into this game of hers? If she could chew her own arm off to get out of this, she would.

What difference would it make? Is Pia Sabel any better than the others? The woman is an idealist, but will she retain those values when she's a trillionaire? Will she be an idealist when she's Yeschenko's age? The Russian is right about one thing: Sabel has been involved in many killings. Yes, the victors write the history books, and her victories absolved her every time. How much of that verdict was due to her money, power, and influence?

Betty realizes she is powerless to stop any oligarch, regardless of their country of origin.

"Jacob has a copy of it," she says, regretting the melancholy in her voice. "I left it for him to find. With the power of all the Sabel companies behind him, he'll get it cracked. That's why I gave him the poison—to distract you, make you back off. I let Symone take the antidote from me, knowing it would give him room to work. When the time is right, he'll come to us."

Yeschenko scrutinizes her again for a stretched moment. "And if your plan fails?"

CHAPTER 54

JACOB STEARNE

I'M HARDLY GETTING MY €500 worth, but our Bolt driver manages to extend his lead to two blocks. In his defense, we did squeeze five people into his Toyota RAV4. Brakes squeal and tires chirp into the corners. The Mercedes roars, the Toyota whines. Were it not for the heavy armor on the G-wagons, they would've caught us long ago.

Symone reports Logan already lost their Russians. She has him heading for the hotel.

"I have been recalled," Joe says, staring at his phone as if it had turned into a snake. "I am to be at the airport in thirty minutes."

He's squeezed in the back with Chris, the girls behind them in the luggage compartment. Our driver takes a corner too fast in the rain and slams the curb. Traffic honks at him. He swears and takes off again.

"Unexpected?" I ask Joe with a glance back between the seats.

He eyes me suspiciously. He's wondering if I really did call President Williams and had him recalled but dismisses that idea as too far-fetched. "I must tell them we have the *Edison Data*."

"Premature," I tell him. "We don't know what's on this. Betty knows I watch her closely and might have set me up with a decoy."

He taps his chin, eyeing me as his doubts grow. "We have a transport flight for NATO staff heading back to Paris. For safety, we should all get on this plane. We will determine the contents later."

As we all know, possession is nine-tenths of the law. I've no intention of letting the French get ahold of this unless I can prove conclusively it's junk. Which it could be.

"Transport. That's how you flew into the country twice without flying out?"

"*Peut être.* Ehm, perhaps."

"Why did you leave when you had already set up the meeting with Betty?"

"Upon arrival, I discovered Russians in the adjoining townhouse. When I relayed this to my superiors, they recalled me. Bureaucracy! Once I arrived in Paris and pleaded my case, they relented, and I returned to Riga. In the meantime, someone murdered the unfortunate young man."

Our driver decides to earn his money by running a red light. Our little SUV spins all four tires on the wet cobblestones before getting traction and sliding between crossing minivans. Kayla lets out a panicked squeal.

"Sorry you've been recalled," I tell him. "But I'm not leaving Betty in Yeschenko's hands. We'll manage somehow."

Chris seconds my sentiment with a frown at Joe.

The Russians see us and mimic our driver's daring move. We have a three-block advantage.

I tell our driver to make a right into a tight alley. I instruct him to go around the block slowly and come back to pick me up. It's the same drill I did with Chris earlier. As he slows, I pop open the door and roll out. Getting to my feet, I see Joe Rouleau has done the same.

"Pop the tires?" he asks.

"You get the front end and the passenger; I'll take the driver."

We take up positions at the edge of the alley. The G-wagon comes around the corner fast. I repeat the operation, only this time, we use small, sticky explosives that destroy the run-flat tires on armored cars. When we toss them under the tires, they blow the treads off. The truck slams down on its rims and stops. The passenger opens his door in time to feel Joe's baton crashing down on his forehead.

At the same time I round the back fender, the driver levels a pistol at me. I zig left, he fires. His round skims my hip close enough that I feel the heat, and ricochets off the paving. I dive into him like I'm sacking a quarterback and slam my last dart into his ribs.

He crumples.

When I stand and check on Joe, his gaze is fixed on a spot over my shoulder. He asks, "She is a friend of yours?"

I turn to find Amit Sofer's muzzle a foot from my nose. Rain falls on her serious face, drips from her long black hair, runs down her black duster, and over her black boots. She looks like Edgar Allen Poe's raven about to say *nevermore.* Her stark Goth beauty would have more appeal without the pistol.

"We're more like acquaintances," I answer. Amit's piercing golden-brown eyes flick to Joe for an instant, then back.

"What was it you said? Women take a shine to you?" Joe laughs. "She does not look so shiny, Jacob."

I can't think of a better way to defuse the situation, so I say, "Amit Sofer, allow me to introduce Joe Rouleau, DGSE. Joe, say hello to Amit Sofer. Mossad, Kidon unit."

They exchange respectful nods. Joe's tightly controlled expression tells me he's familiar with Mossad's assassination department, known externally as Kidon, Hebrew for *spear.*

"If Mossad still considers you an employee, that is." I wait. Instead of answering, she lowers her weapon and shoves it in my ribs. Less noticeable to casual observers. I add, "I doubt they would've sanctioned the hit on Hakim Haddadi."

"Unfortunate," Amit says. "He wanted to borrow my Baretta—but did not ask permission."

I look around the alley. "Is Eli going to join us?"

"He has his eye on the Chinese delegation in Monaco."

"Ah." I look her over while civilians at the end of the alley begin to notice the bodies at our feet. "The CIA thinks you went rogue with Rafael Tum."

"He betrayed us." She spits on the ground. "I infiltrated the Russians briefly, but they know nothing. As usual, you seem to know more than everyone else. So, Jacob, where is it?"

"Who do you work for these days, Amit?"

"Good question."

"Wait," Joe says. "She is after the same thing we are after?"

"Not we," I say, keeping my gaze fixed on Amit. "You said you were recalled."

Amit unleashes a sly grin. "Good to know. It's down to just you and me then."

And her Baretta, she politely fails to mention.

Joe's phone buzzes. He answers it, argues with someone in French. His voice gets shrill as he pleads. Then he clicks off. "I must leave immediately. It appears my orders came from the highest office." He pauses while a frown crinkles his face. "*Merde*, you really did call your president? *Bâtard!*"

I toss him a shrug.

"I understand, Jacob," he says. "You had to do what is best for your country. Allow me to return the favor." He nods at Amit. "It has been a pleasure meeting you, Ms. Sofer. I feel obligated to let you know: Jacob has what you seek—in his pocket. *Au revoir.*"

Bastard.

He whistles as he strolls down the alley and hails a passing cab.

Amit reaches for my pocket.

"It's broken," I lie, "and you don't have the resources to fix it." I wait until she freezes and holds my gaze. "I do. And I need your help taking on the Russians. We can work this out."

She thinks it over, rolls her eyes when she figures I'm bluffing, then shoves her hand in my pocket.

That's the moment my Bolt driver returns. Entering the alley too fast, he slams on the brakes and stops an inch from our shoulders. It's all the distraction I need. With one quick motion, I slap her pistol to the side, wrench her wrist, and spin into her, pinning her against the Toyota's grill. Reluctantly, she relinquishes her weapon from her twisted arm before I break it.

Amit never takes her eyes off me. After following me for twenty-four hours, she already knows the ELA kids in the Bolt and considers them no threat.

What do I do with Amit Sofer? No magic phone call is going to rid me of her. She's as good as I am at this game, so I can't give her the slip. Which means I need to make her an ally. That's like forming an alliance with a cobra. I would've been better off keeping Joe. Too late now.

"We'll do this my way, Amit."

CHAPTER 55

JACOB STEARNE

AFTER SENDING THE ELA CONTINGENT ahead to the hotel in the old Bolt, I summon a new Bolt and put Amit in the passenger seat.

"This friend of yours we have to pick up," Amit says. "What does she have to do with *Chaac*?"

"Nothing. She's a police captain who sent a SWAT team to have me killed."

"I like her already."

"The DGSE is after this, you're after this, we don't want the Latvians after it as well, so the less said the better."

"Then why are you picking her up?"

"I told her I'd help her out." I pause for a moment, carefully considering how much to tell my newest frenemy. "And we're going to need her help."

"You? Need help? Where is the Sabel Army?"

Ignoring Amit's cynicism, I call Marisa.

"Where you have been?" she answers in an angry whisper. "Krollis searches the hotel for me."

"Why would he do that?"

"Kidnapping Betty Bardon—he makes up charges."

It takes me a second to untwist her English. Krollis issued a warrant for Marisa, claiming she kidnapped Betty. He was the only witness to Marisa taking Betty into protective custody, so he's gaming the system. Nonetheless, Marisa's on the lam. While the ironic reversal of fortunes makes me want to laugh, I need her and she needs to be in uniform, ready for a press conference.

"I'll be there shortly," I tell her.

We race to the small stand of trees where she's hiding near the hotel. After a short roll-by, we spot her behind a lilac tree.

She looks miserable in the rain and has the countenance of a wet dog. When she steps out and runs to our Bolt, I see she's taken a fashion cue from Symone: no shirt under her jacket. She slides in the backseat, handing me her plastic bag.

"Emma helps me," she says, pulling out the laptop. "Emma say Sabel Tech make spyware before Krollis picks up. This is smart." She's about to open it when I close it and give her a look. Stunned by my action, she says, "Is OK, I know who killed—"

"Let's keep the surprise for later." I slide my eyes toward Amit in the front seat.

Marisa appears noticeably dulled. It's a side effect of the concussion and there's not much we can do about it. I wonder how helpful she'll be. I can give her detailed instructions, but I'd prefer to have her autonomous and running at one hundred percent.

Distrust twists her expression. She says, "You are wrong about Betty—"

"Yes, and no. One shoe, one bloody print on the stair, someone's framing her. I wanted you to take her into custody to keep her safe."

"This is plan? Put her in jail for safekeeping?"

"I didn't expect you'd get bonked on the head," I say, letting too much exasperation creep into my words.

"I not suspect lieutenant of betrayal."

"To be fair, I didn't suspect Krollis either."

"Yes, deceived everyone. Very bad."

Amit leans in from the front. "Haven't either of you heard of Stearne's Law?"

Marisa, to her credit, pushes Amit's shoulder until the Israeli faces front again. Amit snickers but stays quiet.

"Now I am down to you," Marisa says, as if this equates to living on the street. "I trust no one."

"You suspect more officers than Krollis work for Yeschenko?" I ask.

"How high up does it go?"

"Maybe more lieutenants. Maybe Dubra. Maybe a colonel in International Division—because Russians. I know too little."

She looks out the window as we drive back into downtown Riga. After a long time, she turns to me and asks, "Do you think I am stupid?"

Her tone of voice tells me this is a heartfelt question, not rhetorical, not satirical. Still, I'm not sure what answer she wants to hear or will believe. I don't reply.

"You say, you believe in me." She stares deep into my eyes. "Do you mean this? Or do you say this to save skin?"

"I mean it."

"You tell me look at footprints. I look at footprints. I not understand."

"Yes, you did. You figured it out."

Her face draws back, as if she just remembered she had indeed figured it out. Her concussion is still messing with her.

"Yes, this is right. I did. But I do not get what you mean when you say timeline. Wait." Again, her face contorts with a memory. A look of satisfaction comes over her. "Yes, I do know timeline. Kevin Winn is murdered on stairs same time you break in back door." She snaps her fingers. "Then four policemen arrest you. Seconds after killing. This is timeline, yes?"

"Exactly," I say, feeling a little pleasantly surprised myself. Her mind is coming back.

"Normal response time in minutes, five maybe ten minutes, not ten seconds." She frowns. "But. But you are there at same time. They should not expect you."

"No, they expected to find Betty Bardon. But I watched her and her crew from the beginning. They came in, they drank booze, they had fun, Betty got a call, some of them left. Betty came back thirty seconds later, rifled through drawers in the kitchen, found some loose change, ran back out. A full minute later, I broke in and Kevin came down the stairs bleeding. Who killed him, and who called the cops?"

"This is on recordings," she says, then glances at Amit in the front seat. She recalls I don't want to talk about it in front of my new associate. She holds up a hand. "Wait."

Telling me as she acts, she calls the officer who arrested me. She asks him questions in Latvian, he answers, she clicks off. Facing me, she says, "Krollis stations them end of block. Then he calls them in."

We both know that means Krollis planned the killing in advance. It was a setup: kill one of the kids, frame Betty for it. Then, Yeschenko would swoop in to bail her out—her knight in shining armor. Blackmail armor. Marisa and I look out the windows, each thinking about the ramifications of this devious strategy.

"Why did they call you in on the job?" I ask her.

"I have career desk job. Never field work. They know I prove myself. Give me chance tracking Jacob Stearne and I will not stop until I find him—but they not expect I look at case." She takes a deep breath. "Because they think I am stupid."

"Eager," I tell her. "Not stupid. Who called you in on the case?"

"Dubra." She turns to the window, a finger tapping on her knee. "He ask for help outside Riga jurisdiction."

The driver pulls into my personal entrance for the Hotel Kempinski— the alley next to the trash compactor. Marisa stares through the window, uncertain if her scrambled mind is playing tricks on her or if we're really going in the service entrance.

Amit, who understands how grand entrances work in covert operations, hops out and opens the door for Marisa. As I come around the back, Amit flicks her chin in Marisa's direction and asks, "Head injury? You're being awfully kind and patient. Never expected that from you."

"Thanks—I guess." I lead Marisa to the service elevator with Amit on our heels.

Marisa stops, grabs my arm and pulls. "Not Dubra. Dubra does not call on me to lead search for you. I get call from Interior Minister Anna Krasnova. She say Dubra need help."

She goes silent again as we squeeze in the elevator next to a maid and cart.

After passing the second floor, I ask, "Is that unusual? Getting a call from someone so high up?" When she nods yes, I ask, "Why did she pick you?"

"Maybe Dubra ask for me. He think I am stupid."

"I don't know you at all, lady—" Amit grabs her and spins her face to face. "—but if Jacob Stearne invested this much time in you, you sure as hell can't be stupid. So quit running yourself down."

Marisa's eyes blow open at Amit's intensity. They stare at each other for a beat, then Amit lets go. Marisa glances at me sheepishly.

"Dubra think I do not investigate crime," Marisa says, "only find you. But you have big friend call Minister Krasnova to stop search. She think I am done now."

"OK," I say, uncertain how that fits into the big picture. "Wait, what big friend?"

"American Secretary of State call her personally, not ambassador. He threaten US aid if we hurt *Le Héros de Paris.*"

Amit rolls her eyes, "Did you make her watch that piece of crap?"

"Jealous?" I ask. "Get your own show. Seriously, I just heard about it two days ago. Guess it was big in Riga. No one seems to mind it was fast and loose with the facts."

"What? You don't have a computerized boomerang?" she laughs.

I'd rather see Amit giggle than hold a Baretta on me.

But I can't shake the thought of Secretary Neville Townsend making calls on my behalf. Last time I saw Neville, the President of the United States told him to stay out of my way, and that I would be reporting straight to POTUS. Having been told to stand down, why would the Secretary of State call the Interior Minister of Latvia? The obvious answer: he wouldn't—he doesn't even know I'm here. Or, more accurately, shouldn't know.

CHAPTER 56

JACOB STEARNE

I LET AMIT SOFER LOOK around the Presidential Suite while she does her best to suppress her shock. Government agencies like Mossad don't spring for suites, and her budget with Rafael had to be cheaper than that. The old guy grew up running a revolution in the jungle without so much as a tent. I point her toward the lunch buffet.

Emma had everything belonging to the ELA moved from their house into the connecting rooms. The kids are sprawled across the luxurious living room with laptops. Logan has commandeered the dining table for several of his computers and monitors.

Amit stops me crossing the room. "You're set up in the same hotel as Yeschenko?"

"He hide where least expected," Marisa says. "Under the adversary nose."

Glad to see her alertness improving by the minute, I point at Marisa and say, "What she said."

Not satisfied, Amit tosses a glance over her shoulder at the kids. "This is who Sabel Security employs now?"

What she's doing is obvious: assessing the strength of my team. They aren't the kind she's used to assessing, they're far too meek. She could take them down in a minute if she felt like it. With an unimpressed glance, she tells me what I already know: my chances for survival are slim to none.

I say, "Only one of them works for Sabel. Can you guess who?" I let her look them over for a beat. "Make that two—now that you're on board."

"Me?" Her bewildered voice cracks.

"Two weeks ago, Israeli intelligence told President Williams you and Eli were in North Korea—but you weren't. That means you've been AWOL at least that long. Mossad wouldn't let that go unpunished. If you told me the truth, that Rafael ditched you, you've now lost both rides. That means you're an agent without portfolio, Amit. That can get messy in our line of work." I wait as a series of emotions cross her normally inexpressive face. Her expression telegraphs a wave of nausea when she comes to the realization that she has no choice but to join me. "Welcome aboard."

I slap her shoulder and grin. She looks like I've just taken her mugshot. Before she can say anything, I hail Symone, introduce them, and have Symone take the veteran spy through the company's online paperwork.

Marisa stands slightly behind me on my right. She whispers, "Kevin Winn's killer is right there in—"

"Yes, but we're going to keep that quiet for now."

She looks at me, confused until her thoughts clear. "Keep your enemy close?"

"Something like that. We need more information. I'll let you know when the time is right."

I cross to the dining room, Marisa following like a lost puppy.

Logan and Kayla look up from an array of screens, one with Emma's face on it. Excitement shining in their eyes. Logan says, "They're using a bunch of HPE supercomputers in MPPA configurations. You guys have it going down!"

"Yeah," I say as if I know what that means. "Of course."

I hand him the two memory sticks. He connects them to hardware. Kayla cracks her knuckles, eager for a chance to use her cryptology skills. Emma introduces them to the special squad from Sabel Technologies who will begin cracking the code.

With the geeks babbling in their unique dialect, I turn to my next problem, but Marisa tugs my elbow again.

"What is this?" she asks, pointing around the room.

Before I answer, Amit and Symone cross to us. Symone still can't figure out how to button her top two buttons, which draws a disapproving once-over from Marisa.

Symone gives the captain a right-back-at-ya glance, then says, "You sure know how to rock the dominatrix look … *Captain Redgrave*."

Marisa crosses her arms, tugging her jacket over more of her bare skin. She glances around the room for the plastic bag she brought.

"You expect me to work with a stripper?" Amit says, hooking a thumb at Symone. She leaves her mouth hanging open in disbelief.

"Sex worker," I correct her. "Are you implying state-sanctioned killers have the moral high ground?"

Symone grabs my arm and says, "She tells me her standard rate is €1,500 a day."

"That's hazardous-duty pay. Plus she's experienced, highly trained, and … Oh, what the hell, you can have the same, retroactive."

Symone squeals with delight.

I feel obliged to add, "But I keep the tips!"

She laughs.

"One other thing." I put a hand on her shoulder. "You've been amazing, Symone. What you did in the basement, and how you worked the chase, as a matter of fact, everything you've done from stealing the police car in the beginning—it's all outstanding work. I'm glad you didn't let me put you on a plane for the States. I'm standing here now because of you. I appreciate all you've done. Thank you."

Her arms snake around me before I can stop her. She holds me in a tight hug. When she lets go, her lips twist with a tremble and her eyes glaze over. She turns away before tears of gratitude flow. My praise must be the first appreciation she's heard since turning herself into an adult at fifteen. She goes back to online paperwork with Amit.

Marisa whispers, "Your girlfriend is the sex worker?"

"She's not my … long story."

"She is one who steals police car?"

"Depends. Are you asking out of idle curiosity or as an officer of the law?"

"Answer enough," she says.

Her scowl tells me her faculties are improving, which is good. Unfortunately, she still hasn't warmed up to me.

"What you do not answer," she says, tightening up as if preparing for a fight, "what goes on here? Why do rich, famous, and powerful people—Yeschenko, Bardon, you—come to Riga?"

It's a good sign for her recovery that she's asking. But it's also problematic: I'm not sure if I can plead the Fifth in a foreign country.

"Good question, Marisa. You know the joke, 'if I told you I'd have to kill you?' In this case, it's true with one exception: I wouldn't be the one killing you. One of the many rivals for that—" I point where Logan and Kayla are hard at work "—important piece of a trillion-dollar puzzle, would torture you for information before killing you."

My phone rings. Caller ID shows Betty Bardon. I answer, "Are you safe?"

"No," she says with resignation and defeat in her voice. "But that's not going to change. We need to meet."

"Why?"

"I need your help."

"Help getting out from under Yeschenko, or help getting him what he wants?"

"Don't give me shit, Jacob," she says with heat. "I don't need it, OK? I did what I had to do. I will continue to do what I must. Same as you. You're no different, you know. You convince yourself you're doing the right thing when in reality, there's no difference between Yeschenko and Sabel."

"A lot fewer people dead and damaged."

"Really? Have you done a corpse count? Statistically speaking, I doubt your theory will hold up. Look, I don't have time for this bullshit. Meet me at the Future Café in ten minutes."

She clicks off.

The room around me is silent. They heard my end of the conversation and have guessed who was on the other.

"OK, kids, family meeting." They move like zombies, afraid of what I have to say. Symone, Marisa, and Amit join as well. "We have to talk about Betty Bardon."

I explain Betty's request to meet and how it must be a trap. I ask them to consider whether I should walk into it and hope to walk out—or ignore her and lose the intelligence we might gain. I explain Betty's revolving door of loyalty. The speech she gave about Yeschenko protecting her and how it could be considered a traitor's admission. How she once convinced me her loyalties were to Pia Sabel despite the fact she had already enlisted and trained this crew, the ELA, for her end game. And now, I don't know where her loyalties lie. I wrap up by saying, "I'm telling you this because it is a trap, and that means you're all in danger if I go to this meeting. I won't endanger you without your understanding and acceptance of the risks. Do you want me to meet her?"

They stare at me, hoping I'll say something more. Something that will make the decision easier, or, better yet, make it go away so they don't have to deal with it. I stare each of them down in turn. This is the grownup world and it's time to make a grownup decision.

"Did she kill Kevin?" Francesca asks.

"No," Marisa and I answer in unison.

I give the captain a quick glance to keep her quiet on the topic. She gives me a look that tells me I need to explain what's going on in exchange. I weigh that one. I need both the captain and the murderer for my end game. I give Marisa an accepting nod, letting her know I'll explain it later.

"Are we in danger?" Chris asks.

"Since the day you signed up."

"How much danger is Betty in?" Kayla asks.

"If I don't figure out how to rescue her, I expect Yeschenko will kill her after she serves his purpose."

"What do they want?" Logan asks.

"Whatever is on that drive—decrypted. And they want me to rob Rafael of his piece, the *Chaac Equation*."

"We're not going to give it to them, right?" Francesca asks.

"At the moment, we don't have anything to give them. And the only bargaining chip they possess is Betty. And that brings me back to the question I have for you, as a family: Is Betty worth it to you?"

Silence.

There is a great deal of truth in silence. Support given too freely loses conviction after the first muzzle flash. On the other hand, aid hastily denied leads to regrets that change minds sparking ill-advised missions fueled more by enthusiasm than strategy.

Silence I like.

Amit looks at her watch out of boredom. Lives weighed against the greater good are common decisions for soldiers and spies. For everyone besides Amit and me, this is the first time.

No one looks to anyone else. They stare at the floor. It's a tough call: accelerate the dangers and threats against your own life to save a friend? It's easy to read about people making heroic decisions in books and imagine you'd risk it all if you were in the same situation. But the Holocaust proved how many people in real life were unable to stand up against tyranny when friends and neighbors were rounded up. They knew it was wrong, but they looked at each other and asked the silent question, *Is this OK?* Then they gave each other an equally silent response: *It must be.* And that made it so.

Except Symone. She watches me, her expression announcing she's going to save Betty even if everyone wants to hang the actress for treachery.

"I am not knowing Betty Bardon," Marisa says, "or any of you, but you never leave your own behind. Yeschenko is monster no one deserves. Even if she is traitor, you bring her home, no matter the danger. Deal with rest later."

CHAPTER 57

JACOB STEARNE

As I WIND MY WAY through an art show in Church Square, my team follows, searching for Yeschenko's men in the crowd. Haphazard aisles meander through the homemade kiosks with no discernible destination. A band plays on a small stage near the cathedral. It's not just art; there are a few farmers here as well. One has live chickens in his stall.

I stop and ask the farmer if he has a rooster. There is a bit of a language problem, but after a few exchanges, he raises a reddish-brown animal by the neck. I hold up the smallest bill I have, a €50 note. The rooster squirms and squabbles. With a favorable glance at my currency, the farmer says, "Prepare to go, American?"

I have no idea how much a rooster is worth, but I'm expecting change for the fifty. Nonetheless, a carrier would be nice and certainly worth a few euros. "Yes, thank you."

In one swift motion, he tosses the bird in the air, grabs its feet, slams it down on the table, produces a cleaver, and decapitates the animal. Blood spurts from the neck.

Whoa, homie! Mercury leans over my shoulder laughing hysterically. *You ain't gonna pass that off as a sacrifice, are ya? I mean, c'mon. Where the altar at? What kinda incantations you praying here?*

I'm too stunned to speak coherently. All I get out is, *I, I, I wasn't expecting that.*

Mercury says, *The man axed you if you want it prepared. What'd you think he be axing?*

I'm from farm country, where slaughtering your favorite hog for the holidays is one of many traditions. And I've seen infinite horrors on the battlefield. But something about the startled look on the face of that unsuspecting rooster as his head rolled off the table roils my stomach.

Mercury says, *Maybe cuz it's symbolic of the slaughter you be leading all these young people into.*

That roils my stomach even more. I can't take my eyes off the carcass as the farmer starts plucking. The grocery store is much more appealing, with tight plastic wrapped around various body parts, keeping the vivisection at a distance.

The farmer looks up at me, noting my greenish hue. He's not impressed. I hand him the fifty. "Keep the change and give the bird to someone hungry."

I walk away.

Mercury clamps my shoulder, *Cannot believe you done that, bro. All the times you said you was gonna do a sacrifice and then backs out, I thought for sure you was gonna forget all about that. Oh! But the look on your face was the best I seen in a millennium.*

I say, *Always happy to appease the gods.*

The rain has stopped and a cheerful sun breaks through angry clouds in a few places. The rain left the plaza fresh and clean with the mouthwatering odor of grilled meat wafting from some of the stalls. I've lost my appetite. Several shop owners stand outside their booths, soaking up the warmth.

Amit leads the kids in countersurveillance, having explained to them that "going gray" means blending in, looking like anyone on the street without drawing attention to yourself. She keeps chatter on the comm link to a minimum. They produce a final count of six Russians in standard bad guy suits: a dark blazer barely concealing a shoulder-holstered 9mm Grach.

After several rechecks of maps on my phone, I find the Future Café. It claims a chunk of the square with a canopy, the thick smell of freshly brewed coffee overpowering all other scents. At the far end, at a table pulled away from the rest for privacy, sits Betty, a beam of sunlight playing off her golden mane. A cup of candied coffee in a green paper cup rests at her fingertips. A small vase holds four flowers in front of her.

She's wearing a handsome business suit, not the dress she wore this morning.

My team checks in on the comm link.

Amit says, "You're in luck she still has the hots for you, Jacob. You can tell by her anxious smile."

Symone snaps back, "He's better than that. He showed up seven minutes late to make her want him, not because he wants her."

"He came late," Amit says, "to flush out the Russian observers. They get nervous when you're late and start looking around, wondering if you're blowing them off. Making them easier for us to spot. It's an old trick—and they fell for it."

I hush them both. I need to keep sharp for this conversation.

Two men walk past us carrying a large painting. They lean it against the café and go inside for a cup. I like the art, bright and colorful daisies slashed with a dripping red streak through the middle and probably titled, *Inhumanity.*

Betty offers a hand, to which I bow and shake lightly. A microphone rests in the middle of the flower arrangement. Sloppy. I pull out a seat and drop into it, assessing the situation. Beads of nervous sweat dot her forehead. An icebreaker would be a nice place to start.

Waving toward the art show, I ask, "Why Riga, Betty? Why here and not somewhere like Berkeley or Oxford or Zurich?"

She takes her time answering, adjusting her coffee to just the right spot. "This is where the Russians worked on *Chaac,* you know. I interned for them through the university. I had a great time here."

"Working for Viktor Popov?"

"As you well know, the head of Russia's clandestine service was a jerk. Lucky for me, he was not involved in the operation at my level. Although, he was the one who killed the project when we couldn't figure it out quickly enough to suit him. No, I spent most of my time working with other students and the grad school dean. It was a lot of fun. Why?"

"Just curious," I reply. "If you ask the average American where they'd like to go in Europe, Latvia doesn't usually make the list."

"I'm not average." She scoops sunlight in the palm of her hand. "Besides, they would change their minds if they came, don't you think?"

After an obligatory glance around at the square, I say, "Beautiful. Now I know why you're here. Why am I here?"

Four workers carry a sculpture past us. It's one of those anthropomorphic animal gods, a man's body with an animal head. I think it's a moose. They set it down next to the bloody daisies painting and go inside.

A darkness clouds her face. She leans forward, resting her elbows on the table, one hand folded over the other. "As I said, Mikhail threatened me and the ELA. Then Kevin was murdered. That changed my mind about our chances for survival. If the others found us, they would threaten us as well. I have no options, Jacob. But you do. You have three options."

She waits for me to react. I don't.

"First," she continues, "you could walk away. We're strangers to you. You owe us nothing."

"Except you're human beings, and we're supposed to love our neighbors. Go on."

"Second, you can take him on in a pitched battle." She pauses to gauge my reaction. I give her nothing. "He says you don't know his troop strength. I don't know what that means but he says you do."

He's right; I know exactly what it means. He could have ten or a hundred operatives in Riga. I've no idea. He let me see four at a time in the early going when it didn't matter. We counted six here today. I'm sure he has more, enough to take down my motley crew in seconds. I roll my hand for her to continue. "And third?"

"Or you can do what he wants."

I wait for her to detail what we both know he wants: everything.

After a pause, she indulges me. "He believes you have cracked the encryption by now. He wants the *Edison Data* and Rafael's *Chaac Equation*, delivered by midnight."

"Does he want sparkling or still water with his entrée?"

"It's nothing to joke about, Jacob!"

"If he thinks we cracked a 256-bit encryption scheme," I say, parroting the information fed into my ear by Kayla and our Sabel Tech team, "he's nuts. A sixteen-character password has 17 nonillion combinations. As I'm sure a physicist knows, that's a seventeen followed by thirty zeroes. Cracking that can take our system—one of the three most powerful computer systems in the world—up to five days. But this encryption is different. It doesn't use a password; it uses a 256-bit certificate, an exponential difference in complexity. The possible combinations for the certificate have 600 zeroes after it. The number half that big is called a centillion. They don't even have a word for a number with six hundred zeroes. Using all the computers in the world, you might crack it in several thousand years. You're more likely to vacation orbiting Alpha Centauri than see this decrypted in your lifetime." I pause to consider telling Kayla not to feed me that level of detail. I have no idea what she's talking about other than Alpha Centauri is the nearest star to Earth. "The bottom line is, if he's threatening to kill us all—we're already dead."

The color drains from Betty's face. She fidgets with her coffee cup.

A crew from the art fair drags two half-domes, each as big as an igloo, between us and the café. They set it down next to the bloody daisies and the moose-god with exhausted grunts, then go inside for coffee.

"You have to find a way," she says, desperation in her voice.

"I didn't set unrealistic expectations," I answer. "Did you?"

She grabs my wrist. "Jacob, there MUST be a way."

"Who encrypted it? Did you ask him?"

She shakes her head violently. "No idea. Can't you figure that out?"

Her voice cracks with so much emotion, I begin to wonder if she really expected me to do the impossible. Until now, I thought she'd given me garbage data so I would think I had it and skip town. Her anxiety splatters on me like paint from a brush. She's scared. Really scared.

"We can pray for a miracle," I tell her. "If a miracle happens, we're only halfway there. Why do you think Rafael is going to hand me the *Chaac Equation*?"

"I don't. You'll have to steal it from him."

"No problem there either, Betty." I cross my arms over my chest. I can't even look at her I'm so angry.

My eyes wander to the café while I think but all I can see is the igloo-like art-thing and the moose-god.

I look at Betty, who chews a fingernail. She's always had manicured beauty-queen nails. People who have those don't chew them. Her nerves are frayed to the breaking point. I say, "I'm sure you've met with Rafael. Where did you leave things with him?"

"He's willing to cut me in on whatever deal he makes if I deliver the *Edison Data*."

"Let me guess—your negotiations fell through when you leveled with him that the data was encrypted."

She looks at the ground far away from us. All the answer I need.

"You lied to me," I say while thinking out loud. "You didn't hear Joe Rouleau talking to Yeschenko in Russian. That was you. Yeschenko told you he played me like a chess game. Every move I've made he guided me into making. Finding the *Edison Data*, working on decrypting it, stealing from Rafael—he knew I'd do those things to save you."

She looks up at me with the pitiful face of a child desperate to be saved.

I pull the little flower vase closer to me and speak into the microphone. "If this was your chess game, Mikhail, you just resigned. Not only is what you ask impossible, you've seriously overestimated my interest in Betty."

I lean back, watching tears form in her eyes.

"At least you have choices," she says.

"Can you give me something to go on?" I ask. "Who might have encrypted it? Is this person still alive? Do we have one clue?"

"The Russians kept it encrypted. The key was in a computer with a removable drive. We would tell the professor when we were ready to run an experiment. He would go to the dean's office and get it. We were not allowed to know where it was or who kept it."

"Security measure," I respond while thinking. "You can't steal what you can't find. They didn't trust you."

"They didn't trust anyone." Her eyes search mine. "You have three choices, Jacob. If you walk away, I'll understand."

She knows I won't walk away while Mikhail Yeschenko is on the loose. Any other result will leave me marked for life. Since there are everything from stacks of Taliban fatwas to the Saudis' price on my head you might think I'd shrug off a Russian. But Yeschenko has deeper reach than the others, as evidenced by his presence in an EU country despite warrants for his arrest.

"Should a miracle befall us, where do I find Rafael?"

"He finds me," she says. "I'm sure he'll find you. He probably already has."

My thoughts turn to Amit Sofer's unexpected arrival.

Betty scrapes back her chair while the art-igloo people noisily scrape their project along the ground. They crowd around us, one dome on each side. Before I can react, they slam it down and shove the two halves together. I'm enclosed in their dome when I realize it's not a mistake. They've trapped me with Betty.

Only, they didn't trap me with Betty. In the near-blackout enclosure, small bits of sunlight creep between the cobblestones. It's enough light to see she isn't in here with me. Damn, I feel like an idiot. I knew there was something wrong with that igloo, but I let my situational awareness wander. Distracted by a woman. Again.

I pound my shoulder into the side. Solid.

"Amit! Amit, what's going on?" The silence in my earbud tells me comms are down.

Pulling the tactical blade from my belt buckle, I slash at the igloo. First thing I get is copper threads in a mesh underneath the first layer. It's a damn Faraday cage. No electronic signals get through. Beyond that is fiberglass. Cutting through it would take an hour. I pound my shoulder into it again. Still nothing.

I look around for a tool. The table and chairs are cheap plastic. Betty left a phone on the table. I pocket it.

I slash two holes near the base for my hands. Grabbing it tight, I squat and lift. It's heavy but it moves. I can lift it as high as my knees. Which is good, but I can't hold it and crawl out at the same time. I hear people shouting on the other side.

Suddenly, I see fingers from several hands grabbing the edge. More hands appear and grab the dome and hold it. Rolling out underneath, I thank the strangers who came to my aid. They laugh and pat me on the back as if I'd been the victim of a prank.

I smile, clap a couple backs while listening to the cacophony of voices in my comm link. The downside of using amateurs: no comms discipline. I scan the crowd for Betty.

Her phone rings in my pocket. As soon as I answer, Yeschenko's voice comes at me, "I have no more venom left. You force me to use old-fashioned methods in the Soviet tradition. Midnight, Jacob—no excuses."

He clicks off.

"Shut the hell up!" Amit's voice overwhelms the others in the comm link. When it quiets down, she says, "Jacob, they took Symone."

CHAPTER 58

BETTY BARDON

BETTY FEELS ILL FOLLOWING MIKHAIL Yeschenko into the special room. The room where the inside doorknob has been removed. Waving at Symone's hood, she says, "Take it off. You don't need to fear her in here."

After an approving nod from the boss, the guard unties the cord around Symone's throat and pulls the hood off. Eyes like fire glare back at Betty with such intensity, she turns away. She hears Symone's labored breathing, hot and angry.

"Just let her go," Betty begs. "Please. You don't need her."

"Shut up!" Yeschenko yells. "You screwed up everything. I would've had him at checkmate last night had you done as you were told, you fucking bitch! Since you arrogant Americans have cancelled my travel, I have no access to Fugaku in Japan or LUMI in Finland, the fastest computers outside the USA. Because of you, I am forced to rely on Sabel Technologies. No matter what Jacob says, they can do it."

Symone screams into her gag. To Betty's ear, it sounds like, "No, you're wrong." But she can't be certain.

"Shut up," Yeschenko yells at the girl and slaps her.

Symone kicks him.

Planting his palm on her face, he shoves her to the floor. Her butt lands on top of her bound hands.

Betty steps between the fallen girl and the Russian mobster. "You don't need her because you don't need the *Edison Data*. Forget the whole thing—it'll destroy you. Be happy that you're one of the richest men in the world."

"Rich is meaningless when you can buy nothing more than matryoshka dolls. They never take me seriously. The Americans shunned me in Davos, they ignored me at G20. Russians are footstools to them. That slut Sabel blew up my island in the Azores and the Portuguese never said a harsh word to her." He scowls in disgust. "I need *Chaac*. When I have it working, they will come to me begging on their hands and knees."

He paces to the door being held open by one of his men. Before crossing the threshold, he stops and says, "You will make a fortune too, Betty Bardon. More than Hollywood ever paid you."

The door clicks shut behind him.

Symone sits up awkwardly on her elbows, her face burning with fury.

Betty kneels next to her and pulls the gag off. "Let's get you up and—"

"Fuck you." Symone wastes no time wriggling to her feet. "Get these ropes off me."

Betty looks at the bindings on her wrists. She sees no knot or place to start unravelling them. "I don't see how. There's no—"

"You're fucking useless, you know that?"

Symone sits on the lone chair next to the loveseat. The only two pieces of furniture in the room. She strains and twists until she gets the bindings around the end of her toes. Finally, she pulls her hands around the front of her where she can see them. Betty is right: there is no knot. The ends are fused together. The girl huffs her frustration.

Then she turns her fiery gaze to Betty. "You sold out your friends? You know they just voted to risk everything to save your life. And I voted with them. What a mistake."

"Please, I had no choice. I did what I had to do."

"Before they voted, I told Jacob he had to save your scrawny ass. You know why? Because I felt bad for ratting you out to the Russian. Turns out, you don't need saving. You're in deep."

"You don't know what I've been through. I was pimped out to rich guys when I was a teenager. They made me do things. They always threatened me, even when they put me in the movies. I broke free to finish college and work on *Chaac*. Now they've come back, the rich and powerful, to make my life hell again. I have to do this or he will kill them all, including you."

"Cry me a river, bitch." Symone stands and gets nose to nose with Betty. "I heard kids going down under an assault rifle. Why? Because we love guns more than children. How do you think I feel every time I hear about another school shooting? Santa Monica, California; Roseburg, Oregon; Santa Fe, Texas; Parkland, Florida; Uvalde, Texas—so many shootings people don't even remember them all. Do you hear me whining about it? Do I use that as an excuse to be a traitor to my friends?"

Betty staggers back a step. Symone follows her.

"And now," the girl says, "I'm going to die because of you?"

CHAPTER 59

JACOB STEARNE

CHRIS AND KAYLA KEEP CHATTERING behind me as we wind through the streets and into the hotel. Amit has the good sense to say nothing. When an op goes south, you don't offer excuses, you don't blame anyone; you keep your mouth shut until you've figured out how to fix it. I know how to fix it, but the plan is so risky I want to go over it in my head one more time before saying anything.

I plow into the suite where Logan, who was on my spare comm link, has told Francesca the bad news. She embraces Kayla and they have a good cry. Logan and Chris shrug at each other and grimace in the way of men. I feel like telling Chris not to worry about it—it's not his fault. I should never have left Symone to watch a corner by herself. But that was impossible given the layout of the square. Everyone had a different corner, and we still had blind spots.

Through the primary bedroom's open door, I see Marisa lying on the bed with a laptop in front of her.

Staring blankly, I run my ideas through my head one more time. If every assumption I've made turns out to be correct, everyone wins. Except Yeschenko. If one piece of this puzzle doesn't fit—if someone doesn't answer the phone, if the guilty decide to fight, if one person doesn't show up on time—I'm screwed. Is it worth the risk?

I imagine Symone's eager face smiling at me. I remember the first time she covered for me when the cops were checking us out. I remember having to push my way out of her kiss right after. I remember her stealing a cop car for me—and she didn't know how to drive! Who could leave a delinquent like her in Yeschenko's grip?

Everyone in the room stares at me.

"Don't worry, people," I say. "I have a plan; I'll explain it in a few minutes. I have to do some quick research. Wait here."

Marisa looks up when I stride in the bedroom and close the door. "I heard this about Symone. I am sorry."

I nod at her while I dial up my support team. "Emma, please find the dean of the university where Betty Bardon did her internship in Riga. Text me the answer as soon as you have it."

Emma goes to work.

I cross the room to Marisa. Pointing at the screen, I ask, "What's that?"

"I check department server, see if I still have job."

"I promised you a promotion and you're going to get it. Call a press conference for fifteen minutes from now. Then pull up the murder video. I need to check something."

She eyes me for a beat, then starts typing a group text to the reporters. She's given up asking why, which saves us both time.

When she finishes the text, she sits up, swinging her legs over the edge. I sit next to her.

She points to the time stamp and presses play. "You have seen video?"

"No, but I know who killed Kevin Winn. The guilty always confess without realizing it. But there's something else I need to check."

Four frames show up on the screen, each showing a different floor of the crime-scene townhouse. No cameras in the stairwells. No audio. She scrubs ahead to where Betty and her group leave without Kevin. He's in the top frame, looking around the attic-office like a thief hunting for valuables. He tries the door to the Russian townhouse and finds a brick wall. In the bottom screen, Betty comes back in and goes up to the kitchen. She opens a drawer, takes cash out of a forgotten cookie jar, and turns around. She hesitates, her ear cocked toward the stairs as if she heard something. She shakes it off and leaves.

At the same time, in the top frame, a woman in a hooded cape comes through the Russian's secret door. Her face is intentionally obscured by the angle—as if she already knew where the cameras were. Behind her stands Kaspars Krollis. Next to Krollis is the sinister form of Mikhail Yeschenko. Kevin Winn appears stunned by the caped woman. He backs up toward the stairs while talking and pointing at her. He gestures toward Yeschenko. Unwittingly, he has sealed his fate by recognizing the sanctioned oligarch.

Yeschenko touches the caped woman's shoulder and speaks. She steps forward an arm's length from Kevin. Though she faces away from the camera, the woman takes the posture of someone yelling in anger: leaning forward, her chin out front, her feet ready to spring forward. Kevin runs down the stairs out of camera range.

Yeschenko slaps a knife in her hand, points at the stairwell, and shouts orders. The woman hesitates, then follows Kevin.

Lieutenant Krollis makes a call on his phone. On the video of the floor below, the camera shows the room where the single shoe was found. There are no shoes.

"This is time when Krollis calls for police," Marisa says. "He claims tip from citizen."

Little movement registers for three full minutes.

"What they do in stairwell so long?" Marisa asks.

"Arguing," I tell her. "Kevin caught her working with the Russians. Yeschenko ordered her to kill him, not only to solve the problem but also to test her loyalty. She's trying to win Kevin over, make him join her side. She hoped to get out of killing him. But it didn't work."

"Why would young woman do this?" Marisa asks.

"Nothing terrifies the human mind as much as absolute change. Francesca's dad buys oil, Yeschenko sells it. They've made millions together for decades. This technology would be catastrophic to their industry. They talked Francesca into infiltrating the group who might destroy their business, and with it, her family's way of life."

"She does this for fancy clothes." Marisa shakes her head sadly. Then she scrubs ahead on the video. Within seconds of each other, all the screens fill with movement. The caped woman runs from the stairs, briefly showing her face to the camera, and rushes into the Russian townhouse. At that moment, I sneak in the kitchen. Krollis shuts the fake door behind the caped killer. Then the police burst in on the ground floor, and Kevin Winn staggers from the stairwell spewing blood. She stops it there, we both know the rest.

"Why Krollis call police so fast?" she asks.

"They wanted to pin the murder on Betty," I tell her. "Their plan was to blackmail her, throw her in jail, then Yeschenko could show up like a savior. The price of her freedom would be the *Edison Data*. She could give it up or rot in a Latvian prison for murder." I pause to sigh. "They got me instead, and that messed them up. But the real evidence is that cape. Did you find it?"

"Yes. Was in other townhouse. Much blood. Cape belongs to Betty Bardon. We also have video next day. Killer brings shoe, Krollis plants it at crime scene. He was so confident he only plants one shoe and one bloody footprint on stairs." Marisa points at the screen. "Did you see who you expect?"

"The killer, yes. She was quick to implicate her friends when telling their stories. Twice she asked Betty for the location of the data. She kept throwing shade on Betty, and she wasn't waiting on the sidewalk with the others. But I didn't expect Yeschenko in person. Now that I see how it went down, I realize this was a project he wanted to personally supervise. Too much at stake to leave it to his lieutenants. But that raises another question: How do so many Russians get into Latvia after the invasion of Ukraine? Aren't there supposed to be restrictions?"

"Office of Citizenship and Migration Affairs, OCMA," she says. "Someone there is corrupt. How do we find who?"

"In the spy business, people are corrupted with MICE: Money, Ideology, Coercion, or Ego. We can rule out ideology. Ego is tough, so we look for someone with financial ties to Yeschenko. Or someone Yeschenko could coerce."

My mind chews on that one for a beat. There's an idea just out of reach in that concept. Something someone told me that can unravel the corrupt official. Trying to figure it out feels like catching fog.

"Is this video ready to send out to the press?" I ask.

"Emma makes edited version for email and set up full version on cloud drive." Marisa shakes my arm to get my attention. "I arrest the killer now?"

CHAPTER 60

JACOB STEARNE

WHEN I COME OUT OF the bedroom with Marisa, I pull Logan aside. "Before Kevin was killed, you and Francesca had bottle service in the VIP section of a night club, posted it on Insta. Which one of you paid for that?"

"Neither," he says with a laugh. "Her dad was in town with some businessmen. We went up to say hello, but they were leaving. They left like three bottles of booze, so we partied."

"He works for Olio Completo, right? Who were the other guys?"

"Beats me," Logan says. "It was all in Italian or Russian. Not like they cared about me. Ask Francesca."

I consider this, but there's no need to dig any deeper on that lead. I know what's on the end.

Next, I find Kayla. "When I give you the signal, look at your phone and announce the Sabel team has cracked the code."

"They have?" she asks.

Kids. I'm working with kids.

I put a hand on her shoulder. "You're going to lie. I have a reason, trust me."

"Oh, got it."

"Everyone, gather round." They form a circle around me. "The Russians beat us, and that's on me. We're going to get Symone back. Whether Betty comes along will be up to her. To win Symone's freedom, we will need to give him the *Edison*—"

"You are NOT giving *Edison* to Yeschenko!" Amit shouts.

"I'm not leaving an eighteen-year-old to die."

"You're talking about giving up the future of the world to save one life! There are always difficult decisions to be made, tradeoffs, balances—you know this. You must weigh the fate of the many against the life of one individual. You know the answer."

While all eyes are on her, I give Kayla the signal.

I answer Amit, "We can't leave them behind."

"Today's oligarchs," she says, "the ultrawealthy, are the same as the fascists of the last century. Giving this to Yeschenko is the same as giving Hitler the Chancellorship in 1933. The world will be forced to defer to him like a Saudi prince."

Kayla leaps to her feet, staring at the phone in her hand. "They did it! They cracked the encryption."

The group stares at her, blankly. The news takes a moment to sink in. When it does, Amit's argument becomes the only thing they can think about. Before that, it was an academic exercise—this makes it real. They turn to Amit, then me. Francesca looks overwhelmed and backs away from the group. The others sink in posture. Difficult, adult decisions need to be made.

Emma texts me the name of the university dean in question. Things begin to make sense. How Yeschenko entered Latvia with a crowd of mercenaries. Who controlled Krollis and how they planned to blackmail Betty. Even why the Secretary of State saved me from summary execution during the chase. But exposing this official won't be easy.

"I'm going to save them," I announce. "The only question left is if you're going to help me."

"I will stop you," Amit says.

"You'll try." I turn away, dial a number, and cross the room to find some privacy. "Mr. President, I need a favor."

"I haven't had my breakfast yet, Jacob. You need to respect the time zone once in a while."

"Sorry, sir, but if there were anyone else who could do this, I would've asked them." I go on to explain what I need him to do. After complaining to someone in the background about his coffee, he then complains about taking orders from a civilian. I remind him it's his pet project. He sighs, then tells me he'll get right on it.

The picture of what will happen between now and Yeschenko's midnight deadline has formed in my brain. Everything is going according to plan. Except Amit. She hasn't called anyone. When Kayla made her announcement, I was certain Amit would make a call. Maybe she really is on her own. Maybe her husband is in Monaco like she said. Maybe Rafael really did turn on her.

"Jacob," Chris says, waving me over. The four of them stand shoulder-to-shoulder: Chris, Kayla, Francesca, and Logan. "We have decided to help you. We love Symone, we would never leave her behind. We trust you."

Standing to the side, Amit rolls her eyes and turns away. I'll deal with her later.

"And we have so many questions for Betty," Francesca says.

"What questions?" Marisa asks, stepping forward.

"Like why she killed Kevin Winn," Francesca says.

"She did not," Captain Marisa Redgrave says with authority. "You did."

Everyone, including Amit, gasp. Marisa grabs Francesca firmly by the bicep and turns her to face the others. Francesca's face explodes in fury at the accusation.

"Everyone make elaborate stories," Marisa says, "protecting Betty Bardon. You think she went back to townhouse alone. But that night, while you talk on sidewalk, Francesca went ahead to clubs. She tells you this. She lied. She did not do what she said. Instead, she leaves you, goes to back of townhouse, enters place next door. With help from Yeschenko and Krollis, she put on cape of Betty Bardon, then kills Kevin, then run down alley. She meets you on sidewalk up the street. You think she come back from direction of clubs like she say. But no. She is killer."

CHAPTER 61

CAPTAIN REDGRAVE

CAPTAIN MARISA REDGRAVE LEADS FRANCESCA Bartoli to the lobby with the girl's hands cuffed in front of her. The press has cameras and a makeshift podium set up to the side of the grand entrance. Outside the clouds have closed ranks; rain is imminent.

Francesca tries to hide by hanging her head and letting her hair fall across her face.

Parking the girl beside the stand, Marisa steps up. At the last second, she remembers she still hasn't put her shirt on underneath her jacket. The concussion is still messing with her. That, and the rush to get things done. Touching it to make sure it's at least buttoned in front, she rationalizes, if Sanna Marin, Prime Minister of Finland, can rock this look, why not Marisa Redgrave?

In her native tongue, she addresses the reporters. "Two days ago, I made a grave mistake—I followed orders."

As expected, the reporters' collective attention rose from their notepads to her.

"I took charge of the search for the missing suspect, Jacob Stearne. Those were my orders. I came before you lashing out at Mr. Stearne and instigating a citywide hunt for him. Since then, I have reviewed bodycam videos from the arresting officers. In these videos I found evidence proving Jacob Stearne could not have committed the murder. Further, Lieutenant Kaspars Krollis intentionally misdirected the officers on scene, forcing them to draw the wrong conclusion."

She waits for the reporters to jot those notes. Their surprised faces bobble up and down between their pads and her.

"Discovering the fugitive had been wrongfully accused and detained, I investigated further. I found evidence planted by someone to frame the American actress, Betty Bardon. A tip led me to a laptop that had been surreptitiously recording events at the murder site. With the help of Sabel Technologies, we were able to recover what the conspirators believed they had deleted: video of the murder conspiracy. I have emailed copies of this to you moments ago."

Marisa smiles as the stunned reporters dig out their phones to check their email.

"This is Francesca Bartoli." She tugs at her captive's arm, bringing her forward. "I am holding her as the primary suspect in the murder of Kevin Winn. She appears in the murder video wearing a cape belonging to Betty Bardon. Later, she planted a shoe belonging to Ms. Bardon at the murder scene, also on the video."

One reporter asks, "You used the word 'recover.' Why was that necessary?"

Exactly the question she wanted someone to ask. She feels an increase in confidence that her concussion is under control. She says, "Lieutenant Kaspars Krollis reported the laptop had self-destructed. In fact, Sabel Technologies was able to record him attempting to reset the laptop and erase the video. He will be brought in for questioning."

"Why did Ms. ..." a reporter checks his notes for the name "... Ms. Bartoli kill the American?"

"We hope she will reveal this during questioning."

A voice from the back asks, "Was Lieutenant Krollis working alone?"

The last question was one she hoped to avoid. "Lieutenant Krollis will be given a chance to answer questions and cooperate. He has not yet been charged. It is early in the investigation. However, evidence points to a conspiracy between Francesca's father, Tommaso Bartoli, an executive at Olio Completo, and Mikhail Yeschenko."

"Krollis issued an arrest warrant for you hours ago," the woman in front says. "Is this a retaliatory accusation?"

This is what she feared: the press taking the word of a lieutenant over that of a captain because one is male and the other is not. "He does not have a warrant because he has no evidence of kidnapping. Betty Bardon is not being held by me."

"Is she being held by someone else?" a voice calls out.

"I understood she was visiting an acquaintance. Whether that is by force, as Krollis suggests, or by choice, I do not know."

"Why would Yeschenko and Bartoli commit murder?" the reporter at the back asks again.

All their faces turn to her, leaning in, waiting for her reply.

Jacob filled Marisa in on the connection between the Bartoli father and daughter, and his business partner, Yeschenko. The evidence is flimsy, and she still needs to confirm the sighting at a nightclub VIP section, but it fits. If she spills too much, the others involved might get away. She takes a quick peek at her phone. Jacob has not yet texted her the name of Krollis's accomplice. The right thing to say is: the investigation is ongoing. But that won't strike fear into the hearts of the guilty and force them into the light.

"Bartoli and Yeschenko conspired to stop research and development on a new form of battery that is exponentially better than what we have today. The product would be worth trillions of euros—but it would end the oil industry. They conscripted Francesca into their plan."

A reporter at the back shouts, "They were working with Lieutenant Krollis directly?"

"Krollis was working with someone higher in his chain of command. We will be talking to the relevant parties shortly and expect to have more information—and other arrests—this evening."

Silence greets her last word. They're stunned. Not an easy feat with a pack of rabidly cynical journalists. Marisa feels good about her delivery.

Concussion be damned, she's back.

After a beat, one man clears his throat and asks, "How high up?"

"High enough to allow a banned Russian oligarch into the country."

She gives a tight smile while they chew on who could approve such a thing. At the same time, she feels her phone vibrate. In one quick glance, she sees the name of the official Jacob believes is working for Yeschenko. Marisa is shocked. It cannot be. Can she trust him to be right about this? If Jacob is wrong, her career will be over by morning. He better have evidence. Hard, undeniable evidence.

"Thank you," Marisa says, "I must get Ms. Bartoli booked now."

She grabs her suspect and leads her out the door. Once in the squad car, she sends a text to Yeschenko's collaborator. "Did you see my press conference? Meet me in the cathedral crypt in one hour."

CHAPTER 62

JACOB STEARNE

WHEN MARISA RETURNS FROM BOOKING our killer, I go over my plan to trap the conspirators who prodded the poor Italian girl into doing their bidding. The first thing I notice is Marisa's confidence has returned. A little too much. She argues with me about the details. Eventually, she agrees. It will require complex choreography and Dubra's help, but she can pull it off. To make it all work, I'll have to take it one step at a time.

First up is getting the encryption certificate to unlock the *Edison Data*. Sabel Tech has a team working with our cryptologist, Kayla, and she tells me the certificate could come in any of a hundred forms. It could be as simple as a passphrase, or a retinal scan, or as complex as a specific piece of music. Or all three. With it, I have half the negotiating power I need. Then I'll have to find Rafael and his *Chaac Equation*. If I fail any part of that, the President of the United States and Pia Sabel will be disappointed in me—but Symone will pay with her life.

Marisa and I head out on foot into a dark and stormy evening. The city beats out its endless rhythm of accelerating and decelerating engines punctuated by wailing brakes. Voices call out to friends across the crowd. The streetlights are on, and the cobblestones glisten with rain. In the square, the fabric of the artists' stalls flap and snap in the wind's random cadence.

Emma calls. "I've got the financials for the Latvian officials you asked about. I found a minister who just went into the shipping business—a week ago. I think it's the one you want. Details in an email coming your way. Now, you want Kayla on this comm link, right? No

"

one else?"

"Yes. If Amit wants in, tell her there are technical difficulties."

"Got you covered." She clicks off.

I read the email. At the top is a disclaimer that reads: "This information was gathered without international approval from the governments involved. Do not, under any circumstances, reveal the source."

Sabel Technologies runs taps on the email, phones, and bank accounts of government officials from Tokyo to Paris to Lima—allies and enemies alike—on behalf of the USA. Every conspiracy theorist worth his rant knows about it—and it's up to me to keep the secret?

Reading the contents proves fascinating, though. I find it interesting that a Latvian official would buy an oil tanker outright when all their previous investments had been safe mutual funds.

After walking a block in silence, Marisa asks, "How did you first come to suspect Francesca?"

"She made a few suspicious statements that caught my ear," I say, "but weren't conclusive. But when we went to your house, I had her on lookout duty on a backstreet. One the Russians would never pass by. When we picked her up, the Russians were right behind us. She had to have called them. An ace Bolt driver saved our skin."

"I am not understanding why she do this. After finding the shoe, I thought Kayla because she has many new clothes."

"Kayla wanted to be like Francesca: rich, exotic, and fashionable. She copied everything her Italian friend did. She should've stuck with poetry."

When we reach the cathedral, we make our way down through two basement levels to the crypt entrance. Marisa translates a posted sign that says they close soon.

The cathedral's crypt is exactly as I expected: a small, tight stone chamber with a low ceiling. Like most church crypts built back in 1211, it's crammed full of sarcophagi. It appears the workers dropped their four-ton load when they got tired, not because it was in a specific place. Bare bulbs circle the room on strung wires. My hair brushes the ceiling as I squeeze in. Marisa follows me through the narrow spaces.

A dark figure leans against a marble slab at the back.

As I get closer, I see our contact wears a designer broadbrim hat with a plaid raincoat draped over her arm. She's early forties, tall and lean with auburn hair, wearing a stylish pantsuit.

"Minister Krasnova," I say, stopping ten feet away.

Marisa checks my flank. There are many hiding places for henchmen in this mess of rock.

Anna Krasnova pushes off the monument and takes two confident strides forward, moving with the poise and grace of the privileged class. She stops with her feet apart, arms folded across her chest. "So, *Le Héros de Paris* in person? *Enchanté.* Not as handsome as Timothée Chalamet, though."

I have no idea who Chalamet is, so her insult goes to waste—but not unnoticed. Insults are a sign of insecurity.

"What is this?" she asks. "Why are you here?"

"You sold out to Mikhail Yeschenko."

She huffs. "I have done no such thing. How dare you insult a minister of Latvia. You Americans are so arrogant, you think—"

"You know what tipped me off?" I ask. "When you told Captain Redgrave the American Secretary of State had called on my behalf. Neville and I go way back. If he called you, it would've been to assist in having me shot on sight. I wondered why you would lie to stop the search. Only one person wanted me alive at that point: Mikhail Yeschenko."

"Why would he want you alive?"

"Because he can't get his fingers wrapped around a man named Rafael Tum and the treasure he carries, known as the *Chaac Equation.* Yeschenko figures I could get it. He needed me alive when Captain Redgrave's search party was breaking down doors with assault rifles."

"Mildly amusing bit of fiction you have there. You'll have to develop the characters and work on the plot if you want anyone to care." She shifts the weight of her raincoat as if she were bored. "What does any of this have to do with me?"

"I need the encryption certificate for the *Edison Data.*"

"I have no idea what you're talking about."

"When I asked Betty Bardon why she chose Riga to resurrect the *Edison Data*, she waxed poetic about her time at the University of Latvia. As you well know, she worked on a Russian project for a man named Viktor Popov in the university's graduate program."

"Betty Bardon the actress?" She draws a bored face. "I know nothing of her. How would I know where she studied?"

"What caught my ear was when Betty mentioned the university's dean of graduate studies. Most students would reflect on other students, teacher aides, maybe a professor, but she specifically mentioned the dean."

"So?"

"You were the dean back then. According to a simple web search, you were installed over the protests of the professors. Installed at the insistence of the university's biggest benefactor: Viktor Popov. He insisted on you as dean despite your lack of qualifications. Quite a stir in the press back then. You were involved in his project."

She does her best to cover up her astonishment at the depth of my knowledge.

"Krasnova," Marisa states flatly. "This is Russian name. Not Latvian."

"I was born here," Krasnova spits back. "My parents immigrated from Russia during the Soviet occupation. That's not a crime."

"The Office of Citizenship and Migration Affairs reports to you," I say. "For some strange reason, they let Mikhail Yeschenko into the country despite the EU ban."

"I don't have time to watch every visa application. You're wasting my time with these childish accusations." She faces Marisa. "You are fired."

"You didn't ask how we know," I tell her as she tries to move past me in the tight confines.

She stops inches from my face. "You have nothing."

She's right. I have nothing except a few things Sabel Technologies gleaned from illegal surveillance. I can't tell her where the intel came from without creating an international incident.

So I lie. "Francesca Bartoli confessed."

In my peripheral vision, I see Marisa holding firm to my story even though we hadn't discussed it.

"See she gets a good lawyer to defend her from defamation." Krasnova pushes past me.

"We have Yeschenko's visas," I lie again. I'm getting good at it. "They bear your signatures."

It stops her in her tracks. Speaking over her shoulder, she says, "What is this? Some kind of shakedown?"

"Like I said—I want the *Edison Data* decrypted. You have the certificates on you because Yeschenko is pulling out tonight. You're going to meet him and sell it to him. All I'm asking is for a copy."

"Why do you want it?" she asks, her voice shaky with uncertainty. "Do you plan to sell it to Yeschenko?"

"My boss wants it. If you give it to me, Yeschenko won't know for a year at least. And then he'll have no idea if we used a brute-force decryption or stumbled on the password."

She glances at Marisa. "And you? Does your new American friend reward you in some way I should know about?"

"I am here," Marisa answers with ice, "only to confirm accuracy of story."

Facing forward, Krasnova thinks about it for a long time. Finally, a resigned sigh escapes her, and she faces me. "If I give you what you need, you'll forget about a Russian citizen who wanted to visit a dying relative?"

"I don't care about Latvia's visas."

Krasnova turns to Marisa, "And you?"

"Visa problems are least of my worries," Marisa says.

The minister's face twists while she considers the risks of trusting us. After a beat, she says, "You have a recording device?"

I've been recording everything since I walked in. Play-acting, I produce my phone and pretend to click buttons.

"It's an audio file," she says, "MP4 format. You edit it to this stanza from a poem by Latvian poetess Aspazila. Ready?" She waits for my nod, then inhales like an actress and speaks Latvian for thirty seconds.

We're silent a moment. She gives me a nod that it's done.

"It's part of a love poem," she says. "In English it would be: A new storm of feelings I raised, / New stars of beauty I lit, / I warmed your high hall / By the hot breath of my soul / And snapped your stiffness / With a rustling flood of joy."

"Nice," I say, because love poems are not my thing and I've no idea whether it was good or bad, much less how I'm supposed to respond.

In my ear, Kayla says, "They think it might work, but they'll need to scrub the echo from the room you're in. It'll take some time. They want you to stay with her for fifteen to twenty minutes."

"How do I know this is the real deal?" I ask Krasnova.

"You'll have to trust me." She tosses me a contemptuous look, then strides to the crypt exit.

CHAPTER 63

JACOB STEARNE

INTERIOR MINISTER KRASNOVA DOESN'T LEAVE because the Prime Minister of Latvia steps down into the room. Short white hair and wire-rimmed glasses accent a stark face topping a dark suit and equally dark tie. Stick thin, he moves as stiffly as a Claymation creature. He looks Krasnova over with a cold discerning eye before glancing at Marisa and me.

"President Williams called me," he says, his deep baritone resonating in the stone room. The man is a professional public speaker, and it shows. "He told me to wait outside the crypt until Jacob Stearne called me in. This was a most condescending act for a superpower, the likes of which we've all come to both expect and dread. If we want American aid, we must occasionally dance to their whimsical tune. It pisses me off."

"Nice to meet you, too, sir," I say, adding a little bow.

Off to my right, nearly hidden amongst the coffins, Marisa stares with her mouth open. Guess she's never met the guy before. When she senses my glance, she straightens up, pulls her jacket over more of her bare skin, and puts on her confident professional look.

"I fail to see the international urgency of what I just heard," the Prime Minister says. "Don't get me wrong—giving a visa to a banned Russian is a terrible thing. Anna will be reprimanded."

"Reprimanded?" I can't hide my astonishment.

Aw dude, Mercury says while leaning an elbow on the Prime Minister's shoulder, *you be fighting the wrong battle here. This ain't about right and wrong.*

Yes, it is, I reply. *What she did was wrong. Criminal.*

Nah, man, this be about optics—parliamentary optics. These two ministers be from the same party. He can't make her look bad—cuz that would make him look bad.

He's putting party over country? That's bullshit.

Bullshit, goose shit, bat shit, who cares? Mercury says, *You gots to change your tune cuz right now, if you want to save your girl, you gotta choose being effective over being right.*

Mercury waves an arm at the pair of politicians as if they were discounted jewelry on the Home Shopping Network.

"Yeschenko organized a conspiracy to commit murder," I tell him. "He's on the video Captain Redgrave sent to the press. Ms. Krasnova here let him into the country."

The man stands still for a long moment while he calculates the political angles. He glances at Marisa. "Do you plan to press charges, Captain Redgrave?"

Marisa's eyes light up when he says her name. It's a kick the first time a prime minister knows you without introduction. She says, "Arresting a minister would be problem. This I not do without your approval, sir."

He nods approvingly and gives her the slightest of smiles. Facing me, he says, "Our little country fares well against corruption, Mr. Stearne. Under my administration, we have risen two places in the world rankings of corrupt nations. We're now only nine places behind the USA. A simple oversight involving visas would be torn apart by the more cynical elements of the opposition, which would cause a depressing wave of hopelessness in the civil service. That would lead to a loss in momentum, allowing others to believe the law doesn't matter anymore. We would follow Honduras into anarchy. Our country would crash right out of the European Union. It would be a disaster."

He finishes with the smile of a professional salesman and turns slowly to Marisa for her approval.

She doesn't like it but lacks the power to go against him.

"Corruption is a nasty problem," I say. "I'm glad to hear you've made strides in combating it.”

“Thank you,” he says.

“Naturally, you would want Captain Redgrave to trace the sale of the *Gabija.*”

Krasnova takes a deep and sudden breath. He notices and looks a question at me.

Barred by my company from revealing my source for financial information, I decide to lie about where it came from.

“Not the Latvian goddess of the hearth,” I tell him. “In this case, I’m referring to an oil tanker carrying 340,000 barrels of Russian crude that left Primorsk two days ago and is now parked in the Gulf of Finland, waiting for the new owner’s instructions.”

“Russian oil is embargoed.” He turns slowly toward Interior Minister Krasnova.

“It’s, uhm, just an investment,” she says. “If the embargo is lifted, I win big. If not, I lose. High-risk investment. That’s all. Nothing more. I swear.”

I add, “When the sale closes in the morning, you’ll own 100 percent of the ship and its cargo, Ms. Krasnova. Excluding the value of the tanker, the oil is worth €35 million at today’s rate. The key question here is: How much did you pay for that investment?”

“I don’t see what business that is of yours,” she snaps back.

“It’s my business,” Marisa says.

“Mine too,” the Prime Minister says with an eyebrow raised.

Krasnova’s gaze meets her boss’s for a second, then flicks away. She stumbles through half-formed words before looking at me. “Since you pretend to know everything, you tell us. And tell us your source, as well.”

I can’t blame this one on Francesca. If I do, Yeschenko will think she’s singing like a canary and make her his next victim. I tell them, “When I called the State Bank of Luxembourg posing as Ms. Krasnova’s aide, they were eager to explain the transaction.”

Krasnova gasps.

“They said you invested €100,000,” I continue. “They also mentioned the paperwork for converting the oil’s source from Russia to Norway is already finished. They sent it to you via email with a copy to Yeschenko. That email is what we Americans call a smoking gun. Your €100,000 investment appreciated 350-fold overnight. Yeschenko sold you a tanker at an unbelievable discount. Emphasis on unbelievable."

The Prime Minister's face turns from sickly green to explosive red in less than a second as the implication for his party sinks in.

Suddenly, Latvia's Interior Minister looks a good deal whiter. She stammers before getting a grip on herself. "He made that up. He's, he … What is your game?"

"Easy proved," Marisa says, holding out her palm. "Show us email on your phone. Personal email. If nothing there, he is liar. Otherwise …"

Krasnova's eyes flash around the three of us as her hands ball into fists. A grim scowl crosses her face. She turns and runs to the stone stairs.

Marisa flies through the crypt like a winged ghost. She tackles the minister, crashing them both to the unforgiving stone steps. The captain cuffs her like a champion calf roper and stands, one foot on either side of her suspect. She rifles through the minister's purse, comes up with a phone, and drops the bag.

"What is code?" Marisa asks.

"I'm not telling you!" Krasnova's face constricts with rage.

Marisa tugs Krasnova's hair until her face is off the stone. Holding the phone up to the woman, the phone unlocks on facial recognition. Marisa hunts around the screen for a few seconds while the Prime Minister crosses to her and looks over her shoulder. Their expressions change when they find it. They both look at me with a hint of appreciation, then they both turn to Krasnova with severe disappointment.

The Prime Minister claps Marisa's shoulder. "What is your party affiliation?"

"None."

"If you join my party, you can arrest her right now. If you're with the opposition, it would look like political persecution. I don't want her getting off on a technicality. If you're with me, we are weeding out our own corruption. It would prove our commitment."

Marisa stares blankly at him while her cheek flexes. She's grinding her teeth to keep her outrage in check.

"Being effective is better than being right," I tell her.

After a moment of thought, she agrees with a nod to the prime minister. I help her bring Krasnova to her feet.

"Hold on a second," I tell them.

Taking Marisa's phone, I find her contact group for the reporters and send it to myself. I then send a group text to the reporters that reads, "The Prime Minister and his most trusted officer have just made a shocking arrest at the cathedral. Get there before they leave." I show it to them, and press send.

Marisa rolls her eyes, her head shaking back and forth.

"Well done," the Prime Minister says with a grin. He punches my shoulder. "A little political theater can turn a betrayal into an opportunity. You will be our spotter. Let us know when the press is upstairs so we can make our grand exit."

"No problem," I answer. "You know, it's none of my business, but I noticed you're in need of a new minister. Have you seen Captain Redgrave give a press conference? I've been on the wrong end of a couple and I can tell you she really strikes fear into the hearts of fugitives."

He laughs. "I see why President Williams makes calls on your behalf."

I trot up the stairs, leaving them behind. The cathedral is closing up. One of the Lutheran priests flicks a switch on the upper basement floor just as I reach it and the entire level is plunged into darkness.

Making my way across the stone, I hear footfalls timed to land at the same time as mine. I change my stride to double-check and, as I thought, the shoes behind me miss the beat. It's the telltale sound of someone following me. The sensation of static electricity runs up my spine and creeps into my hair. The back of my neck itches in anticipation of a truncheon landing on it from behind. I stop in the dark. Then I realize who it is.

"I'm glad you're here," I say into the blackness. "I'm going to need your help."

CHAPTER 64

JACOB STEARNE

THREE MINUTES LATER, I'M OUTSIDE striding across Church Square. Behind me, the priest yells at me for letting the reporters into the cathedral at closing time. Walking backward, I gesture skyward, and call out, "I just spoke to God, and he wants you to give them shelter."

On cue, lightning strikes near enough for the thunder to arrive half a second later. The priest flips me off and yells something about family and dinner in a mix of English and Latvian. I want to tell him if he'd gone Catholic, he wouldn't have family problems, but I'm in a hurry. No time for career counseling.

The art fair is now an after-party. A woman hacks a laugh, someone rattles a cocktail shaker, music blasts out of a kiosk. Grilled sausages and wood fired grills scent the air. My boots slap the wet cobblestones as I toss the occasional paranoid glance behind me.

My first call is to Emma. "Monitor my calls and tell the Sabel Tech people working with Kayla about them. They'll know what to do."

"Will your calls be clean?" she asks.

"Squeaky."

"Oh, well. I was hoping to have something to sell the French tabloids now that you're a Euro-star."

"Thanks, Emma. At least you're honest about it." I click off.

Next, I call my psychiatrist. When he answers, I tell him I need to calm myself by reciting a poem. Since Ms. Sabel once ordered him to take my calls no matter what, he obliges. Although he makes it abundantly clear he isn't happy about asking another patient to wait while he deals with the company's prima donna hit man.

"Are you recording this?" I ask. When he says he is, I start reciting the last stanza of a poem by Wilfred Owen called, *Dulce et decorum est:*

My friend, you would not tell with such high zest

To children ardent for some desperate glory,

The old Lie: *Dulce et decorum est*

Pro patria mori.

When I finish, I pause, then say, "Thanks for listening, Doc. I feel better."

"Isn't that an old anti-war poem from the First World War?" he asks.

I'm impressed he recognized it and tell him it is. I add that in prophetic irony, the poet died in battle not long after writing it. Doc is confused about why I didn't feel well and how reciting a poem made me feel better. Professional curiosity, he says. I tell him not to worry about it; sometimes strange things work for us. I click off. I reach the far side of the plaza as another lightning bolt strikes close by.

Catching Krasnova was a high, but I'm reminded of my most important mission: freeing Symone. For that to happen, I need to get Rafael Tum to give me his *Chaac Equation*, a thousand-page document worth a trillion dollars. That ancient revolutionary wants my *Edison Data*. I have three ELA kids with no experience and an ex-Mossad agent who I trust like a venomous snake. This isn't going to be easy.

Turning down the narrow cobblestone streets, I don't hear my shadow behind me anymore. That's not good. Rain brings the visibility down to ten yards. Suddenly, I feel alone and vulnerable. I begin to sense a certain dread. Like I'm carrying a crystal chandelier ready to crash into a million shards at the first whack of a cudgel. If only I could see the future. Just a minute ahead of me. What's around the next corner? Was that dark figure darting into the café a local guy ducking out of the rain— or one of Yeschenko's goons?

C'mon, homie, Mercury says floating along side of me. *Knock off this passive-aggressive shit. You know I can't tell you nothing about what's coming.*

Why not? I ask. *What good is hanging out with a god if he can't spare me a calamity or two?*

First of all, you a walking calamity. Every damn thing you touch gets all calamitous. That's why you so fun to watch—you be like Schadenfreude-a-minute. Second of all, if I tell you the future, then you gonna try to avoid it—and if you do, that means I didn't tell you no future. I ain't letting you make a fool outta me.

Hold up. I stop walking and look around. *I swear on my mother's future grave I won't try to avoid anything you tell me.*

Ain't nobody gonna walk into a trap if they know they's gonna get shot. You'd avoid it, I'm telling you.

What trap? Where?

Oh, dude! Mercury looks pissed. *You done tricked me. I cannot believe I fell for that shit. Nah. I don't wanna be friends no more.*

With that, he skyrockets into the clouds.

That's when I feel the pistol on the back of my neck.

That chandelier crashes and splinters.

Amit Sofer's soft voice comes over my shoulder. "What are you looking at?"

"I pissed off the gods."

"You're an odd one," she says.

"You've no idea."

The cobra has struck. And I was so close to getting back safely. She pushes me into the hotel's loading dock, out of the rain. Kicking me toward the trash compactor, she does the smart thing, keeping her weapon trained on me while staying at a safe distance. I put my arms out to show I'm not threatening her.

"Give me the *Edison Data*," she says.

"This is not going to look good on your annual review, Amit."

"To hell with you and Sabel Security. Don't mess with me, Jacob. I'm not in the mood."

Hell hath no fury like the scorn she's giving me. I twist a glance at the service elevator behind me. I say, "Why would I give it to you?"

"Because you have two options: I kill you now and storm the suite. Chris, Kayla, and Logan will fold the second I put a bullet in the ceiling. The other option: We go up there, you give it to me and destroy any copies." She starts crossing the space toward me. "Which will it be?"

"I like breathing. Let's go."

"Yeah." She stops. "That was too easy. You did get the decryption key, right? That's why you were out there with Krasnova?"

"I'm not going to give the data to Yeschenko," I say. "You know that."

"I don't trust you. You're a man. You'll do whatever it takes to get your stripper back."

"You're right," I tell her. "I'll do whatever it takes to get a human being named Symone Blackworthy back. That does not require giving our Russian friend the *Edison Data*."

"Enough talk. We march upstairs, you give me the data."

"Fine."

"Still too easy. You're up to something." She chews on this concept for several beats. "Your people decrypted the Russian version, then re-encrypted it on the fly."

"You didn't think I was going to leave a trillion dollars' worth of data in the hands of twenty-three-year-old geeks, did you? They'd quickly become as corrupt as you."

"March, soldier," she says. "And drop the insults. I'm not corrupt."

I put my hands up and head into the elevator. When the doors open, I step inside. This is my one chance to overpower her. When she steps in, she'll be vulnerable. But she knows her craft and gestures me into the corner, face to the wall. Keeping one eye on me, she slides into the opposite corner. Her glance at the buttons lasts a tenth of a second, giving me no opportunity. Then she makes her mistake. She pushes her shoulders into the corner and stares me down—taking her eyes off any threats outside.

As the doors begin to chunk closed, the footsteps I heard in the cathedral basement approach. Taser probes zap through the opening. Amit dances and screams to the rattlesnake beat of electroshock zaps.

I grab her pistol and slam the button to open the doors.

"Thanks," I say to my benefactor.

"You are welcome." Joe Rouleau steps in with us. "Fourth floor, *oui*?"

CHAPTER 65

JACOB STEARNE

MY PROBLEMS JUST DOUBLED. IF Amit is a cobra, Joe is a viper. The good news: he's not coiled and ready to strike. The bad news: she is.

I tell him, "I thought I'd lost you."

"You did. I was right behind you through the church, then you ran through that mass of reporters without giving me a chance to catch up. It was like swimming upstream. I almost didn't make it."

The elevator stops on the second floor and the doors open. A maid stands behind a cart; her eyes grow wide at the sight of Joe's Taser. She says something in Latvian that we take for, "I'll wait for the next one."

The doors ding shut, and we resume our upward climb.

"I thought you were recalled to Paris," Amit says to Joe.

"Latvia is a revolving door for me," he tells her. "When I arrived in Paris, I went up my chain of command. The Minister of the Armed Forces took me straight to President Macron's office and told him the terrible stunt President Williams was trying to pull. Our president was not happy to hear a NATO ally was willing to cut France out of the deal. He ordered a Mirage 2000 to fly me back here. While Jacob appreciates me saving him from you, I doubt he wants to know what else Macron ordered me to do."

"Spare me, Joe." I roll my eyes. "Emmanuel already issued a shoot-to-kill order for me once—then had to cancel it and give me a medal instead. We're best buds now."

"No medals this time. Unless …"

"Unless I give you the whole thing? Look, I don't have all the pieces to the *Chaac Project*, and if I did, who owns them and who gets them will be decided by people far above my pay grade. For now, I give you my word: I won't cut you out—again—until our governments come to an agreement."

I sense Joe is reluctantly satisfied with my response. I haven't looked at him yet because my eyes remain locked on Amit. I don't know what an aura is, but hers has changed since Symone was kidnapped. She went from being an infiltrator to assassin in no time. A woman without a country or a conscience is dangerous.

How am I going to get the *Chaac Equation*? The realistic answer is: I don't. There is no way Rafael will give me what I need. I'll have to do something clever.

The elevator stops; the doors open. We march down the hall and into the suite. The three ELA kids look up from what they're doing with stunned expressions. They start to welcome Joe back.

I cut them off. "I'll explain later. Everything on my end worked out as planned so far. Kayla, do we have the drive decrypted yet?"

"Yes and no," she says. "They still have to solve the echo problem, but they're confident it will work. They said an hour, maybe two."

I usher Joe and Amit into the sitting area off to the side. I hold up a finger, telling them both to wait. Then I call Marisa and put it on speakerphone.

"I'm calling to congratulate you on a terrific arrest and great news conference," I say as soon as she picks up. "Well done."

"How you do this, I do not know," she says with a giddy trill in her voice. "Thank you. Everyone is most happy."

"You're welcome. I expect you're trying to round up Yeschenko. If you have twenty loyal officers and can stay by your phone, I'll have another international-headline-grabbing arrest for you."

With an enthusiastic agreement, she ends the call.

"I'm not sure what position the Prime Minister will give her," I tell my distrustful companions, "but I have friends in high places now."

Unimpressed, Amit lets out a great sigh. "I quake in my boots. This is the same Marisa who said she was stupid only hours ago?"

"Be nice, Amit. She had a concussion and a crisis in confidence.

She's over that now. You should be too."

"I suppose I am the international headline you offered her?"

"That depends on whether Rafael wants you back or not."

"Rafael? I told you, he betrayed us."

"Just because you said something doesn't mean I believe you. You infiltrated Remmo Nidal, the Russians, and you think you infiltrated me, but this whole time you've been hunting for the *Edison Data*. Once you have that, the three of you—Rafael, Eli, and you—can sell it to the Chinese. Go ahead, shake your head like that, deny it all you want. No one trusts you. Ten years ago, you moved to Israel just to join Mossad. You didn't walk away from your dream job to pursue the *Chaac Equation*—only to let Rafael cheat you out of it. You're not that bad at your gig. That proves you're in deep with him. So." I toss her phone back to her. She catches it one-handed. "Call him, tell him you're about to be turned over to a Latvian police captain who will detain you—and Rafael, if they can find him—until long after Joe and I clear out of here."

She evaluates my threat. She knows I'm not bluffing. I can tell she's running a thousand scenarios in her head to get her hands on the *Edison Data* and make an escape. That isn't going to happen, and the realization rolls over her. Her only play is to call Rafael and hope he can overpower me.

"You planned this," she says. "From the moment you found Hakim Haddadi, you knew we were playing him. You had him arrested, knowing he'd figure out we were using him. Thanks for that—he tried to kill me in that seedy hotel. From the beginning, you planned to drag me into helping you. Damn it. You let me think I got the drop on you."

I shrug.

"I hate your little power trips," she says.

"If you'd stuck with Mossad, we wouldn't be having this conversation." I marvel at how many people need career counseling this evening. "As it is, you and Eli are bound to the wiliest old man I've ever run across. He has more tricks up his sleeve than you and I combined. What was your endgame? Do you think if you collect all three pieces of the *Chaac Project*, he's going to give you a share? Or are you and Eli planning to cheat him out of it?"

"Trillionaire, half-a-trillionaire, what is the difference?" she asks. "Either way, it's far more than Sabel Security's retirement plan." She noses at Joe. "Or the DGSE. Why don't you two give it up and join us?"

"Some of us work for God and country," Joe says.

Amit scoffs. Then makes the call to Rafael.

In two minutes, the enigmatic professor Rafael Tum knocks on my door. He holds up his arms, ready to be patted down for weapons. Ignoring his supplication, I ask, "Have you been hiding on the roof for the last three days?"

He stays still and silent. I take that as a yes. It's what I would have done.

Leading him to Joe and Amit, I give them a brief outline of how I'm going to get Symone back. I explain what I need from them to make it work. Their skepticism is thick and pasty.

I take them to the window, where they can see that Marisa's officers already have the building surrounded. My threat to have all three of them imprisoned until I conclude my business begins to feel real to them.

Amit and Rafael weigh their options. They don't have any.

"Give me what I need," I tell them, "and you get to leave Latvia. Live to fight another day, as the expression goes."

Joe watches the proceedings with a good deal of stomach-churning concern. I don't blame him. The first time you make promises to your country's president, you do everything in your power to keep them. And from the look of him, he promised Macron a lot.

He'll learn. Guys like us are in it for life—the politicians come and go.

Rafael is silent for a long time. Finally, he says, "You and I will still need to make a deal."

"That's the 'another day' part of this. I promise you: I will not leave you hanging. Give me what I need and leave now. I'll catch up with you later. Monaco, Mumbai, Melbourne, Madrid … I'll find you."

CHAPTER 66

JACOB STEARNE

RAFAEL HANDS ME WHAT I asked for as if I were stealing his children. I walk him and Amit to the front door with Joe in close pursuit. When we cross the living room where Kayla, Chris, and Logan wait for instructions, Rafael stops.

"Mikhail Yeschenko is a formidable enemy," he says. "The Russian Federation will not look the other way if you kill him."

I feel the ELA kids observing me with deep concern. My gamble includes their lives and they're down three members already. I answer, "Killing him would be the wrong result, but not out of the question. Tonight, I intend to bring him down."

"He is too big to bring down."

"Anyone who puts their personal interests over everyone else always goes down in the end. He is his own worst enemy and tonight he will prove it. By morning, the Russians will be too ashamed of him to claim him."

"You're risking everything," Amit says, her dark eyes flashing, "for a stripper who isn't worth it."

"If you think some people are worth saving and others aren't," I reply, "you've automatically put yourself in the second category."

She crosses her arms and turns away.

"If you make one miscalculation," Joe says, "you've shifted the balance of global power to a mad autocrat in Moscow."

"He doesn't miscalculate," Amit says. She faces me and leans in close. "Not yet. But everyone does at some point."

"I'm betting my life on my calculations," I say.

"What about Betty?" Chris asks. "Are you going to save her after what she's done?"

I catch the gaze of each one, individually, "If we left everyone to die for their transgressions, who among us would be left?"

They drop their gaze to the floor. At least I'm working with a group that retains a semblance of humility. That makes me feel better about my chances.

"We were doing this to make the *Chaac Project* public," Kayla says, "so no one profits from what might save civilization. What happens now?"

"A noble cause," I tell her. "But you've learned it will take more than a few energetic young people to triumph over the well-armed and financed factions tracking this down. They corrupted your group before you had the data decrypted. It's time to think of the good we can do in terms of international cooperation." I nod at Joe. "NATO, United Nations, maybe a new international science coalition like CERN or the ISS."

They appear resigned to their new reality. I recall being young and suddenly disillusioned by the world around me. Sadly, it's been a constant state of affairs ever since.

My phone buzzes. Mikhail Yeschenko.

"Your time is up." I wave Amit and Rafael to the door. "If you want to get out of Latvia, it's now or never."

They nod curt goodbyes and head for the door.

Amit grabs my arm, "If you fuck this up—"

"Yeah, yeah, yeah, you'll find me. Got it. Now get moving."

She says something in Hebrew that I assume is a foul estimation of my manhood and strides out.

I answer my phone. "I have what you want, Mikhail. Don't say another word until after you prove Symone is alive."

The hesitation in his breathing tells me my plan is going to work. Men like him hate being ordered around but I've left him no options. He says nothing and turns the camera to take in Symone. He's dressed her like a Latvian farm worker, an ankle-length pleated cotton dress and a long-sleeve cotton collarless top. I might hate Yeschenko with every fiber of my being, but I have to admit he did get her into modest clothes. The fact she hates the ensemble is reflected in her scorching expression. On the floor next to her feet is a large canvas tote bag. No sign of Betty.

The camera turns back to Yeschenko. He says, "13 Zirgu, a place called Radio Bar. Fifteen minutes."

Mercury leans over my shoulder. *Homie, that be the Spy Motel where spies check in—but they don't check out.*

I say, *I need him out in the open, in public. How do I get him to go where I want?*

Same ways you do with all the Caesars. My used god looks at me like I've forgotten my times tables. *If it's his idea, it happens.*

"I have what you want, Mikhail. And you have what I want. But I'm not dumb enough to walk into a trap to make the swap. Somewhere private, without enough time for either of us to set up."

"A nice quiet alley where Sabel Drones can destroy me?" he huffs. "No, we do this in public. This is how it must be."

"I don't want bystanders caught in a crossfire when your people get trigger-happy."

"Then public and crowded. Too crowded to draw weapons. The art fair in Church Square. They're having a closing party tonight. Be there in ten minutes."

"Wait—"

He's gone.

I turn to Joe and the kids. Joe knows the dire situation we're in. The kids are bright-eyed and ready to take on the most murderous oligarch of the century. Dunning-Kruger effect all over again: they have no idea how unprepared they are for the mission. I sure hope I'm not leading them into oblivion.

"Emma sent a box," I say. Chris bolts to the corner of the dining room to retrieve it.

While he does that, Kayla holds her hand out to me. When I reciprocate, she drops seven microSD memory cards in my palm. Smaller than postage stamps, each one has 2TB printed on it with a handwritten number. She says, "The tech team says they're configured in a RAID array, with each one individually encrypted. Do you know how that works?"

"After you decrypt them, you connect six of them at the same time with a special device. The seventh is the unencrypted sample."

She smiles. I'm not as dumb as I look.

Chris hands me the box. I open it and hand out the goodies, reserving an odd bottle of clear liquid for myself. I drop six of the seven memory cards into a special chamber in the bottle and put it in my pocket. I snap a bodycam button—made to match and fit—over my existing button. Everything will be recorded for posterity and the Latvian legal system.

"Emma will explain how everything works," I tell them. "Joe will be your team lead in the field. I've barely enough time to get there, so I've got to run. I'll stall a bit, but don't take too long."

Joe looks his allotment over. In a low voice, he says, "You are certain this will work?"

I take a deep breath before answering him. "No."

CHAPTER 67

JACOB STEARNE

THE RAIN STOPPED, LEAVING TEARDROPS clinging to the edges of buildings, signs, and cars. Dark billowing clouds push across a black sky, offering a rare glimpse of the white moon watching over us like a distant and critical god.

A quarter of the kiosks and stalls are either gone, or in the process of packing up. Friends sharing a bottle fill the rest. Some share several bottles. The party atmosphere is in full swing. Music pounds out of one booth; laser lights escape another.

Traipsing up and down the haphazard aisles, I search for Yeschenko. We failed to set a specific corner. The square is not big, but between parties and moving crews, it's hard to see anyone in the churning crowd. I spot two of Yeschenko's men, obvious for the bulges in their jackets, being overdressed for an art fair, and their vigilant gaze. They try to surveille me casually. An impossible task before an experienced operative like me. I give them a professional nod.

Nothing comes over my comm link. I check my phone and see nothing. No Emma. No Sabel Satellite connections. Only LMT, the local mobile carrier. That's not good.

Between people carrying boxes, I catch a glimpse of Betty's golden hair. After a pair carrying an electric piano move through, I see Symone in the peasant dress holding a tote bag. The women's wary eyes track me. Betty shivers with fear. Symone has no expression at all. Neither speaks.

Taking in our surroundings as I step to them, I spot a Russian at either end of the aisle. A figure huddles against the sky from the parapet atop the nearest building. I hook the rim of Symone's tote bag and glance inside. Six sticks of PVV-5A, the Russian plastic explosive of choice, are surrounded by unopened bags of marbles. The bomb could easily pass through a metal detector. Its blast radius would be at least a hundred feet in all directions. Simple, effective, lethal.

"Are you OK?" I ask Betty.

"No," she says, her voice quaking. "I never thought things would go this far."

I face Symone. No emotion shows in her face. Before I can tell her I'm sorry for getting her mixed up in this, she says in a firm, flat voice, "I'm not afraid anymore."

I'm happy and heartbroken at the same time. Happy that she's conquered her fears. Heartbroken that she's made peace with her mortality. The nightmare she escaped in her childhood has come full circle to claim her. None of us escape the Grim Reaper; we only dodge him for a time. She believes her time is now and has reached the calmness that comes with accepting the inevitable.

I squeeze her shoulder and tell her, "I'm proud of you. Damn proud."

"Jacob, you—" her voice catches in her throat "—should run."

Her only concern is for my safety. I stay quiet. I'm not going to run, nor am I going to argue.

Six detonator leads run from the tote into a single wire that exits the bag and rises to the phone Betty holds in her hand at shoulder level. On the screen is the face of Mikhail Yeschenko with a countdown timer below him. When my gaze turns to the oligarch, he grins. The countdown timer reads 6 minutes. He's calculated the time it takes for me to turn everything over and for him to verify it. The timer reads 5 minutes, 59 seconds. 5 minutes, 58 seconds.

"Everyone is greedy, Jacob," Yeschenko says. "When it comes right down to it, greed controls us all. Even you. People who stop to think about how a few billion rubles would change their lives become quite greedy. But not everyone is greedy for money, are they? Money doesn't move you. Still, you're greedy, aren't you? You're greedy for love, or more accurately, adoration."

He waits for my response. I give him nothing.

"Betty is much the same, you know." His video background changes as he moves around the room he's in. Moonlight streams in a window, lighting the side of his face. I can't tell where he is from the video. He says, "She might tell you she switched sides for the money, the protection, but that's not true. Her mind is on an unstoppable quest for knowledge. Science is her obsession. Her greed is the *Chaac Equation*. Her psyche is wrapped around solving that problem like lichen on a rock. She can't rest until she sees it done."

The timer reads 4 minutes, 19 seconds.

"Greed is my stock in trade," he continues. "It's how I manipulate people. Especially you. Like your pathetic need to be adored by this curvaceous child, or your burning desire to have Betty fall in love with you again. But what's easiest? Your greedy obsession with saving people. From the moment I saw you break into the townhouse, when I watched you on the video feed trying desperately to save that miserable boy, I knew exactly how your greed would let me move you around the chessboard like a pawn. You were driven to save your tiny stripper. Then you had to save that pitiful group, the ELA. At any point in time, you could've left town—but you couldn't because you're greedy for adoration."

Yeschenko brings the camera closer to his face. He swells with hubris, feeling imminent victory within reach. "You're my pawn, Jacob Stearne. The hero of Paris, the savior of the G20, the man who beat the arms dealers—you are mine. I own you. Now give me what I want."

I watch the man through the video feed. His eyes bulge, his mouth twists tight, his skin vibrates with triumph.

"You ordered Francesca to kill Kevin Winn," I state flatly. "Why?"

"All my pawns must prove they will do as they're told. It's a basic requirement. Stop stalling! Give me what I asked for. Do it now."

The answer is simple; the decision to deliver it is not. His timer was an unforeseen complication. The risk is not just to me—my plan was to free Betty and Symone before this point. That won't work. The bomb is more sophisticated than I expected.

Why would he risk blowing me up when I have the data? He thinks it's in a secure form. A typical SSD drive would more than likely survive a blast. Maybe not in one piece, but in recoverable pieces. I didn't anticipate the level of his brutality. I should have.

I weigh the risks. While there are some of his men in the blast zone with us, losing their lives won't bother him at all. The guard I can see over Betty's shoulder must not have any idea what's in the bag or he wouldn't look so smug. And it's not just them. Within range of his explosives are at least two dozen Latvian civilians.

The timer counts down to 3 minutes, 38 seconds.

I give him my answer. "No."

CHAPTER 68

JACOB STEARNE

WHY DID I SAY THAT? My regret wells up the instant I let the word loose. But there's no taking it back now. A thousand variables flash through my mind in an instant. I've not heard from Joe. I have no headcount for the Russian guards. Betty is about to pass out, her face drained of color at my refusal. No emotion registers on Symone's face. I have no choice but to go through with it and trust that my friends are out there, working in the dark.

1 minute, 57 seconds.

I hold up my glass bottle to the camera for Yeschenko to see. "Stop the counter or this, the *Edison Data* and the *Chaac Equation* combined, will be destroyed in the blast. Go ahead—call my bluff."

Yeschenko's face contorts as his mind rifles through his options. He doesn't know what the bottle is and therefore can't determine the extent of my bluff. His head nearly explodes with rage—yet he presses a button.

The pause symbol appears on the timer below his image. 1 minute, 21 seconds.

"This is a bottle of sulfuric acid," I tell him. "And this protective strip separates it from the six chips holding the *Edison Data* and the *Chaac Equation* from that liquid." I pull a strip through a slot in the lid. "Now all that keeps them out of the acid is a small shelf. If I drop this bottle, if I shake it up, if I lose my grip—you get nothing."

Yeschenko chews the inside of his cheek, thinking it over.

"I know what you're thinking," I say. "One of your guys could beat me over the head while the other one grabs the bottle. Maybe you could order your sniper on the roof to take me out and hope your guy catches it. The only trouble with that—" and this is where I have no idea if Joe and the guys were successful or not "—is that you're missing a few of your boys."

Yeschenko scowls, then looks at something offscreen. No doubt, he's checking on his guards on a nearby laptop. I'm bluffing based solely on the fact that the guy who was standing ten yards past Betty is no longer there.

"You see, Mikhail, you only think I'm your pawn. Truth is: you've been mine all along. The second day I was here, Betty came to the hotel for breakfast. She had a plan: the only way she could get out from under your threat was to infiltrate your organization and bring it down. She wanted me to talk her out of it, come up with a better plan. It was risky for her, but I knew her acting skills would allow me to manipulate you. At the time, I reminded her that she was an actress, and a good one. I told her to stay in her lane. And she did. When she visited you, you thought she had capitulated, knelt before you in fealty. In fact, she was putting on an act. It was brave of her; she deserves an Oscar.

"But you! You did everything I expected." I pause for a moment, then hold up a finger. "Except the snake venom. I did not see that coming. That nearly killed me. She's a math genius and ran the survival odds through her head when you gave her the order. She knew if anyone had a chance of surviving the poison, it was me because she knows Sabel agents are given microdoses to build immunity. That's why she injected me instead of Symone."

Symone finally registers an emotion: utter disbelief. Her eyes lock on Betty. "You were working with Jacob this whole time?"

Without looking at the girl, Betty tosses her a shrug.

Symone's gaze comes slowly back to me, deadpan once again.

I continue with Yeschenko. "Here's what's going to happen next, Mikhail: you're going to tell that sniper on the roof to stand down. Then you're going to let me disconnect the detonators from the phone. When I count down, Betty's going to pull the cord. If it goes off, we die but you get nothing. Once that's off, you're coming here—in person—to take these microSD cards from me. That's the only way you get what you want."

"If you disconnect the detonators, the girls will leave."

"Of course the women leave. What kind of impotent man would put them at risk?"

The comm link in my ear crackles. Emma's voice comes in. "Jacob. Jacob, if you're hearing me, nod your head once."

I nod. My head movement will register through my video link.

"We lost you on comms. Joe figured out why: one of the Russians carried a signal jammer. He and those kids stabbed seven Russians with darts. They don't know if that's all of them or half or what, but that's where we are. Oh, and I heard you about the sniper. We're trying to figure out how to neutralize him."

I nod again for Emma's benefit. Joe and the ELA kids have been sneaking through the crowd, getting behind Yeschenko's guys, and stabbing them in the butt with Sabel Darts. But they're nowhere near done.

Yeschenko never left Moscow with less than a detachment of twelve. Since he's been in Riga, he's worked with squads of four. For round-the-clock coverage, he'd use four squads. That means sixteen men, minimum. Joe and the kids have more to find. Joe's a professional; he'd do that same math. He'll be working his way through the crowd right now, but will he finish in time?

"You think this makes me your pawn?" Yeschenko shakes violently. "You're wrong. You're so … Damn it. Fine. The women can go. But I'm not turning off the bomb. Stay right there."

"OK," I say. "I can do a selfie."

I take the phone from Betty and hold it where Yeschenko can see my face and the bottle.

Betty turns to leave and taps Symone on the shoulder. My favorite dancer doesn't move. She stares at me as if she's watching me die. Tears well up in her eyes and begin sliding down the side of her nose.

"Go!" I tell Symone.

Betty takes the straps out of her hand and sets the tote bag on the ground next to me. She tugs on Symone. The girl doesn't budge. Betty pulls harder.

"I can't watch anyone else die," Symone says. "I'm staying here with you."

"No," I say.

As soon as I speak, the image of Jenny running away from me with a bomb, hoping to save my life, flashes through my mind. I had no control over our fates. She saved me but died in the attempt. Her death crushed me. It would have been better to die in that same blast.

Symone faced the murders of her schoolmates without any control over her own fate. It's eaten away at her ever since. Now she controls her destiny. She wants to see if she can look death in the eye and survive. She longs to face the monster. To stand up to those who would destroy us and say, "No."

I know that feeling. I disagree with her conclusion, but I understand how she got there.

Betty tugs on Symone one more time.

"It's OK," I tell Betty. "She can stay."

Betty looks back and forth, sees Symone and I staring at each other, knows there's nothing more she can do. She runs away.

Onscreen, Yeschenko exits a building. I can't tell which one, but a block later, he's in the party on the square.

I must try one more time before he joins us.

"You should go," I tell Symone. "Don't worry about—"

"You should go," she says.

"I know what you're trying to do, Symone. Don't take the risk. You have your whole life ahead of you. Don't throw it away."

"I know what you're trying to do," she says right back at me. Her expression is flat, emotionless. She is fully committed to her logic. "Just like that Russian guy said—you're trying to save everyone or die trying. Well, my life has changed over the last week. No one cared about me before. No one raised me, no one tucked me in when I was little, no one read me bedtime stories. No one kept their promises. No one cared about me, and I didn't care about anyone else. Life felt like a bad joke. Now, it's different. You care enough to risk your life for me. You think I'm worth saving. I like that. But without it, there's nothing."

I don't like it, but we've run out of time for arguments. "Everyone is worth saving. Especially you.”

More silent tears run down her stoic cheeks.

I hand her the bottle of acid. “Hold this. Extend your arm. If there’s a struggle, make sure it goes down first. We’re in this together.”

A small smile cracks across her lips. She takes the bottle, holding it by the cap with two fingers. A little more cavalier than I wanted but effective. Her arm extends to my shoulder. If someone shoves either of us, the bottle goes flying.

Six feet to our left stands Mikhail Yeschenko. He holds up his phone. An onscreen timer shows: 1 minute, 21 seconds. Still paused. He observes the precarious position of the acid bottle.

He says, “I want proof.”

With the detonator phone still in one hand, I dig the sample chip and the special reader from my pocket. I hand them to him. “Samples from both the *Chaac Equation* and the *Edison Data*. Check them out. The rest are spread across a RAID configuration on those six chips.” I nod at the sulfuric acid bottle. “You’ll need all six decrypted.”

Taking the sample chip and the connector, he squints at me. “What is the decryption key?”

“Live voice recognition,” I answer. “Every Sabel employee has a proof-of-life chip that connects to their phone. The phone hears my voice and Symone’s, verifies we’re both alive, then decrypts the chip when she and I recite a poem. That means, she and I go wherever you go until this bomb is deactivated.”

This is the first Symone’s heard of it. Including her was a bluff. I gambled on the concept that she comes from an industry dealing with potentially dangerous negotiations all day long. I knew she would instinctively understand.

Symone remains expressionless when Yeschenko glances at her.

He says something in Russian. Six men push through the nearby crowds. They clear a circle around us. That’s more than I expected. Too many for Joe and the ELA to handle quickly. And the man still has a sniper on the roof with a scope fixed on my head.

CHAPTER 69

JACOB STEARNE

MY BEST HOPE IS THAT Marisa understood my sketchy instructions when we last spoke. If she hadn't been clobbered on the head twenty-four hours ago, I wouldn't worry about it. But right now, because of her concussion, my endgame is a fifty-fifty proposition.

"You know where I got the idea for the voice recognition?" I ask.

Yeschenko counts the heads of his men and wonders where the others are. Quickly returning his gaze to me, he tries not to give away his concern at the low count. He says, "I wait with breathless anticipation."

Emma interrupts in the comm link. "A man with a sniper rifle fell off the roof and landed on the pavement. When Joe looked up, a woman in a long black coat gave him a salute. One less to worry about."

I nod for Emma. She doesn't mention taking down the immediate threat, leading me to believe I'm stuck with the six guards and a man with a trigger in his hand. And I don't see Marisa in the crowd of onlookers.

Around us, civilians peer at our circle with a mix of curiosity and concern. They lean in for a closer look. The Russians stretch out their arms to keep them back. I feel like a fighter in a ring.

"Your other pawn," I tell Yeschenko, "Interior Minister Anna Krasnova, used a Latvian poet and voice recognition as an encryption key. Quite clever of her. I see why you corrupted her. But in case you haven't heard, she's been arrested. Good for her that you already signed over the *Gabija* to her. She'll need that €35 million bribe for her defense."

Yeschenko's face turns redder. He looks one step short of a stroke. "She gets nothing! Until I give the final order, Krasnova gets NOTHING from me!"

That's all the evidence Marisa will need to convict them both. His confession is recorded on my button camera for posterity.

"Mikhail Yeschenko," I announce loudly, "you are under arrest."

He looks confused for a moment, then laughs at me. "You have no such authority."

Pistols appear from the pockets of our surrounding civilians. The muzzles are pressed to the Russians' heads. Officers under cover. A woman, still wearing a uniform blazer with nothing underneath, pushes her way into the circle. "I have this authority! You are under arrest."

Two TV news crews join us to record the proceedings. I assume they were invited by one politically savvy police captain. Marisa's plainclothes officers disarm the Russians while Mikhail Yeschenko watches his world crumble around him.

"Hand me phone," Marisa says to him.

"You cannot touch me!" He backs up, showing the timer still paused. "Latvia is not a country. You're nothing but a dialect of Mother Russia. You're not a real nation."

Marisa yells something at him in Russian that makes him blink and back up another step. She steps forward, a pistol in her outstretched hand. She yells at him in Russian again. Two of her men step in behind him, blocking any exit. She holds her hand out, expecting him to drop his phone—the bomb's trigger—into her palm.

He glares at her, then at me. Then he presses the button to restart the countdown, spins the remaining time down to 20 seconds—and locks the phone.

The timer on my phone is no longer paused. It reads 17. 16. 15.

This is it. This is what Amit predicted: I pushed my luck too far. The countdown is in progress, and the phone is locked. Seconds left. It's over.

There are times in life when so much comes at us at once that time slows down while we sort through the details. Facing mortality is one of those moments.

Surprisingly, a gentle sense of pleasure comes over me. I allow images from my past to overtake my present. I see endless stretches of corn fields and soybeans from my childhood on the family farm. Debbie Grossman giving me a kiss in ninth grade when I didn't think she knew I existed. The flash and bang and blood and hell of battlefields in foreign lands. The civilians on visits back home who thanked me for my service without knowing what that meant. The luxury of vacationing on Pia Sabel's yacht with flowing drinks and five-star cuisine. My best friend bringing me a puppy. Disarming a bomb while hostages watched in horror. Now it's over. I'm finally going to meet Jenny on God's golden shore.

In my peripheral vision, Marisa's eyes have glazed over. She's also seeing her life flash in front of her eyes. As are the rest of the people in the crowd: her officers, the Russians, the innocent bystanders recording this on their phones.

11. 10.

Everyone except Symone. She's given up on living, like a drowning victim whose muscles no longer respond and slips under the water. There is no more struggle left in her, no more will to live. I've seen that look on the battlefield on the faces of both friend and foe, the resignation from life.

But—I'm wrong.

It's not resignation on her face. It's expectation.

She's tilting her head toward Yeschenko. This is her whole gambit. She stayed, convinced that she could face the monster—not because she had made peace with death as I presumed, but because she believed in her hero. She believed with unwavering certainty that I would save her life. Never a doubt.

Yeah. Well. She's right: I hate to disappoint.

I kick Yeschenko in the balls. As he doubles over in pain, I grab a handful of his thin hair and hold his face up. I grab his phone and hold it in front of him. I'm praying he left the facial recognition feature on.

He did, but the timer on his side reads 4. 3.

I click pause. It stops. It still reads 3. Two seconds left over. Plenty of time.

Marisa stares at the display with wide eyes, her mouth trying to form words. A collective sigh of relief comes from the surrounding crowd, even the Russian guards. Symone still has no expression.

I say, "Captain Redgrave, do you have a bomb squad?"

Everyone stands still, holding their breath, until the men in heavy jackets arrive and carry away the bomb and both phones in a solid container.

Taking the bottle from Symone, I hold it in front of Yeschenko, unscrew the cap, and drink the liquid. I shake out the chips and put them in my pocket. With a glance his way, I say, "Couldn't find any acid on short notice, so I used water. Hope you don't mind the bluff."

While his face swells, red and bloated and ready to explode, Marisa slaps handcuffs on him.

"Don't you dare touch me!" Yeschenko yells. "You filthy swine! You have no authority to—"

Marisa hauls off and slams her pistol butt into his forehead. "This is authority."

Her men pick him up and haul him away with the others. Phones recording the proceedings for Instagram and TikTok switch off. People start breathing again.

Marisa gives me a hug. "You not bad in end, Jacob Stearne." She takes several deep breaths, blowing the adrenaline out. "You save us. I not believe possible, but you do it. *Rīgas varonis!* The hero of Riga!"

The onlookers surrounding us repeat the phrase, then cheer and clap. I stare at my feet. The Russian was right—I crave adoration, I just don't know what to do with it when it arrives.

Mercury leans over my shoulder as if smiling for one of the hundreds of pictures being taken of this moment. He says, *Go ahead, homie, tell them who saves you from your enemies. Tell them how I guide your every step.*

I glance at him. *You? Where the hell have you been?*

I just had to duck out for a minute, that's all. He looks disappointed that I would even ask. *Came right back. No biggie. I was at the awards dinner for the Non-Aligned Movement. Not that it's any of your business.*

I say, *You're part of the 120-nation group who are not part of NATO?*

Say what? He looks at me like I'm spoiled milk and he just got a whiff. *Oh my Neptune, no. NAM be the group of all gods who are not aligned with the Christian, Islamic, Hindu, Buddhist oligopoly. See, the Big Four have squeezed the rest of us out of the religion business for going on two millennia now. We have—*

I say, *Not to be rude, but this is my moment. Let me have this.*

Your moment? Mercury frowns. *Ize about to get the best-hairstyle-on-a-supporting-god award. Damn straight. Don't shake your head like that, boy. You'd think I'd win for my toga, but the best-costume award be all about the Lakota gods and their feathers this year. Say, look at them Earthlings lining up for a selfie with you. Go on now, tell 'em all about ME!*

Marisa gives me an extra squeeze and heads out, trotting to catch up with her officers. Civilians surround me, snapping selfies. They get what they want from me and slowly the crowd breaks up.

Betty steps into the space they vacate. Her golden mane glitters in the light of streetlamps and spilled light from kiosks. Life radiates from her as if she found salvation in her recent brush with death. A common experience for survivors. A bright and shiny smile stretches across her face. Music starts up from one of the stalls along with the alcohol-fueled voices of those who had no idea how close they came to dying.

The party is starting back up. Life goes on.

To my left, Symone hasn't moved since the countdown restarted. Her blank stare feels like a grappling hook trying to yank my attention away from Betty. When I face her, I notice her expressionless face has gone quite pale. She lets out an involuntary sigh and all her muscles relax at once. She crumples to the ground like a dropped rag.

CHAPTER 70

JACOB STEARNE

I CATCH SYMONE JUST BEFORE she cracks her head open on the cobblestones. Dead weight is hard to manage, luckily Joe Rouleau pops out of the crowd and lends a hand.

"What happened to her?" he asks. "Was she hit?"

"Don't know." We lay her on the ground, her head on my jacket. As I look her over, I say, "Thanks for all your help, Joe. Without you guiding the kids, I'd be shredded right now. I appreciate it."

"A thank-you is nice," he says with that charming smile, "but France still expects her share of the reward."

As much as I'd like to make a witty reply, there's no discernible pulse in Symone's neck. Placing my ear by her nose, I listen and hear nothing over the party noise around me. Due to swirling air, I'm not sure if I feel her breath on my cheek.

She was fine a second ago. And she's young. Did the sniper get a shot off? Bullet wounds are not always obvious. My fingertips slide around her head, looking for a trace of greasy blood. I pull up her shoulder but don't see any signs on the ground. Joe watches me with increasing concern.

A man taps my shoulder while saying something in Latvian. He's wearing a paramedic uniform and is waving me away. Another man stands next to him with a gurney. I back away and let them work.

Betty taps me on the shoulder. Behind her stand the remaining three of the ELA: Logan, Kayla, and Chris. I explain Symone's condition even though I can't explain the cause of her collapse. We watch the paramedics going through their checklist of procedures while Symone's face grows grey.

The paramedic asks the crowd something in Latvian. No one has an answer but they all point to me. The man turns to me and asks, "Ehm, drugs?"

"No. She was fine, then collapsed."

The man turns back to Symone, whips out a laryngoscope, a metal intubating tube with a light on the end, and expertly shoves it into her mouth and throat. Unfortunately, I've had to use those on the battlefield and they're never a good sign. He gently pushes a tube into her airway and inflates the cuff to hold it in place. Hooking up an oxygen bottle, he forces air into her lungs. He tapes everything in place and double-checks his work.

The two men lift her onto the gurney and snap it to standing. The paramedic turns to me and asks, "Family?"

"Yes," I answer. "Close, anyway."

I turn to Betty, Joe, and the ELA kids for approval. They all nod at me. The paramedic sees their affirmation and tugs my arm.

They wheel her across rough and ancient cobblestones, jostling her with every step. I jog alongside. The oxygen is getting in her lungs, which is a good sign, but I've seen that before. Forcing a body to breathe gives the appearance of life, it's not necessarily a sign of recovery.

The men shove the gurney into the ambulance. The paramedic climbs in with her and motions for me to follow. The other man jumps in the driver's seat and blips the siren.

"What's wrong with her?" I ask, uncertain if he speaks English.

"Stress? Stroke?" he offers.

I'm not sure if he means a stress-related stroke or if he was asking my opinion. We look at each other, awkwardly considering how to bridge the language barrier. We decide not to. He goes back to checking Symone with a stethoscope and a concerned expression.

Observing her with my limited medical knowledge, I can't determine her condition. I don't want to believe she's dying, even though inexplicable deaths happen all the time. I had no idea about her medical condition before I put her in harm's way. Did she have a congenital heart defect that couldn't cope with the stress? Is that the reason for her blank expression throughout Yeschenko's gambit? Was she having a heart attack and I didn't know it?

Mercury puts an arm around my shoulder and, uncharacteristically, says nothing.

I say, *Death is a cruel joke the gods play on us when we are least prepared for it.*

Mercury says, *What makes her life so important?*

I say, *I've mourned brothers lost in combat. I've mourned for the families of enemies who will never see their return. But those are the costs of our deadly game. But she was young and innocent.*

Mercury squeezes my arm. *Ain't nothing but a thin filament connects y'all to this Earthly plane. Though, I axed you what makes her so important.*

I try to think of a logical response. Nothing comes to mind. *I don't know. You're the god, you tell me.*

Mercury says, *All y'all mortals walk the world seeing everyone as a stranger, not a neighbor, not a friend. Ya makes decisions from inside your heads, never knowing—and all too often not caring—what others think or feel. Then once in a great while, you connect with someone on a different level. No negotiation, no expectation, no conditions. Just a feeling that someone needs you just as much as you need them. That's what we gods are hoping y'all reach for: peace and love.*

For the first time in ages, his words make sense. I say, *Yeah, that first moment I saw her from the window, when she made that sign with her hand, she needed me—and I knew it. I was busy running from my problems and didn't appreciate it at the time, but I needed to be needed. Minutes later, she saved me from the cops. Twice. Symbiotic—is that the word? Maybe interdependent. Symone and I were connected from that moment on. Not a sexual connection like she keeps thinking, but a spiritual connection.*

Mercury shakes my shoulder. *Damn, boy, you can grasp the meaning of life sometimes.*

I look at him. *Is that how we're supposed to act toward each other? Is that nirvana, heaven, the peace humankind is supposed to achieve?*

Mercury turns away with a sad look in his eyes. *We got hopes for y'all, but so far, it just ain't happening. Look here, I asked what makes her life so important—and you done give me the 'to you' part. Why is her life important?*

I say, *Because she's a human being. Someone brought her into this world with the implied and sacred promise to care for her—only to leave her wandering alone. She deserves better.*

Mercury smiles and slaps my back. *Dang, homie, if I didn't know better, I'd say you been reading books again. All your bullshit sounds downright poetic. Hold up! I just remembered, you be guided day and night by the god of eloquence. Ha! And you think I never done nothing for you. Check it.* He points at the gurney.

Symone just blinked.

CHAPTER 71

JACOB STEARNE

A WOMAN IN SCRUBS PRODS my shoulder. "You are Jacob Stearne?"

"Yes." My mouth is dry.

"I'm Dr. Linderman. It's time for you to go."

Twitching to take in my surroundings, I notice strong daylight slashing in the window, a hospital recliner beneath me. No longer in peasant garb, a provocatively dressed Symone sits on the edge of the bed with a smirk on her face. I must have a word with Emma about the clothes she's sending this girl.

"What time is it?" I ask.

"Just before six in the morning," the doc says.

It's hard getting used to the endless daylight in this town.

When my gaze meets hers, Symone says, "You were snoring, so they kicked us out."

"No." Dr. Linderman laughs. "The officials told us to send you to the airport."

"Is she …" I try to say more but cottonmouth kills my voice. I smack my lips.

"She's fine. Exhaustion, stress. The body shuts down when you push it too hard."

"I reached 100 percent," Symone says with a smile. "No more reserves."

Until now, I hadn't realized it, but I never gave her a chance to sleep. Soldiers are used to staying awake three to four days at a stretch, but she wasn't ready for that. A pang of guilt stabs me. I let the sting pass.

Pushing up to standing requires more effort than usual. Doc Linderman watches me carefully. It takes a moment to find my balance.

Symone catapults herself off the bed and wraps me up in a tight hug that barely allows me to breathe. She nearly knocks me over. I stagger a step as I extricate myself from her grip.

"You told the truth," she says, tears forming in her eyes. "You said you'd never leave me—and you didn't."

The doctor appraises me with a judgmental eye. I slide her a it's-not-what-you-think glance. She's not buying it. I don't care.

Symone re-hugs me. I stagger back and fall into the recliner. She backs up, apologizing as she goes. Wrenching back to my feet, I take a deep breath and feel the wobble in my posture.

"When was the last time you got a full night's sleep?" Doc asks.

"London." I take the cup of water Symone offers. She has her pack over one shoulder and grabs mine with her free hand. "Three days ago. Maybe four."

The doctor nods knowingly. I know when I'm being given the bum's rush. I don't have to go home but I can't stay here, and wherever I go, the doc wants me to catch some Zs. That makes two of us. I thank her, take my pack from Symone, and head out into the hall. Symone points to the left.

As I walk, I dig a hand in my pocket to make sure the SD chips are still there. They are. Next, I check my phone. Emma texted me, writing: "Hijacked Sabel One for you. It's full of Sabel Capital bankers and the clients they're wowing, I redirected them to pick you up, so they're a little testy. You get the Owner's Suite—up to nine guests, three cabins. Hope that's enough. Pia expects you at Sabel Gardens as soon as you land. I'm going home to sleep. I'm beat."

I make a mental note to send Emma a thank-you gift. What's appropriate for someone who has your operational back for three days straight? A Ferrari maybe. Or diamonds. I can't afford what she deserves, so I'll get Ms. Sabel to spring for it.

"They tried to kill me, but I lived," Symone says and hip-bumps me. "I'm one step closer to being tough like you."

I check her. She's beaming with pride. I want to tell her cheating death is closer to Russian roulette than an achievement. It's addictive and fills you with unwarranted confidence that leads to an early grave. But this is her moment. I let her have it. I stop, hold her by the shoulders, and look into her eyes. "You did well. I'm proud of you."

Her bottom lip trembles, her eyes fill up with tears. She looks away for a moment, sniffles, then looks back with a playful pout. "Watch out, I'm going for your job next!" She laughs, then starts walking away. "C'mon, the others are waiting for us."

"Who?" I ask.

She doesn't answer. Instead, she points to a side room full of couches where families wait for news about loved ones. Betty Bardon, Chris Anrig, Logan Taylor, Kayla Clay, Joe Rouleau, and Captain Marisa Redgrave jump to their feet when we come in.

Although, if my estimation of Latvian epaulet insignia is correct, she's no longer Captain Redgrave. It's Colonel Redgrave now. She rose three ranks overnight. Not bad. Impressing your prime minister pays.

None of them know what to say to me, so they give Symone hugs. Betty stands back, like an ex waiting to see where we stand. I don't know where we stand. She doesn't want me to be her ex; I don't want her to be my ex. But neither of us knows what to do about it. Joe catches her gaze, follows it to me, and back. He takes a step back. Smart man.

To avoid them both, I approach the ranking official in the room. "Congratulations, Colonel Redgrave. Well deserved. Are you the new Interior Minister?"

She blushes, pleased that I noticed. "Not Minister, yet. I tell Prime Minister, for me to arrest Krasnova—then replace her, not good, ehm, optics. I accept for when trial is over, Krasnova sentenced. I come to say thank-you before you leave."

"How did you know we were leaving?"

"You have no visa." She scowls.

"I don't need a visa for EU countries." Suddenly, I remember the doctor said the officials told her to kick us out.

"You do business not stated on entry. Business you still not explain."

She's got me there. And I'm not going to explain it either. Despite getting her promoted, and solving a major crime for her, she's such a stickler for the law that she's evicting me. Nice. Guess we don't have to worry about corrupt officials on her watch. I shake her hand and we exchange smiles.

When I turn to Betty, my feelings for her return in a rush. My heart starts a drum solo. I don't know what to say.

She avoids the heat between us by asking, "Do you think Pia will take me back?"

"Yeschenko was right about you," I reply. "You just want to see this done. You can ask her. She's a bit unpredictable these days. You know, you'll have to swear an oath of fealty."

"At least she has clean boots to lick." Betty slips in close and hooks my shirt with a finger. In her husky bedroom voice, she says, "No matter what, we'll always have Banff."

"Doesn't quite roll off the tongue like Paris." I can't stop my mischievous smile from spreading. My mind buzzes at the thought of another round with Betty Bardon—beauty, actress, physicist, and genius. There's a certain gravity to her that draws me into her orbit. Nothing I can do about it. I should recognize that and tell her how she makes me feel. First I need to get some sleep so I don't say something stupid.

I notice Logan staring at me expectantly, waiting to be noticed. When I turn toward him, he says, "The Sabel Tech people told me I should apply. How do I go about that?"

"If your bags are packed, you get on the jet with me. I'll introduce you at the office and give you a good recommendation."

Chris brightens at this. I turn to Kayla and him, "Are your bags packed? I can't make promises, but I'll definitely put in a good word."

Chris and Logan bump fists with big grins. Kayla frowns and crosses her arms.

"Count me out," she says. "I'm done with this whole thing. Too much anxiety for me. I'm going home to study poetry."

I thank her for her help and wish her the best of luck.

That leaves Joe. His hawkish gaze has been fixed on me this whole time. He says, "You must have one more seat on that jet, Jacob. Macron told me not to let you out of my sight until we have negotiated this whole project."

"I figured as much."

Four uniformed officers appear. Colonel Redgrave directs them in her native tongue. She tells me, "You may be the *Hero of Riga*, but next time, be truthful on entry papers."

She walks off without another word.

Someone told the hospital staff who I am, and a line forms for selfies with *Le Héros de Paris*. Even the cops want in. My smile is tired, and I'm beat by the time we get to the jet. All I want is to get these memory cards into Ms. Sabel's hands so she can hash things out with the various presidents. And I want a nap. Maybe I'll nap the entire ten-hour flight.

Sabel One is a huge airliner outfitted like a luxury yacht for impressing and entertaining the many customers of Sabel Industries. As Emma warned me, the front half of the jet is full of salespeople from Sabel Capital and their clients, bankers from Paris and Rome. They're miffed about being re-routed until Symone tells them I'm a celebrity. Another round of selfies explodes. Finally, I kick everyone I don't know out of the Owner's Suite.

There are three cabins, and one of them has my name on it. I pick the smallest one with the least amount of space. I figure no one will fight me for it and I'll get some peace. As soon as I close the door, I fall face-first into the pillows, fully clothed, and pass out.

Sometime later, I sense a warm body next to me. A warm body with my arm encircling it. Symone. I have my arm around Symone.

I blink several times and take a deep breath. We both have all our clothes on. Thank Minerva.

She rolls over with a smile.

Mercury peeks over her shoulder at me. *Aw, dawg. You are in. This here be what you modern men call consent. That's all you need, right?*

I say, *Consent is not the question. I've made a lot of bad decisions about women in my life—this isn't going to be another one.*

Mercury pulls back, hurt. *Dude, are you serious right now? Symone-a-licious is beautiful, willing, and able.*

I say, *She's young, naïve, and impressionable.*

"I'm not naïve." Symone says blinking in a way she thinks is sexy.

"Whoa! Hold up," I tell her. "You're supposed to be in the primary cabin next door. This cabin is for me. Alone. I need sleep."

"We have such a great relationship," she says.

"True, but it's not the kind that involves a bed."

"Why not?"

I sit up, take her hands, and pull her to sitting. We face each other, close. "Because you're young, your twenties are ahead of you, and mine are behind me. The twenties are when you have drama, adventures in love, drama, sexual experiments, and more drama. You discover new things and destroy old things. I've been there. I'm looking for a relationship with more maturity."

In a sexy, baby-doll voice, she says, "I'll experiment with anything you want."

"Yeah. Um. That's my point. It's like, when you were a kid and you liked *Sesame Street*, but now you're grown up and you move on to more mature things. You—"

"Don't dis *Sesame Street*. Who doesn't love Elmo?"

I palm my face.

"OK, Teletubbies then." I wait for her to frown. "See? You've moved on from Teletubbies. I'm like that with twenty-something relationships. I've moved on. You deserve someone who wants drama and adventures. Like … Logan. Or Chris."

She mimes gagging at my suggestions. "I've gone on a lot of adventures with older guys, and we had a lot—"

"I'm aware those guys exist." I roll my eyes. "I'm not one of them."

"Y'know, that's what Jill Nagle calls compulsory virtue. She shoulda called it imaginary virtue."

"You read Jill Nagle? Never mind. Just …" Suddenly it strikes me that I never invited her on this trip. I invited the others. Where is Symone going? I'm too tired to ask.

"So sue me," I say. "Go on, get out, take the big cabin. It has a shower and two sinks. I'm going to sleep."

Reluctantly, she rises and leaves. I follow her to lock the door behind her. Just outside my cabin, Joe and Betty sit in captain's chairs, talking. Betty sees me and makes her disdain of Symone's exit obvious. Then she touches Joe's forearm, puts a twinkle in her eye, and turns her full attention to him.

That's it. I'm done. I'll never talk to a woman again.

Until next time.

CHAPTER 72

JACOB STEARNE

PRIORITIES. I'M RUNNING THEM THROUGH my head as my boots clomp across the marble hall in Sabel Gardens on my way to report to the boss. Number one priority: taking a little personal time to visit the family back on the farm in Iowa. Nothing helps you focus on the important things in life like surviving a deadly standoff in an ancient square five thousand miles from home. No matter what Ms. Sabel wants, I'm going home.

The door to her home office stands wide open, allowing me into a space larger than most people's houses. I stride in and cross the expanse of polished oak where priceless oriental rugs are strewn like autumn leaves.

Ms. Sabel is an ultra-fit, under-thirty billionaire of considerable athletic beauty. Usually. Not today. Right now, she sits behind her desk in a wheelchair, the room permeated with the scent of antiseptic ointment. She's parked sideways, her leg raised, titanium pins protruding in all directions from every bone in her ankle. They rise through her skin to the surrounding scaffolding. It hurts just looking at it.

When I arrive at the desk, she tracks my transfixed gaze and shakes her head. "Looks worse than it is."

"If you say so. A homeless woman in Maine did this?"

"You'd prefer mobsters?" she asks. She gestures for me to take a chair facing her. Never one for small talk, she adds, "Status?"

"Italian authorities arrested Tommaso Bartoli, Francesca's father, in Milan. As the head of imports for his oil company, he was old friends with Yeschenko, the oil exporter. They didn't want to see *Chaac* succeed. His daughter is claiming an abusive, coercive relationship as her defense."

"For the murder of Kevin Winn?" she scoffs. "I saw the video. Took all of fifteen seconds to coerce her. Good luck with that."

"Yeschenko, Krasnova, and Krollis are being burned in effigy in the center of Riga. A public warning to the Russians. The Prime Minister and Colonel Redgrave are nearing sainthood in popularity. They've been pushing the anti-Russian, anti-corruption angle hard."

"Good for them," she says. "By the way, the Prime Minister wants to give you a medal in a big ceremony."

"Like France did before making that docudrama? I'd like to renegotiate my story rights if there's another film going down."

She laughs.

"Where are you with Symone?" she asks. "Romantically, I mean."

"There is no 'romantically,'" I reply curtly.

She eyes me suspiciously with one brow rising.

In my defense, I ask, "Why can't anyone believe a man can keep his dick in his pants?"

"Ten thousand years of written history," she replies. "From King David to Bill Clinton, the one thing we know for certain—"

Not in a mood for a lecture, I interrupt with, "We're not all Bill Cosby. Symone is one of the world's many abandoned kids. I promised her I wouldn't leave her to fend for herself in Latvia. Nothing more. Franklin says she fixated on me as a savior. Now that we're back here and safe, I'll see she gets established and, um, then ..."

I'm not sure what comes after *and then*.

"In that case, you can't abandon her now." Ms. Sabel appears startled to hear about Symone. As an adopted child, she has her own abandonment issues. I probably shouldn't have used that word. She texts someone, then continues, "You'll take good care of her, I'm sure. Now what about Betty?"

"She's the best physicist for the *Chaac*—"

"I mean, you and Betty ... romantically." She watches me open and shut my mouth several times, unable to voice my feelings. Taking pity on me, she says, "I ask because she's not just the best physicist for the project, she's the only. I want to make sure she's happy and doesn't have any unnecessary distractions. A stable, meaningful relationship would keep her focused." Ms. Sabel's gray-green eyes pierce my soul as if she's measuring my heartbeat at the brain stem. "I was thinking if you're not interested, that French guy might be a good match—"

"No!" I stop myself from leaping out of my chair. Realizing my voice was too loud, I tone it down a notch. "No. I don't think she likes him all that much. He was sleazy back in Riga. Led her on like he was rich and stuff."

Ms. Sabel nods knowingly.

Oh, Dawg! Mercury says from the chair next to me, leaning in like he's telling a joke in church. *You ain't just her pawn, you her gigolo too. She done pimped you out. And made like it was your idea. See, now this be why she's a Caesar and you just a plebeian.*

What am I supposed to do? I ask in all seriousness. *I'm feeling all kinds of workplace harassment.*

Yo, homeboy, you gonna have to take one for the team! Mercury laughs hard and punches my shoulder. *You go file yourself a complaint and whoever reviews it is gonna take one look at you, one look at Betty-the-Bardon, and they be axing you what the problem is. Harassment don't mean the same thing for men as it do for women cuz of the power dynamic. See what I'm saying? Deal with it. What you really wanna do, homie, is wake up and realize if you be serious about winning the heart of a physicist—you gotta do something quantum noticeable.*

He laughs until he disappears.

"Well, Betty's an adult," Ms. Sabel says. "I'm sure she'll choose a man who cares about her."

My mind reels back to the flight home. Joe and Betty, who both had plenty of sleep, spent the flight flirting. I mean, chatting. She wouldn't fall for that clown-faced poser, would she? Oh yeah, and she watched Symone slide out of my cabin. Damn.

I whip out my phone, bring up a florist, and send Betty a dinner invitation nestled in a bouquet.

When I put my phone back in my pocket, Ms. Sabel stares at me impatiently.

"The *Edison Data?*" she asks with greedy eyes and outstretched fingers.

My hand dives into my pocket for the chips. My mind reviews the lies I tell myself: I work for the best, most honest human beings in the world. But those lies don't always work. Right now, I'm asking questions: Am I doing the right thing? I always want to be the hero—is turning this over heroic? Does she deserve this kind of power? I work for her, and she's treated me better than anyone else. Still, am I asking the silent question: *Is this OK?* Then answering myself with an equally silent response: *It must be.* Does that make it so?

"Is there a problem?" she asks.

I find myself awkwardly frozen in place with one hand in my pants pocket, my hips raised to allow access. "To tell you the truth, I'm not sure who owns—"

"It's mine, Jacob." Her face turns crimson. "My biological father was murdered for it. *Chaac* is my birthright!" She slams her fist on the desk. "Why does anyone doubt that? While you were in the air, I spent hours arguing this topic with lawyers and ambassadors. No one else has any claim. It's taken me years and millions of dollars to chase it down and recover it. And all these stinking little presidents of this and that country keep popping up trying to take it from me!"

She sinks back with an exasperated exhale.

Stinking little presidents of this and that country happen to be the USA and France. But that doesn't matter, because in real life it's billionaire versus billionaire. Pia Sabel versus Deng Zhipeng versus Remmo Nidal, or whoever's behind them. In this case, there's a good chance she is better than the others.

None of that matters, it's not my decision to make. I'm just a pawn. I don't mind being a pawn. I'm damn good at it. Knowing you're a pawn is the first step to spiritual enlightenment. And I yearn to be free.

I pour the chips into her hand.

"Sorry," I say, "I'm tired and stressed out. I'm going home to visit the family back in Iowa. I need to rest and ..."

Her attention is elsewhere, her eyes focused beyond my right shoulder. Bootheels clack across the hardwood coming toward us. Twisting in my seat, I follow her gaze.

CHAPTER 73

JACOB STEARNE

Symone strides in, vamping a catwalk. She's wearing her blue Sabel shirt—unbuttoned to the navel. A lacy black bra peeks from inside. Definitely not how she was dressed when we left the jet. In a stage whisper, I say, "I told you to wait in the drawing room."

"I called her in," Ms. Sabel says, and holds up a text on her phone. She reaches out a hand, which doesn't go far because of the wheelchair. "Anyone who can save Jacob Stearne is someone I simply must get to know better."

Symone stretches across the immense desk to shake hands. A significant gap still separates them. She leans way over until she's practically lying across it. She gives a giggle. They shake. Symone remains leaning over the desk for a moment.

"You can put the boobs away," Ms. Sabel says, pointing at how Symone has her assets on display. "Contrary to what you read on the clickbait sites, I'm not gay."

Symone laughs loudly and covers her mouth. "Well. It was worth a shot."

"I like this one," Ms. Sabel says to me, pointing at the girl. "No bullshit."

Ms. Sabel's voice lowers half an octave to prove she's serious as she transitions from fun to solemn. She says, "You can't go to Iowa. You're not done yet. You only brought in two thirds of the *Chaac Project*. You let Rafael Tum walk away with the most important part: the *Equation*. Tania and her crew thought Rafael would be in Budapest—but he wasn't.

Since you let him slip away, you need to find him. Best guess right now is Zagreb. That's based on extrapolated facial recognition. He knows how to avoid that stuff, so we're using artificial intelligence. Anyway. We have Sabel Two fueled with a crew standing by—you can leave within the hour."

Satisfied, she turns back to Symone. "Thank you for helping my top agent. You've already been rewarded with a large bonus. I'm also going to offer you a scholarship and a job."

"If it's that job in customer service Franklin was talking up," Symone says with disdain, "you can forget it. I make the patriarchy pay for their creepiness and have a blast doing it."

"What about a long-term career? Don't you want something you can tell people about without feeling shame?"

"You can feel all the shame you want. Ever take pole dancing lessons?"

"Well, I've dabbled in, uh—"

"Yeah, thought so. People like you get all god-squad about stuff you don't know anything about. Then you live your fantasies—and come down with a case of guilt the morning after. That's your problem, not mine."

Ms. Sabel stares at the girl while she processes her attitude and words. She makes her thinking-face, biting the inside of her cheek while twisting her mouth around.

"Making the patriarchy pay," Ms. Sabel says and slides a glance my way. "Did Jacob pay for anything?"

I want to protest the insinuation, but Symone is quick with her response.

"Hell, no. He suffers from that 'gentleman' pretense—when we all know what gentlemen are thinking when the lights go out." Symone leans in with a conspiratorial whisper purposely loud enough for me to hear. "Believe me, I tried. How about you?"

Ms. Sabel laughs. "I'm at the opposite end of the spectrum. If I so much as smile at a man, they sue me for breach of promise!"

They slap the table and share a laugh.

I don't get it.

"Well, if you don't want a scholarship or a job in customer service," Ms. Sabel asks, "how can Sabel Industries repay you for your stellar work in Riga?"

"Bring a stack of hundreds and watch me dance. I'm going to apply at the Mpire Club downtown. I'm sure they'll hire me." Symone watches Ms. Sabel's face, studying every twitch of her iris.

Ms. Sabel laughs. "The clickbait sites would blow up if I showed up there. As much fun as it might be, I'll have to pass."

"As I was saying," I grumble loudly, "I'm headed to the family farm soon as we're done here. And that's—"

"You're going to Zagreb." Ms. Sabel gives me the not-a-discussion look with uncharacteristic finality. She turns back to Symone with a smile. "Anything else I can do to show my appreciation then?"

A mischievous grin spreads across Symone's face. "I'd take one of those jobs sneaking into buildings, stealing cop cars, and stuff. What he does is like good-guy crime."

"Operational?" Ms. Sabel's voice squeaks with disbelief. "You can handle that?"

"Lady, I held a bomb for you. I didn't freeze, neither." Symone hooks a thumb at me. "I can do anything he can do."

I study my new friend, trying to figure out what she's up to. She's no battle-hardened veteran; she froze more than once and passed out after the bomb episode.

Ms. Sabel hasn't taken her eyes off the girl. She says, "My people are often in live fire situations against some very bad people. What did you think of the showdown in Riga?"

"Oh wow! That was like, such a high—like fire. I got so scared I got horny, then it was over and everything since then has been brighter, clearer, more beautiful. I mean, like, Holy Jesus, that's exciting as fuck." She pauses with an expression of such honesty, I immediately suspect she's up to something. "And the pay was, well, it was almost as much as I usually make."

And there it is. I know where she's going now.

"How much are we paying you?" Ms. Sabel asks.

"Fifteen hundred a day, plus tips."

Ms. Sabel misses the last part because she's snapped a scowl at me. She slaps her palm on the desk. "That's what we pay senior veterans with years of hazardous duty under their belts, Jacob. Every day I'm turning over stock in this company to the employees. My long-term plan is to make Sabel Industries employee-owned. We have employee representatives on the board now. It's no longer just my money we're playing with. We have fiscal responsibilities to others."

I shrug. She's never tried negotiating with a stripper. Wall Street's capitalists have nothing on Symone when it comes to negotiating supply and demand.

She turns back to the girl. "You were something of Jacob's muse in the last operation. You can have that job, but not at that rate. Can you leave for Zagreb within the hour?"

"Hold up," I interject. "I'm not going to Zagreb. I told you: I'm going to Iowa to visit—"

"Zagreb. We settled this," Ms. Sabel says as if I'd forgotten her name.

"No, we didn't—"

"You need him wherever that place is?" Symone asks. When Ms. Sabel nods, she says, "Guaranteed I can get him there. But my rate is $2,000 per day plus expenses and tips."

"Guaranteed?" Ms. Sabel asks, their gazes locked in a serious staring contest.

"Yes."

"Done," Ms. Sabel says. Then Symone's last phrase registers. She looks at me curiously. "Tips?"

"Hey!" I bark. "You can't send her on a mission against Rafael Tum alone."

"I'm not," Ms. Sabel says.

Thank You!

Thank you for choosing my book. As an independent writer, I live and die on word-of-mouth referrals and book reviews. If you liked this book*, please tell everyone you know and leave reviews all over the place. I will be eternally grateful. If you didn't like this book, let's just keep that between us, OK?

If you can't get enough of Jacob Stearne, checkout the book bundles sale priced at https://seeleyjames.com/bundles . While you're there, join my newsletter to get discounts, drawings, news, outtakes, and more about the Sabel Agents club on Facebook! Every month or so (sometimes I'm lazy), I'll let you know about the book in progress, personal triumphs & tragedies, what I'm reading and other fun stuff.

I love hearing from fans. Don't hesitate to email or message me on Facebook to let me know what you think.

*I like you already.

**Now that you've read this book, which one should you read next?
HTTPS://SeeleyJames.com/books**

TRUTH IN FICTION

As an avid reader of fiction, I'm often curious about the facts, physics, and philosophies of the books I read. In this book, I've written some interesting personalities into the story. Because some scenes were derived from firsthand experiences and others from research, I feel you deserve to know what research I've undertaken during the writing of this book. Allow me to address a few commonly asked questions:

1) **How come you know so much about sex workers?** Loaded question, right? Personally, I've always felt the patrons of strip clubs were, by attendance, admitting they had failed to woo women with charm. A sad state of affairs. In my early twenties, I wound up with a platonic (I swear) roommate who was a proud stripper. She started in her chosen profession at age fifteen and served as the basis for Symone Blackworthy. But, I didn't leave it there. I read several books as research that opened my appreciation for an industry I know little about. I recommend these books, which are not erotic but are as fascinating as they are informative: *Playing the Whore,* by Melissa Gira Grant; *This is My Real Name,* by Cid Brunet; *Whores and Other Feminists,* by Jill Nagle; and the most surprising book which I highly recommend: *Whip Smart* by Melissa Febos (who is now an associate professor at the University of Iowa in the Nonfiction Writing Program).

2) **Are there really 250,000 school shooting survivors?** Yes. Shocking, horrifying, and yet gun control is something politicians don't want to discuss. An article by Zusha Elinson, Arian Campo-Flores, Cameron McWhirter, and Dan Frosch, titled "The Altered Lives of America's School-Shooting Survivors," *Wall Street Journal,* June 2, 2022, about the trauma hundreds of thousands of children, some now grown to adulthood, face when the headlines about another school shooting cross their phone screens made me ill. When I was a kid, I had to practice duck-and-cover drills. But nuclear war was so remote due to the world-ending nature of it, that

we found it laughable. In the sixty years since I was in grade school, a very real terror stalks our nation's hallways: us. And it is a uniquely American problem. No other country in the world has suffered more than four school shootings in its history, yet we have had over 2,000 (BrieAnna J. Frank, *USA Today,* "Fact check: Comparison of school shootings in the US, other countries," June 3, 2022.)

3) **Can you really put your car on train tracks and roll?** Yes. IF your axles are the right width. Many years ago, my grandfather told me about doing it in his youth. I challenged him and he dragged the '46 Dodge pickup truck out of the barn, drove it to the nearest train crossing, and damn if it didn't fit. But axles were narrower in the old days. His '72 station wagon wouldn't have worked. For this story, I considered just skipping the details and pretending it would work, but the realist in me wondered about it. So I researched it and—whaddaya know?—the VW Jetta which the Latvian Police use, and the Soviet-era railroad widths (which are larger than the rest of the world) are exactly the same size! HOWEVER, I would not recommend trying this at home. If you try it and wind up dead, don't come whining to me because it's a really dumb idea. AND, the train tracks my grandfather used for his demonstration were used only in harvest season, so we knew there wouldn't be a train for weeks.

4) **Why Latvia of all places?** Why not? You might recall, in *Death & Treason,* Pia Sabel and Jacob Stearne chased her nemesis, Viktor Popov, to the seaside resort of Jurmala, Latvia. When we picked up the pieces left over from that story, as well as mentions from *Death & Secrets*, it was the only logical place for the *Chaac Project.* Besides, you can only set a book in Paris so many times before readers get tired of it. All the locations are real, I checked on Google Maps and read a bunch of travel blogs about it. No, I've never been there.

Still not sure how much of this story you believe? You're not alone. All my life, my 98-year-old mother has been asking me, "Did you make that up?"

ACKNOWLEDGMENTS

My heartfelt thanks to the people who, without hesitation or concern for bodily injury, gave their time and attention to make *LIES* the greatest book ever written by a human. (That's my opinion, and I will not entertain dissention.) Without the insightful contributions of these few selfless, hardworking readers, editors, and writers, the story would teeter on the verge of putting you to sleep better than a Sabel Dart. I am forever in debt to these brave souls:

- **Extraordinary Editor and Idea man:** Lance Charnes, author of the highly acclaimed *Doha 12, SOUTH,* not to mention the DeWitt Agency series: *THE COLLLECTION, STEALING GHOSTS, CHASING CLAY* and, if you like ass-kicking heroines: *ZRADA and ENGAÑO.* I highly recommend his exciting novels, visit http://wombatgroup.com. With his contribution on nearly every scene, this book is a more powerful story.

- **Medical Advisor and Character Diviner:** Dr. Louis Kirby, famed neurologist and author of *SHADOW OF EDEN.* http://louiskirby.com His analysis ratcheted up the tension, and now the bad guy is badder, the good guys are gooder, and the story more engrossing.

- **Amazing Editor and Character Arc Speicalist:** Mary Maddox, horror and dark fantasy novelist, and author of the *DAEMON WORLD* series and the fantastic thrillers: *DARK ROOM* and *HOMETOWN BOYS.* http://marymaddox.com. Her analysis made each character more real and engaging. And also exposed a clue that gave away the ending!

My additional thanks to the beta readers who aided and abetted my endeavors. No amount of proofreading, professional or amateur, can match their diligence in finding the niggling little malapropisms, mondegreens, spoonerisms, homophones, and actual typos: Melissa Krueger, who found meditation where mediation should have been after everyone else was done. Joe Rulo, for whom Joe Rouleau (French spelling) is named, his edits had some brilliant alternatives and ideas. Andrea Neal, who suggested many grammar options that make it easier to read. Rick Tara, who was a mayor in the last book for his great beta reading skills and caused me to search for an excuse to move a small-town mayor from Maine to Latvia. Mike Culpepper, who found several inconsistencies, saving readers around the world a headache. Mike Davis, whose comments bring clarity to the narrative, making more sensible actions and reactions. Marisa "Fritzi" Redgrave, who lent her name to a certain police officer and contributed many as-read thoughts that help me see how the flow is working.

But don't blame any of them for my bad grammar. That's all mine.

Above and beyond the usual acknowledgements, I'd like to thank the many fans who leant their names (and some family members, frenemies, and neighbors) to the character list in this book. Long suffering fan, Joe Rulo brought us Joe Rouleau; Marisa "Fritzi" Redgrave leant her name to Captain Marisa Redgrave; Elizabeth Helm named the dead guy after her ex, Kevin Winn; Clinton Sites thought long and hard to name Symone Blackworthy; Jeff Benton named Logan Taylor; Bruce Anrig chose his son for Chris Anrig; and Kanyon Kiernan chose her best friend to name Kayla Clay. Thank you for your contributions!

ABOUT THE AUTHOR

 His near-death experiences range from talking a jealous husband into putting the gun down to spinning out on an icy freeway in heavy traffic without touching anything. His resume ranges from washing dishes to global technology management. His personal life stretches from homeless at 17, adopting a 3-year-old at 19, getting married at 37, fathering his last child at 43, hiking the Grand Canyon Rim-to-Rim several times a year, and taking the occasional nap.

His writing career ranges from humble beginnings with short stories in The Battered Suitcase, to being awarded a Medallion from the Book Readers Appreciation Group. Seeley is best known for his Sabel Security series of thrillers featuring athlete and heiress Pia Sabel and her bodyguard, unhinged veteran Jacob Stearne. One of them kicks ass and the other talks to the wrong god.

His love of creativity began at an early age, growing up at Frank Lloyd Wright's School of Architecture in Arizona and Wisconsin. He carried his imagination first into a successful career in sales and marketing, and then to his real love: fiction.

For more books featuring Pia Sabel and Jacob Stearne, visit https://seeleyjames.com/books.

facebook.com/seeleyjamesauthor

instagram.com/seeleyjamesauth

bookbub.com/authors/seeley-james